D0916044

Bitter Waters

WITH AN INTRODUCTION BY GEOFF RYMAN
EDITED BY KAREN WILLIAMS

chaz
brenchley

LETHE PRESS
MAPLE SHADE, NEW JERSEY

Published in 2014 by LETHE PRESS, INC.
118 Heritage Avenue • Maple Shade, NJ 08052-3018 USA
www.lethepressbooks.com • lethepress@aol.com

ISBN: 978-1-59021-577-7 / 1-59021-577-x

These stories are works of fiction. Names, characters, places, and incidents are products of the author's imagination or are used fictitiously.

COVER & INTERIOR DESIGN: Matt Cresswell
COVER ART: Elizabeth Leggett.

Library of Congress Cataloging-in-Publication Data
Brenchley, Chaz.
[Short stories. Selections]
Bitter waters / Chaz Brenchley.
pages cm
ISBN 978-1-59021-577-7 (pbk. : alk. paper)
I. Title.
PR6052.R38A6 2014
823'.914--dc23

Contents

The Book You Hold In Your Hands
(even if it's on a screen)

Introduction by Geoff Ryman

THE BOOK YOU HOLD IN YOUR HANDS HAS BEEN WRITTEN BY A MASTER OF PROSE.

Who reads for good prose style? People who want something that captures the heart's secret song on the wing—the rush of feelings and images that fly just below the cloud-level of speech. That *starts out* by showing you what it's like to feel.

Go on. I dare you. Just read the first paragraph of the first story in this book and listen to the universe being born. Unless you find reading difficult (in sixty years' time most of us will) you may well be borne away on Thomas Disch's wings of song. In which case my job's done and you won't need to read this intro.

If not:

Chaz Brenchley has written everything, except perhaps the holy book for a new religion and I wouldn't put it past him. He has published crime novels, romance, erotica (I am told), urban fantasy, children's books, fantasy trilogies (times two; I can't remember the word for a six-book series), science fiction and young adult fiction, a play (produced), essays and poetry. His novel *Light Errant* won the August Derleth British Fantasy Award. He belongs to something called the Murder Squad, which may be why he doesn't always have the same name— you may have read him all unknowing. He has written a Rudyard-Kipling poem, the one that RK would have written had he ever gone to a steampunk Mars. Chaz has written a climate-change story in collaboration with a scientist (without much help from the scientist) and he's written plenty of stories about boats. He knows ships and he knows they are inherently scary. He also finds ways to intersect them with books, ghosts, crime and mystery, buoys and boys.

Boats in this book: a man with morbidly sensitive hearing sets sail to chart dangerous rocks called the Silences. An old family bible unleashes ghosts on a ship stranded in fog. A ship's chandler from among his shadowed stock gives an old friend a true compass that points somewhere other than north. A canal boat with a dubious crew finds another boat adrift—and the body of a battered woman inside it. *Bitter Waters* indeed.

But it's not all boats: a military strategist falls in love with a tea boy in ancient China. A eunuch and his dwarf lover leave the Sultan's harem to visit the baths of the city, poisoned by magic or radiation. A man takes his dying lover to the house of his recently dead uncle. A male prostitute troops home to his magic-infested city after a long war.

The stories, like Chaz's unwinding sentences, build slowly to a punch line. The endings always go further, more movingly than you thought they could. A tender story of friends prepping a corpse for burial ends with his ghost making one sweet final gesture. The first story ends with the most moving use of a mobile phone I've found in fiction.

You hold one hundred thousand words of tale; as much as some writers manage in a lifetime. In all, Chaz has published five hundred short stories. I first met him in 1984 at Mexicon, a literary SF convention that was the brainchild of Greg Pickersgill. Chaz and I were working on a play and it was Like at first sight. I read his work and became at once envious. Since then Chaz has published over thirty books—basically a book a year, all of them joined like fine furniture. This has done nothing to reduce my envy.

Chaz can deliver sentences to live by.

'*Want* is a slippery word at the best of times...'

'Home was just a place to start.'

'The old should hurry more, should be more urgent, they had so little left to play with...'

This book in your hands: it's yours. You've won it. It is yearning for you to read it. It has a heart stuffed full of things, people alive and dead, poetry, realism, fantasy, crime and poetry. And it wants to be your friend.

Geoff Ryman

Another Chart of the Silences

SOME PEOPLE THINK THAT A BREATHLESS HUSH IS THE NATURAL STATE OF THE universe, as darkness is: that sound is like light, a rebellion of angels, a thin and fierce and ultimately doomed attempt to hold back the crushing weight of utter stillness.

They're mistaken. White noise is universal, it's woven into the fabric: the sound of the Big Bang infinitely elastic, infinitely stretched. In the beginning was the Word, and what we hear is still the scratch of God's pen on the paper as he made it, as he spoke it, as he wrote it.

I hear it, almost, on a daily basis. I sit in the Silence Room in the Lit & Phil, the quietest place I know, where even the books are bound and gagged, tied shut with strong white ribbon; and when I'm alone, when I'm not turning pages, when I listen past my lungs' breath and my heart's beat and my belly's churn, I think I can hear the faintest possible scritching sound, inherent in the air. White noise: but actually this isn't that everlasting, ever-fading echo of the slam of all existence. This is something entirely other, contained within walls, within covers. Books telling their own damn stories. I swear to you, it's true. Go in, sit down, sit quiet, you can hear it for yourselves. It's there, it's always there; it's the sound of all those books. Rewriting.

Death is a deception, it's a trick. It's a game that books play. What do they know? They want to keep everything, unchanging and for ever. They take what is liquid, mutable, permeable, life; and then they fix it like a dye, set solid. Historically, what are the three most scary words in the language? *It is written.* You can't argue with that.

But the rules change, surely, when the books rewrite themselves. Somewhere—downstairs, probably, on a shelf in the Silence Room—there's a book that's rewritten the border between life and death, unless it just scribbled something illegible in the margin. Like this:

It was a Saturday morning, and I was alone, content, down there at the large table with my back turned to the room. I had charts spread out before me, and an ocean in my head. That afternoon I'd have the real thing beneath my keel, and I ached for it already; but out there, quite often I would ache for this. When a man can measure his happiness coming and going, he should probably be grateful.

What's good can always be lost, or broken, or taken away: by our own carelessness, by other people's clumsiness, by envy or greed or disregard.

The door opened, at my back.

There were two of them, I could hear that in their footsteps. Both male, I thought: the length of their strides or the sounds of their shoes, perhaps the timbre of their breathing. One was older than the other. By a distance, by a generation.

I heard the squeak of chairs at one of the little alcove-tables, and turned back to my papers.

Then I heard another kind of noise: not incidental, not the haphazard sounds of bodies in motion. Steady, irregular, deliberate.

And familiar, and I didn't believe it. I still didn't turn to look, but I listened, and was sure. Those were the sounds of chessmen being set out on a board. And this was the Silence Room, it says so on the door, they must have seen; and it is impossible to play chess silently.

I didn't turn, but my back was stiff with outrage. They paid no heed. They played, and every move was an offence; and soon—of course!—they started talking.

It's not conversation, exactly, but talking always counterpoints the play.

Some moves have to be discussed, some lingered over like a line of beauty. And this was an older man and a boy, a youth, so the game was a lesson also. The boy had that abrupt, husky teenage way of talking, stumbling over his words; it jarred me every time he spoke.

I could have swept up my papers and stalked out. Perhaps I should have done; hindsight aches for me to do it, for another me to have another chance. *Matthew, I'm sorry. Look, I'll go, and all things will be different for all of us, amen...*

I didn't move, though. Even that would have been a statement, an accusation, awkward for everybody. I stayed, they played, I seethed and nothing further happened until the older man left the room in the middle of their game. He might have been fetching coffee, he might have been visiting the toilet. It didn't matter. He was gone; and some imp of the perverse felt it right that, just as the door swung closed at his back, the boy's mobile phone should ring.

Then I did swivel round in my chair, I was too blindly angry to keep still. The boy knew; he was already looking in my direction, even as his hands fumbled for the phone.

"Sorry..."

"If you were sorry," I said, "you wouldn't answer it."

He flushed, suddenly and thoroughly; and glanced down at the phone, stabbed it with a finger, lifted it to his ear. Hunched over it as though that would help, and muttered, "I'm in the library."

Something in that, the flush or the defiance melted my anger in a moment. All the pent-up rage flooded out of me, leaving me hollow and brittle and defenceless. Then I did have to move; I slipped out and went walking through the library. I went to old friends, old books, sailors and travellers: Hakluyt's *Voyages*, Ibn Battutah.

When I went back down, when I could face it, the older man was packing chess-pieces into their box. The boy was standing by my table, looking at the charts and my own notes where I had left them.

He saw me and flushed again. "What are these?"

Earlier today, any other day, I might have been angry. Now I was past that, in unknown territory. "Nautical charts," I said. "Soundings, landmarks, everything a sailor needs to know. These are contemporary; that one's three hundred years old. Well, you can see," the paper crumbling at its edges.

"Are you a sailor, then?"

"Yes, I am. Don't touch that."

It came out perhaps sharper than I meant. He snatched his hand back as though I'd burned his fingers. So then I had to give him balm, a little. "No harm, only that it's fragile." It's odd how possessive you can be, towards what is not your own. Tom Turner's chart was mine by rights of intimacy; I knew it better than any man alive, I knew it the way you know your lover's skin, their every expression, the rhythms of their voice overheard on someone else's phone. Soon I hoped to know the chart better yet, from the inside.

"So why do you bother with it? The new ones are better, yeah?"

I confronted the intricacies of explaining that marriage of art and craft and science to a teenager, and sighed. "The new ones are more accurate, of course. GPS, satellite imaging, they're exact. But this is beautiful, and it's the work of a sailor, not a machine. This is real mapping, drawn to a human scale, one man's expression of his world and its dangers. It's the original, not an engraving; look, you can see the pen-strokes, sometimes you can see the pencil-lines beneath."

He wasn't interested in pencil-lines. "What dangers?"

Did he really know so little? I took a breath to tell him, but the older man interrupted.

"Leave it, Matthew. You're not meant to talk in here." And then he nodded at me, and walked out. The boy blushed one more time, mumbled something incoherent and was gone.

THE NEXT WEEK, THEY WERE BACK. This time, the boy Matthew came straight over to my table. I had to glance up then; he smiled, put a finger to his lips, set something down by my elbow.

It was his mobile phone. He left it there like a promise, *look, no calls today*. Or it could have been a more aggressive message, *look, it's in your hands now, up to you not to answer it if it rings*.

I fairly swiftly gave up any hope of working, and went to watch the chess.

The old man frowned up at me once. Matthew didn't lift his head. His determination not to was so obvious, he reminded me of me.

Halfway through the second game, the old man left us abruptly, without explanation, as was his apparent habit. As the door closed behind him, I said, "I haven't the faintest idea what to do if it rings, you know. Except throw it at your head, obviously."

"No worries. I switched it off."

"Thank you, then. Though you're not supposed to be playing chess in here either."

"I know, but he won't be told. Thing is, he hates it when people come up and comment, criticise, make suggestions—"

"Uh-huh. While he's gone, then—pawn to king's bishop five."

"Eh?"

"Here." I showed him, on the board. "Just a suggestion."

"Yeah, but—he'll take it, won't he?"

"Yes, of course."

"So what am I supposed to do next?"

"You're supposed to work that out for yourself." I gave him back his own smile from earlier and left him to it.

I sat with a book in my hand and listened to the gameplay. I heard him make that sacrifice, and how he used it to queen another unregarded pawn, and how he won the game thereafter at a merciless canter. I heard the triumph in him; I heard the moment when he remembered I was listening, when he wondered suddenly if I'd give us both away.

Not I. I sat quiet, and he came across to scoop his phone up as they left, and neither one of us said a word.

THE THIRD TIME, HE CAME IN ALONE. He laid his phone down at my side, and then he said, "Grandad can't come today, he's sick."

"I'm sorry to hear that."

"Would you, would you like a game?"

I could have said my work was too important. But that would have been to say that he wasn't important enough: true, perhaps, but cuttingly unkind. Besides, it was working on me again, that gawky charm of the adolescent, the way he laid himself open for the rebuff.

So I said yes when I shouldn't have, I broke a silence where it mattered most, and of us all, I've paid the least price for it. Betrayal can be like that.

CHESS IS A BRIDGE BETWEEN STRANGERS, BETWEEN GENERATIONS. Get them talking, and everything's fair game.

Sometimes the less people say, the more they tell you. Matthew went to school, he went home. He spent time with his grandfather. He didn't want to talk about his parents, nor much about his life. He didn't really want to talk at all. Rather, he wanted to listen. He wanted to hear about my boat; he wanted to know why I spent my Saturday mornings in here with dusty old charts and books, when I might have been out on the water.

"Look," I said, setting the chessboard aside and reaching for that despised paperwork, "here's *Great Britain's Coasting Pilot*, published in 1693. A naval captain called Greenville Collins spent seven years charting the entire coast line. It's our first detailed, practical survey; it changed inshore navigation for everyone. But look, look here..."

I showed him the chart of our own waters, and let him find the problem for himself.

"There's a bit missing," he said. "What happens here?"

There is, indeed, a bit missing. A neat blank square a mile offshore and two miles on a side, where even the rhumb-lines and the bearings break off, where Collins has delineated emptiness. It's unique, throughout the forty-seven charts of the survey.

"The most dangerous rocks on this coast," I told Matthew, "that's what happens there. They've been wrecking ships since Roman times. People around here call them the Silences."

"So why didn't he, you know...?"

"Chart them? Because sailors are superstitious folk, and those rocks have an evil reputation. It's a known hazard, and every captain tries to steer clear; but they say it's like the Sirens, something lures them in regardless. You know about the Sirens?"

He nodded. "We did Odysseus in school. The sailors stuck wax in their ears."

"They wouldn't do it here. Collins' crew simply refused to go near the Silences, they came close to mutiny. Hence this absence. A local fisherman, Tom Turner, made and printed his own chart, here, but that's drawn from observation more than measurement. Tom was a sailor, not a surveyor. If you compare his plan to this, from the Admiralty, which is put together from satellite photos, you can see how inaccurate he was."

Matthew nodded uncertainly.

"I want to make my own chart of the Silences," I said. "I want to do it Collins' way, using his instruments."

"Aren't you scared?"

"Rocks are only dangerous if you're careless. The Admiralty charts are quite clear about depths, currents, the shoals that are hidden at high tide. Though I'll tell you what's interesting, they had to rely on satellite imaging because GPS doesn't work around the Silences. There's some magnetic anomaly that interferes."

"No," he said, "I meant, aren't you scared of the Sirens?"

"Would you be?"

He shook his head, grinning, suddenly all cocksure boy. And then someone else came into the room, and we had to move or else stop talking. He helped me carry all those papers across the corridor to where there was a larger table and permission to speak, and somewhere in the shift and flurry of it all either he begged or I offered, I truly can't remember which. Either way, a day's sailing was the prize.

"Not without your parents' permission, mind."

"They won't care."

"Even so, I'd better come and meet them."

Another shake of the head, this one quite urgent. "Talk to Grandad. Next week, if he's better. He'll be in."

HE WAS BETTER, HE WAS IN; WE DID SPEAK. In the Silence Room, naturally. When sin slides into habit, that's when you'd best beware. Careless talk costs lives.

I said, "I'll just give him a day's run, see if he likes it. I'll undertake to bring him back wet, cold, filthy, smelly, starving, exhausted and intact."

That was good enough. The following Saturday I found Matthew waiting by the kerb outside his house, chewing his nails with doubt of me. He brightened in a moment, jumped into the car and said, "Did you bring any wax?"

"Wax?"

"For the Sirens."

"Oh. No, not today. We're not going near the Silences."

"Aren't we? I thought..."

He'd thought we were heading for adventure, danger, high risk on the high seas. I disabused him.

"Today, we sail in circles. Well, triangles, largely. Way out, where we can't hit anything. You'll learn the ropes, you'll learn to say 'aye aye, skipper,' you'll make mistakes by the yard, and by the time I bring you back, you'll have learned how to sail. Next time we go out, you'll still make mistakes, but at least you'll know what they are."

I was deliberately making it sound like school. He sulked, a little, but that blew away as we came down into the marina.

"Which one's yours?"

"There." I pointed along the floating jetty. "*Sophonisba.*"

"She's enormous," he said, in the tones of someone who'd been looking for disappointment, and hadn't found it. I hid a smile and said, "Big for one, certainly."

"I really will be a help, then?"

"Oh, yes. You really will. Not today, though. Today you'll just be a nuisance."

He grinned contentedly and followed me as I opened her up and showed him over, stem to stern. Then I tossed him my spare waterproofs and said, "Turn off your mobile, before you zip them up. Sailing's about getting away from all of that, being out of touch."

"You mean it's about the silences," he said.

If he thought that, he'd never been to sea without an engine, but I knew that already. He had a whole new world of sounds to learn, from the creaking song of rigging under strain to the slap and hiss of waves against the hull to the half-human cry of a gull over deep water.

Me too, though, I had my own learning to do that day, my introduction to the teenage wall of sound. The groans and curses I'd expected, but not the sudden yelps and whoops, nor the singing in a breathy monotone, nor the jokes, the jabber, the utter inability to keep quiet.

We tacked back and forth until he was comfortable with the sheets and stays and winches. Then I let him take the tiller, while we went around again. He didn't raise a protest when I decided that was enough, and turned for home; he saved that for later, once we'd moored, when I introduced him to the mop and bucket.

I took him home in the state that I'd promised, drained and overloaded both at once. As he stepped out of the car I said, "Next weekend, then? Up for it?"

"You bet," he said, with as much relief as anticipation. "Thanks, skipper."

SATURDAYS, WE PLAYED CHESS AND SAILED; SUNDAYS WE SAILED AND PLAYED chess. After a month I decided he was ready, we were ready, captain and crew. Next week, the Silences.

We started early, in perfect weather, a steady offshore wind and a smooth, swift sea. I offered Matthew the tiller; as he came to take it I saw wires dangling from his ears, disappearing into a pocket.

"What are you listening to?"

"Oh—my new phone. Birthday present. Doubles up as an MP3, it's brilliant."

"Not on my boat, if you don't mind."

"Well, but it's too early to talk. And I can still hear you..."

"Even so. Turn it off, please."

His face was foul, but he did as I asked. And took the tiller, checked the course, did everything he ought to. Best leave him to it, I thought, show some confidence and let the wind blow the temper out of him. I made my way forward, settling into the bows where I could watch for trouble and eventually for the Silences.

At last there were nubs on the horizon that were not other yachts' sails. I called out and pointed.

"Where?" he asked, trying to peer past the mainsail.

"Fine off the starboard bow. Come see; I'll take the helm."

"Aye aye, captain."

I watched him scurry forward, then came about onto the other tack. We'd sail by on the seaward side, to give us both a good look, before we came back inward.

As always, the breakers were easier to spot than the rocks themselves, a sudden stitching of white water in a grey swell. The Silences lay low in the water, but there were no savage currents to beware of, no tidal suck; it was hard to understand their reputation. I took plenty of sea-room none the less, running no risks with my beloved *Sophonisba*. We'd need to be closer on the return leg; at this distance I could barely distinguish rock from spray.

I murmured as much to Matthew at my side. And turned my head for his reaction, and of course he wasn't there, he was all the way forward. I felt as though I had fallen through an unseen door. There was no one in the cockpit with me—and yet for a moment there had been no question about it, an absolute presence.

I couldn't recapture that brief certainty, any more than I could understand it. Let it go, then; stranger things happen at sea. I glanced forward, and saw Matthew coming.

Matthew frowning, puzzled, a little upset. As he jumped down beside me, I saw those earphone cables again.

"Yeah, yeah, I know. Sorry. But I was on my own up there, just looking, and— well, I thought it needed a soundtrack, that's all. It's no good without music. Listen, though, just listen..."

I thought the world made its own soundtrack, but I wasn't sixteen. He held out one of those earphones, gesturing, impatient for me to share. Reluctantly, I listened.

Nothing.

Or no, not nothing: white noise. A steady swish and slurr of interference, the echo of God's heartbeat.

"I think your gadget's broken."

"Only it's new, and it was working fine, and then it just went..."

New toys do just go, sometimes; but I looked at him and remembered what he was clearly remembering, something I'd said before.

"Take the tiller, I'll go and see what's what."

Down in the cabin, no little lights glowed on any of my expensive equipment. No GPS, no radio, no radar.

No warnings, and no way to cry for help. We were on our own.

On our own in clear weather, open water, not a worry in the world. I glanced back out at Matthew and saw him startle as he looked aside, as though he was looking for someone he knew was there and then not finding them.

I did that, I thought.

"Not your phone," I told him. "It's all out, all the electronics."

"You said, that's what GPS does around here."

"I know I said it. That doesn't mean I believed it. Are you happy to go on?"

He shrugged. "You're the skipper."

That meant *yes, for God's sake, why not?* with a subtext of *I don't suppose you will.* I surprised him, then; I didn't let him down. I just nodded, and took the tiller.

Sophonisba was still sailing sweetly, over a sea like glass in motion. The Silences were a presence, but no threat; I wanted to be closer, to see them better, to sketch their profiles from the seaward side. Half a dozen times I caught myself letting her drift in towards the rocks, half a dozen times I nearly sent the boy for a pad and pencils. Each time I checked the motion, checked the words before I was committed to them. In honesty, I didn't want to speak. There was a hush to the air, to the moment, that words would only spoil.

A moment stretched, not ended, becomes momentum. A word not spoken gives us impetus. We ran by the rocks, and it was the easiest thing in the world to throw the tiller over, to gybe, to let her headway bring her around and all the way around, until the sail could catch the wind again and take us back down inside that line of rocks. Sailing can be like that sometimes, where wind and water seem to be unusually willing. Here there might have been currents after all in air and sea together, circling the Silences as a storm circles its dead centre, drawing a path that we could follow.

Between rocks and coast there was room to tack and turn, there was water enough beneath the keel, but a good sandy bottom within the anchor's reach. Now we weren't sailing, we were surveying. We dropped anchor half a mile off the northernmost rock, and established our position as best we could by landmarks and estimate, by telescope and eye. Then we turned towards that chain of rocks and I took bearings on each of them with an authentic period compass, calling the numbers for Matthew to write down.

Surveying by running traverse is a technique as old as the compass rose, and we had practised it up and down the coast till we could do it without thinking.

Suddenly, though, it was hard to keep focus. Water sang past the hull, urging us to movement; wind whispered in the shrouds like a summoning, like a question, *why the delay?*

Only the rocks were patient, and they needed to be. Perhaps they could afford to be. My eye kept shifting, caught by a spume of water flinging high or the eerie stillness in the lee of a rock. My mind drifted another way, into fancies. I thought I heard footsteps aboard *Sophonisba*, out of my sight. I thought I heard cries on the wind, greetings and questions, as one sailor might call to another across a gulf of sea. There were other boats in the corners of my vision, that were only gulls or clouds or nothing when I looked. I could see the same effect in Matthew, the way he shied suddenly and stared around and couldn't concentrate.

I didn't talk to him about it. I didn't want to talk at all. My own voice sounded harsh and alien here, calling numbers; his was an untuned string, a dull vibration, flat and grating.

At last we were done here. We could weigh and set sail, reckoning speed against the clock to know how far we went before we let the anchor go again at the southernmost point of the Silences. That was hard; there was such a temptation to let her run, to come about on that helpful wind and work up the seaward side again, closer in this time...

But I turned her head into the wind, all the air spilled from her sails, Matthew dropped the hook and we were there, with all the work to do again, bearings to be taken on the same rocks from this new position. Later I could mark those two positions on a chart, draw in all the bearings, and where each pair crossed should be definitive, *this rock stands here.*

Find the rocks, take the reading, cry it out. Listen for the boy to call it back— but how much more you hear in the emptiness behind his voice, how hard it is to care for what you tell him, or for what he says...

Was it him who moved to draw the anchor up, or did I send him to it? Were we finished, had I checked my figures, or did I skimp the work?

Did we have an argument, or did I dream it later, whether we should sail round those rugged rocks again? She was my boat and I was captain, but did he win against the odds, to take us southerly, homeward, away?

I don't know, I can't remember. I know that the sun was setting and I was on the tiller, I could see the city's lights tainting the sky ahead which meant that it was later than I liked, later than I could understand. He was trimming the sails, quiet and confident; on that thought he glanced back at me in the cockpit and said, "So when do I get to go solo, skipper?"

"You don't."

"Oh, why not? She's built for one to handle, and I can do it, you know I can..."

"The insurance is in my name. She can't go to sea without me. Sorry."

He groaned and sighed and made faces, as he ought; and then he said, "So how's about that night sail you promised?"

He was right, I had promised him stars and moonlight and the extraordinary potency of the sea at night. We settled on the following weekend; then he dropped onto the bench beside me. "What happened back there, that was really weird, wasn't it? Or was it just me...?"

"Not you," I assured him. "I think you coped better than I did."

He shrugged. "They are haunted, those rocks. The old sailors knew. We should've listened."

"We did listen. Once we got there. But I think the Silences listened back."

That was how it felt, at least to me: that they were attentive, interested, listening. I thought he was wrong, though, it wasn't the rocks that were haunted. The rocks just were. It was the water, the wind, the liminal world about them that held more than it ought to. If there are ghosts, that's where they abide, in the shift between state and state, that blur where you can't say *this is water and this is air* or *this is life and this is death, that was then and this is now...*

I didn't say any of that to Matthew. We were better being quiet, I thought, each of us finding our own place to stow what had happened for mulling over later. Or for rejecting later as a fancy of the day, the rocks' reputation, a desire to be impressed. Strange things happen at sea, but they happen inside our heads as much as they do on the water.

It was full dark before we berthed in the marina. When we were done cleaning up, Matthew reached into his pocket with a half-smile that might have been wider if the day hadn't been so pressing. Still, he was a boy, he'd prepared this, he loved it; he said, "I've got a present for you," and handed me his old mobile phone.

I gazed at it blankly. "I don't use these things."

"I know, but you should. I want you to. Look, we can play chess," and he touched a key and the panel lit up, already primed, *P—KB3*. "We can text moves to each other, see? I'll show you how. And if you never tell anyone the number, then you'll know it's me, every time it rings."

And clearly he wanted me to think this was a good thing. I thought his loneliness was showing, brighter than I'd seen it before; so I let him teach me how to text, and how to make a call and answer one. Then he gave me the charger, jumped on his bike and was gone. I sent a message after him—*P—QB3*—to await arrival, and locked the boat up. Checked the spare key was still hanging on its line below the water—and no, I didn't really think the ghosts had taken it; I always check, it's a neurosis—and then I headed home. Thinking about ghosts, already finding ways to rationalise.

Halfway back, the phone beeped. In Morse, SMS, twice. I ignored it. Five minutes later it rang properly. I sighed, pulled over, picked it up.

"Hullo, Matthew."

"Did you get my text?"

"Yes."

"Only you haven't sent your next move. Aren't you going to bring the queen out? You always bring the queen out."

"One of these days I'll surprise you. But right now, I'm driving."

"Oh. Right. Sorry…"

It wasn't just a lesson in his loneliness, it was a lesson in his youth; at a guess, no one else he might call would have a licence, let alone a car.

When I got home, I sent him the move he expected. And spent the rest of the evening answering his texts, his moves, at five minute intervals. When I wanted to go to bed, I realised that he hadn't told me how to turn the damn thing off. I phoned him to ask; he just giggled, and said goodnight.

A COUPLE OF NIGHTS LATER, I DID HAVE A GOOD NIGHT, I HAD A REALLY GOOD night. Until that damn phone started up. I apologised, didn't answer it, promised to leave it at home in future. Presumptuous of me, she hadn't promised me a future; but she only quirked an eyebrow, and asked if I couldn't turn it off.

"I don't know how," I confessed. "He won't tell me."

So then of course I had to explain, and she pealed with laughter and took it from me and nor would she tell me how to turn it off, but she did switch it onto silent running.

"Vibrator effect," she said. "So you'll know, but it won't bother me."

AND A COUPLE OF NIGHTS AFTER THAT, I HAD TO PHONE MATTHEW AND CANCEL our night sail on Saturday.

"But you promised…!"

"I know I did, and I'm sorry, but something's come up."

"Well, get out of it."

"I don't want to." I might have lied, of course, but it was just too much trouble. "This is too good to get out of."

"Oh, what is it, then, a woman?"

"Yes."

That silenced him, but only momentarily. He was passionate, he was furious, he was almost tearful and pleading; mostly, I thought, he was jealous. Deep-down, fiercely jealous. He would not be placated, I would not be moved; we both said some harsh things before I hung up on him.

I REGRETTED THAT, OF COURSE, THE WAY YOU DO. Not enough to call him over the next few days, but enough to keep the phone charged up and close at hand. It was still and silent all week, until the Saturday. Saturday evening, when for him we should have been out at sea already, watching the stars appear and hoping for the Northern Lights; when in fact I was in my bedroom, trying to decide what to wear.

I was running late already, I didn't want another confrontation; it was my turn to be resentful, that he should try to elbow his way into my evening. I threw the phone onto the bed, and ignored it.

It rang three or four times, in the half-hour that I took to get ready. That felt deliberately intrusive. When I went out, I deliberately left the phone behind.

And had a good, a very good time, and so I guess did she. At all events, she came back home with me. I left her in the living room with Miles Davis and the Macallan, while I made that traditional hasty scour of the bedroom, changing the sheets and hiding what else must be hidden.

And there was the phone, and the screen showed half a dozen calls from Matthew; and I suppose this was part of the scouring, to sit on the bed and listen, not to leave unfinished business hanging over what lay between here and morning.

Half a dozen calls, but only one message on the voicemail. He sounded faint and frightened, far away. He said, "I'm sorry, skipper. Really, I am. I was, I was angry with you, and I thought I could manage her on my own. I didn't mean to come this far. I don't know what happened, I got too close and I couldn't see the rocks but I don't think she hit anything, she just turned over. I'm, I'm up under the hull and I can't get out. I called for help, I tried to call you and then I called my grandad, and he told the coastguard. I think I heard a helicopter one time, but I guess it didn't see us. It's gone now. And my battery's going, and then it's going to be all dark in here, and I'm so cold already, I can't keep my legs out of the water and I don't, I don't think anyone's going to come…"

ANOTHER CHART OF THE SILENCES

THEY DIDN'T FIND *SOPHONISBA* TILL THE MORNING, DRIFTING KEEL-UP OFF THE Silences. They never found Matthew at all. His body should have been there, trapped inside the yacht's hull, but it wasn't. Perhaps he tried to swim out, in the end. They say that bodies are seldom recovered from the rocks there, something in the current holds them under.

It doesn't matter much to me, where his body is. He won't need that again.

Nor do I think the rocks have him, in any sense that matters. Rocks have no reach, no stretch beyond themselves. All their strength looks inward.

I looked for Matthew on my boat, when they gave her back to me. That they couldn't find him, didn't mean he wasn't there. I even sailed her, when she was fit for it, back up to the Silences. I called his name into the wind, but he didn't show. Why would he?

I sold the boat, in the end. She had nowhere left to take me; and I didn't lose Matthew, in losing her. I take him with me, everywhere I go.

I still keep the phone charged up, as he told me to. I keep it in my pocket, mostly. Always set to vibrate, to silent mode. That way it needn't disturb anyone but me, in the Silence Room or elsewhere, anywhere.

Mostly, it keeps silent on its own account. Sometimes, though, quite often, it does shiver into life; and I do answer it, every time. At night, I keep it beneath my pillow and I sleep alone, so that if it wakes me, I can pick it up.

I'm too much of a coward to ignore it. I'm afraid that if I do, I'll find another message on the voicemail. I don't want that. I'd rather be here for him, every time he calls. I'd rather listen to his silence, to his listening: white noise, the hissing attention of the universe, that slow dragging pulse of nothing that—when you listen, when you wait, when you give it long enough, as I have—pounds in your head like surf over shingle, like breakers on a rock, all the surge and suck of the sea.

Junk Male

IF WE ARE ALL, ALL OF US STAR-STUFF, COMPOSED OF THE ATOMIC RESIDUE OF a light long gone to nothing—and we are, believe me, we are—then it follows necessarily that we are all, all of us also nuclear waste.

I like that. Glory turns to stinking ash, and the ash gets up and walks around and does things. I guess you could call it the corruptibility of man.

I WAS LYING ON ONE OF THE LADS' BUNKS, IDLY SCANNING A NEWSPAPER, essentially doing nothing; keeping just half an ear on the sounds and scuffles of the fresh young waste behind me, the occasional thud of footsteps overhead.

I'd been stupid that morning, sent Scuzzy running off to do the shopping. That boy can hardly read, but he knows what he likes, better than he knows what's good for him. So he'd come back with the Sun, along with the milk, the eggs and bacon for my breakfast. So he was still sitting very quiet, very still up front, nursing his bruises; so I was picking through nudie-pics and soap stories, trying—not too hard—to find anything that might masquerade as news. Trying for the second time: we'd only just come out of a long darkness, one of the major tunnels on our route. I'd lain there listening to the boys howl at the echo, hadn't bothered to switch the lights on.

A vicar had run off with a bishop's wife; it sounded like a joke, but I wasn't sure which might be the straight man. A helpline had been set up in the States, for women called Monica Lewinsky; there were probably dozens of 'em, all freshly deed-polled, hot in pursuit of notoriety. It seemed to be what they did best, the Americans, sought reasons to make a public display of their uninteresting selves. Another of them, a millionaire this time, Stephen Learfoot, was holed up on his yacht in Great Yarmouth harbour, with wife Roxanna and two-year-old child Stacy; notoriously reclusive—for the sake of contrast, no doubt, for the sake of the constant pursuit—and claiming to be phobic about lenses, they hadn't been seen on deck for days. Photo of blank deck, to prove it. I wondered why they didn't up anchor and away if they cared so much, if they were so anxious to escape the banks of paparazzi on the shore; but no doubt there'd be more wherever they touched land. No doubt if there weren't, they'd come back to give these a second run. What kind of damage would that kind of lifestyle, those kinds of lights do to a kid...?

I didn't even envy them the boat. I had one of my own, that I liked better. And a hand-picked crew, and privacy, that I liked better yet. I stretched out happily, thought about going up to check on what kind of damage my own sweet boys were showing, this time of the afternoon when I hadn't been watching them for hours. I'd heard no serious fights, though, no men overboard. I could probably afford not to watch 'em for a little while longer.

Just then, though, the noises changed outside, above, around me. There was a breathy call from the bow, and that was Scuz; he wouldn't dare to call above a breath, for fear that I might be sleeping. I'd even heard him try to shush the others in the tunnel. A moment later, anxious mutters from the boys at the back as they woke up to whatever Scuz was seeing. The engine-noise cut to a sullen murmur, startlingly quiet after the steady rumble that had been at my back since lunchtime, since I'd handed the tiller over and come below. Just a lock, I thought, most likely. Any minute now there'd be a clatter and a whoop as boys gathered up lock-keys and leaped ashore, wild yelling as they raced ahead to open the sluices.

Except that that didn't happen, only more quiet talking. I was just picturing the afternoon's route in my head—tunnel to pub where I'd meant to step off for an hour and no, no locks between—when the hatch swung up behind me, and one of the lads came padding down.

"Uh, Skip...?" Geo: big, solid, sensible, worried Geo. Vice-captain, and no pun intended; the boys hadn't got it, anyway. Sharp they were, my latest crew, but bright not. Bright made for problems; I didn't look for bright.

I'd told them not to disturb me before the pub. If Geo thought he had to disobey, he was probably right. I lowered the paper, propped myself up on one elbow and said, "Well, what?"

"There's another boat," he murmured, shuffling bare feet worriedly on the lino, rubbing sweaty hands on his jeans, the weight of responsibility visible on his naked, sun-scorched shoulders. "Wedged right across the canal, we can't get past..."

"Stuck, are they?" It happened: holiday-makers, incompetent with a heavy boat in muddy shallows. "Take the poles, then, and help to push 'em off."

"We can't see anyone, Skip, it looks empty."

"They're probably shagging inside." I'd known that happen too, where the moorings slipped and happy humpers simply didn't notice. "Have you tried shouting?"

"We didn't like to."

Sometimes I thought I trained these boys too well. My fault, if so; I didn't blast him for it. I just sighed, let the paper drop and rolled easily to my feet. Gave him a slap to get him moving, and followed him up the steps and out into dense sunlight, the tense silence of my waiting crew.

A smile would have resolved their doubts in an instant, but I didn't give them that. I glanced around—Benjy on the tiller, Michael and Domino perched on the taffrail, all three in their uniform T-shirts, *cabin boy, mutineer* and *scrubber*, all three warily watching me—and then turned to gaze forward. With Scuz in the bows, there was only one missing from that roster; he was standing on the roof, staring straight ahead and right in my line of sight. He was stripped down to swim-shorts, catching more sun than Geo; I gazed at the lean bones and the honey-brown, money-brown skin of him and almost did let that smile loose, though I kept it out of my voice. "Shift, Shabby."

"Sorry, Skip..." Shaban scuttled to the side, and I had my first clear view of what lay ahead.

As Geo had said, it was another narrowboat lying athwart the canal at an angle, her bow buried in the reeds on the port bank and her stern strayed all the way over to starboard. As I'd suspected, she was a holiday hire, decked out in company livery. Not a full sixty-eight footer like my own *Screw Archimedes*, closer to forty, but long enough to block this narrow waterway. Her engine was still turning over; I could see the dark water threshing into froth around her stern, as the screw drove her slowly deeper into the soft, crumbling bank. I called out once, twice, but there was no reply, no movement. "Must be the *Marie Celeste*," I grunted.

"Skip, it's called *Daffodil*, I can see from here..."

"Never mind, Shabby. Listen, I'm going to bring us up to her bows," waving Benjy away and taking charge of the tiller, stretching one hand to the idling throttle and pushing it one notch forward to give the *Screw* some weigh, "and try to nudge her out of that reed-bank. You and Geo are the boarding-party. Stand by to jump across as soon as we're alongside; switch that engine off, then see if there's anyone aboard. If not, bring her to the bank and tie up. Understood?" If she was a drifter, I'd just have her moored and leave her; let the idiots who'd let her drift track her down, or explain themselves to the owners.

"Yes, Skip. Sure..."

IT TOOK MORE THAN A NUDGE TO FREE THE *DAFFODIL*'S NOSE, WITH HER ENGINE pushing her ever deeper into the bank. I nudged, backed off, tried again harder; ended up having Scuz busy in the bow with a barge-pole, just to fend us away from the reeds to be sure we didn't join her as I flung the *Screw* forward full throttle. I think I heard him yelling "Ramming speed!" as we advanced.

One thing about narrowboats: with a quarter-inch steel hull, they're hard to bend. I've done it, but never in the *Screw* and only against a concrete abutment, which came off considerably worse.

It was the mud beneath the *Daffodil*'s bow that gave way, as it had to: with a sucking sound and a swirl of filth rising to the surface, an almost visible stench that had Scuz suddenly choking and clowning a faint, staggering around and almost losing the pole, almost falling in to join it.

A double thud told me that the boys had leaped over and landed safe as the other boat swung free. We ran slowly parallel for a short way, till Geo cut her engine; I knocked mine back to idle and we waited, no one speaking, while Shabby opened up the hatch and went below.

He was back in short order, looking oddly grey in the sunlight. He glanced at Geo, his mouth working wordlessly; then he turned towards me. "Skip, you'd better come."

"What is it?"

He couldn't tell me, he didn't have the words. I handed the tiller back to Benjy, and bounded lightly across the gap. Shabby's eyes moved between me and the hatchway; this close, I could see that he was shaking.

I took the steps quickly, lowered my head below the hatch and saw immediately what he had seen. It was dim down there, but there was no mistaking, no fooling myself. In the little kitchen area lay a woman's body. A couple of flies were buzzing around the dark pool that surrounded her dark head, that glistened a little in the available light.

This was death, there was no mistaking it. I went in anyway, calling needlessly to the boys to stay outside. Crouched above her, not quite reaching to touch, I saw that she was young, little more than a girl; and I thought her hair had been blonde once in its matted dreadlocks, before the blood had matted it further. Her face was almost gone, it had been so brutally battered.

As I rose slowly to my feet, I caught a movement in the shadows at the far end of the boat. "Who's there?" My voice was sharp and rising. No one answered. I couldn't see a figure, and there was nowhere big enough to hide a man; I was sure of what I'd seen, though, and moved forward slowly, making softer, encouraging noises in my throat. I was expecting a pet, a dog or perhaps a cat. What I found instead, huddled in the furthest corner, mattered more. It was a child, a toddler, a stout and sturdy little boy with huge eyes, his hair cropped roughly, inexpertly short with a pair of blunt scissors by the look of it.

I could have left him, left her, buttoned the crew's lips and moved on; but canals breed dog-walkers, cyclists, lovers. It's better to break news than to be broken. I hoisted him out, held him in my arms; tried an unaccustomed smile and said, "Hi, kid. What's your name?"

"John," he whispered, as the air filled with a rank and familiar odour.

I sighed and said, "Okay, John. Don't worry, you're safe now. We'll look after you, till we can get you home. Come on now..."

I tried to hold my body between him and that other on the floor, but it wasn't necessary. As we passed her, he buried his face in my shoulder, both arms clinging tight around my neck.

IT WAS AN EFFORT TO DISENTANGLE HIM AS WE CAME OUT ON DECK, BUT I managed it at last, thrusting him into the arms of the gaping Geo.

"His name's John," I said abruptly. "He's your charge, for now. Get him cleaned up, he stinks. If you're lucky, you'll find a nappy underneath those dungarees." They were cheap and looked grubby, like the T-shirt he wore beneath; that fitted, I thought, with the girl below.

"Uh, what shall I...?"

"I don't know. Improvise, use what you can find. You'll manage, Geo."

With that vote of confidence, he nodded and reached for a boat-hook to draw the *Screw* closer, so that he could step across safely. Geo had looked after kid brothers in his former life, before he'd left it; he tended to mother the other lads, when they'd let him. That was why I'd made him vice-captain, it wasn't just a joke.

All the boys knew now what lay out of their sight, I could see it in their faces. Shabby must have found some way to tell them, in my absence. I had as much of their attention as I was going to get, what wasn't busy imagining the scene below; I gave orders, snappily.

"Benjy, take the *Screw* and moor up, as soon as the bank gets firmer. Domino, you jump ashore and run ahead; there's a pub less than a mile on. Phone the police, tell them where we are, say we've found a body. Then come back."

"Skip—what about your mobile?"

I just looked at him, for a moment; then, wearily, "People have scanners, they listen in. The police have scanners too. If I call this in on my mobile, they get the number; if they overhear any other messages from the same number, they know who made the call. We don't want that. Do we?"

"Er, no, Skip."

"No. So run. I'll bring this boat behind, Benjy, and moor alongside." I looked for the key to get the engine started, and checked suddenly: it wasn't there. "Hold it!" Just in time, just as the *Screw* started to move away. "Scuz! Over here, now!"

He looked startled, then clambered up onto the roof and ran back to a point where he could jump over. The *Daffodil* rocked a little beneath his sudden weight.

"What's up, Skip?"

"No key. Think you can get her started?"

He bounced down onto the deck beside me, glanced at the control-panel and grinned. "No problem, Skip." I hadn't expected one. Scuz could get into a car, past its immobiliser and away in thirty seconds; I'd encountered him first in my own BMW, with about ten seconds to spare.

He forced that boat's ignition with a penknife, in five seconds flat. I put her into gear and motored slowly in the *Screw*'s wake, until we found a stretch of solid bank. Domino had already made a wild leap to shore, and was barely a dot along the towpath; that boy was the fastest thing afloat.

Ten minutes after we'd tied up he was back, breathing hard, his T-shirt clinging damply to his skinny copper body. "They're coming, Skip. Told us to wait, not touch anything..."

"All right. Just tell them what you saw, all of you," as I scanned their taut, anxious faces. "Nothing more than that. Okay?"

Tight nods, from every one of them.

"Good lads. Here, Benjy, share these around."

I TOSSED HIM A PACK OF CIGARETTES AND WENT DOWN INTO THE *SCREW* TO MAKE sure that Geo was up to speed. I found him quietly cradling John, whispering nonsense into the kid's ear.

"How is he?"

"He's fine, I guess." He was clean at least, wearing one of the boys' T-shirts, its bagginess knotted into a tail between his legs. I wondered briefly what arrangements Geo had made beneath the knot, and decided not to ask. "Except he's not talking."

"That's no surprise, Geo. Given what he's seen." His mother battered to death, most likely, and then her motionless body for however long afterwards. Small wonder, if he found nothing to say about it to the strangers who'd plucked him out. "You just keep him happy, till the police come."

He nodded. "I think he's happier down here, away from the others."

I was sure of it. I slipped him another couple of cigarettes for company and left him, going up to keep an eye on my high-wired crew. Thoughts of the police might quell them, but not for long; they could turn dangerously hyper, if I didn't watch them. Indeed, Scuz was already daring Domino towards the *Daffodil*: "Go on, one quick look..."

"Leave it, Dom. You, Scuz—do you need another lesson in common sense?"

He flinched from the memory of that morning, when he'd brought me the wrong kind of newspaper. "No, Skip."

"No. Good." Come to think of it, his bruises were showing. I added, "Go below—quietly!—and put a shirt on. Fetch one for Shabby, too. And shoes for everyone who needs 'em." I'd have my crew looking spruce and shipshape, before the police turned up.

WHEN THEY CAME, THEY CAME IN WAVES: AT FIRST JUST A COUPLE OF OFFICERS who'd parked up at the pub and walked down, to check that this wasn't a hoax. They took one glance inside the *Daffodil* and called for back-up. That followed half an hour later, in the form of a plain-clothes inspector and a bunch of uniforms. The inspector was quick and easy with the boys, who after all had little enough to tell him; inevitably, he took more time over me.

"Mr Stewart, I confess that I'm a little confused. I gather that none of these boys is related to you?"

"That's right."

"Can you explain exactly what your relationship is, then, how you come to have charge of them?"

"Surely. A friend of mine runs a hostel in London, for homeless lads. They're persistent runaways, all of 'em; troubles at home, of course, and sometimes other problems, drink or drugs or whatever. He takes them in off the streets, gives them food and a bed, a place of safety. So he has a houseful of difficult adolescents, I have a boat; he talks me into giving some of them a week's holiday, come the summer."

I had the paperwork to prove it, and showed it to them. That's the advantage of Mickey's place, it's all very official and above-board. That's one reason why I always go back to Mickey when I'm looking for a new crew. The boys know the score, and so do the authorities. They just don't know that they're singing from a different score-sheet.

Once the police were content with my credentials, they moved on to what they thought were more relevant questions. If anything, though, I was less help than the boys: I'd been below decks for a couple of hours before we'd met the *Daffodil*, so no, I'd seen no one on the towpath. No dog-walkers, cyclists or lovers—certainly no one who might have recently abandoned a boat, a boy, a body. I confirmed that the *Daffodil*'s engine had been running and the key missing; they should check their records, I suggested, see if any holidaymakers had reported a stolen boat. They'd done that already, they said, and had turned up trumps. An elderly couple had tied up for lunch at a canalside restaurant a few miles back, before the tunnel; when they made their way back to their mooring, the *Daffodil* was gone. It wasn't unknown for youngsters to pinch a boat for an afternoon's joy-ride; you can start one with a penknife, they said. Really? Fancy that, I murmured...

They were keeping an open mind, but their best guess lay along those lines: a couple with a kid, from society's margins to judge by her appearance and his, indulging a reckless temptation that was perhaps fuelled by drinking. They took the *Daffodil*, perhaps against the girl's objections; an argument led to violence and the man fled, abandoning boat and child together. It was unfortunate that none of us had noticed him on the bank, but not surprising. He would likely have run on ahead, rather than turning back. There was no towpath through the tunnel, and no easy footpath across the hill it bored through. They would ask questions at the pub, they said, and of any fishermen they found along the way.

I asked if I could take the *Screw* down as far as the pub, and tie up there for the night. They'd know where to find me, if they had any more questions.

That would be fine, they said. Don't let the lads inside, they said that too. I nodded wisely, and assured them that I wouldn't.

JUNK MALE

GEO HANDED THE KID OVER TO THE CARE OF A POLICEWOMAN—DIFFICULT FOR both of them, I thought: the little boy struggled and clung, the big boy looked like he wanted to do the same; I heard him giving her instructions—"He doesn't talk, except that he says his name, he says 'John' when he needs the toilet. Usually too late. I guess he's potty-trained, except that he's so shocked he's half forgotten"— and we went that extra mile at a slow chug. We'd lost half a day on the journey, which meant we'd also lost a full night's work; I spent the time on the phone, making rearrangements.

The sun was setting, by the time we moored. I set Scuz and Domino to cooking, then went to the pub alone; had a couple of pints while I pondered myself and what I'd done that day, what others had done before me. Then I headed back with bounty for my loyal crew, a carrier bag bulging with carry-outs. The police were a watchful presence in the pub, on the towpath, parked a little way up the road and talking to everyone. Clearly they hadn't caught their running man. Likely, I thought, they didn't even have a witness yet. Certainly not a reliable description, or why work the night-time crowd so hard, so hungrily? They'd be here still tomorrow, I thought, and staging a reconstruction next week, as like as not. The girl had looked like a traveller; while students often looked the same, deliberately dirty, they didn't often have little kids in tow. And travellers travel, in borrowed boats or otherwise, and have holes all over to hide up in. I thought their running man might have run far by now, far indeed, and be seriously difficult to trace. I though they might have trouble enough just putting a name to the corpse.

I LET THE LADS SLEEP LATE NEXT MORNING. Now that the schedule had been changed, we had only a short day's journey ahead of us. When they were up and we were moving slowly through the heat, I lay as before on a bunk with a newspaper that I'd fetched myself from a village down the road. A sensible broadsheet this time, it made only small mention of an unidentified girl's body found on a stolen boat on the canal, a toddler at her side. The tabloids might be full of it, as the pub had been full of journos and photographers—another reason the boys had got a carry-out, not to have their pretty pictures on page two: I knew I couldn't trust 'em not to point the finger at themselves, so I kept them below decks all night—but I wasn't curious enough to care.

Neither was my interest piqued by the trouble stirring again in Chechnya, nor the leaking rumour that yon US millionaire's baby was missing, lost or kidnapped or gone overboard. Bombs and bullets far away, who gave a fuck? Dead bodies close to home could cost me time and money both, but not a distant war. And missing kids I knew all about already, their care and resettlement not a speciality but a sideline of mine, a hobby really. Like many hobbyists I took more pains than the professionals, I thought; I did the thing precisely, did it well.

As witness my boatload of boys, moving serenely through the summer's day, dozing and smoking and soaking up sun while they waited for the long, long summer's night to come.

WHEN WE CAME TO THE APPOINTED PLACE, THERE WERE HOURS YET TO KILL before our first appointment. I set the boys to scrubbing up, to mopping and polishing inside and out before I let them think about showering themselves. Clean bodies in a clean boat, that's how I like my crew to be presented.

They were starting to show first signs of nerves by now. Nothing unusual in that. I watched, counting variations on a theme: how this one would go very quiet while that one ramped, how one would pause unexpectedly in his work to gaze at some unseen horizon while another focused intently on his hands and what they did, on a world he could touch and feel.

Nerves were good, I liked to see a boy on edge, so long as he didn't topple over. That kid yesterday, I thought, had toppled far and gone. Too scared even to shit himself, until Skip came reluctantly to the rescue. I wondered if he were talking yet, and doubted it extremely. The paper had one thing wrong, that he'd been found at his mother's side; he'd been as far from her as he could get, and not a drop, not a speck of blood on his dungarees that I had seen. No blame to him for that. I thought of Greyfriars Bobby and remembered a dog I'd killed once, a bitch that had run into the road too foolishly close to my wheels. Driving back later, I'd seen her body in the gutter with a clutch of puppies pressed close. Trying to suckle, trying to wake her or simply trying for some last snatch of cooling, carrion comfort. Animal instinct was one thing, human shock it seemed was something other.

I kept a careful eye on my charges, as the sun sank. Fed them on bread and cheese, not to fill the *Screw* with smells of cooking; sent them one by one into the shower and let her fill instead with scented steam, shampoo and body-wash. No deodorants. The boys knew this routine. They milled quietly in jeans or boxer-shorts, rubbing towels through wet hair and flicking them at bare backs, arguing over the contents of my jewellery-box, adorning themselves with earstuds and cheap gold chains while they jigged and sang along with what music played from the boombox in the corner.

I left them to it once I was sure of their mood, going up on deck to double-check the solidity of the gangplank while I waited for the first customer of the evening to come along the towpath. Wouldn't want him to slip. Slip-ups were bad for business.

He came on time, big and brisk and cash in hand. I waved that aside. Payment on delivery was my policy, always had been; satisfaction guaranteed, or I'd know the reason why. Besides, if they paid upfront they were less scrupulous about tipping the lads after, and I took fifty percent of any tips.

He went below; I listened to the murmur of soft voices coming up through the hatchway and knew how the boys would be preening, posing, trying to catch his eye. The first score of the night was a challenge to them. They laid bets on it; I bet with myself, but only after I'd seen the punter. This one, I thought it would be Domino who got to lead him through to the front cabin, where my double bed was neatly made up with fresh sheets and flowers. Big men went for slender boys, more often than chance would allow.

The lads only kicked up a racket when they were licensed to do it, I'd trained them that well; they were all but silent when a client was aboard and busy. I heard the shuffle of cards, an occasional protesting whisper, nothing more. And smiled, and thought about being *in loco parentis*, as people always assumed that I was, as the police had. What else, with half a dozen ripening lads all of an age, who couldn't possibly all be my own...?

And frowned, and chased that thought a little before I shook it out of my head, no concern of mine.

After a while I caught the scrape of a match clearly in the night's hush, and the whiff of tobacco smoke that followed it, wafting back from the bows. There was no smoking below decks, on a working night; only a boy who'd done his stint was allowed a cigarette, a rest in the open air before he rejoined the others.

So I was ready when the customer came out, a minute later. He settled up, thanked me gravely and went his way; I checked my watch, heard movement in the boat as Geo went forward, heard Domino's bright laugh as he helped to change the sheets. Score one to me, I thought, and smiled lightly as I watched the towpath for another man alone without a dog.

The next was older, sadder; he'd take Scuz, I thought, for that boy's sullen pout, his air of taking on the world and always losing.

I took the pipe from my pocket, for a peaceful blow. As I cleaned it after, my drifting mind remembered something I'd read about gas-companies having a machine that made its own way through their buried pipes, to seal leaks from the inside. That notion triggered another, that I held for a while in my head.

One man left and another came, at steady intervals through the long late evening and well into the night. When the last of them was done and gone off happy, I rewarded my willing, weary boys with crisps and beer and a final smoke before I bedded them down and went through to the forward cabin. Geo had changed the sheets one final time, for me; and had done his best as well against the lingering odours of musk and sweat, opening the windows wide and lighting a rose-scented candle.

I undressed, lay down and thought a little more while I waited for sleep to come: thought of parents and missing children, of boys lost and found, of puppies pressed against the cooling body of their mother.

In the morning, we motored to the nearest town and moored up for a while. I sent Scuz and Shabby off to find a launderette, to wash and dry the sheets; warned the others to behave while I was gone, and went to find a phone. Just for the joke of it, to stamp myself with virtue.

I CALLED THE POLICE, THAT SAME INSPECTOR WHO'D INTERVIEWED ME AND LEFT me with his number. I said, "You're asking questions on the wrong side of the hill."

"Beg pardon?"

"Try the other end of the tunnel. That's where they abandoned the *Daffodil*: put her bows into the tunnel's mouth and jumped ashore, left her engine running. She'd go through on her own, bang the walls a bit but nothing worse than that, they'd knock her straighter every time she did it. You can't get stuck in a tunnel, it feeds you through. It wasn't till she met the curve of the canal on this side that she ran into the bank."

I heard him grunt, I could almost hear him think; I knew the question that must follow before he asked it. "So who are they, then? 'They,' you said..."

"That's right. Is the kid talking yet?"

"No, he's not."

"No." I didn't think he would be. "That American couple, with the yacht in Great Yarmouth—it's true, isn't it, that their little boy's been snatched?"

I heard him breathing slowly, in and out. "How did you know?"

"He says 'john' when he needs the toilet."

"I'm sorry?"

"He had to be American, when I thought about it. It's hard to hear an accent in one word, but it is there. And I bet she's not a Yank: blonde travellers with dirty dreadlock hair, it's a very British thing. And he hadn't been near her, and show me the kid who could do that, who could see his mother killed and keep that distance, never once go up to touch, to claim her back..." And no wonder he wasn't talking else, when he'd been snatched by strangers into a life quite unlike, quite brutal in comparison to what he knew; when that life had abruptly turned brutal for real, under his eyes, a girl battered to death in front of him; when even his rescuers wouldn't call him by his proper name. It must have felt like we were talking to somebody else. He might learn to take shelter in that when he was older, if he remembered this at all. Some of the lads who washed up at Mickey's certainly did; they had their *noms de guerre*, and what had happened to the boy they used to be had happened to a stranger. Or the other way around sometimes, that what they did under their new tag was all acting, all unreal while their true self, their true name was sealed up and hidden deep below. I had both, I thought, aboard my boat right now.

"There are two problems," I went on sententiously, enjoying myself enormously, "two moments of greatest danger when you've kidnapped someone. One is picking up the money; the other is handing back the victim. Money's not so hard now, these days of electronic transfer; you can send it round the world a dozen times in minutes, with the help of a dodgy bank or two. Lose it in charity accounts, wash it whiter than a sheet. People aren't so handy. But say the ransom's paid, the parents want their kid back; what better than to tell them he's in safe custody, the cops have got him already, up the other end of the country? Dump him with a dead girl, some stray you pick up on the road, who won't be missed for weeks; of course people will assume that she's his mother. Pick the right girl, the autopsy will confirm she'd had a kid or two. No one's going to think of DNA tests, not for a while. They'll just go chasing phantoms, a mother-and-child and a father too, and none of them ever existed." It was brilliant, I wished I'd thought of it myself, I loved it.

He did not. "Why go to all that trouble, then, why not just kill the kid if you're prepared to kill a girl?"

Because there was honour among kidnappers? Because no one would pay up a second time, if the victim died the first? Perhaps the one, perhaps the other; but I hoped that neither of those was true.

"Where would be the fun in that?" I asked him, and hung up.

The Pillow-Boy of General Shu

ANY MAN, EVERY MAN CAN FIND HIMSELF PINNED BY A MOMENT, HEARTSTOLEN, abruptly turned around.

The same is no doubt true of women also, but General Shu was not much concerned with women.

Nor, to be honest, had he been too much concerned with men before this, except as units in a calculation. Shu was no master commander, he had no gifts at warfare or leadership; his talents lay in provision, in negotiation, in anticipation of need. The army was such a size, the river this broad: it could be crossed in two days, with this many boats brought from here and here. Shu knew. How and where the boats were likely to be hidden, that too. And he wouldn't forget provender for the men during this delay, nor for the horses; neither would he forget to propitiate the river-gods, to ensure an easy crossing.

A spy captured, a ransom to be paid? Ask Shu how much is reasonable. A city taken, a levy to be raised from its no doubt grateful citizens? Ask Shu how much they can afford. A city not taken, its walls manned and its gates barricaded? Ask Shu whom to bribe and what to offer. This was his genius, and why he had to be a general. He would never win a battle, but he could make any battle winnable, if a well-fed and rested soldiery was enough to win it. If not, he was still the man to buy a victory, if someone on the other side was only prepared to sell.

He followed the army, rather than leading it. Necessarily, he followed close.

This day, heavily astride an indignant horse not accustomed to the work, he huffed into the public courtyard of the provincial governor's great house. The dignified comforts of his carriage were stuck in highly undignified mud a mile behind, and a succession of urgent messengers had only demonstrated how essential it was for him actually to be here. The governor was a fool, and twice a fool to be so swiftly overtaken by his follies; the more military generals, they were all fools too, by dint of long practice. If they were allowed their head—the governor's head, in this instance, along with those of all his household—then the army's forward march would be delayed by a month or more, while it lingered to pacify a restless and unreliable province.

Shu's mount might be unexpected—he kept a saddle-horse for show, largely, the occasional brief parade—but his face and figure were not. A soldier ran to seize the horse's bridle and haul it to a welcome halt; another brought a blessed mounting-stool, to save him the indignity of an ungainly slither to ground.

Fat men should not ride horses. That had been his overriding thought all this way, all the sway and jar of it, every bruised and aching measure of his flesh. Probably, fat men should not be soldiers at all. His bones were padded most unsoldierly, and he knew that he was mocked.

He patted vaguely at his distempered horse's neck, because he was a decent man and truly bore no grudges. Then he had sweat-froth on his fingers, and had to wipe it on his skirts. Horses make poor plotters; their revenges are immediate, though some are lasting. Shu was sore now, and he would be more sore tomorrow.

No matter. A horse was a passing sorrow. What happened here would be enduring, whichever way it went.

As briskly as he could manage, Shu bustled through to the inner courtyard, where the generals would be sitting now in judgment.

In some respects at least, he was too late. There was a bamboo framework rigged up beyond the gateway, with a man hanging from it. What was left of a man. Nothing clung to him except his blood, no vestige of an earthly rank, but still he was no doubt, no doubt at all, late governor of this province.

Well. Shu had not really expected to save him. If a man will stand, will declare his public allegiance to an emperor in fast retreat and close the gates of his cities against the horde that pursues, he cannot expect kind treatment from that horde when his own gates are broken, as broken they will be. What can withstand a horde?

One dead man was not a catastrophe, except perhaps to himself. His whole house was another matter. Trying to stride, Shu scuttled past that foul and dripping scaffold, to where the lords of men—his fellow generals, he reminded himself, and none of them blessed with the seal and authority of the generalissimo, as he was himself—sat in conclave in the shade of a pavilion.

Uninvited, unexpected—they had no doubt been counting on the mud to keep him out of their councils, out of their hair—he sat himself among them, sweaty and disordered and utterly disagreeable. Whatever they wanted to decree, he was determined to disagree with it; and his voice carried more weight than all of theirs combined, for which they would never forgive him.

Not a man to haver or dissemble—not when so simple an act as sitting chafed his thighs, and it was their fault entirely for being so precipitate, for causing him to hurry—he said, "So: you have killed the governor, then. How many more?"

"None yet, but of course his family—"

"Of course his family must be let live," Shu grunted, in a mockery of agreement. "If you slay his family, who had no hand in his folly, then you must slay all his councillors who were as guilty as he; and by the time you have slain their families too, and reached perhaps a little further towards the officers who carried out the governor's orders, then the whole province will be in terror of you, for who among them can be innocent where their masters are so guilty?"

"So they should be in terror," said General Ho. "A rebel province deserves to cower before the blade. Yes, and feel its bite."

Actually, of course, these men here were the rebels, but Shu forbore to say so. Instead, "Will you leave half your force behind, to impose this terror?"

"No, of course not. We pursue the emperor—"

"—With these people at your back, all churned about with hate and horror."

"We do not fear peasants!"

"No? Perhaps you should. It's these peasants who will feed you on the march and through the winter. Or not. Their mattocks have more power than your swords, in the end."

A shrug from General Ho. "We have heard all this from you before, Shu."

"You have. And I was right before, and I am right now, and you know it. You knew it before I came, or you would not have waited for me," blithely ignoring the fact that they had not. "Half the late governor's family would already be dangling from that scaffold in their blood, while you distributed his women among the soldiery, while you kept his daughters for yourselves."

Which was to say *you are all my lap-dogs truly,* and they knew that too, and resented it with a smoky fury that would bring grief soon enough to someone, but not to him.

A boy came with a tray, and squatted in the corner to prepare tea. Good. Tea was soothing for turbulent minds. He himself was hot and thirsty after the discomforts of his hurry. He would be glad of tea, and the chance it offered to speak of other matters. The army's swift advance, the boy-emperor's desperate retreat, the generalissimo's sure success: all of these were proper subjects to be raised and cherished over the perfumed pleasures of the tea-cup.

And meantime here was distraction for the eye too, no need to dwell further on the grisly horror in the courtyard. He could watch instead the boy's slender grace over kettle and charcoal-pot in the wreathing steam and the shadows. Watch as his sleeve fell back as he reached for the tea-bowl, see how a glimpse of line and movement could define the perfection of a wrist...

The boy came forward on his knees to serve Ho and then the others, one by one. Now, watching, Shu was no longer distracted. He was snared, rather. In the grim light from the courtyard, the boy had a still-ethereal beauty, as though death and horror could not mark or mar him. There was no tremble or hesitancy in his fingers, no fear in his eyes, only the shy deference that was proper. His thick black hair was as tame as oil and fingers could achieve, not quite a porcelain smoothness; that privilege was owned by his skin, which was immaculate. Nothing about him was as coarse as his clothes. He was like polished jade, Shu thought, that could never be debased by the sacking it was wrapped in.

Shu shifted his stool a little at the table, to see the boy better when he retreated to his corner, to the kettle and the brew-things. Let the other generals argue between themselves; they could make all his own points for him anyway, and believe them better from their own lips than from his. Let them imagine he was listening, governing in silence. What he wanted was in his sight, more and far more than he had come for, more and far more than he had ever hoped to find here.

In truth, he had expected to find the generals dividing up the house and its treasures between themselves. Having forestalled that, prevented it, now he wanted one of its treasures for himself. A son of the house might have been difficult to claim, but a serving-boy? He could surely manage that, without giving Ho distemper.

He was, perhaps, more obvious than he thought, less subtle than he liked. General Ho was saying unusually little, being altogether too complaisant. Waiting, perhaps, for an opportunity to spring. Well, Shu would not give it him. If Shu knew one thing, he knew how to wait. He could ride away from here on that appalling horse, and send later for the boy...

The boy was coming forward with fresh tea: a forward boy. He was kneeling at Shu's side, his bare wrist brushing Shu's: a careless boy, except that the gesture had been entirely careful. As was the catch of their eyes together, the boy's dark and luminous, enticing, pleading. An importunate boy. And an alert one, seeing Shu's interest and responding to it, seeing something for himself therein. In all of this, a desirable boy; and more, seen closer, still a beautiful boy.

Shu said—no. Shu tried to speak and had no voice, and had to pause and clear his throat before he could say, a little thickly, "Boy. Who rules this house, with your master dead?"

"His sons are gone, lord," fled, the boy must mean, which might perhaps be another reason why the governor hung alone on his scaffold there, "so my mistress, I suppose. If you do not?"

A grunt, and, "Perhaps I do. Smart boy. Where may I find your mistress?"

The boy told him but wouldn't show him, wouldn't follow into the women's quarters. A whole boy, then, and keen to stay that way. Shu sent him instead to wait in the outer courtyard, with the abominable horse; and let the weight of his own authority carry him crushingly over all tradition, into another man's harem.

A dead man's, and Shu made a kinder invasion than it would have faced without him. Which perhaps they knew, these frightened women and their eunuch servants. Word travels swiftly, incomprehensibly, through a house that stands under pain of destruction. They welcomed him as best they could, better than he should have expected. No shrieking, no cowering, only silent and rapid conduct to the new widow in her grief.

She was genuinely grieving, he saw, though perhaps not for her husband. She had closed the shutters, against any view of his dangling body; that was just as well, though nothing could have shut out his screaming. He must, Shu thought, have screamed. Perhaps a lot, and perhaps for a long time.

"A kitchen boy?" she repeated, bewildered.

"His name is Shen." A cautious boy, a deep boy.

"Is it?" She waved a hand vaguely. "Of course, take what you want..." meaning *You will anyway; you have already taken my husband, my life.* And then she said what she really meant, what she really mourned. "My sons...?"

"They are gone," he said, "which was wisdom, and may have saved their lives. They will not be pursued, and perhaps they have not gone far. They may send a message," if they were not too wise to be so careless. "If you have the chance to reply," if they hadn't ridden far and far, beyond all telling, "tell them to lie low until the last of the army has moved on. Whomever we leave here as governor, he will have instructions; they should be safe to return, if my word has any weight behind it."

And he patted his great comfortable pillow of a stomach, to show her that it did.

THERE WOULD BE NO SECOND JOURNEY ON THE ATROCIOUS HORSE. Shu waited until his carriage came eventually to collect him. His brother generals were gone by then, long gone in pursuit of the endlessly-running emperor. Shu might have waited indoors, in comfort, with his boy, but the house was too much troubled already. The last thing its mistress needed was a late-lingering and most unwelcome guest.

Instead, he put the boy to the horse's bridle and led them both out onto the road. Here there were no comfortable benches or blossom-trees to give a perfumed shade, no fish rising in drowsy pools, no gods in niches, watching: only the road, endless and empty. But there was at least a wall at their backs, to screen them from the house and vice versa; there was a post to hitch the horse to, freeing the boy to attend to his new master.

Who was stranded suddenly, his mouth opening and closing like a stranded fish, as he approached and backed away from saying various variously stupid things.

He was master here, he told himself sternly, and he could simply look if he wanted to, if he chose. He did want, but he chose not. He chose to gloss his looking with speech, as if he could draw the lad into an easy, natural conversation, as if a general and a kitchen-boy could ever match mind to mind in comfort. By the side of a weary road, say, after a bad morning, while they waited with a thread-thin patience for a carriage that was tediously slow in coming.

As if he had ever had the skills of common discourse, as if charm and subtlety and insight came to hand, to mind as readily as tonnage and mileage and usage, as if words were numbers and could all be made to march in line...

"Can you read, boy?" It was how he was accustomed to deal with the world, by means of questions, answers, facts.

"No, lord."

"Ah." He had, to be frank, small use for a kitchen-boy. He had no kitchen, nor any immediate prospect of a house to put it in. He might have found legitimate employment for a secretary. Clutching at straws, "You can be taught, perhaps, if you are quick to learn. Are you—?"

A smile, small and quiet, enough to break the heart. "I am told so, lord."

"Good. That's good."

Even so, he could never be quick enough. The sharpest mind needed years to learn its characters; Shu would not have years to justify his boy. Not months, even. He would have no time at all. As soon as the news was out, as soon as the boy was seen in his shadow...

Well. His brother generals had their personal servants, their body-slaves and favourites. He was entitled too. They would laugh only because they always laughed, as people always had. There was no harm in that.

At last, young eyes conjured what they waited for. "Is that your carriage, lord?"

"Is it?" He saw, perhaps, something breast the rise; yes, certainly, a shape coming down, lit by occasional sparks within its own shadow. "I expect so. I hope so. What can you see?"

"It is, it's a carriage. It looks mighty large, lord: wheels higher than my head. And drawn by, drawn by..." He hesitated, shaded his eyes with his hand, looked again, looked around for startling confirmation. "Drawn by *fire-horses*?"

Shu chuckled. "Not quite," though the boy earned credit for the attempt, and for his courage too. Likely this was his first brush with the spirit world outside of gutter-magic, a water-spell or a murky potion. Nine boys out of ten would have been running by now.

This boy stood and stared, and now it did feel entirely natural and easy for Shu to let his big blunt hand with its missing finger rest on that slender neck, to feel bones and tendons and the surge and suck of young blood beneath soft and supple skin. To grip tight enough for reassurance, to shake him gently as a sign of adult authority in this new world, to let him know where he belonged now, here at Shu's side; to murmur, "Don't be afraid, Shen. That is your home now," *this is your home now, beneath my hand,* "and no matter if demon-cattle draw it forward day by day. Only the view changes. You'll learn."

"Yes, lord."

"You should perhaps begin by learning to call me master," as Shen was not a soldier and couldn't be a scribe, could only be, what, a house-boy in this curious snail-shell house.

"Yes, lord," he said complacently, twisting in Shu's grip to press a daring cheek against his arm. Unless it was the defiance that was daring, and the cheek that was complacent. Shu couldn't tell; he had no experience, nothing to draw on. This world was abruptly just as new to him, implicit with things stranger and far stranger than a carriage drawn by unearthly creatures.

It reached them at last, a vast square block of a wagon hauled by six great black beasts with fire in their bones and smoke beneath their hide. Sometimes he thought they were only fire and smoke, and their physical shape was pure illusion. But it was an illusion that held good, mile by mile and month by month. That was solid wrought iron that muzzled and yoked them and linked them to the traces, and those were very real hollows that their hooves left, bitten deep into the road.

Shu had paid his price to have them, and thought them still a bargain. He'd bargained with a demon for a herd to draw the wagon-train, to keep up with the army in its chase; that deal had been made with prisoners' blood. But then he'd needed six more for himself, not to be left behind, and the cost of those of course had come to him.

There were those who thought he'd lost his finger in the war, on his climb to rank. He'd never seen any reason to disabuse them, but actually he'd spent it on the war, which was a very different thing.

SHU HAD DESIGNED THIS CARRIAGE HIMSELF, THOUGH HE HAD NEVER NEEDED TO be so coarse as to say so.

Screens folded out from the walls, to divide the interior into separate small rooms: a reception chamber, a place of work, a bedroom.

No kitchen.

With the screens folded back and his things packed away for travel, it seemed bleak enough, a poor space to offer to a boy even for his own use, let alone as an expression of his master. Shen seemed delighted even so, finding his way swiftly from the clever hinges in the walls to the challenge of the chests, how some of them opened out to make furniture while they still contained Shu's papers and scrolls, his brushes and inks, his clothes and cushions and bedding.

"This one? What does this do," poking and prodding with delicate ineffectual fingers, "how does this unfold...?"

"That one," laughingly, reaching to pull him to his feet where he came lightly, easy to the touch, "that one is just a chest."

NO KITCHEN, BUT IT DIDN'T SEEM TO MATTER. WHEN THE LIGHT FAILED, WHEN the carriage stopped, Shen made tea over a charcoal fire outside. Shu drank it at his desk, reading the reports that were already coming back to him from the vanguard. He made calculations, made notes, wrote instructions in swift clear characters on thin strips of paper. By the time those had been rolled and slipped into bamboo tubes, sealed and sent away with runners, there was food: jewelled rice with egg, hot and spicy and delightful, neatly and delightfully served.

At length—when the bowl was empty, essentially—he remembered to ask, "Have you eaten too?"

"Oh yes, lord. With the men." And, in response to a blankish frown, "I made congee for the guards. After so much work, digging this out of the mud, they needed something hot."

Of course they did. Another day, any other day, Shu would have known it, would have seen to it himself. Today—well, today he nodded, but said, "In the future, feed them, certainly, but take your own meals with me." And, when the boy seemed likely to protest, "It is an order."

"Yes, lord."

And then the boy was clearing away the empty dishes, and Shu need only sit back and watch him move in the lamplight; and he thought this might almost be all he wanted, just to see beauty in action, in private, and know it to be his own.

But there was more, inevitably, more to come: a time when the bed had been laid out and all the lamps dimmed bar one, and in that depth of shadow he could watch as Shen slipped the coarse tunic off his shoulders and let it fall, revealing himself to be entirely the boy, entirely the body beautiful.

And then that same implausible boy—unlooked-for ever, unexpected utterly, irresistible now—stepped forward and put his slim fingers and his urgent attention to undressing Shu. It was a more complicated procedure, with buttons and sashes and lacings to be addressed, but there seemed to be an astonishingly short time—and that to Shu, who was the acknowledged expert in the study of time and work—between those firm, determined hands easing off his slippers and those same hands unknotting his breech-cloth and setting it aside.

And then returning to his body, impertinent, imperious; and if Shu were aware of the contrast at all—the great sagging ageing bulk that was himself, against the lithe slender subtle ivories of youth—it could have been only for a minute, before any notion of himself as a separate creature, a mockable man, was stripped away entirely in the hot damp bewildering wonder that the boy made of his bed.

MESSENGERS CAME, CONTINUED TO COME ALL NIGHT, AS EVER, AND WERE FOR once delayed till morning.

At some time in the night, the wagon-train that followed the army caught up and overtook. This was commonplace, Shu's own order. He liked to bring the demon-cattle through on night-roads where he could, not to alarm the peasantry. The men could rest just as easily by day, and the cattle saw perfectly well in the dark.

What was unusual was his being in his bed but yet awake to hear the creaking of ropes and axles, the hot breath and stamping of the beasts, the low calls of the men who worked them.

In bed and awake and not solitary, that was unheard-of. He would have resented sleep this night, that might snatch away a moment's understanding of slender bones and solid flesh, skin pressed stickily against his skin, a weight sprawled uncomfortably across his legs and a head nestled into his shoulder.

A head that stirred, that lifted, although he would have sworn he had not uttered a sound or twitched a muscle; a body that shifted itself as though reading his discomforts, settling more snugly against his side; a voice that murmured, "Lord?"

"Did the wagon-train wake you? It's nothing, it'll pass by and be gone," as this night would, and all the world be new in the morning.

"My lord was awake," Shen said, as though he had read it in his sleep and so roused as a good boy ought.

"It doesn't matter." Indeed it had been a quiet joy, a treasure to be held against uncertainty, the possibility of loss.

"No, lord," a kiss to his chest, an interlinking chain of kisses, "but now we are both awake," a hint of teeth at his breast, at his nipple, "and it would seem a shame to waste that happy chance..."

Time was a wagon-train, a series of moments, passing by and gone.

IN THE MORNING THERE WAS TEA AGAIN, AND CONGEE FOR ALL IN THE OPEN AIR around the conjured fire, even for Shu—"Eat, lord," laughingly, "eat with us this morning, and this evening I will eat with you"—and so on, the everlasting haul along roads that unreeled like silk from a bobbin but never so smoothly.

Shu sat on his well-padded rump in his well-padded chair, jolted and bumped none the less. He read and scribbled charcoal notes and struggled to think clearly, and every hour called a halt so that he could write his orders properly and send them off via his tail of messengers, and the only unusual thing in that was the struggle, and the only unusual thing in his carriage was the boy, who was the cause of it all.

By day's end they had overtaken the wagon-train again in a familiar game of leapfrog—Shu being happy enough to startle peasants with his own turnout, if it saved him the inconveniences of travelling at night—and all but caught up with the rear echelons of the army, stalled now at the same river that had delayed the emperor. Stalled, but not for so long; the emperor had no General Shu to organise boats fetched down from a lake on wagons that would themselves float like boats to carry troops across beside the bridge that other troops were mending with timbers cut from the woods that fringed that same lake and carried on those same wagons...

All day he had been arranging this and all that it implied. All day he had been talking softly to his illiterate boy, explaining every message received and every message sent, every consequence. It helped, he found, to keep things clear in his own head. Shen was a perfect audience, interested in everything, asking occasional pertinent questions, rolling and sealing Shu's papers as he wrote them. If fingers occasionally brushed skin, if eyes more often brushed eyes, that was more than a perquisite, that was an incentive.

After two days, it was no longer a surprise to find someone else at his elbow, in his eyeline, in his bed.

In less than a week, it was already a habit to look around for him, those times, those few times that Shen was not immediately there: as though something were wrong in the world, a little out of kilter, that needed a boy's light body to rebalance it. He had never strayed far. He might be walking with the guards at the rear of the wagon, chewing ox-hide and listening to their tales of the war; he might be riding up front with the wagoners, learning to crack a firewhip and drive a team of hell-cattle. Boy-like, he wanted to be everywhere, but he always came back to Shu.

By the end of that first week, Shu still didn't have a rank, a position to put to the boy or what he did, that curious mixture of the most intimate services and the most practical. "He is my servant," he would grunt, knowing how inadequate that was, so general it seemed both meaningless and untrue, both at once. And a betrayal, that too.

THE FIRST TIME HE HEARD SOMEONE ELSE'S APPRAISAL, IT WAS ONE GUARD speaking to another: "Where's he off to, then?"

"Who—oh, the general's pillow-boy?"

"Who else?"

"Looking for a duck, he said. For the big man's supper. Promised me the wings if I can find him fresh mushrooms for tomorrow. Not sure I trust him, but..."

But Shu knew for certain sure what he could expect for supper, tonight and tomorrow. And he understood a little more about his boy's systems of supply and barter, and was impressed by how swiftly those systems had been set in place, knowing as he did a little about the subject. And he knew a lot more about how his boy was seen and spoken of.

He wanted to be angry, but that was difficult. Shen was more, so much more than a bed-warmer—but even to Shu, what counted for more? What did he treasure more than the nights, the long slow sleepless nights? The rest of it anyone could achieve, anyone trained to cook and run errands and care for a man's small comforts on the road. The nights, though—well, no one else could suffice for that, because no one ever had.

Even so, Shu resented the phrase and would not countenance it. The first time one of his brother generals used it to his face, he was angry almost to the point of indiscretion. Only a lifetime's training held his temper, schooled his face to its common neutrality, let the moment pass.

Shen himself cared not a whit what they called him. "Body-servant," he said, rubbing oil lingeringly over that great edifice that was Shu's body, "pillow-boy," adjusting the pillow beneath Shu's head, "catamite," dipping his head just briefly to kiss Shu's straining cock, "what difference? They are not here, they don't know what I am to you, or you to me. They can call me what they like."

"And me?" Shu managed, struggling a little for the air. "How should I call you, then?"

A bright smile, and, "You should call me Shen. And you should call me when you want me. I am here."

It was inevitable, of course, that all the army knew he kept a boy. It was inevitable too—because he did not like it—that all the army would come to call Shen his pillow-boy. He learned to live with it, as he learned to live with the boy himself: day by day, moment by raw new moment. When Shen's physical presence was no longer startling to him, when indeed he took it almost—almost!—for granted, he could still be startled by something inside himself, an abstract of Shen, how the boy lay curled within his thoughts and deeper yet, in heart and head together.

Day by day, the boy made his life so much easier. So many little things he no longer had to think about or order: his clothes were washed and mended; whenever he was hungry, there was food; a hundred errands a week, he had only to ask and Shen would run them. A hundred more, he didn't have to ask. The boy anticipated with all the discreet grace of a spirit servitor, sworn and bound.

In all the stories Shu had ever heard, true or otherwise, there was a price to be paid for such service. He had paid his own price for his demon hauliers; sometimes in the darkest reaches of the night, he would dread the day this new price fell due. And reach a heavy arm across the boy in hopes of protecting him, at least, when that day came. Hell is inexorable and debts are not forgiven, but it should not be the innocent who pay.

HERE WAS A MESSAGE FOR GENERAL HO, WHERE HE SHOULD BILLET TONIGHT, where his supply-wagons would be looking for him.

Here was a message for Captain Hao Cho, here one for Captain Lin, one for the quartermaster on the wagon-train.

There could be a dozen such at every stop, and the boy was illiterate. But he only needed telling once, which paper was to go to whom. He would roll them into their bamboo sleeves and seal them and hand them out to the waiting messengers with never a mistake. Shu didn't trouble to check him any more. Perfect trust: it was a rare and a wonderful gift.

And, he was sure, must be paid for.

Sometimes he roused in the darkness and found himself alone, which was unexpected now, new now, terrifying, wrong.

There would be lamplight, though, beyond the bedroom screens. He would call softly, and Shen would come at once, with apologies. He had been sleepless, bitten by the nightmare or roused by the wagons' passing. Better to find something to do when he was wakeful, he would say, than to lie restless in the bed and risk waking his master. He had been grinding inkstone for the morning, perhaps; he was sorry if the noise of it had woken his lord, but he knew a way to make him sleep again...

Perfect trust.

GENERAL HO BROKE THE SEAL, UNROLLED THE PAPER, READ IT AND GRUNTED discontentedly. He hated to lose even a day in this endless chase. Shu was right, though, Shu was always right: he was short on supplies, and the men would benefit from a rest. And be hotter on the trail thereafter, knowing that the emperor had gained a little, not enough.

He gave his orders, then, or Shu's orders, rather:

"There is a dry river-bed ahead. We will drop down into that, and make our way along it to a certain point, described on this map here," an enclosure in the bamboo. "Camp there, where the wagon-train will look to find us in the morning."

And meantime the troops could sleep late, comfortable on soft dry silt; and if the emperor's rear guard had left any spies behind, the chasing army would seem to have vanished from view. They would have no idea where the rebels were, or in what numbers, or where they might reappear.

CAPTAIN HAO CHO, CAPTAIN LIN: THEIR ORDERS HAD THEM MARCHING THEIR squads through the night, to meet up before dawn at a lakeside rendezvous.

This lake was artificial, made by the damming of a river long ago. It supplied the headwaters for a canal now, long and straight, navigable for a hundred miles, more.

The emperor had loaded all his supplies onto barges, Shu's message said; these convenient waters were saving him days, saving his army the work of carrying and hauling.

Only break the dam, the orders said, and the lake will drain itself dry. The canal will have no water, and all the emperor's goods will be stranded in a muddy bottom, all but inaccessible, irrecoverable. Men might work for days to break it, but each captain had a magician in his train. Those two together, working with the men, they should suffice.

THE QUARTERMASTER'S ORDERS ALSO HAD HIM HURRYING ALL NIGHT. Nothing unusual in that, except that the hurry was more pronounced. A hundred of his demon-cattle were needed urgently, as draft animals to clear a calamitous rockfall where the emperor's retreating army had sabotaged the road.

His quickest way to deliver them would be to feed them into a certain dry riverbed here—the point marked on the map enclosed—and have men drive them hard with firewhips, stampede them up. The banks were too steep to climb; the animals would have nowhere to go but exactly where they were needed, faster than they could possibly be herded.

IT WAS IN THE MORNING, THEN, WHEN GENERAL HO WAS LOOKING OUT FOR HIS supplies, that instead he heard first the confused cries of his men and then a dull and rising roar.

When he saw it, dark and thunderous, it was hard to understand: a wall that moved so fast, that engulfed so much, whatever it met it seized.

Men tried to scramble up the banks, and fell back as the soft soil crumbled beneath their weight, and were swept up in the flood of filthy brutal water. Nothing could stem it, nothing avoid it.

A few, a hopeful few leapt onto horses and tried to outrace it. The general was among them, for certainly he should survive this, he who had survived wars and revolutions, a dynasty and its fall.

They might, perhaps, have been lucky, but they met another wall coming the other way: a wall of smoke and fire and hoof and hide, strange flesh, a black stampede.

And hauled their horses cruelly to a halt, and turned to face the flood; and saw hopelessness and death, and turned again. And tried to charge the bank, tried to mount it by sheer force of will and spurs and fury, terror too.

And failed, and fell back, and were consumed.

SHU HEARD THE NEWS PERHAPS EVEN SOONER THAN THE GENERALISSIMO HIMSELF. People needed to be told what to do, and they were accustomed to have Shu tell them.

Also, therefore, he heard the reasons for the catastrophe and deduced the causes, more or less.

And closed his carriage door, and sat down with the boy Shen face to face, with a blade between them as the price that must be paid; and said, "It will come back to me, you know. Of course it will." In all its ugliness and confusion, with a slow and brutal death to follow.

"No, lord. The writing of the orders is ... conspicuously not yours."

"To you, then. It will come back to you," in much the same tone of voice, all doom.

Shen was almost smiling as he shook his head. "You had a fall in the carriage here, my poor fat lord, and hurt your hand," and the bewitching boy's fingers took Shu's hand and laid it out flat and open on the low table, parallel to that lethal knife; and he set his own hand on Shu's forearm so that they sat slender wrist to fat wrist, pulse to pulse, "and all the world knows I am illiterate, no use to you at all in your work. It was a scribe wrote those orders for you, and not at all what you told him to write; he was a wicked man, suborned by a captain with a grudge. They should both have died for it, by now. Orders have been sent. Conspicuously your own orders, justice in due measure."

Shu shivered a little at the meticulous care of his planning, but it could still not be careful enough. "The generalissimo will have his magicians test this, they will ask questions in hell—"

"And will learn nothing to the contrary. I have a promise. And have paid for it."

There was a bandage, a clotted wound on his arm. Shu said, "You told me your knife slipped, slicing bitter melons."

"Yes, lord. Forgive me, I lied to you."

Now, at last, he might allow himself the callous rush of relief, that it must be someone else and not himself—or Shen!—on the cruel scaffold. And then, overwhelmed, appalled, "What are you, boy?" Ghost, devil, what...?

"I was," Shen said, still careful, measuring his words, "I *was* my father's youngest son."

And suddenly—after all these days, all these long miles of looking at him—Shu could see the widow's lineaments picked out in his face, and knew then who his father was and how thorough this deception, how entire this revenge.

And there was a pot of tea on the table, which the boy had freshly made; and Shu gazed at it and said, "Do I need to be careful what I drink, from your hands?"

"No, lord. Never."

He believed him, immediately and completely. But one thought leads to another, one new image to one that came before. Shu said, "You had us all in the one place, around one table, on that day. You served us all. You could have killed us all."

"Yes, lord, but I had no poison for the tea. And you were there," added gallantly, and perhaps a fraction late.

"Gods," with a shudder. And then, again, "What *are* you?"

And here after all was the price to be paid, and not after all Shu who had to pay it. The boy lifted those glorious eyes and looked at him, while his slim hand stayed clamped lightly around Shu's arm; and he said, "I am Shen, the pillow-boy of my lord the general Shu. That is all I am, and all I will ever be."

In The Night
Street Baths

THE WHISTLE WHEN IT CAME WAS SHARP AS GLASS, URGENT AS A WHIP, compelling as a tug on a pierced ear.

It was a summons, of course: expected, nervously anticipated, very much desired.

Teo didn't—quite—spill the beads he was rethreading. He didn't scramble to his feet on the instant; he didn't yelp or whoop or chatter. As far as he could, he did the opposites of those. He became very still and very quiet, as though cast into the heart of a jewel, rapt and trapped. His fingers and his tongue stopped moving, both together. Only his eyes shifted, to find his mistress and look for her consent.

Perhaps he should have looked for her slave instead, her other slave than him. Mirjana's swift and familiar slap stung the back of his shaved head, knocking his cap askew.

"Finish what you're doing, laze. Then make puppy eyes at a soft heart to beg your liberty; not before."

Mirjana's own heart was softer than her hand, if not by much. Under her charge he'd be delayed, and he might carry bruises when he went, but she was at least safe to let him go. His mistress Jendre was more tender, and more careful. She worried when he was out; enough, sometimes, to keep him in.

Not tonight. Her smile was more teasing than anxious; she was half laughing as she said, "Oh, leave him be. He'd be no use to us now if we kept him. Would you, sweets?"

He grinned back at her, and shook his head.

Mirjana snorted. "Go on, then, go. Give your mistress a kiss and come home earlier than last time. And leave your slippers, for I'm not mending them again. I don't know where you go or what you do, but…"

Barefoot, then, he scampered away from her perennial scolding. Half his commerce with Mirjana was play-acting, for Jendre's benefit: which she knew, and took pleasure from regardless. Unless she was only acting her amusement. Life in the Palace of Tears was a hollow thing, a harem of the widowed, a house without a master at its heart; sometimes he thought it an utter sham, where nothing true or real ever came.

Until Djago's whistle came, and suddenly he wasn't playing any more.

Jendre reached out a long arm, to set the cap straight on his head. Her fingers lingered on his cheek, and he smelled the rosewater he had used to rinse her hands after supper.

"Be good," she murmured. "And be happy, and have adventures, and come back with stories for us."

He said, "Yes, mistress," light and dishonest, which she knew; every time he came back, there was less he wanted to tell them, more to be treasured in the secret spaces of his heart. Then he kissed her fingers and was gone.

DJAGO WAITED AT THE END OF THE PASSAGE, SQUAT AND STILL AND MONUMENTALLY patient. Malevolently patient, since he had discovered—no great trick, this!—Teo's swallowed restlessness. Djago himself had swallowed a rock, Teo thought, to gift himself that perfect inner stillness.

Maybe it was just because he was old. Teo said that sometimes, flung it at the dwarf's big head, but he never believed it. Age didn't bring wisdom, he knew that; he had seen it in Djago's mistress, who was old past measure and baby-soft, baby-stupid. He didn't see any reason why age would bring a devastating patience either. The old should hurry more, should be more urgent, they had so little left to play with…

At least Djago had Teo to play with, when he cared to. When Teo was let run to play. Tonight Teo ran and dropped to his knees, put his arms round the dwarf's neck and kissed him; and was soundly cuffed by strong stubby hands, and subsided, grinning; and said, "Where have you *been?*"

"About my business," the dwarf said, which might mean tending to his vacant and beloved mistress, or it might mean something entirely other. Teo could never tell with Djago, and Djago would never tell until he wanted to. "And now I have a little time, a *little* time that I can call my own..."

And a boy too, whom he could equally call his own although it was not true and did not need saying, its being all too obvious to anyone who cared.

A BOY AND TIME TOGETHER MEANT THIS: THAT THEY WENT THROUGH A DOOR that was hidden if not secret, into the maze of servants' ways that riddled the palace like rat-runs. Jendre at least knew that they existed, because Teo had told her. He thought perhaps half the women here did not know, the old dead Sultan's wives and concubines who had never given a thought to how they were served or how such a vast house could be managed.

Djago had been forty years in the Palace of Tears; he knew them all. Teo was learning. This corridor, this narrow turning stair was familiar already: along and down, and a door at the bottom of the stair where he reached over the dwarf's head to work the catch because stretching up hurt Djago's joints.

The door opened, the night awaited: a swift step from the heady incense of the house to the brisk sharp scents of a garden after rain, from smoky lights and shadows to a true night sky. Who needed lamps, though, where there were stars and moon and the Shine to come; who wanted the easy teasing comforts of women's company where he could have the stumping, grunting figure of the dwarf to follow; who would willingly stay sheltered within harem walls, when there was all a city below them to explore?

Nor was it just any city. This was Maras, the glittering eye of empire, the Sultan's own, home to all that was great and terrible in the world. Here in the old palace they stood on a peak and could see it all falling away below them in tiers to the river: tiers of lights tumbling to the broad dark band that was seized by the eerie span of the bridge, tiers that failed entirely within that brighter, stranger glow they called the Shine. That was the city and the empire and everyone within it, Teo thought, caught in a single striking image: safe up high, he gazed at beauty and saw how it was built on the struggle to climb, how it broke apart lower down and was swallowed by despair.

It was no great revelation. His own village had been much the same; he thought the world was much the same. Only that it was brighter here at the heart, everything showed more and mattered more.

Even in a eunuch's life, some things mattered more. Dry of mouth and sweaty in his palms, Teo hung on Djago's heels all through the gardens and down to the wall. It wasn't leaving the harem that made his breath so short, that set a tingle in his skin; he used to run messages for Jendre all through the city, when they lived an easier life lower down the hill, before she was married so high and then widowed so unkindly and so sent here to rot. He loved to be out in the dark, rain on the wind, a dance on the road, freedom under his feet. And he always went home to his mistress, where he belonged.

Now, though: where did he belong now, at her feet or at Djago's heel? He didn't know. He thought there might be two views on the matter, perhaps even two truths. He did know that she didn't inspire this nervous excitement in him, even in her wilder moods. Her maddest exploits were to do with her and hers; he was incidental. These nights out with the dwarf, by contrast, these were all about him, tests to see if he could be trained or broken or delighted. To him they were mysterious adventures, and the core of the mystery was always Djago, and so Teo sweated.

And thrilled, and shivered with the edgy, sweaty thrill of it; and they came to one of the low guard-gates in the outer wall, and he beat a thunder on it with his fists, because knocking hurt Djago's hands. And because he was young, and was tired of doing things quietly. Djago frowned and said, "A little knock would have done as well."

"Oh, but there is no one else to hear, this side of the wall. On the outside, what do they care? They know that we could knock and knock, and never be answered."

"Until he opens the gate."

"Which he will not do, if there is anyone close enough to see. *He's* not a fool."

Which was true, and an impertinence, and Teo might have suffered for it; but just then there came the rattling scratch of a key in the lock, and the smooth swing of the oiled gate opening; and there might perhaps have been a reason for the sergeant to have a key, so long as he never used it, but it was hard to think of any reason why he would need to keep the hinges oiled.

Except that he was an old friend of Djago's, long since bought and paid for. A simple knock would open this gate to the world, and it didn't seem to matter whether Djago knocked himself or brought a boy along to do it for him.

The sergeant held the gate and grunted a greeting. Djago rolled out on the short stiff legs that gave him that rocking sailor's gait; Teo followed, teasingly mocking it, until the sergeant cuffed him straight.

Some nights this would be as far as they came. Djago and the sergeant would sit against the wall and smoke their *khola*-pipes and talk of emperors and battles, life inside the palace and far away; and Teo would sit at their feet and talk as much as they let him, which was not very much at all. And it was good because he loved stories and he loved to watch the city and the stars, and he knew that the *khola* eased Djago's pain; but it also made the dwarf melancholy, and that was not so good.

So Teo was just as glad when Djago exchanged thanks and greetings with the sergeant, promised to be back before his duty ended, and walked on into a shadowed alley. Once there must have been a wide and guarded margin around the old palace, as there was now around the new. Here no one cared any more—the last dead Sultan's womenfolk, locked up to spend their lives wailing their lost lord: what protection were they worth?—and so the city pressed up close against the wall.

"Why don't you have your own key to the gate?" Teo asked. "The sergeant would give you one; and then he wouldn't need to wait around all night, when there's a good comfortable guardhouse at the main gate, and we could come and go when we chose, not just when he had the duty, and..."

Djago chuckled wheezingly. "Oh, you are such a youngling! Listen, brat: it is always, always better to own the man. A key can do two things for me, just the two. It can open one gate, one; and it can betray me. I can be caught with a key. I can never be caught with the key to that man's heart. And because I have that, I can have him do whatever I ask, over and above the keeping of gates. I never have asked anything, beyond a pipe of weed and a night's talk now and then, but I could. What could I ask of a key?"

The old dwarf had the key to Teo's heart too, of course. And others' too, no doubt; maybe many others', maybe he collected heart's-keys and kept each one as carefully as these.

He didn't take anyone else out, though, twice or three times in a week. Perhaps it wouldn't last, but for now, for this while, for tonight—well, it was hard for Teo not to bounce, not to let his legs carry him springing on ahead while his eyes drank in the city's doings all around him and only his hand reached back to Djago, and only then to hurry the dwarf along...

It was hard, but he was good at doing the hard things. Sometimes, he was. In any case, there was no point in trying to hurry Djago. Short legs and pain together made for this slow, grunting progress, with as many pauses as there had to be. Teo had learned to follow, to stifle the impatience in his legs and let his eyes have it all; and besides, there was shelter in the dwarf's shadow, and he could sometimes be glad of that. Djago was known, he mattered. Teo was nobody, except and unless he was Djago's boy.

Which was, after all, what he wanted: to be with Djago, in reach of his hands, of his voice. They didn't have to be alone, neither of them needed to be tender. He was glad enough just to be sat at the dwarf's feet and listening to his stories. Or to be shuffling at his heels like this in the bustle of a bright night's commerce, listening to the rasp of his breath and waiting for some biting comment to be tossed back over his shoulder. A woman's dress, a man's habits, a masked face or a sudden scurry in the shadows, anything might induce a little scathe, a fling of words which might be true or might be pure slander, it really didn't matter. Teo would choke up on his giggles either way, and hug himself in lieu of Djago who was seldom huggable.

Tonight Djago took him unexpectedly far towards the river and the docks, down precipitous stairs and cobbled alleys where soon every step was forcing out a grunt, pain disguised as effort, fooling neither of them.

Teo had never before been the one to call an end to an adventure. Tonight it had to be him who said, "Djago, stop. We'll go back. I don't understand why you brought us all this way, you must have known how much it would hurt you..."

"It would hurt," the dwarf puffed, "rather more to go back up."

"I'll carry you," which was ridiculous in many ways, but mostly because he was a slender youth and the way was steep and Djago might be small but was certainly very solid. And yet he meant it, which Djago knew; and so he earned himself the whisper of a smile, hidden within the snort and the outright refusal.

"You will not. What, shall I ride like a child on your shoulders?"

"Or like a demon on my back. However is comfortable for you."

"No way would be comfortable for me. Anyone who knew me would die to see it, die from laughing. I would die, sooner than let them see it."

He dressed like a fool still, though his court foolery lay decades in his past; he was certainly a slave; his pride was none the less magnificent, far greater than his stature.

"Well, but the further we go, the harder to get back..."

"Not so. Come; not far now."

And on he went, and Teo with no choice but to follow. Djago was cautious down one more uneven run of stairs, even the shallow ones seeming too much now for aching joints, by the way he clung to the wall; Teo finally risked the offer of a hand, so he could cling to that. They were well into the Shine now, the bridge's eldritch light that hung over all the lower town, giving them shadows to walk in and shadows of their own.

At last Djago turned aside, into a narrow lane with little traffic, high walls, no windows. It opened onto an unexpected square which must have been lovely when it was a garden in moonlight, before the trees died, before the moon's light was supplanted utterly by the sickly glow of the Shine. Now it was as tainted as the light, as the air, as the water that gleamed strangely in the sunken pool at its heart.

There were low steps rising to open double doors, people passing in and out; benches in the square that people should have been sitting on, except that no one wanted to linger in the Shine.

Teo said, "What is this place?"

"This? This is the Night Street Baths. By daylight it has another name, but here, now... Give me your arm, lad, up this little last."

That was the first time he had asked. It was a surrender on his part and it felt like a triumph to Teo, even while his mind was swimming. Night Street stories were like the rain, like the Shine: they broke in everywhere that was broken, wherever they could find a flaw, a crack, a breach in the wall.

Privately Teo thought that this whole city was broken, although it was rich and powerful and lordly. He thought the bridge and the Shine had broken it, leaking poison in.

Here was his proof, indeed, just inside the door. Two men—no, two *figures* standing guard, barrel chests and monstrous shoulders, their faces distorted already out of human. *Dogtooths* the people called them, for their jutting jaws and fierce canines, but they might as easily have been called bears or brutes or victims. It was the Shine that did this, that thickened their bodies and changed their bones and ground their thoughts to powder. They had lived too long down here, below the bridge. That was all. The city's hierarchies were imprinted on the bodies of its people. The rich and powerful lived high on the hill, above all danger; those who could not climb so high, the poor and the shiftless lived in the Shine and came to this.

There were none in the harems where Teo had served, because who would choose ugliness and stupidity to serve them, where they could have the opposites of those? And in the streets, running errands, he was light of foot and quick of mind, sharp of sight. Those were enough. He'd never needed to deal with a dogtooth. As with so much of life beyond the harem wall, all he had was stories.

He did try not to stare, because stories he knew were like snakes, they could twist around and bite you.

The dogtooths stood guard here, but barely glanced at him. They looked down—far down!—at Djago, and bowed their heavy heads as though even the slow and massive could respect endurance where they saw it. And he, Teo, he was passed through on the same nod, insignificant but vouched for. The dwarf's boy.

HE HAD SEEN THE GREATEST BATHS IN MARAS, THE SULTAN'S OWN, IN BOTH THE old palace and the new; he had seen private baths and public; he had never seen anything like this.

From the grandest to the least, from marble halls to tiled pools to stone-slabbed sweatrooms to caves with steaming springs, all baths are built on the same essentials, a source of water and a source of heat. No doubt this was too, but its lobby was something else. A marketplace, a meeting-place, of course, all baths were those; but this was a dormitory also, a place to shelter, Teo guessed a place to hide.

In here were benches as there were outside, as though this wide space was a dedicated substitute for the dead garden. Lamps in brackets made a substitute for moonglow, a better light than the Shine. Most benches held sprawled figures, fully dressed and fast asleep. It was hard to be sure, with their faces hidden in their arms or under a cast of cloth, but he thought most of them were dogtooth, more or less.

Elsewhere, between the benches, people stood about and talked, or stood in silence, or moved from group to group with desperate trash to sell, or sat hunched against one wall or another with everything and nothing in their arms.

"Djago...?"

The dwarf had a purse out, and was negotiating with a thin, determined woman. At least, he was offering money which she seemed determined to refuse. He glanced up and shook his head at Teo, gestured lightly: *you go on in, I'll follow, this could take some time.*

On his own, then, Teo did what he would always do, in a strange bathhouse: he looked for the women, which way they drifted.

Following on, towards an open doorway to the right, he found one woman perched on the end of a sleeper's bench, bent over the bundle that she cradled. Her hair hung down to hide both her face and her baby's, but it couldn't mask the sounds that they were making.

The one was a low, heavy keening, the pure sound of a broken heart, the grief of a mother at her child's burying. Teo knew that well enough, he had heard it often and often when he was a child, when he was free, and through the war that had made him otherwise. Likely his own mother had mourned him this way, and never knew what happened to her boy.

The baby's sounds were stranger, unaccountable: a snorting, snuffling whine, broken by sudden high-pitched squeals, like jerks on an unreeling rope.

Everyone ignored the woman, ignored them both. Perhaps the house was used to this.

Teo couldn't do it. He might be outside the wall, but he'd brought his harem manners with him. Unless you'd caused it, you never left another slave in distress; you never passed them by. That was absolute.

He went to her, put his hand on her shoulder, said, "What is it, sister, can I help...?"

Of course he couldn't help. He should have known. He was a stranger here, a boy let slip for a night; what could he do? What did he think, what did he imagine he could do?

She lifted her face and looked at him, and he was too startled to wonder what in the world she was seeing, with her eyes so rheumy. What he saw was the twisted gape of a nose, the thrusting muzzle of a woman turned dogtooth, turned so far that she couldn't talk, she couldn't shape words any more. She did try. Her mouth moved, chewingly; he saw the long loose tongue behind the heavy barricade of teeth; he heard the wet and frantic sounds she made, and could not understand them.

She understood him, his unease, his bafflement. Whatever she wanted, she thought she could show it him.

She lifted it into the light.

It was her baby, cast of her body and too long nurtured in her belly in the Shine, too long fed of her breast since, and still kept here under the dull weight of that poison glow.

If it ever had been human, he couldn't read that anywhere in its bones, as she peeled its wrappings back. The noises it made were animal, its shape was monstrous; it seemed to have been built for pain, as an expression of its people's suffering.

Most of his own people—if they were his people: those who lived behind the wall, the women and eunuchs of the harem—would shriek, he thought, and turn away, and be appalled that such a dreadful thing could be.

What appalled him—and, he thought, its mother too—was that it had not yet found a way into death. Life is tenacious, but some life ought to know itself better.

He looked around for help, for Djago, but the dwarf was still deep in conversation by the door.

"I'm so sorry," Teo said then to the woman, "I'm not the one to help you. You don't need me. You need—"

His voice didn't tail then, it cut itself off dead. He could not say what she needed; only that it wasn't him.

She nodded, and slowly rewrapped her child in its rags, and hunched herself around it, and let her head and her hair fall forward, and began to keen again.

Teo had seen death and dying, a hundred kinds of horror in his own lands before ever he was brought to Maras. He had seen more since. He had seen his mistress's husband the Sultan die in agony. He thought he had never seen anything quite so terrible as this, and he was helpless against it.

Nothing to do now but straighten up and turn away, head for the baths, hope to soak these memories out of his brain before they set hard and inescapable—

—AND WAS STOPPED BY A VOICE BEFORE HE GOT THERE. "Hey, you! Pretty priest, where do you think you're going?"

"I'm not—"

"I know what you're not." He didn't quite know what she was: a girl, a young woman barely older than he was and not noticeably dogtooth, dressed in the shoddy uncertainties that all these people wore, whatever they could find or make from whatever came to hand. Layers of ragged green fabrics, in her case, that were probably not first meant to be clothing. "You look like a priest, though, in your smart grey robes. And you're too pretty to live, at least without someone to lead you around by the hand. You're going the wrong way. The men's entrance is the other side of the hall."

"I'm not—"

"I told you, I *know* what you're not. And what you are. Which is cute, and cut, and a long way from where you belong. And you're still going the wrong way." And she did literally take his hand, and tug him back the way that he had come.

"We," *we eunuchs*, "we always bathe with the women..."

"High on the hill, I know you do. Not here. Men are men and women are women, whatever's happened. Whatever's been done to them. We do things differently, I guess."

They passed the keening woman with her baby; she didn't look up, Teo's new friend didn't so much as glance aside. He gathered that the woman was known, unless it was her kind that was long-known here, trapped in their helplessness. She could hardly have been the first.

Done talking at last, Djago joined them, unexpectedly taking Teo's other hand; which might have been a signal to the girl to let him go now but apparently wasn't, or was not understood as such.

Doubly escorted, then, Teo came to the door into the men's bath. There the girl did drop his hand, and he went on with only Djago for company. Which was how he had come and how he would leave and as much as he ever expected, as much as he ever wanted, but...

But he still glanced back to seek her face again, to ask her name; and found her gone, a swirl of green lost in the eddy of bodies that filled the hall. For once, he wished he was taller. Mostly he thought that he was too tall. His mistress Jendre had said so, from the day that he'd overtopped her. To Mirjana, his constant growing apparently gave an excuse for more rough handling, as though cuffs and slaps would knock him back like dough to a sensible height. Mostly, though, he hated the sense of growing away from Djago. The taller he became, the more the dwarf paid in discomfort. Just to tilt that heavy head back to look up was an effort measurable in pain; Djago would never admit it, but Teo saw it none the less, and felt stupidly guilty, and stooped or knelt or found yet another way to aggravate Djago's sharp-witted pride.

Tonight, in this doubled strangeness—a house full of unknowns, and himself caught the wrong side, among full men where he had never been—he might have wished to be shorter anyway, only to attract less attention.

But at least he had Djago, who was no full man either, by any measure; and he had Djago's hand, which was better; and perhaps he wasn't so far after all from where he belonged.

DJAGO'S HAND HAD A STRENGTH THAT BELIED BOTH ITS SIZE AND ITS DEFORMITY, the stubby fingers and the swollen joints. Unless it was Djago's mind that had the strength, and Teo simply read it in his fingers. It came to the same thing: Djago tugged, and Teo went along.

Once, surely, this had been a finer building than it was. It probably could still seem imposing to anyone not used to palaces, but the arched and tiled passageway was grubby and ill-lit. There must have been a time when none of the tiles were broken and none fallen to leave those gaping plaster blanks, but that was long ago. Now the mortar between the tiles was dark with mould, the gutters that ran either side of the passage were blocked and overflowing, the steamy air smelled more of must than soap.

Here was a robing-room, though, and at least he could slip off his pristine greys and fold them carefully onto a shelf, top them with his little cap, hope they'd still be there when he came back.

Djago took longer to undress, and Teo dropped down to help him: buckles and lacings were hard for the dwarf, and his costume was heavy with both. This wasn't the first time Teo had fussed at him for clinging so stubbornly to clothes fit for what he was forty years before. He only ever shrugged and said that he still was exactly what he had been, he couldn't change his breeding or deny his mistress, and he would wear the dress of her fool until she told him to dress otherwise. Which, as she had lost her words and her sense both long ago, they knew would never happen. He would wear these clothes until she died, that long at least.

Naked, Djago was all the shapes of wrongness, badly made and badly put together. Between his legs he looked like a damaged woman—no cock, no balls, only a mass of scarring ill-hid by straggling hair—but that was the least of it, the last you came to, if you only came to look.

Teo had seen, though, seen and seen. Tonight he wasn't looking: only clinging to that strong hand like a child grown too tall, while he peered through steam and bad light to see whatever else he could.

One side of the passage offered small rooms, increasingly warm rooms where a man or a couple of men or a group might go to be private. If you could be private, where there were no doors. Teo saw men—and creatures who had perhaps once been men—in ways that might have called for better privacy. Himself a slave whose body belonged to someone else and had been cut to suit, he had no modesty to speak of, but even he...

Finally, the passage gave into a space filled with heat and sound and water, little light. What lamps there were swam in steam like moons behind cloud, announcing their presence but not much more.

No matter. He could have found his way, but Djago knew it. There were wooden boards above the floor, which was slick with scalding water; walking on those, the dwarf headed into the gloom, and Teo followed.

All around the walls, there were benches in tiers. They only had to find an empty one. When they did, Djago stretched himself out upon it with a grunt of ease at last, as though the steam and heat were already reaching through his skin to find kinked muscles and aching joints, spreading relief all through his body.

Teo dropped to his knees on the boards and felt the dwarf's fingers stroke the sand-stubble on his scalp, heard, "No, not like that. I want you up here."

So he moved, sat on the smooth-worn wood of the bench, took Djago's head onto his thigh. The dwarf's eyes were closed; Teo amused himself by combing out the iron-grey beard with his fingers, feeling how it softened in the steam. "Can we find a razor? I'll shave your head if you shave mine."

"Never mind our heads. That's not what I brought you for."

"Why did you?"

"Hush. Listen..."

Teo listened; and above—no, below—the gurgle and splash of water being poured, the hiss of water on hot stones, lay the constant murmur of voices. He'd known it already, they'd walked into the flow of words as they did into the flow of heat and water. The dark was full of men; of course they talked. He shrugged, and said so.

"Yes," Djago said, "but wait. At the moment there are two, three men to a bench, and they listen to each other. Soon one man's story will reach further than his own bench. Before the night is over, all the benches here will be listening to the same story. When a man talks, he will talk to us all. Then he may be worth hearing."

Before the night was over, Djago and Teo too would need to be back in the harem, behind the wall. Teo was not at all sure how he was to manage that. Heat and steam would soak the pains out of Djago's body, so long as he was here; they wouldn't leave him fit for the long climb home. What did a bath ever do, but leave you drained and sleepy and luxurious...?

It dawned on Teo—slowly, because nothing moves quickly in a steam-room, thoughts least of all—that he was worrying about Djago, trying to organise his life; and that was wrong, so wrong. Djago was a fixer, he was the man that Teo came to when he needed help himself. Teo was the flit-bird, unreliable and foolish, needing a steady hand; that's why his mistress welcomed Djago's interest, one reason why. She hadn't said so, but Teo knew.

So no, he wouldn't worry. Djago would have a way to get them home. And meantime they were here in the hot wet half-dark, it might as well be just the two of them because no bench was listening to any other, not yet; and he did so want to talk to the dwarf, if only about helplessness, which seemed to be the tune he always danced to; and—

—and Djago rolled over onto his belly, and his body in the steam might look like a string of ill-formed and hairy sausages but that had never mattered, it was the body that held the mind that held Teo in thrall; and Teo's own body—

—"No, stop it, you can't..."—

—was his giveaway, his betrayal, helplessness again. Which Djago knew and exploited at whim but never before where people might see if they wanted to, if they came by, if they cared.

Teo's body didn't care, apparently. More kindly cut than Djago, he did still have his cock and it could still misbehave. It was trained to be tame, as he was, but the dwarf's pudgy fingers had a wicked, knowing way to them. These days, just the sound of his voice could set a shiver in Teo's spine and a stir between his legs.

Tonight, Djago wasn't talking; he had other ideas, what to do with his mouth. While his fingers stroked the scar where they had cut Teo's balls away, while his other hand clenched around the root of Teo's cock, his tongue licked at its tip, his mouth enclosed it.

Stiff and gasping, Teo did stare wildly about him, but only for a moment. He caught no one's eye, was aware of no one's interest; people told their own stories, or listened to their companions', or dozed in the breathy heat and listened to no one.

So he gave up his concerns, or turned his back on them all, rather: folded himself down over the dwarf's head in his lap, wrapped his arms around his knees and found them all the privacy he could, as much as they needed, less than he would have liked, perhaps, but more and far more than Djago seemed to care about, which was really all that mattered.

HOT MOUTHS, HOT BODIES IN A HOT ROOM, HE COULD BE DIZZY WITH IT; STEAM in his head, he could let the world spin away, as it did when Djago let him smoke *khola*, as it had the one time Djago gave him wine.

When it came back, they had moved somehow so that it was he who lay sprawled his length along the bench, Djago who made his pillow. Not understanding, he lifted his head a little and said, "Have I been asleep...?"

"Hush, little one," said the dwarf, his fingers playing at the rim of Teo's ear.

"No, but—are you hurting? You should—"

"Hush, I said," and a firm fat palm closed his mouth while fingers flicked his ear, sharply this time, stingingly.

Teo learned quickly, when pain taught the lesson. It was the way he had been trained. He still wanted to talk, but would not; he subsided instead onto the solid comfort of Djago's thigh, and listened.

There was indeed hush out there, all through the dim gathering, except for the sounds of water and a single reaching voice.

Teo lay in the sweat and the steam-rush, yearning for a cold quench but his bones were hollow stalks and his flesh was leaves, he had no strength to fetch it; and that voice was in his head as the steam was, riding his spirit on its giddy circles, taking him somewhere else entirely:

"...THIS IS HOW IT WAS, THAT THERE WAS A GHOST IN THE WELL-HEAD AND THEY sent for me to drive her out.

"They had known it for years, of course, that the ghost was there. By the time they sent for me, it was too late for some, almost too late for her. Leave a ghost long enough unlaid, unchallenged, she will inhere to the stone, to the earth, in this case to the water; she will become possessive of it, possessed by it, the two conjoined and deadly.

"Fools, they had tried to fetch her out themselves, it's why they were so slow to come to me. Two of them had climbed down into the well, to feel among the silt and find her bones; they thought if they could find them all and give her burial, she would haunt the well no more. Stupid. What do bones matter? Flesh rots, and so in the end do bones. Even spirit frays, like silk in the wind; but like silk on the wind, spirit will find something to cling to if it can. It wasn't her bones that had to be lifted from that well.

"They learned that, those two fools, too late for them. They went down to her, and she kept them there."

"Did they have ropes?" another voice asked mildly. "Or lanterns?"

"Ropes? What good are ropes and lanterns? You cannot rope a ghost. A lantern will not let you see her face."

"To help them climb out again, I meant. Perhaps they only drowned, diving to find their sister's bones in bitter water."

"No. No, I tell you. She took them, she kept them."

"What good are bodies, to a ghost?"

"Their souls were lost to her fury. She sought vengeance against the living world, that had betrayed her. It didn't need me to show her family this; they came to me at last to cast her out."

"And so you did."

"And so I did, yes. As I have learned to do it, with fire and water and sounds that spirits cannot abide, with prayers and powers that spirits cannot resist; and so their well is cleansed, and they are safe to drink from it again."

"But not to clamber down into the dark of it, without the good sense of ropes and lights."

"I have said—!"

"Yes, yes. You have said, and we have heard you. You have said nothing about the lost girl, the spirit. Where can she go now?"

"She will fade, and fail. Silk on the wind, frayed and scattered threads. No more trouble to the living."

"And to herself?"

"I don't know what you mean."

"I mean she was the first victim here, thrown or fallen down a well; and for this you condemn her spirit to utter loss, with apparently no thought at all for her."

"Oh, what would you have me do, beat a vengeful spirit her path to heaven?"

"If you could do that, perhaps yes, I would, if I did not think her vengeful; but you cannot. What you could have done was let her be, tell the family not to disturb her in her well, tell them she was a blessing. Let her do her family good, guarantee them water all summer long. You could have done that."

"She was a curse in the water, and she would have cursed them all."

"So you have said."

"If she had been left in the well, she would have infected the stones that line it and the source that feeds it."

"You have said that too, and I think that is the only true thing you have said all night. A spirit inhabits a building, as it inhabits the body before death; that is not always an evil thing. It is not often an evil thing. Buildings need spirit as much as bodies do. There was a temple once in Maras, where the priest had bought himself a boy to sing at service..."

AND SO ANOTHER STORY, AND ANOTHER; BUT IT WAS THE FIRST THAT STAYED with Teo. He touched Djago's arm and asked him in a murmur which was right, the first voice or the second.

"Perhaps both," the dwarf replied. "For sure they both believe it. Every man tells his own truth here, that's why I wanted to bring you, you who love stories about the world. Each man's world is his own, and his stories bend to suit it. Come on now, if you've stopped listening. I've sweated enough here, I am hot all through and I need to lie down."

THEY WENT TO ONE OF THE SMALL ROOMS WHERE THERE WAS OIL WAITING, WITH thin rough towels and a pitcher of cool water, and room enough for both to lie together.

They took turns to play body-slave, each towelling and oiling the other.

And slept, perhaps, a little, in the warmth and the ease and the stretch of it, the long night slippery between them. And talked, at least a little, about ghosts and women, water, going home. Not at all about helplessness. Teo was thinking that perhaps he was not so helpless after all.

"We can ride home," Djago murmured, lifting his chin on Teo's elbow, "if we go soon. Soon. Some of these dogtooth men, they pull the night-soil carts that take the lower town's waste outside the walls. For a fee, they will take us clean up to the gate we came from."

"With the night-soil? After we have spent all night in the baths?"

"Clean, I said. They have finished their work, and soaked and scrubbed the carts, and now they soak and scrub themselves. But they will take us, if I ask them to. Soon, before the morning."

"You go," Teo said slowly. "You need it. I'll walk up."

"Teo, this is not a time to be nice about your transport. Ride with me."

"No," determinedly, surprising himself perhaps as much as he surprised Djago, not so helpless after all. "It's not the wagon. I have ... something to do, first," now that he had the key for it. "On my own. I'll follow."

"Well. Don't delay. I can't hold the gate open for you, come morning."

"I know. I'll be there. Wait for me, smoke your pipe, talk to the sergeant. I'll come."

HE FETCHED THEIR CLOTHES, AND HELPED DJAGO TO DRESS, AND DRESSED HIMSELF in the sombre grey of his position, body-slave to a widow of the state and eunuch in a great house; saw Djago to the entrance, saw him away in company, the squat rolling figure like a diminutive reflection of the dogtooths who went with him; went back into that broad lobby and towards the women's side, where, yes, the dogtooth woman was still keening over her dreadful child. He knew that: he had heard her at the entrance and on the way to it, he had heard her distantly while he and the dwarf still lay in their little room, not so private as he'd have liked. He'd heard her in his head, all the time that he was listening to stories in the steam and wanting to talk about helplessness.

Straight to her he went, and stood above her hunched misery. He didn't need to speak. As before, she lifted her head, lifted her dull and desperate eyes, lifted the child.

This time, he took it from her.

For a moment she clutched at it, torn, wanting it again; but a voice—not his!—spoke behind him, saying, "Give him the child. He is a priest to us here; he will know what to do."

There was no telling what the dogtooth woman saw, only that it was nothing clear; there was no telling what she thought, though he guessed that the same was true. He stood as straight as he was, as tall as he was, and hoped that his clothing would speak for him, tell better lies than he could.

Her hands fell away; after a little, so did her voice. This was, perhaps, what she had keened for in the end, when she was done with sorrow.

With dignity, with relief, with dread, Teo turned away from her and found that same young woman at his back. He knew that already; he had recognised her voice, although the cheerful mockery with which she'd named him priest the first time had fallen entirely away from it and left it bone-bare, clean and dry and pitiless.

She said, "Follow me. I'll show you ...where you need to go."

Not what to do. That didn't need discussion, nor direction.

THE MEN'S SIDE, THE WOMEN'S SIDE: IN THE CENTRAL WALL BETWEEN THE TWO stood another doorway, this one closed. She opened it, and led him through.

Here was the furnace-room, of course, and those who tended it; here a way in from the alley behind, for deliveries of logs and coal and oil. Here were pumps, raising water from the cistern below Here were stairs that took them down to that cistern. It was dark down there and she fetched a lamp, although he wasn't sure she wanted to. He wasn't sure he wanted it either, but he let it happen.

The stairs led into a broad and man-made cavern, simple but spectacular, a lapping pool beneath a low domed roof. More steps led down into the water, like a summons. He had no resistance, no way to resist; step by step they drew him in, while his skirts at first floated like lily-leaves around him, and then grew sodden and heavy and tugged him further down.

When the water came to chest-height, it lapped at the baby that he carried cradled in his arms.

There he stopped, breathed, looked down at it without speaking—and took another step.

The child struggled hardly at all, as though this ending were as welcome as anything in its short life: more welcome, he hoped, than the life itself, which must have been swaddled throughout in pain.

He held it until it was entirely still; then he opened his hands, and some current in the water took it away from him. It didn't float to the surface, which he had feared. It was simply gone, into the deep and the dark.

He waited another minute before he climbed slowly up the stairs again, to stand dripping on the lip of the pool.

The girl said nothing. He said, "This house could use a ghost, perhaps," if it were benign or grateful: a spirit that might linger, soak into the walls with all the water and the steam, saturate the stonework and be kind to dogtooths and the desperate, well-disposed perhaps to passing eunuchs whether or not they disguised themselves as priests.

She said, "Perhaps," and took his hand and blew her little light out, so that they stood there for a while in the dark before she tugged him upward.

THE WOMAN WAS GONE, WHO HAD BIRTHED AND SUCKLED IT. They had expected that.

What need more talk, now? She kissed him and he left her, left the baths; and trotted up the steps and steep ways of the lower town despite the weight of his sodden chilly dress. So long as he went on upward, he couldn't lose himself. At the height of this hill stood the old palace, the Palace of Tears; and around the palace stood a wall, and in that wall stood a gate, and outside that gate sat Djago and the sergeant, smoking, so long as he could reach them before the sun did.

Which he did, with time enough in hand to let them enjoy a last slow pipe together, one more conversation about how short the years became.

"Ah," Djago said, "but I am a short man already, abbreviated every way I could be. Not the boy here, he will grow tall and taller," with a nudging boot in Teo's ribs, "but I suit the years better than he does. We have seen the best of this city, Master Sergeant; now comes the worst, and as well that it come quickly. Come on, brat," another toe-poke, "inside for us, before the sun catch us wanting."

The sergeant unlocked the gate and they passed inside, and for a few short steps Teo was let hold Djago's hand again as they walked through the deep shadows of the garden.

THE LAST LITTLE WAY HE HAD TO GO ALONE, DOWN THE PASSAGE TO HIS MISTRESS'S rooms. He sidled in to find Mirjana up already, with a single light to work by. And made no apology and no mistake, reading her snort, her gesture; slipping off his robe and cap and coming damply barefoot to the bed, remembering to keep his feet to himself as he slipped into the warm place that Mirjana had only recently vacated, next to the abiding warmth that was his mistress Jendre.

She was sleepy but not asleep, not quite: alert enough to reach an arm around him, tug him lightly by the ear, mutter something about vagrant boys. He took that as the invitation it was undoubtedly meant to be and nestled close, eager suddenly for an enclosing familiarity and finding only that his own oiled body betrayed him, scented strangely as it was.

The Insolence of Candles Against the Night's Dying

"GOD, THAT'S SAD," QUIN SAID, STARING AT THE WALL.

He didn't mean it nicely. Nice wasn't a thing that he did much any more; the thinner his voice became, the sharper it thrust. And it wasn't only his voice. The thinner he grew all over, the edgier his relationship with the world. A razorblade scratching down a mirror, was Quin in that last year we had together: doing no real damage—what could he hurt, after all? Not the image, certainly, and not the reality either, razors can't score glass—but trying hard none the less.

We were standing in the hallway of my uncle's house and both of us were staring at the wall, both feeling further even than we'd come, a very long way from anywhere that we understood.

My uncle Jarrold had been dead six months, so it shouldn't have been him who had marked the wall, the scratches looked too fresh; but what did I know? Maybe erosion worked more slowly up here than it did down south, or else the house had gone into mourning at his death. Maybe more than the clocks had been stopped.

Oh, it was sad, as Quin said, what some unseen hand had dug deep into the paintwork and the plaster. It was the work of some sad and sorry bastard, and it sure as hell sounded like my uncle.

He is gone, he is gone, I cannot find him. It was a cry from the heart, in letters two feet high; and I knew the sound of that bruised heart in all its grief, its stasis.

I knew my uncle's voice as well as any, and sad though it was, though it always had been, I missed it still.

UNCLE JARROLD HAD LIVED AND DIED IN LONDON, IN A BIJOU LITTLE FLAT CLOSE to Parliament Square: a spinster of the Parish of Westminster, he used to call himself when he was in faux-jovial mood. He definitely wanted us to dispute that, to agree with his own unspoken view of himself, that he was a widow, the Widow of Westminster. We never did that even to his face, young and cruel as we were. Behind his back we named him the biggest queen in Christendom.

He lived and died in London and was very much a Londoner, of that type that believes all civilization inheres in the capital; but he kept a house in the country also, like the Edwardian gentleman that he so earnestly aspired to be. It was the greatest sorrow of his life, that he had been born fifty years too late to wear a smoking-jacket and have his boots shined daily by the kitchen-boy.

No, it wasn't. That's a ridiculous thing to say. The greatest sorrow of his life was what defined his life, as so often it is; and though he made a good pretence of yearning for a bygone style and nothing more, he made it oh so clear that this was only a pretence, a diaphanous veil that he chose to lay across his heartache. He always took care to let us see the clear light of his pain, shining through that inadequate curtain.

I say us, but I don't mean Quin and me. Quin never met Uncle Jarrold. In those days, when I saw him often, I rarely had the same partner two visits running. He had the right perhaps to scorn me as he did. Even the first time, when he withered me: even then, with hindsight, he was dead on the money.

It wasn't the first time I'd met him, not by a distance. He'd been a constant Christmas presence throughout my life and an occasional visitor at other times, a fat and slightly foolish man who brought sweets more welcome than his kisses were. Smooth of voice and silky-smooth of cheek, smelling of bay rum and good tobacco, handing down boxes of chocolate and candied fruits: those were my childhood memories of Uncle Jarrold. Later, when I was adolescent, he was more interested in me. He'd take me off for the day and give me lunch in a country pub, making great play of seeking out a table in a discreet and shadowy corner where I could safely enjoy a couple of halves of ale. His words, repeated every time. He always used to claim that he'd taught me how to drink; I never bothered to disillusion him.

The first time I went to stay with him, though, the world had changed, or I had changed within it. I was a student then, and deeply snared in my first affair;

I hadn't seen Jarrold for a couple of years, and it seemed such an obvious move. I wanted to show off my conquest, to glean approval. No hope of that from my parents, they'd have put us in separate rooms and scowled throughout. Not my uncle, though, or so I thought. I thought he'd rejoice in us, as we rejoiced in the wonder of ourselves.

How wrong can you get?

WE DROVE ALL THE WAY FROM CAMBRIDGE, WHICH WAS AN ADVENTURE IN ITSELF: my first car, the classic student rattlemobile made of patchwork pieces and held together with string, kept going with prayer and overconfidence. Two hundred miles was a lot to ask, but we had that faith that flourishes in ignorance, and never thought twice about it.

Like his flat, like his life, my uncle's holiday cottage—his country house he called it, as we did not—was on an island, and largely cut off from the real world. Splendid isolation, he used to call it, though it was neither.

He'd told us about the tides, in the long letter of direction he'd sent me the week before, but we'd paid no attention to his warnings. We'd ignored the enclosed timetable, started later than we'd meant to and underestimated how long the journey would take. When we finally came to the causeway that should take us across, it was deep dark and our headlights showed us only surging water where the road was meant to be.

Never mind, not a problem. Not a problem in the least. We turned the car and drove a mile, back to the nearest pub. If the tide was high now, it had to be low by closing time, or low enough. Take enough beer on board, we could float across if need be; and there'd be no breathalysers out here. One major advantage of the rural life, though almost the only one we could think of just then.

We scrounged a couple of bacon sandwiches from the landlady, ate her out of crisps and pork scratchings, played a lot of pool and drank without rest; closing-time came and went, and it was near midnight before I thought to check the clock.

Then, too late, I thought we ought to have phoned Jarrold earlier. No point in it now; we'd be on his doorstep in ten minutes. I thought.

In fact, it was closer to half an hour. The causeway was wet still, black and glistening as the sea was on either side, a scary drive to a lad unsober and barely three months past his test; and when we did come to the island, while I'm sure Jarrold's instructions were clear and precise, we were anything but. We got muddled, we got lost, we found the wrong cottage twice before we found the right one.

Brutally late and brutally drunk, I suppose we shouldn't have been surprised at the chill of our greeting, but we were. The young are selfish anyway, and drink can make that worse; I was looking for open arms and a beaming smile, a gesture of dismissal to any casual apology we might have offered, perhaps a "pooh-pooh" and no more.

Which shows just exactly how wrong you can be. Uncle Jarrold was fatter than ever, but no jolly green giant, wrapped though he was in a jade silk dressing-gown with a purring ginger cat in his arms. It was sheer temper that made him throw the door open so wide, no welcome in the world; it was temper too that kept him silent as we staggered cheerfully in with our arms full of rucksacks and carrier-bags. We hadn't given a thought to a gift for our host, flowers or wine or whatever. Hell, we were kids; it showed.

When he did finally speak, after he'd closed the door behind us and thrown the bolts across, it was like a tubby kettle hissing steam.

"Don't begin to apologise," he said, which we hadn't thought of doing. We still hadn't even registered our offence: late, drunk, so what? Who wasn't? "If you don't have the decency to arrive when arranged"—his arrangement, not ours, though we were neither of us in a fit state to point that out—"or to phone through that you'll be delayed, there's no point pretending to have decent instincts of any sort. I hope you're not hungry," though his twitching nostrils told us what our breath was telling him, that we'd filled up on rather more than a couple of halves of ale, "your dinner will be inedible. Perhaps it would be best if you went straight to bed, and we all started again in the morning..."

Which we did: up steep twisting stairs to a small room off the half-landing, where a queen-sized bed was squeezed in with chest-of-drawers and bedside table, washstand: all good pieces, he told us, with a watchful frown. Measuring, I thought, to see if we were too drunk to be allowed his guest-room. I almost told him that we were. We had sleeping-bags in the car, and there was plenty enough floor for two downstairs. Far be it from us to trespass where we were unwelcome, among pieces that outranked us...

But he said nothing more, he passed us, if barely; and I was too young or too chicken to force a confrontation. So much easier just to let it go, to listen to his heavy feet climb higher and exchange a speaking glance with Frankie, all apology on my side and long-suffering on his.

Too pissed to suffer long, we slithered in between the sheets and whispered comforts to each other: how we wouldn't stay even as long as we'd meant to, how we'd stick it for a day or two for manners' sake then go on up to Scotland, just the twain, the two of us and let the world go hang, we needed none of it...

SHAGGING ON UNCLE JARROLD'S FINE WHITE SHEETS WASN'T EVEN AN OPTION. We'd come in hot but his icewater welcome had chilled us, and we were unconscious too soon to think about restoking what was quenched. We just snuggled up and drifted off on each other's beer breath and stubble, and I thought my life complete in spite of crosspatch uncles.

BUT COMETH THE HOUR, COMETH THE MAN; EVERY HERO FINDS HIS MOMENT. Uncle Jarrold's came next morning, and he seized it gleefully.

We woke, of course, to monumental grief, two of those hangovers that only the young endure, thank God, because only the young could survive them. Again no question of a good-morning shag: moving was too difficult, moving hurt. Lying still was better, huddled against the warmth of Frankie's weight. When I cracked my eyes open, a bar of hard light lay across the lacy counterpane. I winced. We were going to be as late to rise as we'd been to arrive. I could hear movement down below, and foresaw stormy weather.

Nothing to do but endure it when it came. I was in no condition to play the diplomat, too sore of head and sick of stomach to drag myself out of bed. I closed my eyes, and maybe groaned a little. Frankie's hand squeezed my thigh gently, as much as either one of us could manage and as good I thought as anything was going to get.

Until the stairs creaked, too loud, too soon; the door banged open much too loud and much too soon, and there stood Uncle Jarrold.

With a tray in his hands, two steaming beakers and a pot, real fresh coffee: just the smell of it made my dry mouth ache with yearning.

"Up, you idle creatures, get you up!" He set the tray down carefully on the bedside table, with dire warnings against spilling a single drop on his precious linen; added that breakfast awaited us in the kitchen, which was far more than we deserved but that he was in the forgiving vein today; and swept majestically out.

As ever, coffee was sovereign. We sat up with exaggerated caution, cradled hot mugs possessively and sipped, gulped, poured and gulped again. No way would either one of us have let a drop spill, we needed it more than the bedclothes did.

Coffee does more than ale can, to justify man's ways to man. Inside twenty minutes we were up and washed, shaved—at my insistence: Frankie tried to claim holiday privilege, but Uncle Jarrold had earned so much, at least—and relatively sweet of breath and groping our way unsteadily down the stairs.

To be met by another magnificent scent arising, the mingled odours of bacon and something herby, backed by more elixir, essence of coffee. My uncle was at the stove with an apron around his midriff and a wooden spatula in his hand; he waved it at us with an appalling bonhomie and cried, "Sit, sit! Breakfast is immediate!"

Breakfast was. He set plates before us and heaped them with crisp bacon and slices of black pudding, with sausage and fried egg, with tomatoes and mushrooms too. He set a rack of toast between us and said, "Eat, enjoy..."

So we did that. After a minute—or perhaps a couple of minutes—I managed to remember manners enough to mumble, "What about you, Uncle Jarrold, aren't you joining us?"

"Don't speak with your mouth full, Tom. And no, I had my breakfast hours ago. We don't all sleep the best part of the day away. It's nearly lunchtime. I thought I'd take you to the Queen's Head for lunch. Don't talk, eat. You'll need to line your stomachs. Unless your disgusting behaviour of last night has left you unable to face the sight of a few noggins of ale this splendid day?"

To be honest, I at least was still young enough that the thought of more beer could make me queasy; but I was young enough too to deny it fervently, "Hair of the dog, Uncle, it's the best thing," as I reached for another slice of toast. "After food, I mean. These sausages are amazing, I've never eaten anything like them. What's in 'em, do you know?"

"They are good, aren't they? They're pork, of course, with onion and leek. Sage and thyme are the herbs, I think, though there's another flavour that continues to elude me. Slow cooking is the secret, though. You can't cook a sausage too slowly. These have been on for an hour or more..."

AS HE CHIVVIED US OUT OF THE HOUSE, HE RAISED A MUTE BUT EXPRESSIVE eyebrow at the car, and then said, "I must apologize, boys, for the unwelcome I gave you last night. Your behaviour was atrocious, but that doesn't excuse mine. You struck me in a tender spot, though; I am particularly sensitive to unpunctuality. Pray that you do not, but if ever you spend half the night waiting for someone who never comes home, then perhaps you will understand my reaction a little better."

"Oh, please, don't worry about it, Uncle," I said awkwardly. "It was our fault, we got cut off by the tide and never thought to phone..."

"I agree, your fault entirely. Unfortunately, it played upon my most fragile sensibilities, and so I lost control. When you know me better, I think you will understand."

And his eyes turned to the wide sea, where it battered and sucked at a shelving shoreline.

THE ISLAND WAS A ROCKY PROMONTORY, INHABITED FIRST BY MONKS AND monastery servants. Gradually a secular community had grown up around the religious; now the monastery was a ruin, and the locals lived by fishing and tourism. Pubs at both ends of the causeway pretty much depended on the tides for their trade. We had hardly been the first idiots to find the road awash, and ourselves suddenly with hours to kill before we could cross.

The causeway itself, Uncle Jarrold said, had been laid barely a century before, atop the safest of the several known pathways. Before that you took a boat to the island's fishing-harbor, or else you risked your life on foot across the sands.

"The tide comes in at a sprint, boys, so don't you go tempting fate," he said, with solemn tone and meaningful looks from me to Frankie and back to me again. "Nor is the tide the only danger. There is quicksand out there, quicksand that will draw you down and never give you up..."

And he stared out across the flat sands and the rock-pools, and I was astonished to see tears in his eyes.

HE TOOK US TO THE PUB—A TEN-MINUTE WALK FROM THE COTTAGE, BUT THAT was universal: nothing on the island was more than ten minutes from anywhere else—and outmatched us pint for pint, and on what was for him an empty stomach too. It was impressive. We tried to pretend we were just slowed down by a heavy night and a heavy breakfast, but truth was he could have drunk us under the table, any night he chose.

That lunchtime, it seemed to me that drinking made him maudlin. Later experience suggested that maudlin was his natural frame of mind, or else the state he chose to dwell in. He settled his eyes on us, two young lads sitting closer than we needed to, side by side on a settle, and he sighed mightily. Took a pull on his glass, and turned his eyes to the window, the inevitable view of glistening sand and mud and sea; and said, "You won't know this of me, Tom, your parents won't have told you, but I had a terrible thing happen to me here. A tragedy. A family tragedy, really, only your mother could never see it that way. I lost the one true love of my life, out there on the sands. That's why I keep the house here, why I can never truly leave. This place haunts me so..."

"Unh..." I didn't know what I was supposed to say to that, *do tell?* or what; but it didn't seem to matter. A grunt was enough.

"I wasn't a young man, even then," he went on, "and he was only a few years my junior, but it was a young love that we had; we'd been together barely a year. We both knew that this was the real thing, though, a lifetime commitment. Not like you two, we weren't playing at being men."

I felt Frankie shift in protest, and stilled him with a hand below the table. I wanted to hear this.

"We had arguments, of course, as lovers do. When you've been alone a long time, it's hard to make compromises, and we were both of us stubborn. I have a temper, too—well, that you've seen.

"We had a dreadful disagreement one night; it started from nothing, as these things do, and escalated into savagery on both sides. In the end he stormed out, as he often did. I was too upset to go to bed, so I just pottered around the house and waited for him to return. I knew where he'd be, walking on the sands, cooling off.

"It came on to rain, and I thought he'd come back then, he didn't have a coat. So I fetched a towel for his hair, and waited.

"He didn't come, though. I waited an hour, longer, and still he didn't come. He couldn't have been walking so long, in such weather; I wondered if he'd taken shelter with a neighbor, though it was terribly late. I put on my waterproofs and went out to see. There were no lights burning anywhere, so I went on down to the shore. The tide was coming in strongly, the causeway was entirely underwater already—and there was simply no sign of him anywhere.

"I walked, I shouted his name, I woke all my neighbors and organized a search, but we never found him. Then, or later: his body never turned up. He must have gone out too far in his fury and been caught in the quicksand, or else simply outraced by the tide. It was dark, overcast, he might simply not have seen the water coming until it was too late. It was a terrible death, though, either way; and more terrible for me, I think, having to live on with the memories. Such a love only ever comes once in a lifetime, I can't look for so much luck again."

"So what d'you reckon, then?" Frankie murmured later, as we lagged behind Uncle Jarrold on our way up to the island's height, where he was going to show us the monastery ruins.

"What? Sad story."

"If it's true."

"Frankie..."

"Oh, come on! It's the old 'I have suffered' routine, every faded drama queen has got one. Ask me, if this guy ever existed at all, he just lit out. Hitched a lift off before the tide came in."

"And then what? They were living together..."

"I dunno, do I? Changed his name, dropped out. Emigrated, maybe. Went straight, got married and he's raising kids in Arizona. Wouldn't you? With that to come home to?"

"Frankie, you're a bastard."

"Yeah, right. That's why you love me. But honestly, Tom, it's a fairytale. It's got to be. Christ, he didn't even tell us his true love's *name*, didn't you notice?"

I grinned, and slipped my hand into his back pocket. "We're not worthy."

LATER STILL, A LOT LATER, LONG AFTER THE SUN HAD SUNK IN GLORY BEHIND THE mainland, Frankie pleaded exhaustion and took himself off to bed, leaving me alone with my sad uncle and a bottle of malt. Looking for an excuse to follow, thinking that tonight we might just sully Jarrold's pure linen sheets, I slugged back my shallow share of the whisky and said, "Well, Uncle? Do you approve?"

"Approve? Of what?"

"Frankie. Frankie and me. God, I don't half love that boy..."

And that was when he ripped into me.

"Love? Love, do you call it? Don't insult me, Tom. Don't parade your adolescent conquest and call it by a holy name. You greedy, mocking apes—oh yes, I know you've been laughing at me behind my back, I'm neither blind nor deaf—you animals, what do you know of love? You sit there straining your jeans, your mind's already up there with him, you can't wait, you're almost drooling already with impatience to get your hands on his body—and you dare, you *dare* to call that love? Immature lust, physical obsession—it's nothing, do you hear me? Nothing! A tissue-paper tango, and it'll burn out as fast as tissue-paper burns and it won't even leave ashes on your tongue. Don't talk to me of love till you at least know what the word means, even if you haven't braved its touch..."

And so on and on, a tirade—fuelled by whisky, loss and loneliness perhaps, but a tirade none the less—that shrivelled me, that shredded all my certainties. When the brutal run of his words finally ebbed to silence, to a scornful gesture of dismissal, I slunk upstairs and found Frankie genuinely out for the count; and didn't wake him, only laid my cold body next to his and prayed for warmth.

In the morning we left, we went north and west to the wild Scottish coast, and found no comfort in it. So we went our separate ways instead, to our separate homes for what was left of the vac; and Uncle Jarrold proved to be absolutely right, rot him. Whether he'd sowed the seed of it or not, Frankie and I reaped a fiery harvest the following term, and wrote ourselves into college legend with the force of our mutual destruction.

And no, with hindsight, I no longer called it love, that frail, flickering thing we'd had, that pale light that had seemed to burn between us. St. Elmo's fire, perhaps: fool's gold but no true flame.

IN THE YEARS THAT FOLLOWED I HAD OTHER PASSIONS AND MANY OF THEM, OTHER flames that seemed to me to burn hot and pure and true. Some of them I took to show to Uncle Jarrold after we'd made our peace, after family feeling and some need in me, in both of us had overcome my pride and his. But I never spoke of love, unless he asked me; and even then I was tentative, uncertain, and ultimately right to be so.

BUT NOW HE WAS DEAD, MY UNCLE, AND I WAS HIS INHERITOR: OF THIS HOUSE, and all that it contained. Which was more and a great deal more than furniture and books and bric-à-brac. *He is gone, he is gone, I cannot find him*: but standing there in Jarrold's absence with Quin shakily at my side it seemed to me as though that *cri de coeur* had cruelly reversed itself. Jarrold was dead, and yet his spirit still pervaded this place and hence my life, I might never be free of him now; and Quin was altogether there, slender fingers clinging to my arm for support, and yet I thought that he was all but gone already. I could almost taste the loss of him, and how that too would be a thing of which I could never be free.

"Come on, love," I said softly, "let's get you settled before I bring the stuff in from the car."

No question of the stairs, he didn't have the leg-power for a shallow flight of steps any longer, let alone the steep climb here. We'd brought a camp-bed with us just in case, but memory said there was a luxurious sofa in the living room, and Quin was very used to nesting.

The sofa was there still, little more worn than when I'd last seen it. I turned it to face the windows and saw Quin comfortable upon it, packed him about with cushions and left him with the radio on and a kiss for company while I hauled in all the gear that we had to travel with: clothes and medicines, food and drink, towels and toiletries and chamber-pot. I could carry Quin up to the bathroom when he needed it, but not at night; no room for two on that sofa, and he wouldn't let me sleep on the floor. Not yet, not while he still had the will to resist. *Later* was a promise I'd made to myself, that I hadn't yet shared with him.

When the gear was all fetched in and distributed, upstairs and downstairs and in my lover's chamber, I asked him, "Are you hungry?"

"No," he said easily, almost cheerfully, recognizing the gambit of a familiar game.

"Well, but will you eat?"

"Some soup? Perhaps?"

"Perhaps so."

So I heated soup from our great supply, added plenty of pepper because he tried sometimes to use the blandness of his diet as an excuse not to eat, and added a wallop of yogurt also in hopes of getting protein inside him somehow. Served it up in one of Jarrold's pretty porcelain bowls—one of my bowls, I supposed, now— and stood over him while he ate.

"What about you?" he asked, dipping his spoon and tasting slowly, every mouthful only a taster and a very long way from a full mouth, using almost more energy to get the food there than he could possibly gain from swallowing it.

"Sick of soup," I said lightly, truthfully. "I'll fix myself a sandwich later."

"You've got to eat," he told me, frowning; and oh, that sounded so good coming from him, I could have cried. Instead I went back to the kitchen, sliced bread and beef and pickles, searched out the horseradish and assembled all into a massive bellyfiller. This was how we lived, largely; he could barely eat solids and I wouldn't cook properly for myself alone, so we got through a small reservoir of soup and I snacked on the side. I'd roasted and brought up a joint of beef big enough to last me a week; I had no plans to stay longer than that. We were really only here to sort through my late uncle's things, to decide what to keep, what to sell and what to burn or throw away. If Quin felt up to it, then I'd take advantage of the chance to show him the island and the coast: to try to show him a little of my uncle's life and what it had meant to me, why I really wanted to keep the house. *Expensive memento,* his first comment had been; and it was true, and I felt a great need to justify it to him.

I hadn't expected to find us both plunged immediately into the sad and sorry heart of Jarrold's obsessive grieving. But it fitted, actually, it was apt. This was how Jarrold was in life, he left no margins, no neutral ground. In death, why should he be different?

I ate with Quin for witness, as he had with me, for me. We both needed that kind of watching. It should have been ironic somehow, but to me at least it only felt right. Of course I forgot my own body and my own needs, in caring for Quin's;

of course he took care to remind me. How else should we live?

Reminded, I left him to doze while I went upstairs to get my own room sorted. On the way, inevitably, my eye was jagged by the graffiti on the wall. I paused, and touched my finger lightly to one of the gouged letters. There was an immediate fall of plaster-dust onto the carpet. The floor should have been filthy with it already, and was not. There was a light film of regular dust everywhere in the house; I didn't believe that anyone had been in to clean since my uncle's death.

Well. It was another task for me before we left, and a little lighter than it might have been; no more than that. I trotted up to the old guest-room and made the bed quickly, unpacked a few clothes and necessities, hurried back down to Quin.

Found him lightly asleep, as I'd expected. He did little else but drift these days. I'd never told him so, but I hated to watch him sleeping, lying still and silent with his drawn face slack and empty. It was too potent a foretelling, a premature taste of that time to come when I'd find him emptied indeed, comatose or dead already, and what would I do then...?

The sun was setting vividly outside the window. To save myself sitting and watching him, anticipating a worse vigil, I moved quietly about the room setting candles to burn in all the corners. Strong lights hurt his eyes, so we lived our long nights out among guttering shadows. It seemed appropriate.

I left the curtains open; moon and stars and distant glows delighted him as much as candle flames and firelight. There was an open fire here, coal and logs and kindling all set ready by my uncle's foresight the last time he left, never foreseeing that he would never return. Quin would enjoy a blaze. I turned to attend to that, and saw his eyes open.

I was caught, trapped, as so often at these moments: bereft of movement or intent, free only to be ensnared. We gazed at each other, and my breath was shallower and more tremulous even than his.

He smiled, before I could; and said, "Well. Here we are, then."

"Yes. At last." I'd had reasons in plenty, not to introduce him to my uncle while Jarrold was alive. Chief among them—or perhaps the sum of all of them—was that simple snare that seized me, choked me time and again in Quin's company. Put it bluntly, say it straight, I was in love; and this love I had never been prepared to expose to my uncle's scathing. Jarrold had been important to me once, his approval had mattered, and for that memory's sake I could never bear to see him so belittle himself.

I sank down against the sofa, propped my elbow beside Quin's shoulder and rested my chin on it. "What shall we do? We could nip to the pub later, if you're up for it."

"No. Not tonight, Tom. It's been a long day."

It had. Too long for him, perhaps, though he'd slept through most of the drive up. "I'm sorry," I murmured, "but I couldn't leave you for a whole week..."

"Yes, you could. I've got friends enough, you know that. You just didn't want to leave me."

True, and not true. The whole truth was that practicalities aside, I couldn't bear to leave him for a week; individual days I found hard enough, not knowing what kind of Quin I'd come back to, sharp or dozy, asleep or sick or dead already.

"If you didn't want to come..."

"If I hadn't wanted to come, you'd have sulked and stormed and threatened to stay yourself, to sell the house by proxy, anything to make me change my mind. You know you would. Luckily I did want to come, and I'm glad I'm here. I just can't face company tonight, that's all. Other company than yours, I mean. And that's all the comfort you're getting, and more than you deserve. Get my pills and a glass of water, before you get too comfy; get a drink for yourself and talk to me, okay?"

Better than okay, when such instructions were seasoned with a kiss, as they were. I did all of that and settled down again; and the first thing he said was, "Do you believe in ghosts, Tom?"

Ouch. I didn't want this conversation, not here and emphatically not now; but I never could say no to Quin. Specifically, this time, I couldn't say *no*. "I believe in being haunted," I said slowly. "By the living or the dead, or some dream that was never properly either one of those."

"What, you mean we make our own ghosts?" His voice was a whistle and a whisper, as reedy as any ghost's, a ghost itself of what it used to be. I closed my eyes, and was still haunted by it.

"Well, Uncle Jarrold did. All the time I knew him, he was haunted by his lost love." And now he was haunting me, and that wasn't fair, it wasn't right. I was haunted already, I'd brought my own ghost with me, still barely clothed in failing flesh and blood. My own lost love, and that I hadn't lost him yet was only a confusion of the timeline, or else it was God's little joke.

QUIN WAS WELL USED TO NESTING THROUGH THE NIGHT ON ANY CONVENIENT sofa, now that he was too weak to manage stairs but still too social to keep to his own bed at home like a good invalid should. What he wasn't so used to was sleeping through the night. Another of those little jokes, the ironies of illness: he could sleep at any time of day, all day often, but come the dark he was always wakeful. Sometimes I thought that he was frightened of the dark, scared to close his eyes against it, for fear of that greater dark to come when he would close his eyes and never open them again. I never taxed him with it, though, only stayed with him, kept him company as long as I could manage.

That night I fought off my own exhaustion for a while, for a long time, till we'd burned all the fuel on the hearth and watched the fire die to a sullen glow, barely any life left in it. At last he said, "Get yourself to bed, for God's sake. Christ, I can hear your jaw creak every time you swallow a yawn. You think it does me any good, watching your eyes sink to pits while you mumble like a moron? Christ…"

I smiled, kissed his cheek, put out all the candles for safety's sake except for one wee nightlight on a table, and took myself to bed.

And lay wide awake and fretful despite my weariness and the comfort of the bed; and so was still awake when something cracked in the quiet night. A sharp, destructive sound: I was up in a moment and running downstairs naked as I was, confused and anxious, frightened almost.

Stood in the living-room doorway staring in, and saw Quin's head turn to find me. Sobbed one breath in relief, the first I think since I'd heard that sound; and took another, far more calmly, as his acid voice said, "Sorry, sweets, you look nice as anything I've seen for months, but I'd be no use to you tonight."

Nor any night now, not that way, but never mind. "What was it? That noise?"

"I don't know. It was outside, in the street. I'd say someone had put a window out, except I didn't hear footsteps. It wasn't me, at any rate, I haven't broken yet. I haven't broken anything. Go to bed. And sleep this time, will you? Or you'll be no use to me in the morning."

OBEDIENT AS EVER, I WENT TO BED, I WENT TO SLEEP. And woke in the late morning, and found Quin dozy but demanding, no change there. I fetched him pills and the coffee he was not allowed to drink, in exchange for his promise to essay a little porridge, which I made. It was an hour or more before I could go outside.

It only took a second to spot what had cracked in the night. The car's windscreen was starred in one corner, as though someone had flung a pebble at it; but out of the crazed glass ran lines of fracture, and those lines spelled out a run of words, *he is gone.*

I stood there looking for a time, for a short time that seemed longer than it should. Then I got into the car and with my elbow I knocked out all the glass in the windscreen, before I went back indoors to phone the RAC.

THAT AFTERNOON I TOOK QUIN FOR A DRIVE AROUND THE ISLAND, STOPPING wherever I thought I might be able to beg some empty cardboard boxes: the few shops, the tourist information office, even the parish church. We finished the tour at the pub, which did us proud with crisp-boxes. It seemed only good manners to have a drink while we were there. Quin had a Bloody Mary, the evil of the alcohol—which he was absolutely not allowed to drink—offset, we decided, by the virtues of tomato-juice. I had a pint of my uncle's favorite ale, for old times' sake, and a quiet chat with the landlord. He'd known Jarrold since my uncle first arrived on the island, and offered a tradesman's conventional sympathy for my loss; said he was pleased that I was keeping the house on, and hoped to see plenty of me in the years to come. Plenty of me and my friend, he said. I didn't disillusion him. Instead, I asked the question that had been burning in the back of my head for years, ever since Frankie had set it to smoulder, the question I had never quite dared to ask while Jarrold was around; and yes, he remembered well the night that my uncle's lover had disappeared. Remembered the morning after, at least, the search: had joined in, indeed, as many locals had. Such a sad story, he said, and Mr. Farnon had never really got over it, had he?

No, I agreed quietly, he never really had.

BACK AT THE HOUSE, I PILED MY BOOTY OF BOXES WHEREVER I COULD AND SET about packing up Uncle Jarrold's things, under Quin's acerbic eye. The books he approved of, at least in theory, though some of the titles justified their existence by drawing a dry chuckle or a snort of amused contempt. The ornaments earned nothing but scorn, even where they were porcelain figurines that carried the stamp of Meissen or Worcester. Quin had no patience with prettiness for its own sake, nor for the sake of market value. I was less precious; all this was money in the bank for me, and Quin was expensive.

I'd meant to leave my uncle's bedroom for the following day, but the work went faster than I'd expected, and having built up a head of steam it seemed a shame to waste it. Besides, that was the one room in the house into which I'd never ventured yet. Curiosity drove me up the stairs, reluctance held me only a moment with my hand on the door before I pushed it open.

It was a dark room, even after I'd flicked the light on: heavy oak furnishings that must have been a trial to manoeuvre up the stairs, faded brown velvet curtains, bare boards with a scattering of rugs. A tester bed, a massive wardrobe—*his clothes, what to do about his clothes? Leave them for now, that's what. Sort them later, give them to Oxfam, whatever*—and another case of books, a dresser with more pretty things on doilies to arouse Quin's happy ire.

The dresser had a mirror. I saw myself reflected, and thought it likely that I was the first young man to be so framed since Uncle Jarrold's tragedy. I'd been feeling glad, in a strange and not very comfortable way, that the story had proved true, at least in so far as there had been a young man and he had disappeared. It seemed almost to validate my uncle's obsessive sorrow, to justify the emptiness of his life. Ghosts need to be real, to take the bathos away from a haunting.

But now, as I stood there thinking those charitable thoughts—and thinking too, thinking inevitably of Quin and my own haunting to come, which could itself prove lifelong—I saw words form slowly in the mirror, letter by letter, as if an invisible finger moved between the glass and the silvering.

He is gone, he is gone, I cannot find him.

And suddenly I had no sympathy and no pity in me, nor any trace of fear, only a blazing anger. I remembered how Jarrold had hacked at me in my own first gripping passion and I turned it all back on him, on whatever was left of him in this empty house.

"Oh, you shit," I whispered. "You sad, sorry little shit. You had your love and you lost him, yes, to the sea or to a pathetic argument, whatever; and you huddled around that little light and kept it feebly burning, you used that as your excuse against the world for all the rest of your life; and now you dare, you *dare* to shove it in my face, when all you had and all you lost can't hold a candle, not a bloody *candle* to what I've got waiting for me...?"

Tears stung my eyes, but I dashed them away in fury; and snatched up a shepherdess who might very well have been Dresden, only that I didn't stop to examine the base of her, I only flung her full force at the mirror.

More than the glass and the ornament was shattered, in that moment. More than shards of glass and porcelain fell crashing to the dresser, to the floor. I stood breathing heavily amid the silence until I'd stopped shaking, until I had some kind of weak control.

Then I turned and walked out of there, walked softly down the stairs, down all the stairs and into the living room, that Uncle Jarrold had called his parlour and I would not.

Quin was sleeping, his face turned away from the light. Briefly—as so often at these moments, as ever—I thought he was gone already, I thought I'd never find him again.

Parting Shots

When you're burying a man, you can give a lot of time to what he wears, how he looks, what he takes with him. That last, especially. You don't have to get all Ancient Egyptian on his ass, he's probably not Tutankhamen, but—well, it's a thing. You can do it.

Us, we stood around his bed and cracked a litre of Stolichnaya. Shot-glasses straight from the freezer, the way he'd taught us all to drink it: we drank him a toast of parting shots, wetted his forehead, opened his wardrobes and set to work. Dressing Miss Daisy, Micky called it.

We'd already washed and shaved him, we were good at that; it was routine, we'd been doing it a year already. I would've liked to have his hair cut, but none of us was competent with scissors and who can you ask, to do that? We were sending him on shaggy, then—but we did touch up his roots, not to let him go greyly.

Underwear was simple, a pair of his favourite Calvins; he'd seen a banned advert once, dissolved into hysterical lust and never wore anything else after. Clean black jeans and a silk shirt, the Issey Miyake jacket with the mandarin collar that he loved, all of that was straightforward.

We argued over footwear, because he hated his smart shoes. For preference he went around in sandals and socks, and we all hated that and always had. He'd have been thrilled, to know that we were still fighting over his feet. In the end, we decided he could go barefoot. Clouds are fluffy, and the road to hell is notoriously well-paved; he'd be fine, either way.

We crossed his legs for comfort—"sorted for ease," Sally said—and because we were all settling in to make a night of it, and because he'd always been a crusader. We laid his hands across his belly, fingers linked, because he used to do that when he was drunk or tired or bored enough, when he was just sitting back and listening while we bickered and flirted and debated great matters all around him, and you'd think we did it entirely for his amusement. Likely we did.

Then it was all about decoration. His favourite rings, that had grown too heavy for his fingers: they could go back on now, the jet and the jade and the skull-knuckle silver ring. They were too loose, but that didn't matter any more. He wouldn't be flinging his hands around to make his points again, his stillness did that for him.

No watch—he used to say there never was that much hurry, that a man had to carry the time on his person; and I never knew him late, though it was odd how often the rest of us turned out to be early—but we plaited leather thongs around his wrist, and each of us tied a knot in the trailing ends to hold them.

Around his throat, what he liked to call his giveaway: "I'm a creature of the seventies," he used to say, "medallion man to the core." Only his medallion hung on a fine silver chain and was silver itself, a moon in crescent, the bulk of its disc black and secret, with just that sliver shining. He loved that.

A silver Bajoran cuff on his right ear, with the finest imaginable chain linking it to the sleeper in the lobe. In his left, a stud of white gold, which was all the gold he ever had or wanted: one of a pair, and these days Gerard wore the other. Gerard wasn't there. He'd given this to us to do, which was either acutely generous or an acute surrender, and I wasn't sure which.

We'd already ruled out a post-mortem tattoo, even if we could have found someone to ink it. We had discussed it, though. He'd have liked that.

Nothing left, then, bar what went into his pockets or into the coffin with him. Much of that was standard, those things he always used to carry in his jeans when he was still able for it, when he was up and about: his purse with all his credit cards in case he needed money, house keys in case he wanted to come home. A corkscrew, a toothpick. Loose change. He liked to jingle a little as he went.

In his right-hand outer jacket pocket, a fresh pack of Winstons and a lighter, because he hadn't been able to smoke for a long time now and he'd want that; left-hand outer pocket, a flask of Lagavulin. The last thing he drank in this life, first drink in the next.

Left -hand inner pocket, a wallet of photographs: his mum, his sister, us. Some of us individually or in twos and threes, the ones he'd taken himself; and then the team photo, all of us together at the foot of his bed on the day he came home from hospital, the day we started nursing him ourselves. All of us bar him. He took photographs, he didn't appear in them. He used to say he wasn't interested in how he looked to other people, only in how they looked to him. It wasn't true, of course, which is why he found it necessary to invent.

Right-hand inner pocket, his passport. We'd renewed that for him just six months ago, when he was long past leaving his bed. He'd need it now, wherever he was going.

In the same pocket, because every journey involves longeurs, he'd want a book. We gave him—no, we let him keep—his copy of *Religio Medici*, a slim Victorian edition with the leather long since worn to a butter softness. That'd see him through.

Tucked under his arm, of course, a cuddly toy. How not, when it would infuriate him to find her there? Besides, she had a function: this was Vespa, the vast fluffy wasp we'd bought him years back and hung on the back of his door to remind him never to go out without his epinephrine.

THAT, OF COURSE, WAS THE MOMENT THAT ALIX YELPED, AND SCURRIED OUT OF the room; and came back a minute later, blushing and laughing, with his EpiPen in her hand. We'd almost sent him off without it.

SO THAT WENT INTO HIS JACKET POCKET WITH THE FAGS, BECAUSE THERE WAS nothing he liked better than a smoke after a crisis; and then we were done. The vodka was gone, but hey, there's always another bottle. And this was a wake and a houseparty and, what, did anybody imagine we were going to bed tonight...?

AT SOME UNCERTAIN TIME DURING THAT LONG NIGHT, WHEN THE OTHERS WERE all out in the kitchen, concocting some witches'-brew punch to welcome Gerard home, I slipped into the front room—laughingly renamed the parlour, just for the occasion, because that's what he would have done—and I added one little memento of my own, slipping it into his pocket with the rest of his loose change. My lucky silver dollar, that I'd been carrying since I was thirteen, since my astronomer-uncle sent it to me from Mount Palomar: the design showed an eagle with an olive-branch in its claws, descending on the moon. It was a sharp counterpoint to his own moon-medallion, and I wanted him to have something that would hurt one of us, at least.

LATER WE GAVE GERARD SOME TIME WITH HIM ALONE, WHILE WE WENT OUT walking in the dawn mist and the chill of it, climbing a hill and passing a bottle from hand to hand, drinking one more toast on the summit. And then—at last, too soon, whichever, both—it was properly tomorrow, and we had to let him go. See him off. We had to be good in public, dress as sober as he was and act as quiet in church and at the graveside and over sandwiches and squash in the church hall after. His sister presided, while his mother sat quiet and proud and miserable in her wheelchair at a table in the corner. One by one we all went over to do the dutiful by him as well as her, listening to her and failing utterly to recognise her son in anything she said.

And when that was over, we could go home and there could be wine in plenty or whisky for those that wanted it, the rest of that bottle of Lagavulin; and it turned out that I was the only one who wanted it, so I did that, I applied myself to what I wanted most.

Then Tig started rolling joints and sending them around, clockwise and anticlockwise each in turn, so I got them coming and going; and eventually between the whisky and the dope it was me that was going, losing contact, drifting hard.

AND WHEN I WAS ROUSED, WHEN GERARD ROUSED ME EVERYONE ELSE HAD GONE, seemingly; and he said, "Not so much a wake, more a sleep, eh? Bed for you, sweets. I've made up the spare, so shift yourself."

So I did that, I shifted myself upstairs: through the bathroom on autopilot, toothbrush and towel, and so to the little boxroom where I must have dossed a hundred times when we were sharing shifts, while he was slowly slowly dying in the room below, breathing no more than a leaf breathes, heedless and fractional.

I tumbled into bed and slept, or passed out if you're not polite; and woke in the deep dark, to a terrible sense of presence.

I hadn't thought to pull the curtains, and I could see him, almost, as a shadow against the stars. I hadn't closed the window either, and I could smell him like rain on the road outside, like the risen roots of matter.

I lay very still and didn't speak, didn't breathe; felt watched, watched over, not free after all. As though there were still expectations, and I had better not disappoint.

And then he was gone and I could breathe again, like a child at Christmas who has been desperate not to let his father guess that he was still awake, not to spoil an adult's pleasure in a supposed secret; and I was still dizzy unless I was dizzy again, and I went spinning away again into incoherent dreaming, and didn't wake again till it was full day.

AND WHEN I DID, WHEN I ROUSED AND SAT UP AND FUMBLED FOR MY GLASSES ON the bedside cabinet, the first thing I found was my lucky silver dollar, laid gently down for my fingers to discover, clean and cool and misted with the breath of leaves.

Up The Airy Mountain

UP THE AIRY MOUNTAIN,
Down the rushy glen,
We daren't go a-hunting,
For fear of little men
—from "The Fairies" by William Allingham

THE DEAD ARE HEAVIER THAN THEY USED TO BE, BEFORE THEY WERE DEAD. That's not what the scales say, but it's a fact none the less. Life is anti-gravity; the earth may suck, but we spit back at it and snicker, and walk just a little taller than we ought, step a little further, not float but—well, you get the picture. You live the picture, you should know. Every cell in your body resists that tug a fraction, and that's a lot of resistance.

The dead don't have the same privilege, it's all switched off. Meat, bone, body: heavy stuff. Even blood has weight to it, when the fizz has gone.

And when you're dying, when you're neither hale and whole nor wholly here, when your cells are slowly, slowly shutting down—that's when you start to acquire that extra weight, what can't be measured on the machinery but only in the minds and muscles of those who care for and about you, either or both. The dead are worse, the dead can overtopple a man with sheer mass, but anyone on that journey starts to acquire drag, momentum, matter, call it what you will.

We're all of us dying, of course, from the moment that we cease to grow; only that some of us go faster, and too soon.

AS GLEN, AS HE LAY UPON HIS BED AND TURNED HIS HEAD TO FIND ME AND EVEN his gaze weighed more than it used to, even his lightest thoughts had substance now.

Life is anti-gravity, and so am I; I hated to see him grave, portentous, sinking.

"Who is that," he said in his horsehair voice, a fibrous scratching of it string on string, the only noise he had remaining to him, "who's there?"

Who is that one who always waits beside you? Except, be fair, I thought, it might have been any one of us.

"Glenda honey," blood brother, lazy angel, open your eyes, "it's me."

"Daniel?"

"Yes, lover," and the third time that he'd asked today and it was hard to hold my patience except that I would, of course I would, what in God's name was I here for unless to do the hard things?

"Daniel. I want you to do me a favour. Big one..."

What, more than my being here and doing this? I'd fetched him bedpans until he couldn't manage, until so little movement hurt and he hadn't the control in any case. He was in big man's nappies now, and I changed them for him on my turn of duty. And I held buckets that he could gout blood into when that was needful, when he haemorrhaged inside and it had to go somewhere and generally came up; and I endured the hellwatch of his dead eyes, which was worse, and bathed them hourly in glycerine and water. And still turned up on time, on schedule, day or night. I caught a lot of night-time watches, often on my own. And came because he was my friend, or had been, and one of us at least had not forgotten. I couldn't imagine any favour greater than that.

"Daniel?" Seemed he hadn't forgotten either, or not right this minute. Sometimes he had never known me, ever; sometimes we were still bed-bunnies in his head, flashing rumps across a disco floor. Occasionally, rarely, we could be simply what we were in my head: old friends together, patient and nurse, one who claimed and one who paid the debts of long-gone loving. Those times he recognised my voice and called me by my given name, as now.

"Right here." Sitting on the high bed's edge and laying my fingers lightly on his own, as much contact with the world as he could bear.

"Listen."

"I'm listening." Every word cost him pain and effort, precious coin; neither one of us would waste them.

"You remember that dog, where we put it, where we dug it under?"

"Christ, Glenda—!" As often as not he couldn't remember me, and yet he clung to the death of a dog, a nameless stray...

Well, yes. If I was Daniel, he was still or again my Glen, and he'd always held that animal in mind. Why else would I have remembered it myself?

"Yes, love, I remember the dog, and I know where it's buried. What of it?"

"Dig it up, Daniel."

"What? What for?" Old dead bones that he'd broken himself, knocked all out of kilter even before the worms and the weight of soil and rock got to them; what was he going to do, cast an augury?

"There's a body, a boy underneath."

"Oh, Christ." He hissed, as my hand tightened; pressure hurt. How much had this hurt him, how long? "What is this, confession?"

"Absolution."

Glen, man, don't be in such a hurry... But he was, he had to be, of course. His time grew shorter, every breath he took; every moment's struggle wore him down.

"All right, then. Who's the boy?"

"I can't remember. You find out, Daniel, give him back to his family, let them bury him for real."

WHEN WE WENT, WE WENT AS A TEAM, AS WE WERE NURSING GLEN: HIS FAIRY band reformed, all but silent under the weight of him when we were in the flat together and utterly silent now, crammed into Henry's 4x4, compressed with news.

Henry, Jody, Tim and Blake and me. Tosh had stayed behind, hospital duty, nothing could break that schedule; something of him had come in the car regardless. We carried his curiosity along with his crowbar and shovel, along with our memories of the boy he used to be. We were all of us bonded, beyond the abilities of time or change to part us.

Once we'd been young and foolish, young and rowdy, high on the delights of city life and our own sweet selves, the damage we could do. Once we'd been wild together, following Glen or trying to grab the lead from him and never quite achieving that but loving him regardless.

No longer. Now we were a team again despite him, because of him; we didn't have a captain.

If we'd been kids still, eighteen, twenty, we'd have been arguing as we drove, wrestling for that elusive leadership: every band of fairies needs its Oberon. Grown men, it seemed, could get along without.

I might have claimed the crown for a while, at least, for a little while. It had been me that Glen had turned to; it was me that knew the way. The others only knew the story. For a wonder, they hadn't been there when the dog died. Seeking a little transitory independence, perhaps, looking for a new order, or simply sipping city lights on their own to find out how they tasted apart from Glen's direction, my own more subtle influence. Whatever. They'd been off without us, and they didn't know what I knew.

"Where now?" Henry demanded, slowing as the headlights showed him how the road divided, left and right.

"Up," I said unhesitatingly. "Just keep going up. I'll shout, when we're near."

THE ROAD CLIMBED THE HILL, A HIGH MOOR NORTH AND WEST OF THE CITY. It had been a night like this, I thought, when the dog had died: cold and clear, stars and a bright moon, the planet spinning us relentlessly towards a terrible uncertainty. Only difference was, in those days I'd seen hope and wonder in that spinning, in every dawn and sunset. Very heaven, I'd thought the world to be; and myself lieutenant to a power, a principality who held the keys to every pearly gate. I was young, I was a believer: music, dance, drugs, sex, whatever came along I gave it credence, I had faith. I believed in myself, my body, every way it made me feel. Money was votive, it allowed the opportunity to feel more, or feel differently. Even my hangovers I cherished for their immediacy, their potent seize.

Outside my skin I was less certain, perhaps, but I believed in the band, our brotherhood, its tangibility against an insubstantial world. Above and beyond them all, I believed in Glen. He was that little bit older, that great gulf wiser: wherever we went he'd been there before us and knew his way about, whatever we came up against he could find a route through or over or around.

Even now, I supposed, he was leading the way, going first. Checking out the other side. If death was the last taboo, he meant to break it. He'd said that, more than once, before he got too sick to be clever.

Actually, I thought, he'd broken it already, long ago. Swift and hard and meaning every moment, and I'd watched him do it, I'd been sitting right beside him as he did. For a while, later, I'd thought it was for my benefit, a baptism of blood, a lesson given and learned. Now I wasn't sure.

THE NIGHT COLD AND CLEAR, MOON AND STARS OVERHEAD BUT OTHER LIGHTS were brighter, nearer, the whole of the city laid out before us like a playground, like a school; just the two of us in Glen's big car, and I felt special, selected, exhilarated. This didn't happen often, and it was treasure to me. Whatever he had in mind, I was up for it.

I thought.

We drove down the hill from his place towards the city centre, going slow; his eyes flickered constantly off to the side, to where long terraces and alleys fell away towards the river. Suddenly he knocked the indicator, spun the wheel, dived across the flow of traffic. Horns blared behind us, but he showed no sign of caring.

We were in one of the alleys: high walls of brick on either side, wooden gates and redundant coal-hatches, black bin-bags spilling garbage under our wheels. Ahead of us, eyes shone briefly pale in the headlights. A stray dog, young and hungry, all legs and ribs as it scavenged in the gutters; good street-sense it showed, cringing back against a wall to let us pass.

Glen steered straight for it.

It turned and trotted into its own long shadow, staring back over its shoulder; its eyes gleamed again, bright and empty. For a moment it reminded me of us, any one of us, skinny and scared and bathed in light, running into the dark.

It was running for real now, senselessly down the middle of the alley, forgetting what wisdom it had learned. Glen grinned, or showed his teeth at least, as he stamped on the accelerator.

And me, I just sat and said nothing, did less, didn't even breathe. I was out there with the dog, sharing its thoughtless terror; I was in here with Glen—my friend, my mentor, my idol—and not sure if I were sharing anything with him. Either way I was trapped, inconsequential, the entire victim.

WE THOUGHT WE WERE THE CHILDREN OF THE NIGHT; LOOKING BACK, I THINK perhaps we were all of us victims, all the time.

"THERE. BY THAT OUTCROP, THERE'S A PLACE YOU CAN PULL OFF TO PARK."

Probably we weren't meant to park there, it was an overtaking spot where the single-track lane widened suddenly and briefly between its enclosing dry stone walls; but there was no traffic this time of night, we'd met nothing coming down as we went up. And no traffic wardens, of course, no watching eyes.

That was, that had always been the idea.

We climbed out slowly into the road and stood stamping and huffing, swinging our arms the way you're supposed to, the way you learned to do by reading it or seeing it in other, older men. The way we learned most of our adult habits: from books and magazines at first and then from men. It's a boy thing, unless it's just a fairy thing. Perhaps we were enchanted; God knows, we always felt that way.

Blake, Blake the builder reached back into the 4x4, dragged out a canvas bag of tools and passed them around. Pickaxe for Tim, crowbar and sledgehammer for Jody; for me it was three spades and carry-the-bag. Henry got nothing but a heavy torch. Henry had a banker's belly now, was furthest gone from lean and whipcord boy. Besides, it was Henry's car, he'd driven it, he'd done his share. We'd always been more socialist than democratic, dividing up the portions with a grand inequality. From each according to his ability: let him hold the light now, let him act as witness if we need one. Not objective, not neutral, never that—one for all and all for one, we few, we fairy few, immutable and indivisible and us—but he had the status we still lacked, he could speak for us if occasion demanded. Better he didn't have mud beneath his nails at the time. Real mud or figurative. It might not make a difference, but it might.

I led them up to the outcropping rock, to where a buttress thrust suddenly up from earth.

"Here?" Henry asked, breathing heavily.

I shook my head. "Not enough soil, it's bedrock six inches down. We tried it. Look, see that solus rock on the skyline there?"

They looked, saw, confirmed it with grunts and nods.

"Twenty paces, on a direct line from here," and my hand slapped the buttress, "to there. That's where we put the dog."

"That's a bit...specific, isn't it?" Tim murmured at my back. "A bit *Treasure Island*, X marks the spot in crutch-lengths, Long John Silver?" Tim the Crim, he was a lawyer yet, sharp to spot unlikely detail.

I shrugged. "That's how Glen wanted it. He wanted to know, exactly; he said it was important. You couldn't just dump a body and forget it, he said. Even a dog's body mattered."

I stopped, listening to myself on half a second's lag and shivering suddenly for better reasons than the night could offer me.

"He was setting you up, Dan. Just in case. Christ, he even told you so. Dogsbody, right?"

Well, at least he'd said that I mattered...

UP THE AIRY MOUNTAIN

THE DOG DIED IN SILENCE, AS IT HAD RUN, PRETTY MUCH AS IT HAD LIVED, I thought: lurking, sneaking, the opposite of presence. It was the car that made the noise, a thud that shook all the windows and rattled the doors; it was my mind that held it, that has held it ever since, one of those pivots a life can twist around.

Glen had been iconic, up till then. Suddenly he was something more, darker-stained and incomprehensible and human. We understand our idols all too easily, because they're invested with public virtues and public vices and nothing else. Only real people have private lives. Glen had just admitted me to his.

Though even then it was obvious that this was not habitual, he didn't kill stray dogs for a hobby. He stopped the car, as quietly as the dog had stopped; he got out and paused for a moment, looking at deductible damage—a bend in the bumper, a wet smear and a ripple on the dirty white bonnet—before he moved back up the alley to look at what was a fixed cost, no deposit and no return.

This was what I was there for, though I couldn't figure why. The sums wouldn't add up. Some kind of initiation, surely: maybe he put every boy through it, before they could melt seamlessly into his little band of brothers...

And swore them to silence after? Well, maybe. I didn't believe it, though. One of them surely would have said. And what was so significant about a dog's death, anyway? To us, who were not dogs—far from it, we were gorgeous, radiant, the height of delight—and dealt in worse fates daily? We knew all about death already, though he hadn't yet plunged among us in red braces, *greed is good*, as he would a few years down the line. The milieu we moved in, of course we knew. We danced on a deliberate edge, for the thrill of it; other boys had fallen off.

Still, I thought this was a message, expressly for me. I went to join Glen, where he stood above the mangled body; he said, "There's a blanket in the boot. Want to fetch it?"

The boot wasn't locked. I found the blanket, ancient and moth-eaten, waiting for me. Beneath it, I found a spade. None of this was normal, in Glen's car.

He made me do the messy work, down on my knees in the gutter, getting blood and muck on my dancing-clothes as I wrapped the dog in its ready shroud; he made me carry it back and stow it in the boot. I saw him smile faintly, as I wiped my hands on a corner of the blanket.

"Blood washes off, Daniel," he murmured. "Everything washes off in the end, and there's plenty of water in the world. Come on."

He drove us out into the country, north and west. He parked on a high moor, found a landmark, paced a counted distance before he tossed me the spade and told me to start digging.

He didn't say much else, then or later, after he'd taken me back to his house and washed me thoroughly, teasingly, laughingly, working hard to win a laugh out of me; nor after he'd taken me to his bed, when we lay languid and weary and needing another wash. If any or all of this was a message, I thought it was missing me. If it was an exercise in bonding, bondage, I thought it was unnecessary. He should have known that I was bound already.

THESE DAYS HE DIDN'T SAY MUCH AT ALL, AND LESS THAT MADE SENSE. If this was an exercise in futility, I thought I might face a little grief from these old fairy friends of mine, here or in the car going home. If they let me get in the car to go home. They might leave me to walk if I'd dragged them up here on a fool's errand, in pursuit of fool's gold, buried treasure, buried bones.

Not my fault, but they'd blame me anyway, I thought. I was catching one or two looks already as we paced and counted, hefted hardware, faced the reality of chill air and frost-hard ground.

It wasn't that hard to dig, once you'd broken the crust of it; I remembered that from last time. And told them so, and caught a glare full-force from Henry. It was only the torchbulb glaring, I couldn't see his face, but it carried intent enough for anyone to read.

"Glen dreams," he said. "Hallucinates. What the fuck are we doing here, anyway?"

"Looking for a body." *You brought us, you know.*

"What body? Anyone here missed a boy? It's just Glen, he's half mad with it, lesions in his brain..."

"Maybe so. He sounded clear to me," and maybe it was my fault after all, maybe I did deserve all the grief I might yet receive, if I couldn't tell when the captain was seeing true and when he was simply babbling. "Let's just dig, shall we? See where we get?"

Tim swung the pickaxe; Jody cracked the ground the way he used to crack doors, safes, whatever, with swift and judicious use of crowbar and sledge. I plied a shovel, as Blake did beside me.

Soon Jody abandoned the crow and grabbed the last of the spades. We built up a quick stack of spoil; I was relieved when Tim yelled out, I'd just been starting to wonder if I'd struck quite the right spot after all, because surely I hadn't buried the dog that deep.

"What?"

"Pick went through something. Not earth, it didn't feel right. Dig here. Henry, give us some light..."

We dug there in the circle of torchlight and scraped soil back off the rotten remnants of a blanket, with the rotten remnants of a dog beneath, snapped bones linked by slimy stringiness. Only the skull seemed whole, and only for a moment; it crumbled as Tim worked the pickaxe blade beneath.

I made some noise, I guess, some protest. He said, "We're not archaeologists, Dan. Nor priests. This isn't what we're here for."

No. And it was only a dog, in any case, and never mind that I'd seen it die and thought now that it might have died for this precisely, to be what people found if they should dig here.

Even so, "Treat it gently," I said, "show some respect. We've got to put it back after, whatever else we find."

"It's dead, Dan."

"That's my point." A sacrifice, a victim: we all knew how that felt. I felt understanding settle like the silence, all around me. We shifted that dog in spadeloads—Tim was right, we were not archaeologists—but did it as gentle as we could manage, and laid the bones all together in a separate place. We wouldn't get them back in any order, but at least its ghost could find itself again.

Beneath where the dog had lain, we needed pick and crow once more, to work through hard-impacted earth. A forensics genius, I thought as I hacked uselessly with the spade's edge, an expert with light and time and tender loving care could say this had been stamped to such solidity. We had none of those advantages, but worked a little slower as it started to make sense. I felt happier, less happy, both at once. No trouble in the car, perhaps, but plenty after.

Even doubting Henry watched us closely now, slipping torchlight under every clod of earth we raised, looking for another gleam of bone.

And spotting it, first among us all, and crying out to warn us. We stepped back in a moment, rested on our tools, rubbed hot sweat from our faces and felt the cold touch of the night come back to claim us.

"There," he said, pointing with the torch, close as a finger, "see it?"

We saw it, just a streak of pale in the dark; and now I did want to play archaeologist, I wanted to get down and grub with my fingers in the dirt.

That was too much respect, we couldn't afford it. More cautious spadework then, the most care we could manage; in ten minutes we'd laid him bare, we and the years of worms between us. A boy, as Glen had promised: huddled close around his death, laid down with his knees drawn up tight against his chest to make him dog-sized, make him fit the grave. He still had rags of skin and flesh and tendon, as the dog did; he still had rags of clothing also. His trainers had survived the worms, as had his nylon jacket. The rest was shreds and patches.

"There's a tarpaulin in the bag, Dan," Blake said. "Lay that out, and let's see if we can lift him."

"Why bother?" Henry asked. "We've found him, okay; what are we going to do with him now? Cover him up again and leave him, that's my suggestion."

"Henry, we've got to find out who he is. Give him back to his family. Glen said."

Henry's face suggested that we'd done enough for Glen already, and too much perhaps. "We could give the police a tip, let them come and fetch him."

"And let them find what we can't, some clue to lead them back to Glen? No way. We'll do this ourselves, as anonymous as we can make it."

I thought we'd end up dumping bones in a box on someone's doorstep. Not pretty, but we'd done ugly things before. I'd do anything, I thought, to make these last days easier for Glen. Never mind how hard they were for the rest of us. There was a debt, our bright and shining tiger-years, we owed them all to him. Now in his grey descent, he could ask more and far more than he had thus far.

WHEN WE GOT BACK TO HIS PLACE, HE WASN'T ASKING ANYTHING. Like consciousness, lucidity came and went in tides, as though there really were a lunar link. He could be aware, he could be self-aware, but the rhythms of both were different and they were rarely in sync one with the other.

Tosh didn't want to see what we'd brought back with us, and no blame to him for that. I didn't want to see it myself, in the bright garage-light where Blake was laying it out on a pasting table, like a makeshift morgue. Plenty of space in there, we'd long since got rid of Glen's old car. We had joint power of attorney, all six of us; Tim had fixed that six months before, when we made this pact with Glen. He wasn't dead yet but his estate was ours none the less to keep or sell, to divide up as we chose. I'd thought his car, his house, his books would be the most of our responsibilities; I hadn't thought we might take possession of his history, his skeletons, the bodies he'd left in his burning wake.

I hadn't known there were any literal bodies, though it didn't come as too much of a shock. Thinking about it, looking back, I was only surprised that all six of us survived him in the one sense, as he had been then, and again that we would all survive him in the other sense, that he would be the first of us to die. The Seven Sisters they used to call us, we used to call ourselves, but he was always more than elder sister and guiding light. Devil, tempter, bully, scourge—all of those and more, he whipped us wild and we were too young to do anything but dance maniacally at his heels, spinning faster, skidding further, desperate to outdo him if only to show that we could do it too. Boys did die, then as now; one of us surely should have died, perhaps we all deserved to. It seemed bizarre sometimes that it was Glen who was dying now, before any of us had had the chance to nip ahead of him. He always used to lead the way, but he'd had intuition or seemed to, he always seemed to know just where to stop.

No great surprise, then, that some other boy had died, a greater sacrifice. I was only shocked that I didn't know, that none of us had known. I slid my hand beneath Glen's, and gazed reluctantly into his eyes. When he was truly living, when he was light they were gravity, blue and potent, blinking at nothing. Now they glittered dully, crazed and smeared, frantic behind a veil of murk. He was blind, we thought, as near as we could tell; for sure he didn't see us, nor anything we tried to show him. In losing sight or just forgetting how to see, it seemed that he'd forgotten how to blink also, or else lost sight of the point of it. His tear-ducts were dry, his fund, his reservoir exhausted; we bathed his eyes to keep them moist, to soothe them.

Trying to soothe him if he should need it, if those trapped and frantic eyes weren't doubly deceptive, saying no more than they saw, I gave him senseless words to match his senselessness: "It must be a weight off your mind, my love, that must have been some burden to carry all these years..."

I didn't think Glen had carried it at all except as a fact, one little historical detail, a truth that he remembered: *I killed a boy and buried him in the hills, Daniel knows where.* He'd left it to us to carry, as we carried him now and the ever-increasing weight of him, as we'd carry his coffin between the convenient six of us when he was dead. I thought Glen might even have planned that. Perhaps that was why we none of us had died, he'd known that he would need us at the end.

As it turned out the boy wasn't hard to name, and only a little harder to identify. He'd carried a purse in his jacket, in a zipped inner pocket; it was barely marked, despite the years of rotting. Inside the purse was a cashpoint card.

"Mr D B Tunnicliffe," Henry read out, holding the card between fastidious fingers that had been scrubbed and disinfected like my own, like everyone's; dirty boys once, we'd all learned to be scrupulously clean. "Mean anything to anyone?"

We played with the name, the initials, as we would have done before. DB— Dirty Boy, Dust Bin, Dave Brubeck, Dandelion & Burdock? Dog's Breath, Dog's Breakfast? (Dog's Body, but I kept that to myself.) Tunnicliffe—Tunk, Tuna, Tuna

Fish? Tinkerbell, if the kid had been a fairy...?

Nothing tinkled any of our bells, though. Henry slipped the card into a pocket of his suit and said he'd make enquiries.

TOOK HIM LESS THAN TWENTY-FOUR HOURS. The following evening, we had the lad all lined up, named and tagged and wrapped up, ready to return.

Derek Brian Tunnicliffe, according to his records: seventeen years old when his account fell into disuse, presumably around the same time that he fell into that dark hole on the moor. Not living at home, not officially employed, not in a steady relationship (amazing, the details that banks record), he seemed to have been gone a while, a lag of a few weeks between the last transaction on his account and the police putting him down as a missing person. Even then, they had apparently done little more than fill in the paperwork. One more gay boy skipping town, and so what? He might have been running from his dealer, his pimp, one of his clients, anyone. Happened all the time: boys came, boys went, it made no difference. They all looked the same to the law.

Seven years later—exactly on the first day they were allowed to—his parents applied to have him rendered officially dead. More paperwork, no passion, and the account was closed. Records had only been kept this long, Henry said, because of the unusual circumstances, against the remote chance of his returning. Officially dead didn't necessarily mean defunct, and his bank was covering its back as banks do, Henry said, the world over.

He sounded as though he approved. In this case, so did I. We had the parents' last-known address, we could dump the bones in a cardboard box and give them back their boy, however little they wanted him.

Except that I didn't want to. That was what Glen had asked and all that he had asked: a local habitation and a name, find out who he was and give him back. He hadn't suggested going further. Well, he wouldn't, would he? He'd known the truth himself, necessarily. If he'd felt no need to share it over all these years, why should he want it shared around now, even if he could remember? He wanted the ends tied off and tucked away, nothing more than that.

I wanted more, and didn't believe I was alone. I used to follow Glen without question, but no longer. *How?* and *why?* were beacons blazing in my head, and the man who had the answers neither would nor could tell me now. We had a tame GP to supervise our nursing, but he wasn't really one of us. We couldn't take him to the garage, show him bones and ask him to tell us how the kid had died, stabbed or strangled, what. I doubted his ability in any case. I thought a specialist with a lab at his disposal might have thrown his hands up in defeat. There was too little flesh remaining to give any easy reading, and we'd hacked the bones about some despite our care, as we dug them out. Blake and Henry between them had done more, washing the mud away while I'd sat with Glen. Likely they'd washed off a putative scientist's last chance.

Why was another matter, and we had perhaps some hope of working that out. Gifted the boy's full name, Tim remembered him, and prompted memories in the rest of us. Glen had loved Python, so we had too; we'd called the kid Brian, with a giggling tag-line, *he's not the messiah, he's a very naughty boy...*

More than naughty, he'd been a sinner by our lights. Good boys steal, of course they do, but never from their mates. Brian had been compulsive, unless he was simply stupid. When he was around—in bars, in clubs, at parties; jealous of our own company, we'd kept him at what distance we could manage—we were always careful to keep a hand on our purses and an eye on our bags. At a gig one time I'd been dancing, I'd stripped off a favourite silk shirt to sweat half-naked under the lights, under the beat; when I went to cool off, the shirt was gone from where I'd left it. Next time I saw Brian, he was wearing it.

Compulsive or not, he was definitely stupid. I took the shirt back, left him with bruises for a finder's fee. Any bright kid would have taken the lesson with the lumps, and been grateful. You needed to be bright, to survive that world we lived in then; when Brian vanished, I guess some of us wondered if maybe he'd been dimmer than we knew, if he'd turn up in the river one night with bad drugs in his blood or worse than bruises on his body. Both had happened before, both would happen again. When you took yourself to market the way we did every night, you needed to be part of a conglomerate, you needed at least one buddy to watch your back. Brian was always peripheral, always alone.

Now we were wondering if maybe it had been a different story, though the ending was the same: if the little toad had wangled his way into Glen's house, and tried to make off with something. Glen had always been protective of his assets. My shirt had cost Brian a serious beating; it took little imagination to write that just a little larger, to remember Glen's temper and his sheer physicality, the strength those extra years had given him...

"What I don't get, though," I said slowly, "if that's what happened, if he laid into the jerk and Brian died, then okay, he thought he'd bury the body and stick a dog on top of it in case anyone saw the disturbed earth and came to check, fine— but why drag me into it, why make me dig the grave, or start it? Why make such a ritual of it, something I was bound to remember?"

"That's easy," said Henry, as Tim had before him. Smart boys, these professionals. "He was setting you up. Glen could lie for England, but not you. That's why you got a record, Dan, while the rest of us stayed clean; your face is like a signed confession. Anyone came asking questions about a grave on the moor, you'd blush and stammer, give yourself away without saying a word. It'd be clear as day that you knew something, where it was at least. That would've been enough. You remember what the cops were like back then, go for an easy target and fit him up if need be, if they couldn't find the proof. And Glen knew you'd say nothing, he'd be safe."

I shook my head, more a plea than a refusal. "He wouldn't do that. Not to me."

"Why not? You didn't have fifteen years of history together, not back then. You were the last of us to join up, remember, the last one Glen found. He probably hadn't known you six months, you certainly weren't a fixture yet. Why would he give you a break? He used us all, Dan, you know that."

And was using us still, and we still let it happen. That was the hold he had, the debt we owed. Henry was right, of course, I'd never have grassed him up; I'd have served his time if I had to and thought myself a martyr for the doing of it, thought it a far, far better thing than ever I'd done before.

Even so it was a cold picture that Henry painted, a banker's view of the world, investments and returns and selling short. I didn't want to believe it. Neither, I thought, did the others.

Lord, I believe; help thou mine unbelief. Please? Make it flourish, make it strong...?

In pursuit of that, perhaps, I urged them all to do some serious thinking, to drum up whatever memories they could. We'd been living half in that world anyway for months now, back in orbit around Glen again as we had not been for years; we carried it with us daily, and fresher every day. There must be more stories about Brian, someone surely must have spent more time with him than I had. He was a toe-rag, but a persistent toe-rag. A barnacle, even—as witness how he was clinging still, despite being fifteen years dead. Any little thing might help.

MYSELF, I WENT TO SIT WITH GLEN A WHILE, TO TALK HIM THROUGH THIS LATEST revelation. And had nothing back from him besides his nerveless stare—he was failing fast now, the doctor said he'd likely not pull himself into proper consciousness again—but I didn't mind that. I was scared, I think, of what he might say if he could get a grip on what I was telling him. *Yes, Daniel, it's true, you were my fall-guy if I needed one.* Or worse, perhaps, he might deny it and I'd never believe him now. It was true, he was a born deceiver. His greatest gift was to lie by misdirection, to let drop a word or two and watch how people misconstrued him. I used to envy that so much, trapped as I was in my own directness, where I said no and my whole body said *yes, that's right, officer, take me away.*

IN THE END I TOOK MYSELF AWAY, I LEFT GLEN TO BLAKE'S MORE PRACTICAL CARE and went home, went to bed. Stayed away all the next day, losing myself in my own memories, rebuilding us in my head the way we used to be, less brightly shining now, more tawdry in perspective; and was woken the morning after by a phone-call, early.

"Dan, it's Jody. I'm at Glen's." Of course he was at Glen's; it was his watch. I didn't need to check the rota, I knew it by heart, and I wasn't on until that evening. For a moment I thought this was the call we were all waiting for, all dreading, *he's on his way, come now if you want to say goodbye.* But Jody went on, "Tim's supposed to take over, I have to be early at work today; and he hasn't turned up, and his wife doesn't know where he is, he didn't come home last night. Can you stand in for him?"

"On my way," I said wearily. I was the one among us who didn't work, at least not nine-to-five. Hence I was the one among us who got these calls day or night, the permanent standby as well as a regular lead.

Never before for Tim, though. Tim was the guy who lived his life to a metronomic standard, who was always where he should be when he said he'd be there. For Tim not to show was disturbing; if his wife Lisa couldn't find him, that made it serious. I wanted to say *call the hospitals, call his office, call the police,* but she'd have done all that already.

I GOT TO GLEN'S SOONER THAN JODY HAD EXPECTED ME, LARGELY BY VIRTUE OF not showering, not cleaning my teeth, forgoing coffee and turning up in yesterday's clothes, if any of those are virtuous. Virtue must be relative, I guess.

"How is he?"

"Quiet."

I nodded. That was what they'd told me on the phone yesterday, so I was more or less prepared when I looked into the room we'd set up for him on the ground floor, back in the days when he was still occasionally mobile but couldn't manage stairs any more. He lay quite still in his high hospital bed; someone had persuaded his errant eyes to close, and I couldn't see the least movement in the sheet that covered him, I couldn't see his breathing.

"Glenda, love..."

I licked my finger and laid it lightly on his upper lip, felt the faintest touch of air. The doctor had warned us about this, had said that he could slip into a coma at any time and linger maybe for days before he died. He hadn't eaten for a while now; we had a drip going into his arm, enough to keep him comfortable, pain-free, hydrated, not enough to keep him alive. He'd said he didn't want that. "When the time comes, let me go," he'd said.

Well, we would do that. Slowly, reluctantly, but we would.

I SAT IN THE CHAIR BESIDE HIS BED, PUT MY HAND ON TOP OF HIS AND FOUND THE fluttering pulse that lingered there. Like a bird on a wire, like smoke in a breeze, it gave not the least promise of permanence.

Well, no more could any of us. If the most solid, the most settled, the most reliable of us could fail wife and friends and solemn oath and all—hey, we're all friable under pressure, it's the human condition. Glen had his pressures, we had ours. I wondered what Tim's were, beyond the ticking of a mortal clock: *time presses* was one of his most lawyer-like catchphrases, I'd heard it a hundred times this year and we'd all watched the truth of it being acted out on Glen's body. I wondered if that were the problem, if he'd suddenly reached his limit, simply couldn't bear to witness these last days, the end of a long song.

And didn't believe it, couldn't make that coalesce with what I knew of Tim. Besides, even if he wanted to run out on us, why would he run out on his wife also? It didn't add up. So instead, inevitably, I wondered if there might be a connection with what else was new, a boy's body brought to light and laid out in the garage.

TIM HAD ALWAYS BEEN THE FOCUSED ONE AMONG US, THE ONE WHO COULD party tonight but still keep an eye on tomorrow. For a while all he was looking for tomorrow was another party, but that changed. Quite suddenly he signed up for a college course, and then university after; while we dossed, he studied. He'd still come cheerfully to market with the rest of us, selling himself along with an acid chaser for the extra cash, but renting wasn't a career-choice any longer, it was just a means to supplement his grant and have some fun along the way. Inevitably, he found other ways to have fun, in other company; it wasn't much of a surprise to me when he faded away after he'd qualified, after he'd got his first job. Nor when he turned up again, only to invite us to his wedding.

It was always going to be Henry who missed him most. Those two had been the closest among us, the ones who seemed almost enough for each other until

Tim started reaching further, the ones who didn't really need to follow Glen. Once Tim had gone, I'd watched with a kind of cynical amusement as Henry aped his journey into respectability. Not into marriage, never that: but first he took a daylight job as a bank clerk, then he started taking courses—to improve his prospects, he said, to advance his career—and before long we never saw him except in a suit and tie, even around the clubs.

Those of us who were left had settled slowly into other lives, the way you have to as entropy sets in, as the fire starts to cool. We were all of us cooler now, fallen out of orbit and *fear no more the heat o' the sun*: Glen was a vast red giant, all-engulfing and all but entirely burned out, too close to collapse. Swallowed within his dimness, his gravitational suck, it was hard to remember quite how brightly we'd burned.

One of us, though—I thought one of us must have flared once at least like a sun through a lens, to make a blister-point all unnoticed while the rest of us danced our wild wasteful scatter.

HENRY CAME TO RELIEVE ME, ON TIME AND IN CHARACTER, THE BUTTON-DOWN banker. Half-drowning in *nostalgie de la boue*, I made a mad effort to see him as he used to be, short and skinny and fiery in orange jeans, glitter in his hair and his mascara. Hopeless; only the height remained, or the lack of it. Otherwise he was like the rest of us, a victim of the ever-turning world.

I fetched coffee and whisky and a second chair, so that we could both sit with Glen while we talked.

"I don't think it was Glen killed Brian," I said bluntly.

"No?" His frown made his cheeks pudge out to emphasise the weight he'd accumulated, his hard-won gravitas. "How not? He sent us to the body."

"Oh, he knew. He must have helped to bury him. After he'd killed the dog for cover—and yes, all right, after he'd set me up. Double indemnity." This might not be the first time Brian had been laid out in his garage. They must have stored the body somewhere until I'd done the spadework, the groundwork, laid the dog down in the first instance for them to slide Brian beneath. "But I think he's doing the same thing again, only setting himself up this time. If the story leaks, it can't hurt him, how could it?" Henry was shaking his head; I said, "Look. If one of us had killed Brian, for whatever reason, skip over that for now—what would he do? Back then? We were kids, remember. When we needed help, where did we run to? Every time?" To the source, inevitably: to the mythmaker, to the guiser, to Glen.

Now he was nodding, not following me, trying to skip ahead. "You think—

Tim? You think that's why he's vanished, in case it all came out?"

Oh, he was quick. Quick with his sums, at least, though he had no imagination. I almost smiled, as I said no. "No," I said softly, "not Tim. Think about it. Brian was a thief; what could he ever have stolen, that Tim would give a fuck about? Tim didn't care. He knew where he was going, and how to get there. Nothing else mattered, not to him. There was only one of us who was desperate to hang on to what he'd got." I gave him a moment, then went on, "What did he steal from you, Henry? What was so important, Brian had to die?" When he didn't answer, I added, "There's only the three of us here, and Glen's not listening. No tapes, I'm not wired for sound. Trust me."

That far, I thought he would. And I was right. He sighed; he sipped in rotation, glass and mug; he looked at me and said, "Brian was stealing my life."

"Explain?"

"It was watching Brian that made Tim think about the way we were, the way we'd end up. Dead or addicted, or scavenging on the margins. The rest of us were too busy to look that far, or too stupid, or else just dazzled by Glen, thinking we could all be like him. Small chance of that, he was the exception; and even then he was only a survivor. Everyone's a survivor, until they lose it." One rapid glance aside, to show me just how badly Glen had lost it in the end. "Tim wanted better than that. It was Brian that drove him, every day; he used to tell me so, *Brian's my criterion,* he'd say, *it's Brian who makes me work to get away. I could be Brian so easily, we all could, we're halfway there already...* And he was right, I knew that, but I didn't care. I was young, I liked what we had and I wanted to keep it, I wanted to keep it all. Tim too, Tim especially. If I lost him, I knew I'd lose you all sooner or later, and likely soon. I wasn't ready for that. So I thought, if I got rid of Brian, Tim might lose his impetus and we could all go on as we were..."

And when it didn't work, when Brian's disappearance was a spur if anything, he cut his losses and went after Tim, rather than cling on to what was already fraying. He didn't need to say that, I understood him all too well.

I sat and watched him drain his glass, put down his mug; I watched him walk away, I listened to the door close behind him and his car start in the street outside.

There were questions I hadn't asked him, but again I didn't need to. *Whose idea was it, to line me up as fall-guy at need?* Glen's, it must have been; Henry didn't have the imagination.

More importantly, *where's Tim?*—but I knew where to find Tim now, if I chose to go looking. Again, Henry had no imagination, He'd use Glen's old tricks one more time, double indemnity, once he'd seen the danger. Tim had to go for fear of what he might remember, how many times he'd talked about Brian and what Henry had said in response. He was too lawyerly to let the memory slip, for old times' sake; he might not betray Glen, but no one else was safe. Usefully, he could be set up in his absence, with his absence. And if that pointing finger failed, he could still be hidden where people would stop looking before they got that far. For Glen's sake, *give him back to his family,* I thought I might write a postcard to the police. With gloves on, not to give hostages to fortune. I thought I'd tell them to go dig on the moor—where it was easy, freshly turned, not too hard a labour for an unfit man—and when they turned up a dog's bones they should just keep digging deeper, however hard the soil had been stamped.

IT SEEMED AS THOUGH I HAD A NIGHT WATCH NOW, TO FOLLOW MY LONG DAY. I poured myself another slug of whisky, turned to Glen—and found that Henry had turned thief despite Tim's care that he should not. He'd stolen from me the one thing I'd been hoarding, what I'd worked for all these months.

Glen was gone and I'd missed the moment, the chance to see him off. Only the weight of him remained, star-stuff without a hint of shine.

The Light of Other Eyes

THERE WAS AN OLD MAN AND HE HAD A GLASS EYE
And he spent all day looking up at the sky
There was an old man and he had no eyes at all
And the world is surely getting smaller
(Irish, trad)

SOMETIMES IT FEELS LIKE TRESPASS, WHEN HE LOOKS AT US. How else, when it is seldom us he sees? Not ever our fault, no one's fault, of course not; even so it makes us feel as though we stand in other people's proper place, in skins not rightly ours.

We want to apologise for not owning, not belonging to the names that he calls us. Sometimes we do. *Sorry, Quin, it's not Mickey, I don't think I know Mickey. I'm Don, I work with Charles, remember?*

Of course he doesn't remember. Today he remembers Mickey, from ten or fifteen, twenty years ago. We correct him, every time; that's policy, not to lie for his comfort or for ours. Hard on him, we can be hard on ourselves also. It makes no difference. What he sees is what is real, for him, for today, just now. Sometimes his reality leaks out a little, to infect us too.

You are what you wear; wear another man's name for a while, and see where it gets you. Some place else: looking through a stranger's eyes, not quite comfortable with your fingers or your friends, acquiring just a little distance.

LIGHT-YEARS ARE FAMOUSLY A MEASUREMENT OF DISTANCE. Sometimes there aren't enough, and never can be.

THE WORLD IS SHRINKING, PEOPLE SAY THAT ALL THE TIME. It's still a shock to see it in real time, to watch someone's sense of scale fall in on itself, on him. The universe is meant to be expanding in compensation, but not his.

Once he held all creation in a bead of glass, in his hand. *Look, this little lens, this bubble: it's nothing, it's a marble, it's a toy. We could play catch. Whoops! We could drop it, lose it in a gutter, crush it in a moment. But come close now, hold it to your eye, see what there is out there. You can see it all, or could if your eyes were better. That's everything, everything there is, and you're looking at it. The planets, the suns, the constellations, the galaxies, all the way to the furthest edge of time. Right now, this moment at this point in space, trapped in a tiny perfection. Hang on to that. No one else will ever see it quite the way you do tonight. Take another look tomorrow, in an hour, blink and look back now: it's measurably different. You can't step into the same river twice, and who would want to? You can never go home again, but this is your compensation. It's a journey. Measure it in time or distance, it doesn't matter, they're the same thing in the end. We use light to measure them, either one: how far the light has come, how long it's taken. And measurements are all we have, to know a thing is true. All things that are, are lights.*

So high, so wide, so deep he was; so far he stretched. Not now. Now all his horizons are bounded by the borders of one room, and he has shrunk within it. How he lies, he can't see out of the window; he says it hurts when we try to raise him up, to show him sky. I'm sure it does.

We did stick luminous stars across the ceiling while he slept one time, but I don't believe he ever saw the joke. If he saw the stars, that would have been a bonus.

They say that light-years are a measurement of distance, not of time; I say it's false economy to insist on a distinction. From me to you, how far is that? Three hours or three days, depending how we go, but it's still a hundred miles since I saw you last. How long since you saw him? Time is distance, as near as we can figure it; vice versa, the sums still work as well.

The nearest star to ours, next sun over is Proxima Centauri, 4.3 light-years from where we stand. In other words, we look up at it today and what we see is a moment from four years ago, four years and a little more, an extra hundred days. How is that not a measurement of time? Four years ago, a hundred days meant a hundred days to party, to frivol away in search of the perfect hangover. These days we are more abstemious, we don't have a day to spare.

But anything that can be measured can necessarily be contained, at least within the bounds of an equation. Sidereal time we count out by the grand sweep of stars across the sky; his time we could count out drip by slow drip of the fluids we pump into him, or by measuring what little good they do. Sometimes I like not to look at Proxima Centauri, or any star that I can name. I like to take my eyes off the numbers altogether and let the whole array, all the breadth and the reach of it tumble over me, tumble me over. I could drown in stars, if only I didn't have to count them.

THEY SAY THAT HE WILL LOSE HIS SIGHT ALTOGETHER, IN THE END; THEY SAY that he will lose his mind. Blind and mad, that's the doctors' diagnosis, and he's halfway there already is what they're saying now.

To us who have to live with him, it doesn't seem like that. Rather that he's being peeled, stripped back: think onions, think tree-rings, pearls, anything that accretes in layers. It's a process of abrasion, necessarily of loss and we are the lost, he's lost us. This is time travel in one direction only, in reverse, and he's gone far enough now not to know us yet. He looks at us and sees old friends, old lovers emerging from the dust. Where and when he thinks he is, he can't say and we can't tell; only that it is not here, in his bed, his bedroom, our reluctant care. He's a long way short of here, and receding all the time.

Those strange eyes of his must show him something, what time he has them open. What it is, I would not try to guess. He is a living lesson, or a dying one: that none of this is certain, that we can stand side by side and share not even the moment. How can I show you what I see when I can't even describe it, only the negative, *I don't see what you see?*

BEFORE HE DID THIS TO US—BEFORE HE SHOWED US HOW FAR AWAY WE WERE, WE could be, he was getting—he took us up the hill with him, one more time the old invitation, *Let me take you up the hill, show you the stars, you'll like that.*

More accurately, I suppose that we took him. Not how it used to be, but we were getting used to that inversion of dependency. Time was, he ran this filthy old estate and we packed in like puppies, spilling his papers onto the floor, filling the seats and the luggage-space and offering to ride on the roofrack, making more noise than the engine and to far less effect. And he ignored us magisterially while he manoeuvred us out of the dull sick glow of the city, and then there was no other traffic and nothing else that glowed beneath the fierce scatter of the sky, only his own headlamps, full beam all the way; and he would be talking, pointing, teaching while the engine thumped and strained against the weight of us, while we argued, elbowed, stretched and pointed and appealed. Always doing that, always appealing: he was our court, our arbitration, source and seer. He took us up the mountain and showed us all the kingdoms of the world, and all worlds else. Young as we were, greedy as we were, that seemed to be enough.

Now it was our turn, payback, one last brief trip before his bed could claim and keep him. We loaded him into Jed's old Land Rover and squeezed ourselves into the back, unnecessarily many of us, as much like old times as we could make it. No room for the wheelchair that he was using already, that he would soon be too sick to use. *Don't worry*, we said, *we'll get you there and back again, we'll help.* And so we did, of course, as much as we were able, not enough.

We drove the old road up to the observatory, and unpacked him at the door. University rules and ancient custom said that the keys were his, he was our St Peter; so we propped him up while his thin fingers scratched and fumbled, all grace long since departed.

In at last, we carried him up and around the gantry, and down into the well. It felt like a procession, as though we bore our saint in effigy. Hard to say we didn't, looking back; even at the time there, it was quite hard not to be humming Bach as we went. *Schweigt stille, plaudert nicht*—oh, yes. We were not made to be quiet, but we were always almost prayerful that first minute, coming in under this great dome. With him in our arms—too light, too ungainly, too little of himself—we thought we ought to tiptoe, we were so overset by the silence, the gravitas, the weight of the space of it. If there had to be noise, creaks from the flooring and the shuffle of our feet, I would very much have liked a little Bach.

It's the only appropriate music anyway, to watch stars by. We used to keep a stash of CDs up there, for party nights like this; we used to party often. Not these days. *Too tired* we say, when what we mean is *tired of each other*, unless it's *tired of ourselves*. These days we do our shifts together and go home. Some of us come up to the observatory with our own sets of keys, a process I suppose from shift to shift. I always have something in my car, the St Matthew Passion or the Art of Fugue; if music is mathematics in the third dimension, then astronomy is the same thing in the fourth, and Bach is its prophet. If we had any ham we could have ham and eggs, if we had any eggs; if I'd been in my own car I might have played the Passion, if I'd thought to bring it in. Not regular party music, perhaps, or not ours, but this was not a regular party. They might have lived with it; they might have let me live.

None of us could let Quin live, but we could show him a good time, if a short one and out of his reach. We could sit him in his own old seat, where his narrow fleshless thighs didn't fit the impression that he himself had made, so many years of sitting just exactly so; we could uncap the eyepiece for him, and help his awkward fingers with the focus; we could say, *Look, see: here is everything that matters, everything that is. You showed us this, you taught us; we have not forgotten, we could show him that. We still get a kick out of this,* we could say, popping the tops off bottles of Grolsch and clinking them together in salute, finding a carton of juice with a straw for him to suck, looking round to check that we'd all of us forgotten to bring any music, which we had. There were no CDs in the Landie, there being nothing to play them on. Still, we could have a good time regardless, let him see.

And let him look, let him feast his fading eyes. This was his last real chance; from now on it was photos from Hubble downloaded off the NASA site and an occasional television documentary trying to skip lightly where you had to sink or swim, in the deeper mathematics of dark matter. That would have enraged him once, except that he used never to watch television. Now he does by necessity, because we do, and it's the rage he can't manage. Unless he simply doesn't see, or understand.

That night he was seeing well enough. He broke all his own rules for proper observation, he had us redirect the telescope a dozen times to find him favourite stars or clusters, little scatters of bright dust he could only find hereafter on the star-charts back at home. He had spent his life looking at those far few lights; spent it or wasted it, for precious small returns. He used to say that it was only ever the universe could give him any sense of perspective. That was a small return at the time, perhaps, but it was precious now. That was why we'd brought him here, one reason why: a last reminder, an inoculum against a looming loss. *Still there, still bigger than it was last time you looked, how big is that? It's all there is, and you are so so small a part of it, what can you possibly matter...?*

Except to us, he mattered much to us. But we partied anyway, without the music; and when he was tired, when he fell asleep in his chair we partied a little longer, just to make the point that we could still do this, with or without him.

IT WAS SOON AFTER THAT HE STARTED CALLING US BY OTHERS' NAMES. He was going slower suddenly, or we were speeding up; either way, we were drifting out of phase. And he's been falling further and further behind us ever since. I thought it was just a doppler shift, some kind of crucial red-eye; but it's not only the speed now, it's the distance, it's the time. His gaze may move around the room; it isn't us he follows. He's seeing ghosts, like we do through the twelve-inch on the hill, the light of what's long gone. Look into his eyes and there's a glimmer there, but he doesn't shine for us. That's a light has taken twenty, thirty years to reach us, a spark struck ages since and deep, deep down.

Maybe that's a spark was struck for you, how long ago you saw him, how far away it was? Maybe if I looked, I'd see your face rising in reflection.

LISTEN, I'M TIRED, AND THE WORDS STOP MAKING SENSE. Or else it's just a phaseshift, doppler, I'm starting to slow down. Whatever. I'm through with this.

As he is nearly, nearly through with us. Blind and mad, the doctors say; but actually that's all right. I say it's only distance. I can live with that.

And come the ending, and it will, he'll be not blind and mad. Just nothing, a fire in a box and no one there to see it; and that'll be all right too. You could say he burned out long ago, I wouldn't blame you for it. Perhaps he did. There's no universal clock, no absolute time to say what happened when. Near or far, you see things differently, and seeing's all that counts. Being there is incidental. We've been close, we've had the last of the heat of him; he's fading now. And heat is only light in close-up, quick-time shine. Come right down to it, everything is wavelength. You can measure that by time, you can measure it by distance, either way. All things that are, are lights.

Septicaemia

LOVE IS A DRUG, BUT DRUGS ARE SAFER. WHEN THEY COME IN PILLS AND POWDERS, in nightclubs and alleys and Turkish baths, when you're sweating cold despite the heat of dance or sex or steam, when you know what you've put into your bloodstream.

EVERY TIME I OPEN HIM A BOTTLE OF WATER—WHICH IS OFTEN: IT'S ALL HE'LL drink now, Volvic, clear and blue, blue and clear as he is now, we keep a case of it under his high bed, hospital bed here in the living room, bedroom, dying room, call it what you will—every time, I think of stag beetles and worse.

LOVE IS A DRUG, BUT SEX IS SAFER. Sex can be controlled. *Do this, I'll do this, we won't do that.* Paisley patterns of memory, paisley with my lenses out, bright but soft, swirling, incoherent, unattached. Which night and with whom, the details are lost; it's all habit now. Everything's contained.

WE TOOK HIM TO THE SHOW IN HIS CHAIR WHILE HE WAS STILL ABLE FOR IT, WHILE he was still interested. The water-bottle was the first thing we saw: Volvic, small, clear and blue, lying on its side on a white plinth, seal intact.

Inside it, in the water was a beetle. Massive and horned, legs splayed, drowned and dead.

Nice, he said.

Next was the demijohn with the air-trap in its throat, bubbling slowly, making scrumpy. With a rat in it, floating, rising and falling more slowly than the bubbles were. *Traditional,* he said.

Then the cold cabinet, white wire shelves and the hum of the chill of it and the little jars of lumpfish roe, red and black, each with a fish's head staring out at us through the smear of eggs; and between them a big three-litre plastic supermarket thing of milk with something murky in it that we couldn't see, something dead of course, and much wider than the neck was wide.

How did he get that in there? we asked, as we were meant to; and, *what happens when the milk goes off?*

Last was a rack of tins, unopened, soups and beans and such. The label at the side said that each had its intruder: larva, pupa, imago. Butterflies and moths and dragonflies, it said, in all their stages. How could we know? Open a tin, you kill the mystery; and mystery is all that's left to play with. Answers are dead ends. Schrödinger's Catastrophe, we called that. He smiled, and said nothing. I used to hate his silences; now I could welcome them almost, as a forerunner, a taste, rehearsal time.

LOVE IS A DRUG, BUT WORDS ARE SAFER. Words can bury anything. Words could even bury him, if I would let them; but I drown words, I store books in bowls of water, ink in solvents. Or rather I do not, but I wish I would. Words fix the world too firmly, books describe what ought to be beyond description, sacrosanct.

HOW LONG I CAN LIVE LIKE THIS, I AM NOT CLEAR. The trick will be not to fail before he does. Which is a monstrosity in itself, tingeing each day's sullen beat of blood with a whisper of poison, *perhaps this will be the last, perhaps I need hold out no longer than tonight, one day more, I can manage one more day...*

LOVE IS A DRUG, BUT I THINK I'VE GROWN IMMUNE. It's too much, a lifetime of love, loving, being loved; I have drunk it and drunk it, tentative sips and great draughts I choked to swallow, spilling from the corners of my mouth. When he fell sick I stopped drinking, too late for either one of us. My name is what it is, and I am what I am: I am a lover. Please, no applause. It's not that praiseworthy.

WHEN HE BLEEDS, WHEN HE GOUTS BLOOD INTO A BUCKET—IT'S A THING HE DOES, the artery that feeds his liver starts to leak and then there's nothing else he can do but spout forth, utter it, words reduced to a liquid sense—when that happens, he breaks his containment and my own. What comes out is dark, splashy, messy and hard to catch, everything that he tries so hard not to be. Sometimes it gets everywhere, as he does.

That's what he doesn't know, or at least I hope so, though I find it difficult to hide at such a time. I want him not to see how permeable I am to him, to the essence of him. We wear rubber gloves at his insistence, but they are no defence; what he spills out is more than blood, does more than stain the carpet. I am soaked through and through with what he is, with what he has become. It's not so different to the way we were before, except that if he guessed he'd think me hurt, infected, harmed.

Which I am, of course, of course I am; but not in the way he'd think. I only hate what he hates, the stink and the filth, the indignity to us all. That apart, I would drink him and drink him; even that I can swallow, as I must. And change the sheets beneath him, scrub the floor, make play with disinfectant. My fingers wrinkle despite the gloves and I reek of pine, as close as ever he'll come to landscape now. I am his view, as he is mine; I wish that I could show him trees or running water, anything not closed in or sealed off.

I wish that I could tear this paper mask away and breathe his air unfiltered, strip my hands naked before I turn to stripping him again. I want to give him back normality, but he refuses. He made these rules for our sakes, so he says; for his sake I comply, that he not see what he has done to me, how my veins run with him.

LOVE IS A DRUG, BUT IMMUNITY IS DEADLY. My mouth is dry, although I share his water. There's nothing else left that we can share, and that only for a little while now. What happens when the bottle's empty, none of us has asked.

IT SHOULD BE HIM THAT'S FRIGHTENED, BUT IT'S NOT. He lives in a bubble, hermetic, eremetic; nothing of the outside can touch him, as it seems, and that's where fear thrives. Nothing of the inside touches me. He has filled me like a swelling, swallowing bubble that cannot burst, it is too full of matter. I feel him in my throat and in my belly, I hear the shiver of his heartbeat below my ribs, the suck of his blood in my ears. Nothing remains of me within my skin, he's left no space for it.

LOVE IS A DRUG, BUT DRUGS ARE SENSELESS, RANDOM, WORSE THAN BLIND. They don't discriminate, they can't foretell. I knew what I was getting into, only not how deep I'd have to go.

I GIVE HIM NOT EVERYTHING HE NEEDS, NO, BUT EVERYTHING HE'LL TAKE FROM me. I have become a master of the needle, of the intimate cartography of veins. I draw his blood in measured millilitres, and it seems that he can barely spare so much; in return I give him clear, pure liquids against the desert that his body is become. I fix his drip, I raise him up and help him swallow pills as the clock dictates. I used to bring him illicit cigarettes and wicked whisky, but the fun died with the conversation; he has nothing to tell me now, nor I him. Or only the one thing, that I will not say however much he needs it.

LOVE IS A DRUG, AND YOU GET IT ON PRESCRIPTION. If you have to ask the price, you can't afford it.

The Cupboard
of Cold Things

WHAT DO YOU DO, WHAT DOES ANYONE ACTUALLY DO WITH THE POSSESSIONS OF the dead?

Oh, you can put the house on the market, shred the accumulated paperwork of decades, pass on the physical bequests and give the books to charity. Roll up the carpets and leave them out in the alley; someone will come by before the council can, to carry them off for uncertain purposes. Invite people round for a takeaway, have them take away anything they fancy. First come first served, finders keepers, no returns.

And still, after all of that, you find yourself left with things. Less than a skipful, and you can't just chuck them anyway. These are the things that no one wants because they're claimed already, they still belong to the one who's gone. You see them, you touch them, you know. They're *invested*.

Some of them are obvious. The love letters from thirty years ago, the painfully erotic ones all heedless of what's coming, seeds of mutual death inherent in the text? You can't shred those, nor publish them, nor pass them into hands less scrupulous or tender than your own. The recipe book half filled with his mother's handwriting, half with his own. The photographs from forty years ago, unindexed, unattributed: people in hats, people in jeans, people in formal poses or high good humour, people who used to mean something. The silver napkin-ring inscribed with the name he never used, a gift from godparents he never saw, perhaps the last object on the planet to record that name and that relationship.

The teddy bear, of course. What can anyone ever do with an orphaned bear?

And then there are those things that he collected or kept that are orphaned of intent now, sometimes orphaned of meaning. An odd assemblage of brass tubing and blu-tak that he could take to any party, that turns any innocent empty wine-bottle into a bong for the better smoking of dope, except that he hadn't smoked for years and nor do any of the rest of us, but still. A wooden half-shell under a pewter lid, with indentations chiselled into it, never quite the right size for a pack of cigarettes and a box of matches; it used to be a party game of two parts, trying to figure out what it was really meant for and any other use it could practically serve. A game without a winner, always his favourite.

A dog lead that always hung on his bedroom door, although he never ever had a dog. Try not to think about that one.

The shells he used for *coquilles St Jacques*, that weren't scallop shells at all; he claimed them for river oysters, said he swam for them himself when he was young. We were always careful not to let a marine biologist anywhere near, for fear of hearing that story disavowed. Some myths are a pearl beyond price, where the truth is a shabby bead.

Shabby beads, strings of them that he might have worn to any of a dozen festivals he might have gone to. We all knew too many stories that didn't quite jibe with each other, that couldn't all be true. But still, the beads were true.

Stories coil and tangle like beads on a shelf, dusty and inextricable. Take them by the handful, or not at all.

Things accumulate. Once there's one that can't be thrown away, there's always more than one. Another and another, a man's life expressed in what he loved or kept or couldn't throw away. So what do you do, with things you do not love or want to keep and cannot throw away?

Stow them, for now. Find a cupboard, make space, think about it later. Promise yourself that, promise each other. Later...

I MADE SPACE FOR MYSELF BY LEAVING. LEAVING THEM ALL, LEAVING EVERYTHING; crossing oceans, working away.

A promise is a promise, though. No escaping that. *I'll be back,* I said: and here I was, coming back. Flying in on a warm front, while snowmelt flooded the ground below; the metro and my own feet carrying me to Gerard's new front door. Slogging over damp and grimy pavements, thinking as I went about the persistence of ice. How time and change had cleared the way—by and large, give or take—but still there was ice beneath the puddles, still great stubborn slabs of filthy snow at random at the roadside.

It ought to be a metaphor for something, I remember thinking that. As though it mattered, as though it were foreknowledge, ominous.

Gerard's door. My feet wanted to go the old way, to the old house; my mind had to keep remembering that wasn't his any more and wasn't ours, that we had no claim now, we'd sold up and walked away.

I had to check his e-mail more than once for directions how to walk this new way, where to turn. Which door.

And even so I found myself reaching for my own keys on his doorstep, and having to remember once again that I was a stranger here myself. And ringing the bell instead, and even that made the wrong sound. I knew the call of Gerard's bell; this wasn't it.

Still, it called him and he came. He opened the door and we were instant family again, awkward and uncertain with each other. Did we kiss, did we hug? We used to, but that was then. Should we shake hands, perhaps, like an acknowledgement of distance travelled? With strangers and with friends, these matters resolve themselves. It's family that you have to think about. Even when that family is a tribe of choice, brothers by adoption. Someone else's choice, but hey.

In the end I did kiss him, yes, dry and perhaps ironic. Then I handed him the dutiful litre of duty-free whisky and let him show me around.

Kitchen, bathroom, utility. His bedroom, the spare bedroom which was mine for the duration. Dining room, living room, hallway. That was it, neat and spare and functional; and all the way there was something missing. One more door, a false wall, something.

He knew. Of course he did, we were family. Even so, he waited; I had to say it myself. That's what family does, leaves things lying until it's almost too late, except when it is actually and absolutely that.

I said, "No piano?" and his face twisted into something that might almost be called a smile, if a smile is a measure of what's bitter.

"No," he said, no more than that. What he meant, what we both meant was that there was nothing of Quin's, nothing visible, anywhere in the flat. All the years I'd known him Gerard lived with Quin, in Quin's house, amongst his stuff. This, now: this was more than different, this was opposite, an exercise in absence. I could look and look and only ever see what wasn't there.

It was...almost overwhelming. It was what Quin did while he was alive, he dominated, he overbore us all; he was older for real and bigger in our heads, he had a longer reach and a stronger voice, he had opinions and taste and experience where all we had was grabby hands and appetite.

Dead now and gone away, moved out, Quin was still all-encompassing. Still not letting go. He used to fill Gerard's life with artefacts, with evidence; now he had me searching for it. Which turned out to be the same thing in reverse.

Gerard knew. He put that whisky to the best use possible, a glass in my hand and another in his, the bottle between us and the cap lost somewhere, left behind, tossed out. You maybe can't actually drown jetlag, but you can surely drown it out.

Other things, questions, are also not susceptible to drowning. I said, "Where are you keeping his stuff, then? It has to be somewhere here."

"Of course. There's a cupboard. In your room, as it happens. We can swap, if you like. If you don't like the thought of it."

"No worries," I said. I was the one with inbuilt distance, thousands of miles'-worth, years of time. He had to live with things daily, nightly;. If he chose not to sleep with them at hand, I wasn't about to force him into it.

Besides, I really wasn't worried. Nothing of Quin's had ever worried me in his lifetime, so why should it start now?

WHISKY, THEN. AND WORDS, TALKING, THE WAY WE HADN'T TALKED FOR YEARS. It was my first true sight of Gerard without Quin, and he concerned me. He was like the flat, I thought, marked out by absence: nurturing the hollow at his heart. He hadn't lost weight in the body, but in his mind, in his substance, yes. Everything he said seemed to delineate an edge, a new limit to his reach, *thus far and no further, I can't go there*; and all those edges together made the shape of Quin, an emptiness exquisitely cut out.

Or I was over-imagining, seeing what wasn't there in more senses than one. Whisky and death and reunion: they're notorious all three for stirring up sentiment. Add the toxic shock of displacement, crossing half the world to find an old friend in the wrong place, and small wonder if I thought he carried damage. Of course I would have expected loss, if I'd come with any overt expectations. Grief is lossy by its nature. And after so long seeing Quin at the heart of everything we did, the puppet-master for us all, of course I'd see his absence writ large all around me. Of course I'd see Gerard reduced, missing the better part of himself. Of course I would.

Two positions, two points of view, and I oscillated between them until the bottle was empty and my giddy mind couldn't keep a grip on either one. My feet were steady enough to carry me to bed, so I went there.

SHIFT HALF AROUND THE WORLD, IT TAKES TIME FOR TIME TO CATCH UP WITH you. My body-clock was running hours slow, and pouring whisky in the works didn't help at all. I did sleep, or at least I passed out for a while; but I still woke up in the deep dark, in the heavy silence of a sleeping house.

Woke up cold, densely and deliberately cold. That was how it felt, at least: that I was cold by intent, someone else's purpose.

That would be the whisky talking. I could feel it still seething in my system like the suck of a salt tide, tangled up with jetlag and exhaustion and whatever dreamstate I'd been stumbling through.

Stories tangle like shabby beads, and so do legs and sheets. I made a sorry mess of scrambling out of bed. And stood there violently shivering as I grabbed clothes at random in the dark, my own grubby travelwear and a bathrobe my fingers found on the back of the door as I jerked it open, as I groped my way out of there.

I was moving almost by instinct, just to get away. Logic said that the rest of the flat would be just as cold, but logic was wrong and my legs knew better, seemingly. Even the hallway felt warmer, an end to that vicious chill. By the time I reached the living-room I was comfortable, at least on the surface, skin-level. The bitter icicle bite in my marrow took longer to ebb. I was still shuddering as I blundered about the kitchen trying to boil a kettle quietly, making instant coffee as an act of desperation, drinking it black and hot enough to scorch.

When I was steady again, when I could think again, I wanted to think that it was just dreamsickness, an act of unconscious imagination. Of course the room couldn't have been that cold.

And yet, and yet. I couldn't convince myself: not without going back. Which I was weirdly reluctant to do. I had all the excuses I needed, jetlag and caffeine together; I was obviously not going to sleep any more, so why go back to bed? But I have a lifelong habit of doing those things that are branded by my own reluctance.

Back I went, then, with a second mug of coffee in my fist. Opened the door and stepped inside and felt it instantly again, all the chill of winter. And laughed at myself for leaving the window open when there was snow on the ground, and drew back the curtain—and found the double glazing closed and locked, and ice on the inside of the glass.

On the *inside*, and too chill to melt when I dragged my finger through it. Not frost, not condensation: clear ice.

Bewildered, I gazed around the room and saw of course the cupboard in the corner, waiting for me. Never mind the chest of drawers and the bedside cabinet and the bookshelf, never mind anything. The world is all that is the case; in that room, right then, the world was in that cupboard.

When Quin came into a room, he drew the eye.

The eye and then the body after, irresistibly. We used to cluster around him, all his acolytes, his fanboys: quarrelsome and jealous of each other, sparring for his attention. He'd scold, but privately I always thought he loved it.

The cupboard's handle burned with cold. I snatched my hand away, then shook my head, reached back, gripped again and tugged.

And here, yes, in the fall of lamplight: here were all Quin's things. The essence of him, what makes or describes a man. Here they were, arrayed on shelves and caught in a nimbus of air so cold it was almost visible, almost tangible.

My mind wanted to play with thoughts of deep freeze, of cold storage, suspended animation; but the animus coming off those shelves was nothing playful. Hard and bleak and savage, rather, frost on an iron blade.

It was terrifying, appalling, it spoke grimly to the grimmest heart of me; and it was very real, no whisky-dream, no fancy of the night; and I was very, very glad I hadn't agreed to swap rooms with Gerard, because it was also pure Quin. Once gone, what else would he do but rage? And where else do it but here, among his things? Accustomed to our worship, he always did hate to be left out or left behind, those rare times we did that to him; and he always did have a temper like a whip.

Standing there, shivering in that bitter fall of air but not running this time, thinking it through, I almost felt that I faced him down; but it was Gerard I was angry for, and not myself. He didn't deserve this. Knowingly or not, he'd shifted all Quin's things as far as he could bear to, nowhere near far enough. Months and years he'd lived here, on his own, no one close to notice as Quin flayed him from within. What we did see, we'd all put down to widowhood and grief. I had myself. Who'd think of a flensing-knife, all ice and malevolence, cutting that perfect hollow replica, eating out the core of a good man...?

Or I was over-imagining, seeing what wasn't there, only a cupboard full of relics and an old familiar sorrow—but this I knew for certain, that I was bloody cold. So I closed the door and went back to the kitchen, kept myself warm and worried until the world turned and the sun rose and so did Gerard.

I DIDN'T SAY A WORD TO HIM. Stories tangle, words knot themselves into muddled meanings, and our own history was too complicated to pick apart even without Quin's winding through it and through it.

I did hug him, though, and felt how brittle he was. And wondered if I were too late already, but there was nothing I could do about that. He needed to rebuild himself; he might or might not have the chance.

I fed him breakfast the way I always used to after we'd been up all night with Quin, and saw him off to work, and let him go away thinking that it was only jetlag that had me so wide awake and restless so early in the morning, only whisky that had made me so sentimental.

And then when he was safely gone I went down to the corner shop and bought all the padded envelopes and all the wrapping-paper they had, all the packing tape and all the labels. Then I came back and started making parcels. One by one, all of Quin's things, each one separately addressed to any one of Quin's many friends worldwide. I had them all, listed in my laptop. I sent them e-mails to warn them, and then I carried packages to the post office, in batches. Stood in the queue and sent them off, this way and that, local and long-distance and international, by common post and carrier and courier.

His teddy bear I kept, my contribution.

Stories tangle like strings of beads, but you can always cut the string.

True North

THERE'S A POINT—A THORN, PERHAPS, A CARDINAL THORN?—MISSING FROM the compass rose. A fifth quarter, another direction, somewhere worse to go. It stands at an angle to everywhere else; its scripts are undeciphered, its maps incomprehensible from here. You'd need to be there, standing in its different light and looking back. If you could bear to.

It doesn't have a name; at least, we don't have a name for it. How could we fit a label to something that we can't describe, that we can't even point to? We know it's there, is all. I know it; so do you.

It's that place in your head that you can't quite bring yourself to look at, the step beyond, into the dark and on your own. It's where the monsters come from when you're a kid, that sidle under your bed and wait to grab you. Every child knows it's only ever one false move away, one moment's inattention: a blink or a breath at the wrong time, a word in the wrong ear. Adulthood is learning resolutely to look away, to give it no credence, pretend it isn't there.

We're good at that. As a race, as a species, we're very good, but only once we're adult. That's why it tends to take the children.

CITY IS AS CITY DOES, ALWAYS. City is a spirit, sui generis, something more and far more than a tendency, a propensity to gather. We think we build our cities to suit ourselves, but you could say that entirely the other way around. City draws us in, to fill its empty spaces. We're a city people now, evolved to suit.

IF YOU WANT TO BE LEFT ALONE, COME TO THE CITY. Everyone knows that, bone-deep. Surround yourself with strangers, they'll act like insulation, guard you from your friends.

I did it the wrong way round, came here for the company, but city did its thing regardless and here I am, alone.

You were the company I came for, and this flat is a hollow thing without you. So am I. And I have no right to protest it; of course you had to leave me. That is understood.

And what has happened here since you left, here and elsewhere, everywhere, to me: that may be vengeance or it may be an appeal, or it may be something I cannot measure in a language I do not speak, but for sure it is an act of bitter irony.

That too is understood.

WHEN WE MET, YOU AND I, IT WAS IN ANOTHER WORLD. Softer, kinder, though we couldn't see it then. Dark and true and tender is the north, and we thought this was it, we were there.

Specifically, we were at a party, and acting ten years younger than we should. Ten years at least. At least, I was. You? More like twenty.

It was a big house, a busy house and a good party. As witness, Marx Brothers showing on a loop, in an improvised cinema in the basement. By midnight they were showing only to you and me, giving a soundtrack and a milieu to a sudden and unexpected flirtation.

I was surprised, amused, enjoying myself. Enjoying you. You were startled, uncertain, determined; what more would be for you to say, and this isn't the time. Time's long gone and the world has changed, you've changed and so have I. Let it go.

Perhaps I should have let you go, right then, that night? Perhaps I should. I know I had the chance. In the early hours I went upstairs for another bottle, maybe to scout out the possibility of a room. The house was still all full of party, but our hostess found me none the less.

She and I were friendly, though not strictly friends; it was her husband that I knew well. She said to me, "Do you know what you're doing?"

I was still delighted and intrigued, loving your dogged bewilderment, loving my own casual enticing charm, loving the discovery that the whole party was talking about us. I said, "Sweetheart, apparently everyone knows what we're doing." Which was talking, to be fair, barely anything more than that; but there is talk and talk, and some of it has to be done close and quiet, while other people slowly notice and slip away if they're courteous, or if they're bored or resentful or lonely on their own account. Sooner or later one of those is likely to apply. Apparently, with us that night, even the Marx Brothers would have made an excuse and left.

She said, "He's *married.*"

I knew that; you'd told me. Besides, I'd read it in your wedding-band. And in your shoulders, your eyes, your voice. Marriage is all-encompassing.

I said, "I've shagged more married men than—well, than you have. And more straight men, too."

"I don't doubt it," she said. "This isn't a pissing-contest. But he's got a daughter, and—"

"—and whatever he does or doesn't do tonight is not his wife's choice, or his daughter's either," I said. "Nor mine, as it happens. This isn't a seduction."

"Oh, is it not? He's on his own, he's drunk, he's out of his depth. You've got all the advantages down there, and I don't think it's pretty."

I thought she was wrong, on every count. You weren't on your own, and neither was I. Neither one of us was drunk, though we had certainly been drinking. Alcohol is fuel sometimes, and not an intoxicant at all. We were splashing about in the shallows of something, with the depths of it barely glimpsed yet on the horizon; and whatever it was, wherever it was taking us, I thought it was beautiful.

I thought you were beautiful, and I came back down to tell you. It seemed a shame to waste the opportunity.

SMALL CHANCE OF BORROWING A ROOM WITH OUR HOSTESS SO DISAPPROVING, and small need either. I had a credit card, the city has hotels. The best of them are down on the quayside, in old adapted warehouses from the days of sail and coal; so we could walk along the river in the glamour of an early summer's dawn and talk a little, touch a little, recognise the slow inevitability of what lay—what had always lain—at the end of all this touching, all this talking.

You were not so much frightened, I think, as awed. Overawed, perhaps, that something so shattering could still seize you up, late and imperative. You had been faithful, and you had been straight; that night, that morning took both those words away from you.

If that was a loss, perhaps I should have felt guilty after all. I was the knowing one. Before and after, though, I spent time arguing otherwise. Wrapped in the sodden tangled boldness of your body, how could I not? There was nothing in the bed with us but gain.

Even so. I argued too well, perhaps, I persuaded myself. You needed no persuasion, once the thing was done; you had to believe me, or remorse would have eaten you. Remorse and self-disgust. Me, I could have walked away. I should have done. One night of wonder and send you home a wiser man, a deeper man, even perhaps a better husband and father.

But I was greedy or desperate or else unexpectedly in love, if that last can be distinguished from the other two. I stayed: in the city, in your life, in your thoughts. I bought a flat, I bought a bed. You talked at last to your wife, to your daughter; something irreparable broke there, and you came to live with me.

FOR A WHILE, FOR THAT LITTLE TIME WHEN WHAT IS NEW CAN DISGUISE ITSELF as needed, when change can claim to be happy chance and get away with it. Not long enough for that different life to settle into your bones and become a part of what you are. Happiness needs to be mined for; that first flush is excitement, passion, hope. Enquiry, wonder. Touch. The skin of things.

And now you're as gone as you can be: not just gone away, gone back. And I'm caught here, as stranded as you and none of it is anybody's fault, we're all helpless in the face of horror; but I wish, I *wish* your dreadful daughter would let me be. Let her come and trouble you.

SHE WAS THE ONE WHO ABSOLUTELY COULD NOT OR WOULD NOT SETTLE IN THE new dispensation. No blame to her for that: twelve years old, her life must have been hard enough already, without this. Without me, taking her father away from her and making him into something other than he had been. That must have been how she saw it. I don't know, she wouldn't talk to me and hardly to you, but surely so. Whether it was her mother pushed her there, whether it was her friends, whether she found or built her own rocky path to a savage crest, I can't say: but there she was, windblown and blind with rage, screaming or spitting or sullenly contemptuously silent.

Once a fortnight, there she was. I did my best not to be there myself, to give you time with her alone. Not to win her over, just to find some place to stand within the wither of her glare, where she had still to acknowledge you her father. What comfort you found in that, I could never calculate. Nor learn from you, however hard we tried. Some mysteries are unbridgeable.

But there she was, mysterious and hating, souring the weekend twice a month. Perhaps it was cowardice as much as kindness that took me away those times. As we're being honest. Perhaps it was just distaste. How could I warm to someone whose face twisted when she looked at me? Or at you?

It was my flat, though, my life was there; I couldn't always be gone. There were bad words and brutal meals, tears sometimes that were not always hers. If I couldn't or wouldn't go away, she would: as soon as might be, calling her mother for a lift or her friends for a coffee, company, a convocation somewhere in town, anywhere that was not here.

WHEN I WAS YOUNG, I THINK I WOULD HAVE LOVED IT HERE. Leather sofas, a vast television with cinema sound and movies on tap, picture windows with the wide river and all the bridges of the city laid out below. I'd have seized it, claimed it for my own and filled it with my friends to make that claim secure.

Not her. She came alone, she left alone, as soon as could be arranged, as though we had a taint she dared not share among her clan. Or else she simply couldn't bear to be seen in our company. You weren't even allowed to drive her home. If her mother wasn't free, she'd take a bus. You used to watch her through the window as she stood in the shelter waiting, a slim colourless slip of a figure like a needle in a glass, a silent accusation, unkindly sharp.

ONE DAY SHE LEFT, YOU WATCHED, THE BUS CAME AND BLOCKED YOUR VIEW; IT went, and she was gone. Empty shelter, river, road. You turned away from the window. We talked, I cooked, you played Bach. We filled the flat with things that were not her or hers, things she would not touch.

After a time, your wife phoned to ask if she was here. To say she was not home.

She would be with her friends, of course, in town; but she wasn't answering her own phone, and none of the other numbers that you knew could find her.

The hands of time hold razors, every little tick catching at your skin, cutting you newly.

WHEN THE DOORBELL RANG, IT WASN'T HER COME BACK, NO. THE POLICE, RATHER, a woman in uniform and a man who was not. Your daughter's backpack had turned up. Intact, with phone and purse and all things proper to an adolescent style. Maybe she'd lost it, maybe she was searching for it, maybe she was crying in corners with a friend who was off your radar and her mother's too—but this didn't feel good, to them or to us. Probabilities were starting to balance the other way, and could we please be as exact as possible—individually, please, in separate rooms—about this morning, her mood, her departure. Had we argued? Had we seen her onto the bus? Had either one of us been out of the flat since she left...?

No, we hadn't, but now you did. Of course you wanted to see your wife; the wounded huddle together. Of course it made sense for you to stay with her, so that the police had just the one point of contact. Of course I understood.

Of course.

SHE DIDN'T COME BACK, SHE DIDN'T TURN UP, NO ONE FOUND HER.

No more did you come back, because how could you? There were whole monuments of guilt and sorrow, valleys of loss that could not be negotiated or abridged. Once there, you were condemned to stay within the pale, in that communism of grief where each gave all they had to the collective pot. I had not enough to offer and was condemned to the other thing, exclusion. Isolation.

God bless the Internet and the mobile phone. I couldn't have called your wife's landline, just to talk to you. I wouldn't willingly even call you unexpectedly, when every ringtone must be a blazing moment of hope with a catastrophic disappointment to follow. With e-mail, though, we could fix a time, you could make sure to be private and prepared, we could talk undisturbed.

No, that's a lie. We were both of us disturbed, and there was a great disturbance between us. Even then, when neither of us dared look to the future, I had a creeping sense of inevitable doom arising. There was a shadow that I couldn't see past, that we couldn't talk our way around; I sat alone in my comforts, and already they felt barren.

It was fear and uncertainty, I told myself, no more: let your daughter only turn up, the way kids sometimes do, and you'd come back to me. Wiser and more wary, perhaps, better prepared. Our rebuilding could be stronger than before...

I told you none of that. What we built the first time had been determinedly founded on truth; I couldn't lie to you, then or now. I listened to the distance as it grew between us, you on your side of terror and I on mine, and I thought that even if she did come back, she couldn't bridge this gulf.

SHE DIDN'T TRY, AS IT HAPPENED. When she did come back, no kind of bridge, she came to me.

IT WAS, I DON'T KNOW, A FEW DAYS AFTER YOU LEFT ME. A few days after she went. Too long for any comfort, almost too long for hope. I've heard them say it on television, that if they don't find a kid in twenty-four hours, they're pretty much looking for a body. I don't know if anyone said that to you. It was the thing we didn't talk about, those times I could get you on the phone. Which left us of course with nothing much to talk about, because you had nothing in your life except her absence, and I had nothing except hers and yours.

And then nothing except yours, because she was suddenly not absent from me any longer.

THE FIRST TIME, THE BEGINNING, I WAS AT HOME, ONLY BECAUSE I HAD NOWHERE to go without you. I do obsession as well as I do self-regard. Those may be the same thing; they do say we fall in love to reinforce our own self-image. For sure, if I loved your daughter, it was because she reflected an aspect of you; if she hated me, it must have been for the same reason.

I had a world of work I might pursue, and I was chasing none of it: only pacing the apartment, hoping you'd phone and knowing you wouldn't. Checking local news constantly, on television and radio and the web, in case of a miracle that continued not to happen. Watching the river, the tide, the occasional water-traffic.

And watching the road, of course, between me and the river, only because it was busier, there was more going on, agitation draws the eye more than calm, more than stillness...

IT WAS HER STILLNESS THAT CAUGHT MY EYE, JAGGED IT LIKE A NEEDLE. Still and stiff, standing in the bus shelter, hood up and head down, she might have been any scrawny adolescent.

Truly, she might have been any. Including the one that she was. My eye knew her by clothes and stance and a soul-sharp certainty. I was suddenly breathless, as still as she, achingly anxious: should I bang on the glass, hurl the window open, yell down to her? Or should I run, too urgent for the lift, nine floors and fetch her up, by force if need be?

What I wanted, of course, was to phone you.

And what happened, of course, was the bus. Before I could choose, before I could move, it came along and cut off my view of her entirely. I might have screamed; I think perhaps I did. And then the bus moved on, and of course she was gone.

And then I did phone, because what else could I do? You first, but only got your voicemail; so then the police, frantically, *she's on the bus up from the Quayside, no, I'm sorry, I didn't see which number, one of those new electric shuttles...*

I GUESS THEY TRIED, I HAD CREDIBILITY ENOUGH FOR THAT. They didn't find her, on any bus nor on the CCTV feeds when they checked those. They talked to me, and overrode my certainty with their own doubts; all I'd seen, after all, was a solitary kid, and they all dress alike. It might have been any, they said. And the fact that no kid at all could be seen to board the bus at that stop, that time of day—they thought that was evidence in their favour, evidence against.

I disagreed, but mutedly. I talked to you and was muted too, one more raiser of false hope soon dispelled; I felt that I'd failed you twice, neither returning your daughter nor letting you rest in her loss. You wouldn't hold that against me, I thought—I hoped!—but your wife would, of course. Hold it and use it too. She'd need that, something, anything. I could hardly hold it against her. The urge to harm is instinctual, and I'd made her such a gift...

My only remedy was to understand, to play detective in the face of disbelief. I didn't expect to be lucky twice, to see your daughter again; but if I could diagnose why she had come this close, perhaps I could track her back to where she'd come from. She'd seemed well, as far as I could tell from one short sight of her. She'd seemed free. Call her a runaway, then, the most hopeful of options, and try to figure out what she wanted.

It was chance that I'd seen her, but not chance that she'd been there, at that bus-stop. Perhaps she had come looking for her father, and her nerve, her finger had failed on the doorbell. Perhaps she had only been hoping for a sight of him. Either way, he was on her mind, and that was good. If he wouldn't be hopeful on his own behalf, I could be hopeful for him. And I could act: I could distribute flyers at all the likely stops on the bus-route, I could put up posters, I could talk to drivers, passengers, shopkeepers...

I COULDN'T TALK TO THE PRESS; THAT WAS YOUR TASK, AND YOUR WIFE'S. They ran their stories anyway, of course, about the missing girl's estranged father, his gay lover, our luxury hide-out on the river, but at least I didn't feed them. My role was to be freelance, on the streets, proactive.

The second time I saw her, I was coming home from one more long day, making her face public while I tried to keep my own private. There were press outside this building, front and back; I could see them from a distance, so I paused, leaned against the railing, looked out on the river. Gave myself a moment, before

I had to run that particular gauntlet.

I don't suppose it was a garbage scow, I don't believe we dump trash directly in the sea these days, but that was the phrase that came to mind. It was long and low in the water, open-bellied and heaped with something foul-smelling that might have been dredgings from higher up the river, and she was sitting on the prow.

All alone, like a figurehead, proud and still and gazing forward. Again she had her hood up, and I could barely see the line of her face in profile, but it was her.

I stared. I started to walk, to run, to keep pace with the slow determined vessel; at last, I called her name.

She wasn't so far away from me, twenty metres perhaps, no more; and sound carries over water. Even above the guttural mutter of a diesel engine, my voice must have reached her. Reached and reached.

She didn't turn, she didn't look my way.

Ignored, desperate, what could I do? I ran, I waved; I tried to catch the skipper's attention on the boat's bridge at the back, but if he saw me he ignored me too. I phoned the dedicated helpline as I ran, and must have sounded mad. Once I'd identified myself, I expect I sounded madder. Reporting a second random sighting, far less likely than the first: no great wonder, if they didn't believe me. Certainly there was no sudden wail of sirens on the road, no swoop of police cars, no launch chasing down the river.

Downstream was our direction, away from the lingering reporters. I couldn't grab them, show her to them, have them point their cameras for evidence. I did try grabbing passers-by, and was punched and bruised and screamed at, no complaint.

At last the scow picked up speed just where a tributary came into the river, where I had to turn away from the bank to find a bridge across; and I was out of breath already, starting to lose touch. Gasping, defeated, I watched her go.

When I was calmer, when I could be rational, I reached for my phone again— and put it away, didn't call you. I'm sorry for that, but what could I say? Another failed sighting, fleeting and inconsequential, I couldn't make it credible. Perhaps I was sheerly selfish, but it seemed to me more generous to keep this to myself. Just as it was a cruelty in the world to be showing her only to me, when I wanted her only for you.

THE THIRD TIME, I STARTED TO THINK THAT PERHAPS IT WASN'T THE WORLD after all, perhaps it was her; perhaps it really was deliberate.

One thing for sure, they were increasingly unworldly, these glimpses I was gifted. Suddenly I could start to doubt myself, except that every time I saw her more, more of her.

The bus-stop had seemed almost likely; the boat was the opposite of that, almost impossible. Perhaps there was some community of feral children, living wild on a landfill at the river's mouth and hitching rides on all the river's traffic—but I didn't really believe that. Let alone that I alone should know it, I should be the one to discover it, in pursuit of your lost daughter. It was the stuff of fiction, and no weave of the world we actually lived in.

And yet I had seen her, and seen her again, and she must surely be hiding up somewhere.

They say the third time pays for all, but it isn't really true. It just confirms the debt.

I was at home, but I couldn't bear it: the silent telephone was a mockery and a temptation, a devil's lure to disaster. How you endured that same silence I couldn't begin to imagine, except that your wife was with you and I had no wish to imagine how you filled the empty hours with her. They were hard enough for me alone, too hard. I snatched up my messenger-bag full of flyers and headed out. Again.

As I walked down the corridor, I was aware that the lift was there waiting for me, doors wide, someone in it already.

They must have seen me, must understand that—from the ninth floor!—I would most certainly want the lift. I barely speeded my pace, just enough to show willing.

I wasn't really looking, but after a few more steps my sidelong mind had diagnosed the figure: adolescent, scrawny, female, hooded...

Then I was looking, really looking.

It wasn't raining outside, but she was dripping wet.

Then I was running, calling; not quite daring her name, and what else do you call out, running in those circumstances...?

"Hey, hold the lift!"

Then, at last, she lifted her head. Not to see me, not to acknowledge me: to let me see her, rather, to make my own acknowledgement.

Then I did, I cried her name to her face; and then the lift doors closed, and she was gone.

NINE FLOORS, AND I TOOK THEM AT A HECTIC, HURTLING SPRINT, CRASHING DOWN the stairs, bruising my shoulder at every turn.

When I reached the foyer, the lift stood open as before, and she was gone.

There was a wet patch in the corner, where she had been standing. It was muddy, and smelt of the river and its tides.

THERE SHOULD HAVE BEEN MUDDY TRACKS ACROSS THE FOYER, TRAILS OF DAMP in the carpet, but there were none.

My building had security, almost to the lengths of paranoia. There should have been images of her on the CCTV, but again, none. The key-codes on the doors had been changed since her disappearance, after a determined journalist bribed a cleaner; she shouldn't have got inside without being buzzed in and logged at reception, but no one there had seen her.

She surely, absolutely could not have slipped past the press cameramen still staking out every entrance. They worked their equipment frenziedly as I approached them, looked blank when I asked about the girl who had certainly gone in and presumably come out again. In exchange for the promise of an interview, they showed me their haul of pictures, everyone who had passed through every door that morning. Not her.

IF SHE HADN'T TAKEN THE LIFT DOWN TO RECEPTION, IF SHE HADN'T COME OR gone, there were still apparent options. I spent a long time checking every other floor for muddy traces, finding nothing. I tried to persuade myself that she was living secretly somewhere in the building, perhaps with the connivance of someone on security. I imagined trying to persuade the police of the same thing, or trying to persuade you. My imagination failed, before my persuasion had the chance to try. I didn't believe it for a moment. Stranger things had happened, yes—but not this, not here, not to her. To us. It was a beautifully malevolent fantasy; she might have the malevolence—she was twelve years old, and viciously unhappy; malevolence goes with that territory, nowhere better—but it called for organisation, a network, contacts that she surely couldn't muster.

Even so, I went out less often and spent more time just wandering the building. Using the lifts as often as I could, just in case. Discovering roof-access and basements, meeting staff and other residents, asking idiot questions. Learning many things, and finding no trace at all, hearing no whispers of your daughter. No surprise.

AS TIME WENT BY, I HEARD LESS AND LESS OFTEN FROM YOU, TOO. Again, no surprise. I had been an adventure, catastrophic, the embodiment of loss. Now in your distress, in your mutual distress you and your wife were settling back into old habits of dependence, leaning on each other, looking inward to that emptiness you shared.

If you never actually told me you'd gone back to her in the marital sense, it was only because you didn't need to. It was written in your voice, more loudly in your silences.

THE BED OF COURSE WAS FAR TOO WIDE WITHOUT YOU. Sleep was hard to come by anyway, and solitude made those long watches harder to endure. A radio makes for small comfort, mock-company, bodiless and unresponsive voices.

Even so, I used to listen all night long: doze and wake and drowse again, to the thin and constant stream of others' talking. It was better, marginally, than the great hushed hollow cavern of the dark all unrelieved.

One night, waking, it was something else I heard: or something more, overriding the newsreader's murmur. There was a low but steady splashing, as though I'd left a tap running in the en-suite. Or as though you were there, perhaps, not left yet, taking a shower.

Of course I rose, I went to see. How not? I thought a tap washer had split, perhaps, or a pipe-joint burst somehow. I thought I had plumbers in my future. I could have lived without it, but at least I knew the men in Maintenance now. They'd fix this. If I was worrying, it was about my downstairs neighbour's ceiling...

THEN I WALKED INTO THE EN-SUITE AND WAS HIT BY THE SMELL OF IT, THE STINK of tidal mud.

THEN I HIT THE LIGHTS, AND WAS BRIEFLY JUST BEWILDERED. There was a figure in the bathtub. Someone small and fully dressed, and simply sitting there, in the dark until I turned the lights on.

Then she lifted her head.

Then she pushed back her hood.

It was your daughter, of course, I knew that already. Unchanged, just as I had seen her three times now. Dripping wet again, or still, but not from bathwater any more than it was from rain.

Her mouth was open, and water was running out of it. Running and running as though she were a gargoyle rainspout in a storm, only nothing so clean as that.

Foul water, filthy water, black and heavy with silt and rot. Clogging the drain and swilling around her legs already, putrid and rising and still coming from her mouth, from her *mouth...*

I THINK I SCREAMED, PERHAPS. And then I didn't know what to do. I backed out of there, trembling, but had nowhere else to go, so long as she sat in my bathtub; I went back in. Turned the light off and then on again, as though I could reboot the room. She was still there, and her waters were still running.

I said her name, and she looked at me. Her face used to twist when she did that, fury or loathing or disgust. Now she was—like this, come to this, and it still did. Her mouth gushed horror and I supposed she must be dead, and she still saw me as something lower, lesser, to be condemned.

I slid down the wall and sat on the floor, because my legs wouldn't sustain me. I talked to her because one of us had to do something, and she was busy just spilling over.

I had little enough to tell her, though, except that she was loved and missed. That had carried little enough weight before; none now. Otherwise, all I had for her was questions: what had happened, where could we find her, why was it me she had come to when her parents loved and missed her so much more?

Death famously has no answers to offer to the living. Perhaps it brings no revelation, even to the dead. For sure, it brings no forgiveness. She looked at me and spouted, was a spout, and the dark waters rose all around her.

Then, when I thought the bath would flood, must flood the room and the flat and the building entirely while she would go on sitting there letting it all flood out of her, at last she closed her mouth. She rose, stepped out of the bathtub, stepped over my legs and walked out of the en-suite, dripping water all the way.

Me, I just sat there listening to the slow, vile gurgling from the bath as what she'd left behind her struggled to drain away.

When I could stand, when I could grope my way out of there, I found a trail of sodden carpets and slime, all the way from my bedroom to the lift. Where she'd gone then, it was impossible to say.

YOU'VE CALLED ME ELEVEN TIMES SINCE THEN ON MY MOBILE, AND I HAVEN'T picked up once. What can I say to you—your daughter's dead, and I'm the one she haunts? I have nothing to offer but a useless truth, a horror with no resolution: no body, no story, no proof.

I have nothing to offer her except apology and regret, just as useless. All she can give me is dread. We're all caught here, in a helpless spiral of loss.

I CAN'T SAVE YOU, OR HER. *Sauve qui peut*: I can only save myself. Or hope to. I see her constantly, but only here on the riverside, on the water or nearby. I daren't stay in my flat now. High ground might be safer, but a river runs through her, and all this city is river-built.

If I leave, if I go somewhere else, far and dry, perhaps I can leave her behind me. For sure I have to leave you, but you have left me already; it ought not to hurt as much as it does.

How far I go depends, perhaps, how fast I travel. Whether she comes with me, or tries to follow, or maybe lets me go.

Sometimes I think, wherever I go, I can only ever come closer to her. I think I'm off the compass already and all roads, all directions are the same now, and she's been that way before me, gone ahead.

Hothouse Flowers: or The Discreet Boys of Dr Barnabus

IT HAS BEEN RIGHTLY SAID THAT TRAVEL AS YOU WILL, SEEK AS YOU CAN, RISK what you dare, never will you find anything to match the horrors that you left behind at home.

I HAVE BEEN A SOLITARY MAN AND A RESTLESS ONE, BY NATURE AND BY PRACTICE both. Being blessed in the possession of a good fortune and far, very far from the want of a wife, I found myself able to indulge both those predilections as far as I chose. At the age of twenty-one I engaged a man of business and left my affairs cheerfully in his competent hands, to nourish as he could. Myself, I promptly departed this drizzly demi-paradise with a thousand pounds in gold and notes and promises—it seemed a fortune to the callow youth I was—and the firm intent of returning only when I lacked the funds to keep away any longer.

THAT NOBLE EXPERIMENT TOOK ME THIRTY YEARS TO REALISE.

I DID COME BACK AT LAST, AS I HAD ALWAYS KNOWN I MUST. The John Furnival who stepped off the packet steamer in Southampton was as light of frame as the boy of the same name who had departed the same way three decades sooner, if not so light of heart. He was more sallow of skin, malarial, and inclined to limp in damp weather; he carried a record of his adventures in scars both public and private, both visible and otherwise; he had a fund of stories on which he rarely drew, and nothing of value besides, except experience dearly bought and highly prized.

I rode north, two days on a hired hack. My destination was a spa town in the hills, whose name need not detain us. Once there, and with my pockets entirely to let, my first enquiry was necessarily for my man of business. He, it transpired, had in my absence become a company. I paid a call, then, upon the firm of Alshott, Stroud and Alshott; presented my card and asked for Mr Alshott and was ushered into the presence of a stripling, a mere youth whose efforts at gravitas were mocked by the very desk he sat behind.

"Ah," I said. "I think, perhaps, your father...?"

The boy laid my card—cheap Indian pasteboard, florid print, in itself sufficient to declare my history, my status and my recent impoverishment to anyone with eyes to see—upon his blotter, rose to his feet and walked around that imposing edifice of a desk, smiling ruefully.

"My father is in Sussex, sir, enjoying a very comfortable retirement. I am sure he would wish me to remember him to you; had we but notice of your coming, I am sure he would have written. I am Sylvester Alshott."

We shook hands, but I was shaking my head. "You were...not born, I think—heavens, I think your father was not married!—when I left England. And retired now? Good grief! I had not supposed him to be ten years older than myself."

"Oh, barely so much, sir. A number of happy years in the business induced him to relinquish an active role with us far sooner than might otherwise have been the case. Or at least, to relinquish a *public* role. His name, you have seen, remains on our letterhead; he himself remains deeply interested in our activities. It might fairly be said that his retirement has been more comfortable for him than for those of us who toil beneath his vigilance. If you are concerned about your own investments, Mr Furnival, let me assure you that my father has been assiduous in overseeing my endeavours on your behalf, and that your position is...robustly healthy, shall we say?"

By now I was laughing internally, and trying to disguise it for the sake of his *amour-propre*, while still being grateful to his father for that careful and no doubt onerous supervision.

"Thank you," I managed, knowing the little phrase to be hopelessly inadequate to the occasion—either of the two occasions, indeed, his injured pride or my own relief.

He offered me sherry, of course—that utterly English ceremony that I have acted out a thousand times, from Gibraltar to Kuala Lumpur to Hong Kong—and bade me sit with him at a fireplace, where we could talk without that monumental desk between us. We spoke of trade, of 'Change, of my various properties and his investments on my behalf; at last, rather diffidently, I asked whether I might still actually have a house.

"Of course, sir!" For a moment there, he looked like a startled owl. Had we not been speaking of houses, among other benefits, all this half-hour gone? "Did I forget to mention that Minscombe has been let this last year on most advantageous terms?"

Minscombe was my childhood home, a bare ten miles north of where we sat, and he knew quite well that he had not forgotten to mention it.

I smiled at his blushing awkwardness, and shook my head. "I'm sorry, I have confused you now. I have been attending, I promise, despite this intriguing sherry," and despite the more simple pleasures of watching young Sylvester Alshott as he strained to impress upon his most senior and unexpected client how very much he justified his father's confidence. "What I mean is, do I have a house that I can actually live in, without dispossessing any of my tenants or disrupting your other arrangements? Preferably a house close at hand, that I might occupy this week? Tonight, even? To be frank, Mr Alshott, I find myself embarrassed—*temporarily* embarrassed, thanks to your excellent stewardship—to the point where even a room in a posting-house is a strain on my resources."

Again I had startled him, again he had to struggle a little with his composure. This time, I thought, he was trying not to laugh. My mind had perhaps not yet caught up with my new, my *resumed* position. After one has spent many months counting every copper coin and ekeing out every meal—after one has spent the better part of a year, indeed, travelling overland because the cost of even a third-class sea-passage had been beyond one's means—it is not easy immediately to shrug off habits of parsimony.

"Mr Furnival," the boy said earnestly, with a glance at the clock, "it is too late now, but a visit to your banker in the morning will resolve any such difficulty, and should quite set your mind at rest," in a way that, to his clear chagrin, he had failed to accomplish himself. He was back to thinking me a little simple, I suspected. "In the meantime, I hope you will consider yourself my guest."

"No, no, there is no need for—"

"Please," he said. "I insist. My father bequeathed me his house when he departed for the salt air of the Suffolk coast, and to be blunt with you I rattle in it alone. I should be glad of the company, and you will find it more comfortable than any hotel in town, let alone a posting-house. That is, assuming that you can tolerate the bachelor lifestyle...?"

It was rather neatly done; that question of course made it impossible for me to refuse. So I laughed at him and drew his attention to the fact that I had myself lived the bachelor lifestyle for more years than he had been alive, and a rather rougher version of it recently. Then I graciously allowed him to buy me dinner, on the grounds that my fortune had been the foundation of his father's and hence his own. Conversation proved easy, and by the time his front door had closed behind us both we were on the way to becoming fast friends; by the time the sun surprised us the next morning, we had ventured rather further.

IT WAS NOTHING BUT CURIOSITY—MY BESETTING SIN, I CONFESS IT—THAT TOOK me north the following week, on a borrowed hunter of my host's. I meant no more than to overlook my former home from a convenient hill, a childhood haunt of mine. Minscombe was let out now to a philanthropic gentleman, Alshott had told me, who took in orphaned boys; I had half an idea that I might run into some of the lads playing as I used to play myself. Perhaps I wanted to find one alone, who might stand in for me exactly.

The oak was there yet, the particular oak that overhung the cliff above the house. I used to sprawl panther-like on a branch some days for hours together, to the voluble horror of my anxious guardian, just watching the slow passage of life below. My tree was untenanted that day, though, as was the hill entire. I took my mount as near the edge as was comfortable for him, and looked down. The house seemed as empty as the countryside around. It had never bustled even in my time—my guardian having been of a retiring disposition—but I saw not a soul at work in the grounds, not a servant crossing the yard, not a boy running through the park or capering on the leads or indeed anywhere about.

Perhaps they were all at luncheon. My pocket-watch had stopped and I kept misreading the sun, forgetting how low it lies even at noon in northern latitudes. Or perhaps the philanthropic gentleman was a tartar who laid all his charges down for a nap in the early afternoon. Or he was a generous soul, and had taken them on an expedition for the day or for the week—there seemed no more life in the stable-block than there was in the house, neither hands nor horses shifting the light—and the staff was taking advantage of this opportunity to idle. Or...

I could list half a hundred reasons if I cared to. Nevertheless I thought it curious, unless I was simply disappointed not to find that analogue of myself. Perhaps I had built too much on a dream of continuity, as though there must always be one lonely boy at Minscombe, hopeful and bereft ...

One lonely horseman on the road below drew me down unexpectedly. It might only have been that the glimpse of movement in an otherwise still world acted as a trigger to my own need to move, or as a reminder that I could not sit there all day gazing into the pool of memory and speculation. It might have been coincidence that I emerged from Home Wood just as he rounded the last hedge before the boundary wall.

His horse shied at the sight of me, but she was nervous already. That was his doing, I thought, the fat man who sat her, who sweated in her saddle and shied more dramatically than she did.

He huffed with relief when he saw my face, when he saw that I meant no harm, or else perhaps when he saw that he didn't know me. I saw that he was clumsy with his horse, but not unkind. Once they were both settled I saw another thing, that he had a doctor's bag strapped to the saddle at his back.

"Is someone unwell here, sir? One of the boys, perhaps—or their benefactor?"

It was a fair guess. This road was practical no farther than Minscombe, petering out in farmland that bordered the river, which offered neither bridge nor ford for three miles in either direction. And illness would explain the quiet, perhaps.

His eyes narrowed none the less. "Do you have some connection with the house, sir?"

His question was equally fair, and I might fairly have said *no, none at all.* Certainly I had no legitimate interest in my tenant's doings, so long as he paid his rent and kept his children orderly. Still, I had come too far this morning to be willingly balked; I took advantage of the way the question was framed. "You might say so, sir, as it belongs to me."

He frowned. "I understood the owner to be expatriate?"

"Indeed. I have just now returned to this country, after a life abroad. My name is Furnival."

"Ah. Barnabas, Rowland Barnabas."

We shook hands, there with our horses restless beneath us. I said, "You are a doctor, I collect? Unless the shape and significance of a man's saddle-luggage has altered radically since my last days here." When he still hesitated, I added, "I have no connection with the Minscombe tenant, sir, except that he lives in my house; but I confess to a growing curiosity, and perhaps a hint of unease. And, well, he does live in my house."

"Yes." He came to a decision, visibly. I had been confident that he would. He was a few years younger than me, I thought, and not a confident man himself. He carried a burden he would like to share, once he was sure of my *bona fides*. Perhaps he wanted to confess; he looked to me unquiet in his conscience.

He said, "You are right to be uneasy. Your tenant"—he was quick, I thought, to attach me to the situation—"is not a man to inspire ease of mind. Nor are the orphans thriving in his care. My whole concern is for the boys, you understand," in a sudden outburst.

Mine too, but I did not intend to say so. "Will you explain it to me?"

He was hesitant again, thinking perhaps of his Hippocratic Oath and his duty of confidence. At last he said, "I would prefer to show you, if you will come in with me."

I thought he would be glad of company, as well as of witness. "I think," I said, "my tenant would find it difficult to keep me out."

"So do I, by Jove! Come on, then!" His mood suddenly and inexpressibly lightened, Dr Barnabas actually led the way down the road, that last hundred yards to the gatehouse.

The gatehouse was unoccupied and the gates stood open, as they never had in my late guardian's tenure. The drive, I was sorry to see, was weedy and the park unkempt. Did my tenant's lease not require upkeep of the grounds, or was he a cheeseparer, had he endeavoured to save money by depending on his boys to do the work? If so he must have been disappointed, and so was I.

We rode to the house, where all the windows were shuttered or shrouded, as though there had been a death. Again that would explain the stillness, but I thought my companion would have forewarned me. Something there was, that he wanted me to see for myself; I thought death did not fit the case.

Nothing here seemed to fit the case. We rode around to the stable yard, and no one stood to our horses' heads, no one came to the house door to ask our business here. Dr Barnabas clearly expected this neglect, sliding ungainly down from his mare and himself leading her to an empty stall, loosening her girths, fetching her a bucket of water. I did the same by my own mount, apologizing to him the while for the inadequacies of service. He was a fine animal, and deserved better. Meanwhile, the stout doctor was apologising to me: "I am afraid it is always so these days. Mr Royce seems quite unable to retain a servant, inside the house or out."

"Ah. Mr Royce is my tenant's name?" Matters did not bode well for Mr Royce, if he wanted to retain his lease. I had not especially wanted to live at Minscombe myself—I had no particular fondness for the place and, while not a great house, it was a monstrous edifice for a man alone, who had neither interest in nor prospect of children—but I would not willingly see it fall to rack and ruin.

Doctor Barnabas confirmed the name but said no more, only beckoning me to follow him in through the house door.

"Oughtn't we to announce ourselves?" I murmured. "A knock, perhaps...?"

"There is no need, no point. No one would come."

It felt strange to walk in uninvited, even here; it felt exceedingly strange to heel another man into what had been my home. After the first minute, though, the strangeness was entirely the other way about. This place was not my home, and everything I saw reminded me of that.

To begin with, the house was cast into unutterable gloom, even at this height of the day. Never a broken beam of sunlight found its way in to play with the dust—and there was a great deal of dust. Filth, too. Mud beneath our boots, tramped heedlessly into the house.

Well. Barnabas had said that Mr Royce could not keep a servant. I would have countered that boys can sweep and scrub as well as maids, if they are put to it—but perhaps he lacked the discipline to do so. Or perhaps there was another reason. The doctor was here for the boys, after all...

More mildly than I meant, I said only, "Do they never draw a curtain in this house?"

"Nor open a shutter, sir, no. Daylight is an affliction here."

Lamps and candles stood everywhere, with tapers and lucifers to hand, but there was enough indirect daylight to show us our way; more than enough to show me the grimy state that Minscombe had been allowed to fall into. I should have been angry if the doctor weren't so imperative, if he hadn't given me to understand that there were worse things here than disregarded dirt. Besides, to criticise my tenant was to criticise my man of business, and I was disinclined to do that. Soap and water and elbow-grease would soon restore Minscombe to her rightful state; no house falls to ruin in a single year.

Dr Barnabas led me up the back stairs, up and up to the servants' rooms in the long attics. He puffed and gasped at the climb; I reflected that Mr Royce was not generous to his orphans in their accommodations. With no one else in the house, he might decently have slept them in the guest wing, even in the family wing. Perhaps he was a practical man, not wanting to give them ideas above their station, which must inevitably be disappointed when they moved on into the world beyond the gates? Or—with no servants in the house—perhaps he was practical in another consideration, thinking that the sparse comforts of the attic rooms would be easier of maintenance. Or—if the boys were indeed sick, as Dr Barnabas' presence and anxieties must suggest—perhaps this was a measure of quarantine, mark of a sensible man...

The good doctor sweated and hauled his bulk upward, and needed a minute to recover at the head of the stairs, before we ventured the jute mats of the corridor. At least, he wanted me to believe so, lifting his hat and patting a handkerchief across his brow. My suspicion went unvoiced, that in truth he wanted only to delay the moment of discovery a little longer.

Even up here, the dormer windows had been masked with some thin stuff that kept the sun at bay, though it did let in light enough to see by. Dr Barnabas opened the first door, to what had been a housemaids' room in my day. Here were the twin iron beds, the worn rug on bare boards, the washstand and dresser, just as I remembered.

And here were the promised boys at last, one to a bed, pale and clean in the shadows: quite startlingly clean they seemed, in all this gloom and grime. Their nightshirts too were brightly, unexpectedly white.

"I have my girl wash these," Barnabas murmured, fingering a pristine collar as though he read my mind. I hoped not so; he wouldn't have liked where my mind went next, as his fingers strayed through the boy's dishevelled hair.

The boy didn't wake or stir beneath these attentions. Nor did his brother in misfortune, though Barnabas was heavy-footed, heavy-handed too, and made no great effort at discretion.

I opened my mouth to ask what ailed them, what could keep lads seemingly unconscious but not apparently sick otherwise, in no apparent need of nursing. Barnabas forestalled me, moving to the door and beckoning, *onward, more to see...*

Indeed there was, but it was all the same. Room after room, two or three boys in each and each of them asleep or comatose, oblivious. It needed a dozen before at last I could stop Barnabas and put the question; he needed me to see, I think, the scale of what faced him.

"Dr Barnabas! What disease is this?" Something infectious, surely, to strike so many—and yet he seemed quite unconcerned about his own danger, fussing intimately over each of his patients, touching where there seemed no need to touch.

He sighed, straightened, shook his head. "I...do not know. It is like anaemia in some senses, a peculiarly pernicious anaemia—but anaemia does not produce an aversion to sunlight, photophobia, such as these boys exhibit. Even in this state, if I pulled back that scrim across the window, you would see them flinch. They will rouse at evening, a little: enough to take whatever medicines I prescribe, but my best endeavours do no good. One boy was so weak, I transfused him with my blood, my own," and his big hand stroked the arm of the boy he stood above, while his eyes gazed at the blank of the window, while his mind I thought saw another boy altogether, "but he died regardless. He might have died anyway, there are five in the churchyard now," death after all and he had not warned me; "but for all I know, my actions helped him on his way. I cannot tell. I am..." *I am out of my depth*, he meant to say, but a shake of the head was all he had to offer.

"And their guardian, Mr Royce? What does he say?"

"Little enough. Nothing, in recent days; I rarely see him. He pays my bills, and perhaps thinks he has done his duty. And, true, they are only parish boys who would be in the poorhouse else, but I feel their loss most dreadfully, I for one..."

The only one, he thought himself. I thought he was probably right.

And might have thought little more about it, except for wishing this were not happening in my house and wondering how soon we might revoke Royce's lease, Alshott and I between us—but Barnabas went on, speaking half to himself, touching another boy at the throat. "They have these contusions, too, these sores that form on their necks; I've never seen anything quite like them."

"What? Show me!"

It must have come out in a bark, most unlike my previous sickroom mutter. He startled physically, but turned back the high collar of the nightshirt to let me see.

I looked, I saw.

He said, "Your face...! Do you know what this is?"

"I...have seen its like," I admitted, though I hated to hear the words come from my mouth. "More than once. In India, years since, and in the Carpathians just this winter gone. The snows came early, and closed the road; I was obliged to overwinter. The valley folk were kind to me, but they were much afflicted by just such a plague as this. Happily, I was able to offer my assistance."

"How, oh, how...?"

I am a hunter: the words were on my lips, but I was merciful. What would he benefit, from knowing? I shook my head and said, "Because I had seen it before, in India. Come, Dr Barnabas. We can do no good standing over these poor boys. You have done magnificently, but it is not a case for you," *you are out of your depth.* "Let me gather what I need to treat this scourge and I promise you, by the time of your next visit, your boys will be on the mend."

It took more work than that to remove him from Minscombe, but not much. He was frankly eager to be gone, only that his professional curiosity was piqued and perhaps his pride also, in a way that flattered him less. I gratified neither, keeping as obscure in my responses as I could achieve.

I put him on his horse and saw him off the grounds and away down the road. Then I turned Alshott's fine hunter to the fields and a wild ride, partly for his satisfaction and partly for my own, to chase the megrims out of my head. This was no disease—no wonder the doctor had been baffled!—but a devil: a foreign devil, by all that ever I knew or dreamed. I had never thought to encounter such a thing in my own county, in my own house yet...!

Here it was, though, and at least I knew what it was. And how to address it. Horror might drive me, but it was tempered by experience.

We came hot and hard into Alshott's yard, his horse and I. I tossed the reins to his stable-lad and jumped down, to be met by the man himself in his doorway. His face showed disapproval, as he gazed at heaving flanks and a sweat-soaked crupper; he said, "I suppose I should thank you for giving him a good work-out, but truly, Furnival—"

He cut himself off abruptly, as he saw my own face for the first time. "Good God, man, what is it? What's happened? Your house...?"

"Minscombe is very well, or will be when I have her in my care again. Her current tenant, though—he is the devil!"

"Oh! Have I been mistaken in Mr Royce?" His expression changed again, as he thought himself at fault. The young are so mobile, and so revealing. Therein lies their charm, I think, far more than in personal beauty. "I might have taken more care over his references; but he settled so quickly on the first sum I asked, I was perhaps too hasty..."

"No, no. Be easy on that score, his references could have told you nothing." I would much have preferred to have done the same thing exactly, told him nothing; but I had said too much already, in my heat. There could be no backing away now. I consoled myself briefly with the thought that I knew my host already to be a sportsman, a huntsman, and one who kept a vigorous and testing stable. He would not resile from a grim task, if I could only bring him to trust me.

I thought I could do that. I believed it, indeed, profoundly. I had amassed evidence enough, these days beneath his roof. Sylvester Alshott was a young man who inspired confidence, and deserved it.

Even so, I begged his indulgence while I washed and changed my dress. Nothing could happen yet in any case, and whether or not he believed the tale I had to tell him, it would be briefly told.

In my absence he'd had his man clean and press my evening clothes, and lay them out ready for me. I had grown unused to such service in recent years; now I felt an unexpected surge of sentiment, as though somehow I had come home. It was inappropriate, of course, in another man's house. Also, it was all too easy to see it in relation to the danger that would confront me this night—confront us both, if I was any judge of men—and still I was absurdly moved by such a little, such an ordinary attention.

I couldn't speak of it, of course, when I met him in the library. Besides, we had other graver matters to discuss. I cursed his lawyerly sherry and demanded a brandy and soda; he laughed at me and mixed a strong one, but would not be bullied—he said—into joining with my barbarity, when his father had laid down three dozen of a fine oloroso and this was the last of it.

Unchallenged, then, by each other's tastes, we sank into heavy leather chairs and a brief silence while he waited, while I reached for words.

"I have travelled," I said, "far and far. I have seen strange things, dreadful things, most of them the work of men. This, though: this is something other. Bear with me, while I try to explain—and if you can, suspend your rational mind, which must revolt at what I have to tell you.

"There is a...creature, a spirit; a more godly man than I would call it a demon, no doubt. It inhabits the dead, I think. Certainly it is not human, although it can look so, although it is intelligent enough to pass. Certainly it kills. It feeds on the blood of the living. I have met it in the slums of Calcutta, and again in the mountains last winter; I told you of that before, though not in these terms. Not honestly. I spoke only of a beast that must die, an endless hunt through snow and storm. You must forgive me, but I did not see the need for more, where more is always worse.

"Now there is a need. This day I have seen its spoor again, at my own Minscombe, and I would ask your help."

"Of course," he said. Instantly, unquestioningly. Ignorant as he was—and knowing exactly how ignorant he was—he yet gave me blind trust, quite untrammelled.

I might have melted, I think, if I hadn't had the fires of Hell in mind.

I leaned forward, nursing my glass, and told him punctiliously what lay before us, what we would have to do. If we could achieve it.

He listened gravely, nodded, laid his life in my hands.

I would have prayed not to abuse that, if only I believed in anything good enough to pray to.

SO IT WAS, THEN, THAT TWO MEN RODE OUT LATE THAT NIGHT, STILL IN EVENING dress. He had protested, laughingly, until I pointed out that black clothes would help us pass unseen on a moonlit night, and in the shadows of a dark house. After that he was quiet and thoughtful for half an hour together.

Minscombe had been my childhood home, the setting for all the adventures of my youth. Of course I knew where we might leave the horses in a grove of trees, where a natural spring would give them water, where deep grass would offer them both forage and rest. Of course I knew the path that would bring us unseen from there to the boundary wall.

Minscombe wasn't a bridewell; the wall was high, but still a statement as much as a barrier. As a lad I used to slither over it without a second thought, to save myself the trek around to the gate. Sometimes, indeed, to avoid questions at the gate. I didn't always want news of my excursions to reach back to my guardian.

Alas, that boy was long ago, and my body had seen hard uses since. Alshott eeled up the old stone with a young man's easy grace, then perched atop and reached down a hand to help me. I might have ignored it, might have snorted pride and hauled myself up alone; I may be twice his age, but a rugged life keeps a man limber. That I chose not to do that, that I gripped his hand and depended on its warm steel grip as I scrambled to the top, I think that says as much as I need to about trust and commitment. On the night, I think it said it all.

Side by side we let ourselves down the other side, into the moonshadow of the trees. Broad lawns stretched between us and the house, but no need to expose ourselves: again I knew a way, my old poacher's path home, following the treeline until it met the wall of the kitchen garden. As a boy I'd have shinned over that and helped myself to a peach or a pair of apples on my way to the scullery window with the broken sash, paid for them with a rabbit left in tribute on the long deal kitchen table for the cook to find in the morning.

Now, though, we had another end in view. Literally in view: there was light in the old library window, where the shutters had been flung back. Some creatures love the night.

I beckoned Alshott forward. We crept along the wall to my guardian's sacred rose-bed, let run now to ruin in neglect. Runners tangled our ankles, thorns ripped at our trousers: no matter. I was overdue new evening dress in any case, and I suspected that Sylvester's had come down to him from his father. Certainly from a man broader than he was, and not so tall. My memories of the elder Alshott were grown vague with the years, but would accord with that description. Also with that habit of mind, to pass on an old suit to a newgrown son rather than send him to a tailor. Parsimony is no doubt a useful trait in a man of business— but I thought I would ask Sylvester to recommend me a good tailor, and then take the boy along. I could legitimately point out that he had ruined his good clothes in my service, so I was duty-bound to replace them...

I should probably not have been thinking about clothes, just then. Nor plotting my way through an inevitable argument with young Mr Alshott. The human mind is a curious artefact, in both what it is drawn toward and what it resiles from.

I did not want to look through that library window. But we were here now, just beneath the stone lip of it, and we had come for this. Exactly for this. I lifted my cautious head above that lip, and looked. And ducked back down, and would have kept Sylvester from looking if I could: only that he needed to see it, to confirm his faith in me and the needs of the night.

So he looked, and I watched his tender young face change in what lamplight spilled out of the window. He shuddered and dropped back to my side, wordless.

Silence was just as well, because such creatures have preternatural hearing. I had told him that. Everything that I knew, I had told him and he had seemingly accepted, at least to come this far on an adventure. Nothing that I said, nothing that I could have said would have prepared him for the actuality of that room that night.

It was worse for him than for me. I had seen such sights before, and grimmer ones than this. Also, he had seen my tenant in other guise, the man he knew as Royce.

No one could mistake the creature for human tonight, for all that it wore a human shape and human clothing. It seemed nothing more than beastly, as it hunched over the white-gowned body of a boy; nothing less than demonic as it lifted its face from his neck, its mouth and chin painted with fresh blood.

I was glad, I had to be glad that Alshott my companion had seen this; I could be nothing but sorry that Sylvester my new young friend had had to see it. I wished that my hand could express those opposite feelings, both at once, as it gripped his upper arm. I did think that perhaps he was sensitive to my wishing, that at least, as his fingers closed over mine.

WE HAD NO MORE TIME FOR SENTIMENT. I led him away from the window, softly,

softly: back through the rose-bed, back to the walled garden, this time over that wall and swiftly up to the house, confident that the scullery window would still be just as yielding. I could only hope that some at least of the boys now resident had had the chance to discover it before the monster's teeth began to steal their joy, their energy, their life's-blood.

What will let boys out, will let grown men in: even if their shoulders have grown broader than they knew. I went first, by my mute insistence. It took more squirming than was perhaps dignified—especially as Sylvester had my rear half to watch, my helpless kicking legs—but I was through soon enough, and had the resentful pleasure of watching him ease after me as if he'd been greased for it.

That was the last of our light for a while, what moonlight fell through one small window that we couldn't leave open. Again, though, I had all the years of my boyhood to draw upon. Nothing in this house was a stranger to me in darkness. Or the whole house was strange now, rather, a devil's home and not my own: but the walls and doors and stairs remained untouched, the furniture was all the same, more or less all its arrangements. I could find my way, and Alshott could follow me.

To be sure of him, I took his hand and set it on my shoulder, held his gaze until he nodded compliance.

Like that, then—the blind leading the blind, except that I was blind but knowing—we made our way through the kitchen to the back stairs. The monster in the library would never come this way; it would be beneath his dignity to use a servants' passage.

There was a greater danger that we might meet a boy. The one we had seen in the library would never move again, but Dr Barnabas had said that his patients grew more lively in the evening. Even so, I was not expecting to find them careering about the house in the dark.

And did not: wise or lucky, we made our way unchallenged to the Great Hall on the first floor.

The name was a joke. My guardian and I had felt—or I had asserted, and he had agreed—that an establishment so large as Minscombe merited a great hall, and that our own dignity demanded it. Lacking anything suitably baronial or mediaeval in a house that could claim nothing older than ramshackle Jacobean—and that was doubtful—we had settled eventually on the ballroom. Neither of us was much inclined to dancing. So my ancestors' surviving weaponry and military paraphernalia went up above the fireplace, eked out—I have always suspected—by judicious purchases on the part of my guardian, and the Great Hall became an established fact. On wet days my friends and I enacted battles all up and down its length, to the constant complaint of servants who had polished its sprung floor for a generation or more.

The maids and footmen were gone now, but little else had changed. I had counted on that. I picked up a candle on the way, I had a lucifer-case in my pocket; Alshott closed the doors at our backs and I struck a light.

Chairs lined the walls, and there was a stack of tables at the further end. Otherwise the long room was clear, as it always had been.

Alshott took the candle and made his way methodically from one wall to the next, lighting every lamp and sconce and candelabrum that he could.

"If we're going to have light," he said, "we might as well have *enough* light."

There was sense in that, of course. I didn't argue.

There was danger in it, too. There was danger in everything, in our simple presence here and in every telltale. The least glimmer of spilled light could catch a wary eye; the lightest footfall could carry on a quiet night; the best-laid floorboard could creak unexpectedly, the best-laid plan betray. Even the smell of a smoking candle could reach too far.

The library was directly below us. I watched the high doors almost in expectation. Surely, however little we spoke and however carefully we trod, surely he must hear something...?

I suppose we must have been right, I suppose he did; but for all my vaunted knowledge of the house and of his kind, still he confounded me.

We were watching the doors, waiting for him.

He came through the window.

Our eighteenth-century ballroom was mirrored—forgive me!—on the famous *Galerie des Glaces*, at least in its barest bones. It couldn't hope to rival the ostentation of Versailles; happily it hadn't tried. Nevertheless, there was the run of mirrors along the inner wall, standing opposite a matching run of windows. Outside our windows was a balcony, where guests could cool off with fresh air and long views over the park.

He must have heard us overhead and come the quick way: out through the open window and up the wall, scuttling like some spider-thing, inhuman; and so over the parapet and onto the balcony, and then straight in through the window.

Through the *shuttered* window, through glass and wood and all, monstrous strong and monstrous unheeding. Any man would have turned aside from such a mad decision; any man who persevered would have taken dreadful hurt in the doing of it.

This creature came through in a tempest of shards and splinters, as careless of its skin as it was of its clothes.

Its eyes glittered in all our lights, as we swivelled around to face it. Was that manic fury that twisted its face, or manic glee? I couldn't tell. Perhaps it was nothing at all, perhaps the creature was beyond all such human emotion.

Certainly it thought itself beyond us, unreachable.

It charged, directly for Sylvester. It moved dreadfully fast, but even so I managed to interpose myself and what I carried. Neither of us had time to think, or to change our purpose.

It ran, then, directly onto the point of my spear.

I have enjoyed my share of pig-sticking in India. I was ready for the shock of the body striking steel, the sink of blade into flesh.

I wasn't ready for the cold bitter intelligence that glared back at me from a six-foot distance; nor for the mocking gleam of its smile.

The spear's blade was steel, and it takes wood to slay such a creature, wood piercing its dead heart.

I smiled mirthlessly back, and pushed harder.

The spear's blade was sharp, and my strength was desperate.

The spear's blade might be steel, but its haft was ash.

I had no idea whether this would be effective, but I drove that spear right through the creature's body until the blade stood out between its shoulders, and what pierced its heart was good plain wood.

It stood its ground, stood on its feet and stared at me, transfixed.

Perhaps it had no idea either, whether it was dead again or not.

It took Alshott to decide the matter.

Alshott, swinging my guardian's old cavalry sabre, taking Royce's head clean off his shoulders at a blow.

THEN THERE WAS MESS, A FOUL MESS. Neither of us was much inclined to clean it up, but needs must. I don't wish to say too much about that: only that there was a sack from the gardener's shed, and a pit dug far from anywhere that mattered, and something slung in and buried deeply.

"We," Sylvester said, and stopped; and tried again, speaking not quite at random, not quite. Said, "We should go up, and see to the boys. Don't you, don't you think...?"

"Like this?" I said, with a gesture to show him his clothes, his condition, mirrored in my own. Ripped fabric was the least of it; mud from the digging mattered not at all. What mattered was the grue that had spilled from the creature that we slew. No neat dissolution, no crumbling into age and desiccation. All the blood it lately swallowed had come erupting out, mixed with less wholesome effusions, acid bile and I knew not what sprayed from its pierced body and its severed neck. I had been in trouble often and often for spilling on the ballroom floor, taking off the polish. Now I thought nothing would do but to take up the boards and begin again.

Sylvester and I had been sprayed as much as the floor. We both stood in urgent want of a bath. To be blunt, we stank, and our clothes were stained where they were not soaked. We were neither of us in any state to interview sick children, to whom we would be entire strangers. Sylvester acknowledged that, with a rueful expression.

"Besides, they'll be asleep," I said. At least, I trusted so. They'd need sleep more than anything: wholesome sleep, not the induced trances of their late master. With his influence lifted, I thought they ought to drift from the one state to the other, first steps on the road to recovery.

"First thing tomorrow," I said, "I'll bring Dr Barnabas here. They know him, they'll respond to him far better than to two filthy strangers in the dark."

"We could light lamps," he said mildly. "We could wash, even."

He didn't mean it, though, he didn't urge it; he was as keen as I to remove ourselves from that house. Also he was as reluctant as I to leave the boys unwatched, unguarded, but I thought the alternative was worse.

One thing we could do, we must; together, we laid out the dead boy on the library table and left him wrapped in a linen sheet, cleaner than we were ourselves.

Then back to the grove and the horses. A quick splash in the stream there because neither of us could bear the state of ourselves any longer, though we made the upset of the horses our excuse; and our first move when we reached his house was to fill the copper and boil water for a bath. Sylvester didn't so much as offer to rouse his man. We could perfectly well do the work ourselves, and attend each other.

Our dress suits both went into the furnace, to make their last contribution to our comforts.

CLEAN AT LAST, THERE SEEMED SMALL POINT IN BED. We lit a fire simply for the comfort of it and sat talking over stiff brandies until the easterly sky turned pink. By then Sylvester was sitting on the carpet at my feet, drowsing against my leg like a much younger boy. I smiled, took my hand from his shoulder and sent him upstairs, pointing out that Barnabas knew only me and wouldn't need two of us to conduct him to Minscombe.

So I rode out alone, and roused the good doctor from his warm and solitary bed. I told him something of what had happened, an abbreviated tale with no mention of a supernatural monster, or of a body flung into a pit; rode with him to the unguarded gates of my house; and bowed reluctantly to his wisdom when he plied my own logic against me. The boys knew only him, he said, and wouldn't need two of us to wake them. If they could be woken, if they weren't too far gone. The dead child in the library would be his care, he insisted; truly, he said, he would prefer to go on and deal with this alone.

I didn't doubt him for a moment. Neither that the boys would prefer to have him and him alone to deal with, for all that I doubted his motives. A known face, a kindly soul would always be better than a stranger.

I left him, then, and rode back to Sylvester.

"What will you do about Minscombe, John?"

In our ongoing attempt to feel clean—"clean on the *inside*," Sylvester said, "where I feel most befouled"—I was introducing him to the greatest pleasure of a spa town, the public steam-bath. It was late now and we had it to ourselves, but the servants came and went in the swirling, unpredictable fog; we were accordingly as discreet in our conversation as we were in our persons, sweating a yard apart and swathed with towels.

I said, "I'm not sure. There's no hurry, at any rate; but—well, if Barnabas offered to rent it for the sake of those poor boys, if he felt it would be best to keep them there, I would have no objection. I don't feel any great yen to live in it myself, if that's what you're asking. I don't know where I will go, but no doubt you can find me a house."

"I don't need to," he said definitely. "You'll stay with me, of course." And then, stumbling over his own eagerness, "I mean, that house is far too big for me alone, and, and..."

"I know what you mean. And thank you. I'd like to stay." I had almost depended on it.

I was determined at least to give Barnabas some time alone with the boys, to recover those he could. If he needed me, or when he wanted me, he knew where I was to be found.

Days passed, a week, two weeks. I heard nothing. When I did encounter the good doctor, it was by chance, and at first I failed to recognise him. I was meeting Sylvester for luncheon, at an hotel close to his place of business. With time on my hands and eager only for his sweet company, I was irredeemably early; but there was a man already at table, eating alone, making swift work of a plate of rare sirloin.

One ought not to criticise the manners of another. It was a remarkably large plate, though, and heaped high, and he was—well, gobbling. I did look twice, I confess. The second time—

"Dr *Barnabas*?"

He looked up, almost as startled as I was; I wondered if he had come in so early in hopes of avoiding anyone he knew.

It took him a moment to remember the courtesies. Belatedly he set his cutlery down, rose to his feet, held out his hand. "Mr Furnival! You must excuse my not having called on you before this, but, well, my charges are demanding of my time, and..."

"And I think you have been unwell, my dear doctor," I said. "Please, do continue with your meal. Don't mind me; I'm meeting Alshott here, but not for an hour yet. I'll sit with you, if I may," taking a chair before he could think to offer it. I beckoned a waiter over and ordered a pink gin, to root myself in place. Barnabas had a bottle of claret, and had made fair inroads already. "Tell me truly, doctor, how do you do?"

Truly, he looked terrible. He had lost extraordinary amounts of weight in such a short time, but men who drop stones are supposed to be the better for it. Barnabas seemed utterly fagged, dragged down; *drained*, I should have said.

"Oh," he said, applying himself to his meat again with that most extraordinary appetite, "I may have slipped a few pounds. Those young devils take it out of me, you know. Still, I have such a hunger on me, I'm safe to make it up again."

"The children thrive, I trust?"

"Ah. Some of them. Only some, alas. Others I could not save, they were too far gone. I have seen too much of the vicar. He wanted to come round and bless each of the surviving boys, but I could not have that, no, I could not have it..."

He rambled as he chewed, and I grew more and more worried the more I watched, the more I listened.

Dr Barnabas ordered another plate of beef, and despatched it as keenly. Then he called for the bill, rose, made his excuses and left me.

By the time Sylvester arrived, I was on perhaps my third pink gin, perhaps my fourth. He greeted me cheerfully, said, "You look as though you were mulling over something terribly serious, John."

"Yes," I said, in no mood to equivocate. "Yes, I was. I'm sorry, Syl. Will you take a ride with me, this evening...?"

AND SO WE FOUND OURSELVES RIDING OUT AGAIN, THE SAME MOUNTS ON THE same route. They seemed almost to pick their own way to that private grove, and to settle happily to an hour of their own company in the grass there.

I led Sylvester by swift familiar ways to the wall—no nonsense this time about my needing help, or his offering it—and thus the kitchen garden, the library window. It had to be the library. I knew it, and so did he.

Light spilled from the window, as before. We rose and looked together; and ducked back down, and stole away again without a word, without a thought of staying.

We rode halfway home in silence, before he said, "What will you do?"

I said, "I know...some people, who should be here in England now. Former soldiers, from my India days. I will find them out and install them in the gatehouse, with instructions. And let the doctor know, what those instructions are."

"And they will be?"

"To let no one in or out of the grounds, except himself. They have *shikari* skills; not the most lightfoot boy could get by them, where they have set themselves to patrol. And each of them is a killer, that's why they were sent home."

He mulled that over, at last said, "You will let them live, then, if you can keep them penned."

"Syl, they're *children*. If he can...keep them fed, I can let them live, so long as they threaten no one else."

Which was the closest we came, the closest we could ever come to discussing what we'd seen: how the doctor sat in the library chair, willingly, arms and legs spread, while half a dozen boys swarmed all over him, biting, lapping, sucking...

One For Every Year He's Away, She Said

WE CAME INTO THE BAY ON THE WIND AND THE TIDE, WITH THE RED LIGHT OF sunset in our sails. The captain was with us on the quarterdeck, the first mate down in the well, roaring at the hands through a megaphone. My own work done for the moment, I leant on the taffrail and watched as they brought us into harbour. Not journey's end, of course, only one more call on a journey that had no end, only one more bead on a rosary, another turn of the wheel; but it was always good to touch land after weeks at sea, just as it was always good to break free again with the dealing done. We sailors are never really comfortable with an unchanging horizon, but we need regular reminding of it. We forget else, we get hungry for stone walls and fresh food, warm beds and hills with a bit of solidity to them, somewhere to stand and fix yourself and see how the world doesn't turn around you.

Briggs the harbourmaster was first aboard to welcome us, as soon as we were tied up at the quay. I hung back politely while he exchanged courtesies with the captain; but he came to me next, his hand outstretched and his thin face smiling his pleasure.

"Martin! You've changed ships again."

"Of necessity, I'm afraid. The *Seaswift* foundered in a gale, away to the south. Three years since, that would be."

"Ah, that's bad. Many lost?"

"Most."

He nodded solemnly, then smiled again and struck me on the shoulder. "But not Martin, eh? Never Martin. We'd thought you lost, it's been so long, people have been saying you must finally have met a storm you couldn't master; but I should have known not to listen. I should have known you'd be back, when it suited. Ships come and ships go, but Martin sails on forever."

"I've been lucky," I agreed quietly. Then I handed him a copy of the *Gentle Lady*'s manifest and a list of our needs, with good water and fresh fruit at the head; and we arranged to meet early the following morning in his place of business, for the inevitable haggling. The captain wouldn't want to delay two days if we could have the business done in one, but on land and after nightfall my time was my own. That was clearly understood between us.

So I bade the captain a respectful goodnight, touched my hat to the quarterdeck and followed the harbourmaster ashore; and already, even before my feet had touched the planking of the quay, it was clear to see that much had changed in this town in the seven years I'd been away.

If I still had a home other than the sea then this was it, it was this bay and this busy port I came back to time and again, in my own ship or another's. But when last I left it had been a sullen, suspicious home to me and all its people, doors bolted in the twilight and never opened till the sun was up. Strangers were unwelcome and deeply mistrusted—and this in a trading port that depended on strangers for its business—and even old friends were eyed askance. Even I caught my share of black looks and murmured imprecations.

Tonight the streets were thronged, the houses burned with light through open shutters; I could hear the taverns' noise even down here on the quay.

"Your—trouble's over, then?" I inquired, indirectly, as the habit had been in those difficult years.

"Eh? Oh—oh, yes. Yes, God be thanked, it's over. Almost forgotten, tell the truth, except for the folk who lost their own kin, and you wouldn't expect them..."

"No." You wouldn't expect anyone to forget the blood-drained body of their child, liver and kidneys and delicate flesh cut away and the residue dumped in the street for the dogs to chew on. "Did you catch the man, then," I asked, "the one who was doing it, the killer?"

"No, we never did; but you must have seen the last of it, the very last. There's not been a, a sign of trouble like that here since that summer you were trading up and down the coast and we had you here for a week in every month. Seven years, it's a long time, no one worries now. He died, or moved away." And then, after a judicious pause, "That lad you signed up then, to crew in *Seaswift*, he's not with you still? Young Toby, the widow's boy from the tavern?"

"No, Toby's not with the *Lady*."

"Did he go down, then, when the *Seaswift* was lost? Ah, someone should tell her, if..."

I shook my head. "He didn't sail with us more than a season. I don't think the life suited him."

"Ah. Well, then."

"Why," I asked mischievously, "what's your interest in Toby? Or is it his mother you're interested in?"

"What? God, lad, don't say things like that, even in jest. No one here meddles with the widow. No, it was only remembering that summer put me in mind of him. The *Seaswift* here, and him signing on to be a sailor when he'd never shown an interest before. But you would remember the odd things, wouldn't you, with it being the last summer of the troubles, and not a hint of bother since, in that way?"

I LEFT BRIGGS TO HIS OWN AFFAIRS AND WALKED SLOWLY UP THE COBBLED wagonroad, past yards and warehouses to the thronging centre of the town. I leant heavily into every step in the swaying walk of the long-time seafarer, feeling the immutability of land against the plunge and roar of water in my bones, the lasting rhythms of the sea. And yet every sailor knows that the sea may be changeable day to day, but she never truly changes; and land may give you firm footing today and the same for your children tomorrow, but the sea can shift it in the end, the sea can swallow anything.

I went through the town and climbed higher, up the hillside behind, almost to the crest; and the last low roofs, the last lights I came to were the sheltering roofs and the welcoming lights of the widow's house, the tavern on the hill, where Toby's mother looked down to the port and out, far out across the bay, where her boy had gone to sea with me seven long years before.

This was no busy, bustling place like the rowdy taverns down below. The widow's reputation saw to that. I ducked my head under the lintel and walked into a quiet, smoky room, the customers scattered in tight little groups among the shadows in the corners, no one braving the fierce light of the fire. Some would be travellers from out of town, nervously learning that they should have found somewhere else to stay tonight; the rest undoubtedly were smugglers and thieves, with worse perhaps hidden away in the private rooms. Bandits and murderers, men with valuable heads and a talent for keeping them attached.

I strode unheeding across the room, and hammered a fist on the bar.

"Service here, service! Where are you, sluggard, you whore? Service!"

The low hissing of secret conversations died to nothing, while those self-absorbed groups looked around with a slow curiosity, interested to see what might happen to such a fool in such a place as this.

There were heavy, unhurried footsteps on the cellar stairs, and the widow heaved her bulk up through the trap behind the bar.

Dressed in her usual filthy black, she had a little more grey perhaps in her wild hair than when I'd last seen her, her skin was mottled more and her jowls hung lower. But for all the changes she was like the sea, she was still unchanged. Her small, dull eyes strained to focus through the smoke to where I stood in shadow, and she slapped one meaty hand down on the bar with a noise like wet canvas snapping in the wind.

"Who called?" she demanded, and her voice boomed as it always had, and the room was utterly still. "Who *called* me so?"

"I did," I said mildly, as if it were a matter of no moment. "I'm salted through from throat to belly, and I'll take a jug of your best ale now and a meal later, and a bed if ever we get that far. If you've got one with no fleas, that is, my blood's not for sharing."

"Martin?" she wheezed, suddenly breathless. "Martin, is that you?"

"In the dry and bitter flesh, it is."

"Hah! I knew it. I knew you'd be along, when you were ready. Let them say what they like, with their soft bellies and their soft minds, I knew you wouldn't be drowned. Not Sailor Martin, let them hope what they like. And they did, you know, they were hopeful. You frighten them..."

And while she talked, she drew a deep jugful of ale, carried that and two tankards in one hand, a bottle of spirit and two glasses in the other; rolled around the bar and over to a table by the window. The pane was too dirty to see through, but this was my table nonetheless, I always sat here. Today it was empty, but she'd thrown men off before, thrown them out even for daring to be sat at my table when I came in.

I sat with my back to the wall, where I could see every door and every corner of the room, every conversation. She pulled up two stools, set them together and lowered herself with a little more care than she used to take.

Two shots of spirit were sloshed into the glasses, and we toasted each other silently, tossed the drinks down. Oil and fire, as vicious as ever, and as effective.

Then the glasses were topped up, tankards of ale were poured and tasted and approved, and she leant her massive arms on the table and said, "What of my boy, then, my Toby, what of him?"

"I'm sorry," I told her. "I've no news, none since he left my ship. And that was within a year of his signing on."

She grunted, sweat glistening on her doughy face. "What, and nothing since, no rumours, even? Not a word?"

"No. Truly, nothing."

"Well." She paused and thought about it, sighed and said, "Well, perhaps that's just as well. Only a sailor-boy, after all, and why should they be talking about one sailor in thousands? That's why he left, after all, why I chased him off, to get him away from the rumours."

"Indeed." That was why I'd agreed to sign him on. I'd been first mate on the *Seaswift*, I'd had the authority; but I wouldn't have done it if she hadn't been pressing in her anxiety, if the talk hadn't been growing stronger day by day. Death by death. I'd taken Toby on to save his life; but a piss-poor life it was, and not worth the saving except for her sake, to see her happy. He was a strange and secret lad with stranger appetites, and the ship had been well free of him, even if her luck hadn't got any better after.

"He'll come back," the widow was saying now. "When he's ready. What's seven years, to a boy like that? I count them, but he wouldn't. He's off discovering the world, it'll be a while yet before he notices how time's passing, before he comes back to see his mother. And it might be safe now, but he's not to know that. He'll likely be cautious, wait longer than he wants to, to be sure. He'll be back, though, sooner or later. When the time's right. He'll come whistling up that hill, gold ring in his ear and all the arrogance in the world, I know you sailors."

"Oh, you do that," I agreed, toasting her again. "Indeed you do. None better. And how's business, then?"

"As you see," with a jerk of her head towards the wide room. "How I like it, quiet. No trouble. You'll be with the *Gentle Lady* now, is that right? I saw her coming in."

I nodded. "Supercargo."

"You'll be wanting supplies, then?"

"Please. But we can talk about that in the morning."

She smoked and salted meat, to supplement her takings at the inn; but I was never sure how much she needed the money, because she didn't encourage customers for either business. She worked just enough to keep her occupied.

Otherwise she ate and drank and talked, laughed and fought and won every fight she was mixed up in.

And, presumably, watched the sea these days, watched the wide sea and every ship, every boat that sailed it for signs of her son's returning.

I remember a fresh bottle being cracked open, and at some point I remember a meal, thick stew and good fresh bread. And there was always ale in the jug when I reached for it, though I remember reaching and pouring many more times than a single jug could satisfy.

I don't remember being led to a room, but certainly I woke up in one, sprawled on a straw mattress still in my clothes, with a pounding head and the widow's rough fist pounding on the door. "Up now, Martin," and she laughed raucously, "time to get up now. We've business to discuss."

"Business?" I blinked against the soft dawn light, dragged a hand down across my face and said, "What business? Pay when I leave..."

"Of course you will," she said, gripping my arm and hauling me bodily to my feet. "But you want meat for your ship, don't you? Salt pork, sausage and dried beef?"

"Talk to Briggs. I'll tell him, buy from you, I'll tell him..."

"Oh, now, Martin. A good officer never buys blind, you'll want to see what I'm selling. Come on, this way..."

She steered me down a passage and through an open door, out onto the hillside behind the inn.

"Where are we going?"

"To the smokehouse," she said, and cackled. "Nothing in there for you, nothing ready yet, but I want you to see it, I want you to see what I've got."

I didn't understand the feverish mood that was on her, the childish excitement, secrets to show or tell; but I went with her stumblingly, while the wind and sunlight cleared some of the fuddlement out of my head.

She led me to where two wooden doors, one squat and the other tall and wide, were let into the hillside. There was a pile of hickory logs beside, and each door leaked a little smoke between its planks.

She opened one, the low one, and coughed in a sudden cloud of smoke. Peered, and threw in a couple more logs. "Mustn't let it get too hot," she grunted, reaching a long metal poker in to rake the embers. "Slow and sweet, that's the way. Slow and sweet, not to cook the meat. Fire in there, do you see, Martin," slamming that door closed and pulling open the other to create another swirling cloud around us, "and the smoke's drawn through into here. Hang the meat for a few days, let it dry, let the smoke get to it. I'll leave the door open, it'll clear in there, you can have a good look."

And she took my hand and pulled me into her smokehouse.

My eyes smarted tears, and my lungs all but cracked my ribs with coughing; but the smoke did clear slowly, and eventually I could see.

I saw sides of beef and sides of pork and strings of good fat sausage, all hanging in neat rows in that artificial cave; and finally, down at the far end, I saw what she wanted me to see.

I saw a young man, barely more than a boy, hanging naked among the meat, his arms bound tightly to a crossbar.

"Doing nicely, that one," the widow said softly beside me. She reached to grip the lad's tangled hair and jerk his head up from where it was slumped against his chest. I faintly saw a movement in his red and staring eyes, faintly heard a noise from his cracked mouth.

"He's still alive?"

"Oh, yes. They do better if you smoke them living first. It dries them out, you see," and indeed there wasn't a trace of sweat on him even in this stifling chamber, barely a hint of moisture even in those terrible eyes. Smoke had stained his skin as darkly orange as the meat around him, and his flesh had shrivelled up tight around his bones. A skeleton in leather, he looked like. I'd seen one once before, a drifter in a boat we found out on the open ocean, baked by sun and salt. The only difference was, this one was alive.

Temporarily, at least.

"I don't know how long they're to keep, you see," the widow was saying, pinching at the boy's flank and seeing how the skin stayed rigid long after she took her fingers away. "That's why I sweat them so. It could be years yet, and the drier the meat, the longer it keeps. Doing nicely, this one," she said again. "He'll live another day or two, I guess. Tough lad. Then I'll open him out and dry him from the inside too, and he'll be fit to hang for a good long time, he will."

"Where did you—?" I had to break off to cough; even with the wide door open, the acrid air in there was harsh on my lungs. "Where did you get him from?" *Won't he be missed?*

"Oh, he came to me. Looking for work as a pot-boy. On the run from something, I'd guess, jumped ship or skipped his indentures. I didn't ask. Came in the early morning, he did, no one around." *No, he won't be missed.* "It's always like that, there's always a loose boy you can pick up on the quiet. And I only take one a year, and strangers mostly. No one worries, no one even notices." *Not like when my Toby was around, with his strange appetites,* she was saying, *and it was local children being taken, and their carcasses just dumped in the street. Not like that at all.*

We came out into the sweet air again and shut the door, shut the young man in with his slow death; and then she took me back to the inn and down to the cellars and back, far back under the hill.

It was cold down there, with a cold that had never known it might have an enemy in warmth. We were swallowed into cold dark tunnels, and neither the cold nor the dark were touched by the flaring lamps we took with us.

These were the widow's storerooms and famous in the town, the tunnels and the many doors that opened off them. Every smuggler on the coast knew and used these tunnels, for a fee. Worse men than smugglers too, or so the rumours went.

Even the rumours didn't speak of the widow or what use she might be making of her own space. Even rumour-mongers had better sense than that.

But she took me down, and showed me. Opened one door among many. Beckoned me in and let me see.

"One for every year he's away," she said.

I have seen dried birds for sale in Eastern markets, chickens and ducks, where the body has been opened and the bones exposed, so that they lie like a pattern on a flattened disc of flesh.

I'd never seen it done to a man before.

Take your body and gut it, cut off head and hands and feet. Cut through the breastbone, map the ribs and the clavicles, and with a little more knifework you can open the chest out like a flower. After that it's easy. Slice and peel, slice and peel back; and before long you have a man turned inside out, all his bones revealed, clinging to his flesh as his flesh used to cling to them.

Then you can really smoke him.

She'd done that, the widow had, and she showed me the results, six leathery curtains hanging with their bony frames uncovered. Six down here, and the seventh in the smokehouse above, *one for every year he's away.*

"A mother should provide for her boy," she said, stirring a vast barrel of brine in the corner. "She should have something in store, to welcome him back from sea." Something rose to the surface briefly, rolled and stared at me, smiled and sank. She didn't waste a thing, the widow.

"Of course, it's not what he liked, quite," she said, "he liked them young, and fresh; but he can't have everything. I don't want the trouble starting up again when he gets back. And he's a good boy, he'll eat what he's given."

I nodded politely, thinking, *Ah, if only.* If he'd eaten only what he was given, I might have brought him back with me last night, and returned him to the suspicious glares of his neighbours and his mother's loving clasp.

Young Toby should never have gone to sea. Sailors are a tolerant folk, by and large—but strange appetites should only be fed on strangers. He should never have stolen the heart of the captain's favourite cabin-boy. Neither the liver and lights.

As first mate on the *Seaswift*, I was the one who gave the order that hanged poor Toby, hanged him high and slow from the yard-arm. And sailors are superstitious, so I was the one who hammered a precautionary stake through his chest before he was sewn into a sail and cast overboard with no prayers other than the twenty-four pounds of lead at his head and feet to hold him there.

And now I stood with his mother in that larder prepared against his returning, and remembered that she'd married very young. Formidable though she was, she was a long way short of fifty yet; she should have a deal of active life before her. And of course she had the contacts to buy any service she wanted even after her strength had gone, and probably all the money she'd need.

One for every year he's away, she said.

I smiled my compliments and shook my head in admiration, and followed my hostess upstairs to pay my bill, thinking it was as well that the tunnels ran deep and private.

Keep The Aspidochelone Floating

"WELL, THEN," SHE SAID SOFTLY, MENACINGLY. "Give me one good reason—one—not to kill you. Here and now."

I don't take prisoners, she was saying, *I don't collect ransoms. The living are too much trouble.*

There were heavy splashes from astern, as the captain—the *former* captain—and his officers went overboard. No trouble at all.

I said, "There's only one ocean. One. All the waters of the world, all intermingled, all *talking* to each other; and they're under us right here, right now. Listening to you. Weighing you, weighing me. Is that good enough? Big enough?"

"It should be," she said. High sun glinted off the pocked blade of her cutlass. Another splash came from aft. I didn't look around. Down below, someone screamed: thin and hoarse, I thought it was a man. Or had been.

Her eyes didn't flicker, her blade didn't twitch. I was counting on that. She was solid: sure of herself, sure of her crew. Nothing to prove.

"It really should be," she said again. "Enough. But—you don't buccaneer. No one ever called you Pirate Martin. Did they?"

"No," I said. "No, they never did."

"No. And I don't carry passengers. So..."

The blade was like liquid sunshine in her hand, hot and ready. She'd do this herself if she had to; God knew, she must have had practice enough. She really didn't want to, but she thought she'd do it anyway. She'd be famous, maybe: the one who put Sailor Martin down, the one who sent him to the bottom at last.

That's why she didn't want to. It's not the kind of fame a person looks to carry, even on land. Out here, on the attentive waters—well. If she was hesitating, that was why.

Unhurriedly, I said, "I can cook, though."

Now I'd surprised her. She blinked, took her time, said, "You can?"

"Yes, actually. I can cook for you." Not buccaneer, but feed her and her crew: that, yes. Nothing in that to sear my conscience or darken my long story more than it was dark already. I wouldn't be feeding prisoners, conniving at their capture. What my new shipmates did to those they took—a swift blade and a splash astern—would be on their souls, not mine. I was comfortable with that.

I'd be hanged regardless, if we were taken.

I was tolerably comfortable with that, too.

"Good, then." Her cutlass slammed back into its sheath, and she turned towards the poop. "Help my people get this mess cleared away, I want to round Dog Point before sunset. You're ship's cook, but I carry no idlers; you're starboard watch, and you'll scrub and stow and haul like any of them."

"Aye aye," I said, "cap'n."

For once in my life I was aboard a naval frigate, rather than a merchantman; for once in my life, I was on the passengers' manifest, rather than the crew's roster. I'd come aboard at Port Herivel, seabag on my shoulder and my name like a whisper rolling up the gangplank and across the deck before me: *Sailor Martin, that's Sailor Martin; he'll be luck for us, good luck in tricky waters...*

The captain welcomed me to his poop deck and his table, would perhaps have given me his cabin too if I hadn't insisted on bunking in the gunroom with his junior officers.

"Those pipsqueaks? Unbreeched boys, I warn you, they'll keep you up half the night demanding stories."

"That's my intention," I said cheerfully. "Perhaps I can teach them something. Youngsters listen to me."

He grunted and didn't argue, for whatever brief good that did him. Not half an hour later, I was followed up the gangplank by a woman in black veils and her two servants, one a dusky matron and the other a boy.

I stood by the taffrail and watched while the captain and his first lieutenant went to greet her. After a minute, the captain called for his steward and there went his cabin after all, gifted necessarily to the lady. He took her through to view her accommodations; her servants followed with the baggage; the first lieutenant came thoughtfully up from the afterdeck to join me.

"Who is she, Number One?"

"Florence, Lady Hope. Says she's sister-in-law to Sir Terence Digby, king's man at Port St Meriot. That's barely out of our way, and we're only running cargo anyway; the old man said we'd take her. Between you and me, I don't believe he likes the idea, but..." A shrug said the rest of it: that even the Royal Navy bowed to politics, and a wise captain did nothing to aggravate the civilian power.

For a little time, I thought of reclaiming my seabag and treading spry down to the quay again, seeking another ship. I knew Sir Terence, by more than reputation; I knew why the king had sent him to Port St Meriot, and why he'd gone. I knew he had no family, in or out of law.

But I was ever curious, it's my besetting sin and why I can never quit the sea. I held my tongue and settled into the gunroom, amused the lads and tried not to interfere too badly with ship's discipline while I kept a weather-eye on the lady and her people.

She herself kept her cabin, didn't join us for dinner, rarely showed abovedecks and never without her veil. She was in strict mourning, seemingly. Gunroom gossip said it was for her husband, or else her lover: either way, the man who had brought her from England and then had the discourtesy to die of yellow fever, leaving her with no alternative but to fling herself on the charity of an unfortunate but obliging relative.

Her boy had little enough to do, and was apparently glad—at first—to have the freedom of the ship. I found him everywhere, from the lower hold to the higher rigging, gambling with the idlers or racing the midshipmen from deck to masthead and down the shrouds again.

After our second day at sea, though, I saw him mostly in the company of the boatswain. Who was a bully, as are so many of his calling; and the boy looked less than happy now, red of eye and bruised of spirit, bruised of body I suspected as he slunk about, obedient at the big man's heels.

Well. No doubt that would be a lesson learned. No doubt he'd find it useful. Myself, I spent my time in pursuit of the abigail as she laundered smallclothes in a barrel of fresh water, stood over the cook in his galley, sat to her needlework high on the foredeck in the late of the day.

Her name, she said, was Delia. Tall and broad-shouldered as her mistress was—convenient, she said, for fitting dresses—she was good-natured and open with it. Firm of purpose, knowing her own mind, finding her own course in life and cleaving to it. Free to do that, serving her mistress because she chose to: "I was never slave. I wouldn't have stood that. A person should be free. If she ain't born to it, she should take it."

As she spoke, her eyes roved the ship, the crew, the set of the sails, the horizon. I didn't need to keep watch myself; I could depend on her to do it for me.

NO SURPRISE, THEN, WHEN THE LOOK-OUT HAILED THE DECK: "A SHIP! Hull-up, two points off the starboard bow!"

Really he should have seen her sooner. I rather thought Delia had, though from the foredeck we could make out only the scratch of her masts on the skyline. She was adrift under bare poles, so the man had some excuse, but even so I thought he'd probably face a whipping come Sunday, when his officers would have leisure to attend to it. A warship with a skeleton crew such as ours, reduced by disease and desertion, too few to work the ship and man the guns at once: she needed fair warning above all, to close with friends and keep her distance from any threat.

I should probably have said something to the captain, that first day. Too late now. Captain and first lieutenant both were halfway up the shrouds, telescopes in hand, to see for themselves.

Before their polished boots hit the deck again, I could see the first smoke rising from the other ship, a greasy smudge against the sky.

"She looks to be a whaler," the first lieutenant confided, while his captain paced the windward side of the poop alone, considering. "A derelict, in trouble. We'll go to help. It's our duty."

Duty could bring a rich reward, salvage-fees on a vessel full of sperm-oil and ambergris. I held my tongue. Nothing about this captain impressed me, from his own indecision to the quality of his officers to the manners of his crew. I wouldn't interfere now. I distrusted even his ability to run away.

Even the wind was a conspirator, lying handsome off our aft quarter; in less than an hour we were drawing alongside. Even in his cupidity, the captain wasn't entirely stupid. He'd had the guns loaded and run out, so that we had at least the appearance of a wary warlike vessel in His Majesty's vigilant navy. Every officer bore a loaded pistol, every man went armed.

Even so, that was just routine. The ship was really not expecting trouble.

Even so, I was still exploiting my privilege, lingering on the poop with the officers of the watch, just to see what happened.

What happened first was that Delia swung up the companionway to join us. There was no sign of her mistress, nor their boy.

Delia might be free but she was a woman, a passenger, a servant. The captain merely stared; the first lieutenant moved to evict her as swiftly as he might, as rudely as need be.

"Madam, by all that's holy, you may not—!"

She forestalled him, with a swift nod of her turban'd head towards the other ship. Where a plain red flag had broken out astern, and a boil of men erupted from below.

"My God, sir, they're pirates! Hard aport! All hands, bring us about!"

Delia said, "I'm afraid you'll find that my man has cut your steering chains." Her man, she said, not her boy. I pictured her supposed mistress, as tall and broad of shoulder as she was herself, veiled in solitude. And wondered, a little, what the boy was up to.

The man at the wheel cursed, as it spun freely in his hands.

"Belay that order! All hands to the guns! Fire as they bear!"

"Unfortunately," Delia said, "I don't believe your guns will fire. I'm afraid my boy has been fooling about in your magazine since we boarded, mixing powdered glass into all your gunpowder. He's a skittish lad, so you may be lucky; but if he's done his work properly..."

The first lieutenant tested that, jerking the pistol from his belt and levelling it straight at her face at no more than two yards' distance. She simply stood there, waiting.

He pulled the trigger. There was a flash in the pan, a sullen smoke, no more.

He flung the pistol furiously at her head. She ducked, and when she straightened she had a cutlass in her hand, drawn through some cunning slit in her skirts.

She was just in time to meet his blade with her own. She was a big woman, but even so: a hanger with a man's weight behind it should have been enough to finish her quickly. Somehow, it was not. They fought from leeward to windward, and when they came bloodily apart at last it was she who stepped back and he who slumped boneless to the deck.

That the captain and his other officers had only stood and watched, transfixed—that said all that was necessary about the ship's command. By the time they saw their brother officer fall dead, it was too late to recover. A man in skirts came bulling up from the afterdeck, with his veils thrown back and pistols in each hand; grapnels were already flying across the rail to drag the doomed frigate closer, while the pirate crew came swinging aboard on ropes.

There was fighting down on the quarterdeck, but none up here now. Everyone waited for the captain; what they saw at last was his sword-belt hitting the deck as he let all slip.

AND THAT WAS THE BATTLE, MORE OR LESS: HOW HIS MAJESTY'S FRIGATE MILFORD fell to a pirate queen, with never a shot fired in anger.

And how I found myself eye to eye with her, shortly afterwards; and, "Will you spare the boys?" I asked.

"Perhaps. If they swear to follow me, and if I believe them. Boys can be taught. Don't waste your time pleading for the men. You might be better served by pleading for yourself."

"Perhaps, but I don't plead. Ever. You know my value, you know what I am. You choose to keep me, or you don't."

"Well, then..."

AND SO I FOUND MYSELF SHIP'S COOK AND STANDING A WATCH, EVERYTHING NEXT worst to a pirate true. I saw the boys I'd slept with herded over onto the bait-ship, where no doubt they'd be tested and tested. I watched, and wished them luck, and hoped that some at least might survive, for a while at least.

One boy remained, as Delia took possession of her new flagship: the lad she'd brought aboard. I saw him come up from below, scrupulously cleaning his knife. A little later, I saw men carry up the bloodied ruin of what had been the boatswain.

Well, small blame to the boy for that. I remembered the screaming, and still blamed him not at all; I had a fair view of what he'd done, as the men swung the body overboard, and still not. I never did like bullies.

The boy came up and glanced at me, and seemed surprised; turned to his captain with a questioning glance, "Why's he—?" and won the only proper response, a quick cuff to the ear.

"He's our new cook. And you're his galley slave, till I say otherwise. Get below, the pair of you, and see to the crew's dinner."

HIS NAME WAS SEBASTIAN, HE SAID. That was the most of what he said for a while, caught in a fit of the sullens as we scrubbed and chopped. He held our captain too much in awe to disobey even my commands let alone hers, but he was bitterly resentful. He really didn't understand why I was still alive, let alone why he should be set under me.

Matters eased between us when I contrived to let him think that he was really there to watch me, to stand by with that good knife of his in case I tried to poison his captain or set the whole cursed ship aflame.

After that, it was easy enough to get him talking. He was barely twenty yet and mightily pleased with himself and the wild tangle of his life, bubbling over with it, spilling stories. He'd been a stable boy in Jamaica and then tiger on his lady's curricle, until he was snatched in a tavern and pressed into service on a buccaneer. Twelve years old, stolen for his pretty face and given the same choice that faced those boys on the bait-ship today: swear fealty to a pirate and knuckle under, or else die.

Sebastian had sworn, smart boy, and survived. Longer already than most pirates did; and somewhere in that lucky life, he'd fallen in love with it. Like any boy he could be vicious and fearful, passionate and sentimental by turns, hungry for adventure and hungry to sleep in the sun. Playing cabin boy to a pirate crew had fed each of those urges and more; serving Delia had brought him to the point of worship, her total devotee. I could have found no simpler way to win his heart myself, than to let him talk about her.

I hadn't planned to win his heart at all, I hadn't planned to stay—one cruise, one port, I'd be away—but even after so long at sea, the sea can still surprise me.

So can a boy. Even after so long, so many boys.

I had him stir the porridge for loblolly, not to let him ruin his precious knife hacking at the navy's salt beef, harder than the barrels it was kept in. In the end I fetched a mallet and a sharpened caulking-iron. Between my pounding and his giggling, we agreed that it was wondrous condescension on her part, that she would eat this with her men; and that let me ask, "How does she come to lead a crew of men, white men, in any case?" There had been women freebooters, there had been black freebooters; probably there had been black women; but not as captain. I was sure of that.

"We elected her, of course. It's the tradition." Then he pulled a rueful face and went on, "I think it was a joke. Our last captain was no use, he lost us too many prizes and sailed us into trouble, time and again. We were hiding out, hungry and afraid, with the navy at our heels and hunting. Delia had been the captain's doxy, that's why she was aboard. She was sensible, someone to listen to. Even so, it was a joke. We wanted rid of the captain before he got us all hanged, but you never call for a vote unless you know who's going to win it, and there were too many men who wanted to. That's dangerous. Nobody dared stick his neck out until Double Johnny got drunk enough. He called the vote, the captain asked who stood against him—and Johnny named Delia. Because he thought it was funny, or because it was a measure of how much we despised the captain, or because he was so drunk and the rum so bad hers was the only name he could remember, hers the only face he could make out. I don't know. I think it was a joke.

"But he named her, and when the captain had quit laughing, he asked if she would stand. And she said she would. He already had his hand on his cutlass, he knew just how this would go: of course he'd win the vote, and then he'd kill her, and then Johnny, and that would be that.

"Only he lost the vote. We all hated him that much, and we all loved Delia. So we voted her in. And then he tried to kill her anyway, but she was ready for him. She had a loaded pistol in her skirts, and she blew his head away.

"I think we thought she'd stand down after, and let us have a proper election for a real captain. Only she didn't do that. She took it on herself to be a real captain. She found us safe harbour and led us to a prize; and then we wouldn't have let her stand down if she'd wanted to. She's hard on us, but she's kept us alive all this time. And now we have a warship," unthinkable bounty. And he might want to give all credit to his captain, but he still did keep a little for himself, how clever he'd been, playing servant all those days while he quietly sabotaged the gunpowder and never gave himself or his companions away.

He wanted my applause, so I gave it him; then I traded stories. Soon enough his eyes were bugging out, as he finally understood just who I was. Or thought he did. He'd have known it sooner if he'd listened to the crew of the *Milford*, but he was a boy: full of himself and his own daring, listening at first to nothing and nobody but his captain. And then to nothing and nobody but his own sorrows, once the boatswain had him. I had apparently entirely passed him by. I might have been wounded, if I didn't understand him all too well.

Still, he made up now for that neglect. I was famous, all around his limited little ocean. He'd heard the common stories about Sailor Martin and wanted to test them, to hear them again from the source. *Did you really...? Is it true that...?*

He was a boy, he could readily be squashed at need. For now I talked more than I ordinarily do, I told him more than I was entirely comfortable with. I wanted an ally, perhaps a spy, certainly a bunkmate. He was still pretty; he'd do.

PRETTY AND WILLING AND TRAINED, AS IT TURNED OUT. Better than willing, awed and grateful. I had worried that the boatswain might have killed his pleasure in the act, but one night's careful negotiation took us past that. Gentleness was a revelation to him; so was anything that didn't directly marry my cock with his arse. Soon enough he was melting-hot under my hand, far past caring how roughly I handled him. He was rough himself, with the unexplored strength of the young; making me grunt was a triumph, apparently. Even if it cost him extra chores in the morning.

I TOOK CHEERFUL ADVANTAGE OF HIS BODY, DAY AND NIGHT, THIS WAY AND THAT: any excuse to fuck him at any opportunity, any excuse to heap work onto his wiry shoulders. The more I left to Sebastian, the more I could sprawl at my ease on the foc'sle on a bed of coiled rope in the sun. The captain didn't mind, so long as she and the crew ate three times a day; and she'd been light on crew even before she had to divide it between two ships. Really, feeding those she'd kept on the *Milford* was no burden. Not to me, at least. Sebastian grumbled, but even he didn't seem too outraged.

Our consort, the *Nymph Ann*, showed herself to be a true old whaler by her lines, when she wasn't pretending. She'd probably never been much of a pirate, but she'd made a good bait-ship. Now she offered a good shakedown to new crew, those navy boys. From my rope throne I could watch them being put through their paces, up in the rigging and around the deck, swabbing and holystoning and hauling sail. I saw one of them flogged on a grating, two dozen strokes of the cat; next day I saw a rope slung from the yard-arm and thought I was about to see one hanged.

And so I did, nearly—except that they hung the boy up by his heels and just let him dangle, for punishment or amusement or I know not what. For a while he writhed and begged shrilly, loud enough to carry across the water, while the old hands laughed at him. Soon enough he fell quiet and only hung there, and they grew bored and left him.

They might have left him too long, he might have died, if a boy can die of a blood-flood to his brain; but he saved himself at last, pointing and squealing, trying to cry out as a good boy should.

Someone looked, and called a proper warning to the ship's master at the wheel. He responded with a bellow that sent hands swarming up aloft; I suppose one of them must have taken the time to cut the boy down, if only because he was in the way of the fore course's falling.

The *Nymph Ann* veered close on our starboard, within hailing distance.

"Whale, cap'n! The boy saw her blow!"

"Where away?"

"North and two points east. If he could see her, the boats can reach her."

The captain hesitated, but only for a moment. Then she nodded, yelled her approval, started yelling orders to our own crew.

A simple cruise makes a decent shakedown—but hard sudden work, the chance of danger and the chance of profit makes a better. Pirates and whalers are close kin, half of them have been the other thing at some time; we had enough experience between the two vessels, maybe enough boats too.

What boats there were went overboard, and collected crews to row them. Harpoons came from the *Nymph Ann*, cables from our own locker, courtesy of His Majesty.

"Sailor Martin: do you whale, if you won't buccaneer?"

"I've served," I said, "on a whaler."

"Take a seat in the gig, then. Pull an oar, if you can't throw a harpoon."

I could, but not as well—I was sure—as the lean tattooed creature crouching in the bows of the gig as we pulled away. The whale must have shown again, because voices called down to us: directions, exhortations, blessings on the day. Nothing excites a crew like first sight of a blow.

Nothing is harder than to catch sight of your whale from a little boat on the swell. We rowed to where we thought she had been seen; our ships were no help, having to work up against the wind, soon left behind.

We rowed and craned our necks around, seeking and seeking. We were a fleet of three, the ocean is desert-vast, and whales can swim far and far underwater; I thought we were safe to lose her. I thought we had lost her already. It was almost a relief. Our crews were learning their work, whaling or pirating or both together; and Sebastian was in *Milford*'s other boat, and if we found no whale then he was at no risk. That sat more easily in my mind and on my stomach. I hadn't expected to worry for him, but—

"There! There she is! She's logging!"

She was; and she was a cruel unlucky fish, that we should find her adrift, asleep in the water, almost impossible to spot from a boat unless you come right on her, as we had.

Once spotted, a logging whale is easy to spear. We coordinated by voice and eye, gathered all three boats together, hit her with three harpoons at once.

She dived straight down, our cables whipping out hard and hot, fit to take a man's arm if he tried to grip one. But she couldn't stay down long, she couldn't go deep, she'd had no chance to breathe; soon enough the cables slacked as she rose and breached.

Rose and breached and dived again, and now she was dragging us, and what could three cockleshell boats, two dozen men do against such a monster? This was the perilous time, when a boat can swamp or turn turtle, when a whale can turn against a crew, a fluke can splinter planking, men can die.

We hauled on the oars, legs braced: backing water until the shafts bent and our shoulders popped, until we had to yield or something broke. Then we let her pull us, until we'd recovered enough to strain again.

We worked her and worked her, each boat in turn or all together; she hauled us hard, worse when she stopped diving and only swam because she needed the air. Our little boats sheared through the swell, flew off the peaks and slammed down into the troughs, again and again. I never thought they'd survive. I never thought we would. It's always a surprise after a Nantucket sleigh ride, to find yourself and your mates intact.

If you do.

I watched Sebastian's dory when I could, when spray wasn't cutting at my face like knives, when the gig wasn't flying or smashing into the whale's wake or tossing so hard we could do nothing but hold on. We lost oars, we lost sight of anything outside that eggshell, we lost hope; we never lost the whale though I thought we must at any moment, the rope would break or the boat would break or the harpoon's barbs would tear free of her blubber and strand us in mid-ocean.

None of that. She slowed, the world lost its madness, the sea settled back beneath us; we recovered what oars we could and backed water one more time.

You can brace and look about you, both at once. Heaving, I turned my head and looked and looked. There was a dory, there were men in it, braced as we were, bending their oars against the whale's pull. Salt spray blinded me and I had no hand free to wipe my eyes; sun was setting, and I had no good light; I had no breath to bellow his name. Nothing to do but haul and wait, haul and wait until that fish at last stopped fighting.

Then, when she lay floating, as still as we had found her, wheezing in great bubbling salt-stink gasps; then we could call from boat to boat. I held my tongue, having nothing useful to say, but youth is loud. I heard Sebastian exult at finding himself alive yet, nothing worse than wet and sore.

I heard him call my name across the water. I heard him hushed peremptorily, hoarsely: "Quiet, lad, no chatter now. You'll start her again. Who has a lance?"

From beyond the dory, no answer. I wasn't sure if there was still a boat.

Our own harpooner fumbled in the shadow of the bow, found a lanyard, pulled it in. Blessedly, it hadn't snapped in the fury of the whale's wake or any of the impacts of boat on water. At the end of that rope rose a long iron shaft, cruelly bladed. Once that had been in the gig with us; I hadn't seen it go, being too busy keeping myself aboard. Lucky it hadn't taken one of us with it, or at least an arm or so. A whaler's lance is wicked sharp; it needs to be.

The dory had apparently lost its own. Poor whale. The harpooner stood in the bows as we rowed slowly in beside the floating monster. She was aware, I think, that we were coming; her fins stirred, but feebly. No danger of Sebastian's voice starting her now. I thought she was utterly overdone, we'd exhausted her beyond recovery. Even so, she had maybe sent one boat, eight or nine men to the bottom, if they weren't just lost on the water; and all whales are female, like ships, but this one truly was. A bull would have been half as long again, maybe twice the weight. More spermaceti in its head, more ambergris in its belly, more oil in its blubber—and twice the power too, many times the temper. Never mind boats, full-grown bulls had sunk ships in their time, in their fury. I doubt we would have survived a bull, any of us.

The dory pulled up beside us at the whale's flank. Sebastian didn't risk his voice again, so recently scolded, this close to the monster's shadow. He didn't risk standing, either, let alone the leap I was half dreading: from one boat to the other, his to mine. I saw an arm wave wildly, that was all, and knew him in the murk—and, God save me, I did wave back.

And then very suddenly needed both hands for holding on again, because the harpooner plunged that vicious lance in through the hide of the whale, deep in, probing for lungs or heart or anything that mattered. The great beast spasmed, though she lacked the strength to surge beneath the water. Perhaps she only shrugged in pain; perhaps she meant to swamp us. One small eye caught the last of the sun, gleaming in the vast dark bulk of her head, making her seem more intelligent than she was. Perhaps.

That little movement raised a wave that forced us from her side. Our harpooner left his lance jutting from her flank, preferring to let go than dangle, ridiculous and at risk. By the time we'd baled and caught the oars and pulled ourselves back in, the dory had our place and a man there had the lance.

A man? No—a boy. Sebastian, of course: on his feet and taking a man's task, wanting to impress me. Pulling the lance free of her flesh's suck with one swift draw, that sweet unsuspected strength resolved into grace in shadow; letting the dory's drift carry him a yard down her flank before he drove it in again, power and spring and determination, knowing himself under my eye, coiled at the heart of my anxiety.

Again she flung herself about in the water as that savage needle struck deep into her innards. Again, her wash forced the boats away. Sebastian was too slow to let go, too young to understand the need or else too focused on twisting the blade, probing for her heart, wanting to be the one who slew her cleanly. He found his platform suddenly gone altogether from beneath him; I saw him hang by both arms from the dipping lance's shaft, and then I saw her roll him underwater.

And then me, me too, as though her one movement had carried us both down. I swear, I never chose to dive. There I was, though, swimming through the dark in quest of him. Something on her hide glowed phosphorescent, like moonlight trapped in water; weed or living creature, I couldn't tell, but by that faint illumination I found his shadow as he sank.

Of course he couldn't swim, what sailor can? Apart from me, of course. Rumour says that I could log like a whale and drift like a derelict and never need to shift a finger in effort, that the sea would bear me up.

Rumour is an ass. In this and many things. I swim because I learned to swim, the way I learned to handle boats: with work and time and practice.

I swim for the same reason that I sail, because I love the sea, not it loves me. Because it is dark, because it is salt, because it is deadly. Because it is bitter, and because it is my heart.

Dark, but not obsidian; deadly, but not mortal. Not necessarily mortal.

Bitter, but not unbearable. I saw Sebastian, by the grace-light of the whale's hide. I struck down and reached him, found him still clinging to the shaft of the lance where it jutted from her body. Desperation or good sense, whichever, I had cause to bless it now. If he'd let go, he'd have sunk; if he'd sunk far from that gentle light, I never would have found him.

He wasn't about to let go now, even though I'd found him. I wasn't about to allow him. If he ceased to clutch at the lance, he would clutch at me instead; then we'd both sink. I have seen men drowned by their friends, and I didn't mean to join them.

The whale meant for both of us to join them, but I too can be dark and salt and deadly. The beast had rolled deliberately, I thought, to hold Sebastian under the water. His eyes were screwed tight shut, so he was no trouble to me, if no help. If he'd been looking, if he'd seen me, he'd have lunged, I think. I didn't even touch him. I only laid my own hands beside his, and twisted that lance as sharply as I might.

Poor thing, she'd been trying to shake the boy loose and shed the pain. Now here it was again, worse than before; what could she do but roll up to the air again, and breathe, and suffer?

Sebastian's death-grip was tight enough to fetch him out, no chance of shaking loose. I hung on by grim purpose, through the wrenching tug of that roll; and there we were, breaking back into the world, gasping and coughing and holding on, still holding on as we dangled and kicked above the surface of the ocean.

And there was the dory, seeing us, pulling back to the whale's side: giving us something to drop into, if Sebastian would only let go.

At least his eyes were open now. He stared at me, wild, frantic—and then twined his legs around my waist, a death-grip too late to do harm, and swung us both back and forth.

Working that lance-head in the whale's innards, back and forth...

Finding something, I know not what. Something that mattered. Slicing into it. Bringing one last brutal spasm from the beast, and then a groaning stillness.

The dory came back for us again, and this time I let go, this time it was my turn to practise my death-grip on the boy, wrapping my arms around his shoulders so that all my weight hung from his determined hands.

He laughed in my face, and held on that one last second, long enough to kiss me. Then he let go, and we fell.

Bruisingly, into the crowded boat: oars and benches and other men contributed each their share of bruises, but mostly mine came from Sebastian. He seemed all elbows in my grip, and all deliberate, and all delight. Wet lithe muscled boy, once again exultant and alive; I had to cuff him hard to make him let go, and then again just to calm him. He spat blood and grinned dizzily up at me, settled between my legs there on the boat's boards in the awkward cramping space between the rowing benches and other men's feet, and said, "What now?"

Said it to me as though I were captain, as though the decisions were mine. It ought not to have been true—but the dory fell silent, as though all the men there were waiting on my answer. Across the water I could hear the silence in the gig too, matching.

Into that delicate moment, dying or dead, the whale let rip an abrupt and tremendous fart. Which shattered the tension nicely, throwing us all into gales of laughter; and in the subsiding cheerful chatter that followed, I took an easy charge.

Got a rope around the whale's tail, not to lose her in the encompassing night; joined both boats together with another, for the same reason; said, "We'll just sit out the darkness, lads, and wait for the captain to find us in the morning. She'll come. She'll have to: can't hardly handle one ship without us, let alone two."

"How's she going to come, then, if she can't—ow!"

I suppressed my boy handily, amid another ripple of laughter, and asked who had rum or hard tack in their pockets, tobacco still dry in a pouch, anything to share around to see us through the waiting.

LATER, WE SANG. Later still we slept, those who could, sparing only those on watch. Sebastian could most likely sleep through a hurricane; I hoped to have the chance to prove it, another day, another voyage. For now I cradled the slumped weight of him, felt the slow seize of stiffness in my joints, learned that it is possible for a man's parts to be both numb and excruciatingly painful, both at once.

WHEN HE WOKE, HE WAS YOUTHFULLY, OUTRAGEOUSLY LIMBER. Also he was youthfully and outrageously heedless, teasing me and disturbing everyone, knocking men out of their slumbers as he mocked and stretched, making the whole boat rock as he scrambled to his feet to peer into the dawnlight for his beloved captain.

In the end I pitched him overboard, left him to squawk and splash for a minute before I let a man thrust out an oar for him to snatch at.

As we hauled him in dripping over the gunwale, he was still squawking, but not in protest now. He'd swallowed too much water to be coherent, or else he was just too angry—but he was a good boy, he kept pointing and making noise until we turned, until we looked, until we understood.

The sky was pearling to the east, the other way, the way I'd pushed him. Westward was still dark, but it was too dark. Not sky-dark, not even storm-dark: a rising arc of shadow split the night, cut away the stars. Now, in the hush of experience, I could even hear the sounds of surf breaking against solidity.

I had not thought we were that close to land, but the whale had hauled us far and far, out of all reckoning.

"Good, then," I cried, pounding Sebastian between the shoulder-blades as though it were his achievement, as though I didn't just enjoy pounding the lad. "Landfall will make our wait more comfortable. There'll be water, sure, and green timber to raise smoke, to tell the captain where we are. Out oars, lads, and haul away. We'll haul our catch to dry land, and be dry ourselves..."

SOMETIMES I AM WRONG AND WRONG. Even now, even still: wrong and wrong and wrong. We came ashore in the false dawn, with our false hopes high; and found ourselves cast on a hard rock, hard and bare and empty. No trees, no habitation and no water. One of the hands talked of an island he'd seen rise overnight, a seething volcano building itself in fury from below; but that had been far to the east, half a world away. There were no such stories here, save the ones he told. In the end I sent him to the high bleak rounded peak of this rock, to keep watch for the captain. He'd have no way to signal her, but she should come in any case, as soon as she sighted land.

If she were anywhere on our trail, anywhere near, she'd come. Even if she knew what little comfort this place offered, she'd still come. Any sailor would. We love the sea, and turn to land like a needle to the north. She'd know to find us here, sure as storm.

Meantime—well. There was no fresh water, and no timber for a fire except what we'd brought with us, and no sailor would ever burn a boat. Even so, more than one hand sat on the ridge-rock shore and dangled bare hook-and-line into the tugging sea. Hope springs eternal, and you can always eat fish raw; and it was always possible that the captain wouldn't come.

That was a possibility we didn't talk about. Every man held it private, in the back of his own skull, with all that that implied.

To one boy, it didn't occur at all. Sebastian was full of excitement, empty of doubts. As full as he needed of rum, perhaps, that too: I thought the men had been topping him up, for his reward for being first to cry land or just for their amusement.

He was a happy drunk, happy and confident and trusting, almost impossibly pleased with himself. He couldn't keep still, but he didn't want to walk. The rock felt rocky under sea-legs, and his triumph floated large and alluring just off shore; he wanted to row around the whale's corpse and relive the whole adventure, show me the jutting lance and tell me how clever he'd been, how kind I'd been to come after him, how wonderfully we'd worked together.

I didn't mind, so long as he did the rowing. One lean lad shifting a heavy gig: the work of it would burn the rum out of his bones and maybe even still his restless tongue. Also, we'd find a privacy on the water that I hoped to celebrate, in the whale's shadow and down between the benches, doubly out of sight from shore. The men would speculate wildly and mock cruelly when we came back to them, I hoped with every justification in the world...

Sitting in the stern, manning the tiller, I got to watch his face as he pulled: all strain and anxiety until he had her moving, until his confidence came back. Then concentration, the determination to do the thing well, not to catch a crab, above all not to splash me more than he could help; then awe at the simple size of the thing, his achievement, the tales he could tell as we came into the windshadow of the whale. A more simple smile, when he looked at me.

An unreadable expression, when he looked over my shoulder at the island at my back. He had no breath spare, but his eyes were speaking for him. I twisted around and saw a sea-cave rising broad and high, just a little way along the coast from where we'd come to land.

"That," I said, turning back to the boy, "looks big enough to shelter the *Milford* and the *Nymph Ann* too. You may have found our new hideaway, lad."

"Oh, I didn't..."

The protest was breathless and instinctive and utterly meaningless; he thought he did, I could read that all through him. The mighty adventurer, slaying beasts and leading us to treasures.

"You were the first to see it," I said, feeding his imagination along with his self-content. "We'll call it Sebastian's Cave—"

"—Sebby's Cave, they'll call it, only you call me Sebastian. You and the cap'n—"

"—All right, Sebby's Cave, but we still won't go in there till we have torches. It's dark, and anything could be hiding out already."

"I want to go now." A dead whale, a tale told had lost all its attraction suddenly, in the face of an adventure not yet lived. It would be the same with me, I thought. Right now I was all the world he lived in, as the captain had been before me; sooner or later, I would be a tale told.

It was a boy's life, that was all. Sooner or later, perhaps he'd be a man.

I felt unutterably old, and played that hand as I had to. "I know you do, but we'll still wait. You don't want them calling it Seb's Folly, because it's where you went to die. It looks like a mouth, half-open, ready. Just pretend you can see teeth hanging down, and wait till we have lights. Now row me round to the other side of this fish."

He pulled a face, but then he pulled the oars. Still a good boy.

Still a boy: he sulked, and complained about the stench of it. I laughed, and said, "You should be used to that, sleeping down below. You should *get* used to it. Wait till we flense this fish, before you worry about smells." *Then wait till we fry it,* but I didn't say that. One step at a time. Little by little, let him learn. "Now ship those oars, and come here."

TIME AND TIDE, THE MOVEMENT OF SMALL VESSELS ON GREAT WATERS. Sex in the scuppers. It's all one.

While I had his clothes off, I gave him his first swimming lesson. Unless the whale had done that, and all I had to do was reinforce it. All I wanted him to learn was not to panic—which made it really a lesson in trust, which started as it had to, with trusting me. "Let go of the gunnel, Sebastian. Just let go. It's perfectly safe. I'm here, and I won't let you sink."

Eventually I had him with his arms hooked over a floating oar, kicking furiously for shore. Soon enough, I thought he'd trust himself; sometime after that, he'd learn to trust the water. And probably start calling himself Sailor Sebastian, thinking himself immortal, *the sea will hold me up.*

At the moment he was all effort, more splash than surge, and that good oar was all that held him up. I paced him in the gig, one slow stroke and then another, easy work. I was ready to pluck him out if he exhausted himself entirely, but I thought the whole crew ought to thank me if I brought him back weary to the bone. He could sit in the sun with his good knife and make himself useful as well as decorative, pick limpets from the rocks, give us all something to chew on while we waited for the captain.

WE COULDN'T MAKE SMOKE TO GUIDE HER, BUT OH, SHE WAS GOOD. Not four bells in the afternoon watch, there was a bellow from the peak, a wildly waving figure, our watchman running and slipping and sliding down the long slope, risking bones and softer parts to bring us news.

"I'd have sent the boy up to you," I murmured, once we had him safely gathered in, "if you'd only waited."

Sebastian just looked at me, and went on sharpening his knife. I grinned. "Go on, then. What did you see?"

"She's coming, she's there, she'll be with us by sundown..."

"No. What did you *see*?" There were other ships in these waters, and few of them were friends to us.

He saw the point, nodded, stuck to his guns despite: "Two ships, mast-high. One warship and one whaler, I rate 'em—and don't tell me I don't know the *Nymph Ann*, for I do."

"She might have been gathered in by a king's ship. Which might have sunk the *Milford*, if the captain made a fight of it. If she could. Or the king's men might have taken both, hanged everyone, might be coming now to hang the rest of us."

If they were, there was little enough that we could do about it. Still, we all trooped to the peak to watch the ships' approach. Of course they were the *Milford* and the *Nymph Ann*, that was clear soon enough; we had to wait to see the scarlet shock of the captain's flag, to be as certain of her.

WE HAD HER GIG; WE HAD TO ROW OUT TO FETCH HER. Sebastian insisted on pulling an oar, only so that he could lay claim both to the whale and his cave, before any other hand got the jump on him.

Cap'n Delia could manage him, better than any of us. Better than me. She gave him everything he deserved, in due order: praise and encouragement; mockery; a stinging slap to the head when he wouldn't subside.

Finally, after she'd seen all that we had to show her, after we'd brought her to land, she said, "Well, then. There's work to do. Food and grog for all you marooned lads and the lads who came to save you; Martin, see to that. Use the galley on the *Milford*; people will be busy on the *Nymph*. She still has all her try-works from her whaling days, but they're down in the ballast, largely. Someone wriggly needs to haul them out. Sebastian, that's you, and those boys we took from the navy. You'll be in charge down there, but that's not an excuse to slack. I want everything out and set up tonight; you don't get your grog until it is. Don't drink the bilge-water meantime. Sorry, Martin, but we need to boil down that fish before it starts going bad. You'll be on your own today."

THAT WAS NONSENSE, OF COURSE, AND SHE KNEW IT. You're never alone in a ship's galley. Even with half the crew on another ship and half the remainder ashore, with the watch reduced to a bare skeleton few, there's always someone with time on their hands and oil on their tongue, hoping to wheedle a jot of rum, or else a handful of soft tack and a dip of it in the slush.

I had company, then, and I could put them to work, but I did still miss my boy. Which was unexpected and curious, interesting to watch in myself, not easy to understand. Not easy to shrug off. Boys are like deep-ocean swell; they come, they go, there's always another on the way.

This one—well. Apparently I wanted to ride the wave awhile.

I could do that. I could afford the time. That's something I've never been short of.

A HASTY DINNER FOR ALL, THEN, AS EACH MESS OF MEN WAS RELIEVED IN TURN. No time for the salt meat to soften, so I gave them hasty pudding. When every mess had been fed, I watered rum for the grog and took that up on deck to serve it out. Last in line, as ordered, came the boys: sodden and stinking, exhausted, elated. Arms around one another's shoulders, leaning into each other even before the rum hit them.

Last of all was Sebastian, proud of his command and proud of their work, determined to show me. I'd seen it all before, but still: for his contentment, I let him row me ashore one more time, a lamp in the gig and fires on the shore to guide us. Not till after I'd dunked him in the sea one more time, though, in the tropical sunset glow. I called it a swimming lesson, and forbore to fetch the scrubbing-brushes.

The men had roamed all over this rock-bubble island while I was busy, and found no beach. Some way down the coast from Sebby's Cave, though, the rock shelved out almost level, like a lip. Here they'd hauled the whale ashore already, secured her carcass with rocks and ropes, drained the spermaceti out of her skull and begun to flense her carcass. Come morning, they'd open her belly for the ambergris; in the meantime, no reason not to start rendering the oil out of her blubber.

The *Nymph Ann* was too old to have try-works built into her deck, all bricked about for safety, as the modern whalers did. The great iron pots had been set up ashore on tripods, with empty barrels stacked behind and slow fires already lit below them. Those would burn night and day now, until we ran out of either blubber or barrels, depending.

"See, these are the blanket pieces, these long strips we cut straight off the fish. I did one myself, this one I think," nice boy, honestly laying claim to the least of the stacked strips, the shortest and most ragged, "till Twice Tom took the flensing-knife off me. Then we cut 'em into blocks, the horse pieces, I don't know why they're called that; and then they're sliced down for the pot. Bible leaves, Tom says these sheets are called. He won't let me cut those, he says I'll take my hand off..."

He was likely right. I was grateful to Twice Tom, and impatient to quiet my boy, to stop him bubbling over with what I already knew. I knew too well what the bubbling pots would smell like, all too soon; I'd sooner be back aboard before then, or at least on the other side of this island. The reek of rendered whale-oil clings to clothes and hair even worse than the smoke of a smudgefire, and I'd only just washed him.

I kissed Sebastian, then, to silence him, and guided him away uphill. He was too tired for the long haul back to the ship, it'd only make him quarrelsome if I tried to take him far from his triumphs; too tired to sleep, he could yet be charming company if I only flattered him a little and taught him a little. The island offered no softness, but we'd contrive.

"Sailor Martin."

Hers was the one voice I couldn't ignore. She was sitting alone in a blaze of starlight, halfway up the slope. I swallowed my sigh, settled on a rock below—the perfect courtier, attentive and obedient and not threatening her status—and tugged Sebastian down at my feet, let him settle against my legs, played with the damp straggles of his hair while I waited to hear what was on her mind.

"I had a look inside that cave," she said, "after the men's dinner, before my own." I knew it; her lamps had been lit from my galley fire. "It's not as deep as I've seen them, but it's even higher inside than it is at the mouth. It'll take both ships with ease, even at the height of the tide, and not a sign to see outside. I wouldn't want to be caught in there in a storm, mind, but if we need to duck a king's ship, that's the place. Hell, I don't think this rock is even on their maps; it's not on mine." And hers, of course, had been the king's before. She'd have nothing more recent or more reliable than the *Milford*'s charts.

"That's good news," I said, which was true, but irrelevant: good news for her, of little interest to me, not what she meant to tell me.

"Yes. Somewhere to run to. All we need now is a reason to run." Here it came. "The *Nymph Ann* doubles very nicely as a whaler, and now we have an honest cargo to prove it. We don't need to take it to Port Royal and let those thieves bilk us for a tenth its value; we can head for Port St Meriot and deal openly for once. Only, not with me on the quarterdeck."

Well, no. News of a black woman pirate captain might have spread through the islands already; even if it hadn't, news of a black woman whaler captain would still raise too many questions. It wouldn't be believed.

"The master can stand in for you," I said.

"He can—but so can you. Everybody knows you, everybody trusts you—and you know Sir Terence Digby. I thought we might pay a call. Word on the water is he's giving a ball."

Likely he was. Everything in its season, and this was dancing weather. Light muslins damped with sweat, candlelight on gold brocade, military boots and dainty slippers, scents of jacaranda and musk in the fevered air.

I understood her perfectly. I said, "I still don't buccaneer."

"You don't need to. You only need to be there, in port, visible. Master of a whaler with her holds full to bursting. Of course he'll invite you to his dance. Of course you'll ask to bring your chosen men: your mate and the surgeon, the specktioneer and the skeeman. A couple of likely boys you think the navy might like to look over. That's your part, all I'm asking. We'll do the rest."

I could imagine the rest. She'd be in the kitchens, with a few more men: fresh fish from the harbour, perhaps, or vegetables from market, rum and sugar syrup from the hills, something. And all Sir Terence's guests in all their glitter, the finest jewels for a thousand miles—and no prisoners, no hostages. She wouldn't change her customs on dry land. The cream of the navy would be at that ball, all the senior officers and most of the young hopefuls; why would she ever leave them living behind her, knowing her face now and hot for revenge? They'd scour the ocean till they ran her to ground. Better to hew a hundred heads at a stroke, leave the navy and its government rudderless and adrift, leave no one to come after her.

"That's not what I signed up for," I said mildly. "I'm the cook."

"You are. And, for the moment, a man of mine." If that was a warning, it was pleasingly oblique: no threat, simply an observation of what was owed and owing. "Think about it. We'll be days here, salting that fish down."

She rose and left. I'd have stood to see her off, but Sebastian had fallen asleep with his head in my lap. For a long time once she'd gone I only sat there thinking, watching the stars wheel slowly around the sky while the moon dallied with the horizon.

WHALEMEAT FOR BREAKFAST—OF COURSE!—WITH BISCUIT-CRUMBS FRIED IN THE grease. The crew gorged, men and boys together; the only one not groaning as he rose was Sebastian, and only because I'd rationed him.

"Oh, why?"

"Swimming lesson later, and I don't want you seizing up with cramps. You've eaten enough. The cap'n wants to move the *Nymph Ann* into your sea-cave first, then the *Milford* after, see if they both fit. Go climb the mainmast, try if you can touch the roof as she ducks under."

He went off happily enough, knowing that if he went up aloft on either vessel he'd be raising sails rather than fooling with the cave roof. The master was a disciplinarian with a ready rod, and the captain was probably worse; and half the men were ashore wrestling with the whale, so it'd be a lean crew managing some tricky sailwork. In honesty I thought it'd be easier to put the men in boats and tow the ships in, but there was pride at stake all around.

Pride has never been my problem. I cleaned up in the galley and then went on deck to watch the *Nymph Ann* through the cavemouth. Looked for my boy but couldn't spot him: not high in the cross-trees, he was probably hauling ropes down below. No matter. Even a vigorous swell couldn't lift the whaler anywhere near the roof; the master kept her on a perfect line and she headed slowly into ship-swallowing darkness.

The *Milford* would be next, but not me. I've headed often enough into damp uncertain nights, I didn't need another. The little boats were all busy, ferrying the working crew from the *Nymph Ann* back to the *Milford*; I gave Sebastian—and everyone else, but I did hope that Sebastian at least was looking—an object lesson in the confident swimmer's entry to the water. One neat dive, down and down into the measureless ocean; I could almost see the island from its underside before the water threw me up again, up and out like a breasting dolphin, vigorous and free.

I swam ashore and dried off in the sun, walking over rocks. First to the try-works, just to see how the men there were coming along: to stand upwind of the seething pots and counsel care with the ladle there, count the barrels filled and sealed, count the exposed ribs of the flatulent giant carcass.

And then away, up the rising curve of the hill that was the rock that was the island; and soon enough down again, to a high cliff-edge that I sat on with my feet hanging over. And leaned down to look and no, not a cliff after all, the mouth of another great sea-cave. And I thought about that, and the stars in their slow shift last night, and the way the moon had seemed to drift on the horizon; and I was almost expecting Sebastian's hail when it came, in that way that lovers do anticipate each other. I was almost commanding it, indeed, that way that lovers can reach out *in extremis*.

I said, "The captain let you go, then?"

He sat contentedly at my side, swinging his bare heels above nothing: utterly trusting, utterly vulnerable, soon to be utterly betrayed. "She said the men at the try-works don't want me and nor does she, and there's no point leaving more than a watchman on an empty ship, so she sent me to find you."

"Uh-huh." He was, I guessed, my bribe or my persuader, a little of both. She held him in her gift, and offered him to me. He was ignorant but willing, sweet and savage and desirable. I was something close to desperate, even this close to the sea. Normally, properly, that's all that matters; but nothing was quite normal now.

"Go back," I said, holding my voice steady with an effort that I could only hope he was too young to hear. "Go to the captain and say I sent you, tell her this: that Sailor Martin says there's a storm in the offing and a king's ship nearby. Tell her to bring back all the men she can, and stand by. She may need to move both our vessels out to open water, but she shouldn't do it yet. Just be ready. Tell her that. You take an oar and help to ferry, get everyone aboard if you can. Tell her

He too would have seen nothing

that we'll watch the try-works, keep the fires going, feed the pots. Just the two of us, we can manage that between us. Leave the gig with the *Milford* once you've got them all aboard, and come back with the bumboat. Then we can get to the cave when we need to, to bring word of the storm or the king's men. Tell her that."

He stood, straight and slender at my side; he stared around the long horizon; he said, "I don't see a storm. Or a ship."

I said, "Sebastian. Which of us is a green brat, and which of us has been at sea for ever?"

He grinned. I waited, and soon enough I saw that smile slip as the weight of what I'd said, the reality of it sunk into his head.

I nodded. "Tell her nothing is immediate, but it'll blow up fast when it comes. She needs to be ready now. She should fetch the look-out down, if she doesn't want to maroon him. I'll keep watch. Go."

This time he went, urgent and easy, trusting me as he trusted the rock beneath his feet, as he trusted his captain too.

THERE WAS A LOOK-OUT HIGH ON THE MOUND OF THE HILL, WATCHING ALL THE wide ocean. He too would have seen nothing, neither storm nor ship. That didn't worry me. He didn't have my name. The captain might flog him just on my word, that something was coming. It wouldn't be just, but no pirate looks for justice.

Besides, I didn't think he stood in too much danger of her whip.

I sat brooding on the brow above that sea-cave, waiting for something to show. Too long, I thought I'd waited, before at last the sea seethed and surged below me to speak Her coming. She was late, She was slow on her own behalf. I guess it takes time, all night and half the day, for the heat of slow fires to scorch through a shell as thick as rock, as hard.

Her head was as massive as a ship itself, thrusting forward like the ram of some unimaginable galley before it rose clear of the water on a neck too long, too monstrous. Her eye might have stood for the rose window of a cathedral, if those were ever glassed in black, a single untraced lens.

She looked right at me; I could see myself reflected in that glossy horror, just as a diver sees his own self rising in the stillness of a pool before he breaks it.

I thought She didn't even need to eat me. Her eye would swallow me down.

SHE'D NEED TO BE FASTER THAN THIS. I was already running, while She deliberated. Over the rise of Her unthinkable shell and then down, down to where smoke smudged the air, where the bumboat rocked in the water, where nobody yet knew anything.

Where a figure stood waiting—and a second, rising to stand beside him. Two men, two: and neither one slim as a willow, neither one rushing to meet me.

I was coldly, painfully breathless; it took time even to gasp, "Where's Sebastian?"

"Cap'n took him. She said he's your boy, and you're cook; it's his duty to polish the ship's bell, she said, and he could do that while we all waited for you. Is it coming, then, that storm o' yourn?"

She knew, then. Not the facts or she'd have one ship out by now and be working for the other; but she knew something, not to trust me, something. She was changing her habits after all, using long-established custom to hold one boy hostage. For now, for this little time I had.

Not long enough to take the boat and row that little way, to find any useful truth to tell her. Not long enough to do anything but get there, whichever way I had.

I turned my back on the bewildered men, left them to their smoky fires and seething pots—not long!—and ran again.

Along that flange at the water's edge and up the shoulder of Her shell, to the high edge above what we had taken for a sea-cave: where our two ships lay in companionable stillness, where their crews had gathered in secrecy and darkness. Where I had sent them, to a cold destruction. Where the captain held Sebastian, but would not hold him long. One way or the other.

STRAIGHT TO THAT HIGH EDGE, AND STRAIGHT OVER.

I HAVE DIVED INTO WATER SO STILL I COULD SEE MYSELF COME AT ME. I have dived into the steady swell of the deep ocean, where nothing but myself disturbed the water for a thousand miles all around.

This was...not like that. Even as I went, I could see how the sea's surface bent and stretched below me like a mill-race at a sluice, as great things shifted out of sight.

Down and down I went, purposeful as a hurled knife. As I plunged through the broken surface, I felt the water's familiar grip, tight as a sleeve closing about me; but I could feel the first slow tug of dreadful currents too.

Too fast to be seized, I went down and down, as far below as I had been above; and further yet, far enough that I really could see Her underside this time, the plastron of Her shell. Clad in barnacles and weed but unmistakably floating, more like a vessel than an island; and here came Her flippers, ponderously unfolding to pull Her down below the surface, to cool that fierce hot spot on Her back.

Unfolding from behind those great arches we had taken for cave-mouths, that I'd only understood late and slow, and too late now. What must it be like within the shell there, on board ship and still not understanding, knowing only that the great cliff of the cave-wall was moving, lurching forward, crushing one ship against the other and both against the inside of Her shell, heedless as a man crushing snail-shells underfoot?

What must it be like in the captain's head, thinking *He knew; Sailor Martin saw something, knew something, sent us all into the ships exactly for this, because he knew...?*

Never mind the captain; I was looking for my boy.

Either one of the ships might have been lucky, might have been popped out like a bottle from a cork—but I'd have seen the shadow of her overhead if she was, parting company from the vastness of the turtle, bobbing away. I did look, up into the brightness of the sea-sky.

No ships, no. The great broad blade of Her flipper, undelayed by whatever ruin She had wreaked on its way—and here came the first fringes of that ruin, splintered timbers and twisted ironworks, heading for the bottom.

Timbers and ironwork and a boy, floundering, frantic. Sebastian, with the ship's bell on a rope around his neck, a terrible brass weight to drag him down, sounding his knell for him as he went.

She hadn't even bound his hands or feet: just belled him and thrown him overboard, as soon as she felt the trap close about her. Let him struggle as he would, the bell would bear him all the way, irresistible. That was a cruel touch, one last vengeful fling at me, though I ought never to have known it.

Except that I was here, and down he came towards me; and she had taken his good knife, of course, but I had mine. I caught the bell first, and severed that rope with a slashing cut; then I caught my boy.

And shook him hard, and held him until he remembered his lessons, not to panic, not to flail about; and then held him and kicked for us both, kicked for the surface.

We were too deep, too short of air. Even I don't have gills, to breathe salt water; and I couldn't breathe for him. His mouth was closed yet, but his eyes were bulging. He couldn't last. And there were men in the water all around us, not all of them broken or dying yet, dead yet; and those jagged plunging timbers, those were a danger too, though the men were worse; and—

Men in the water and a woman too. Of course she'd never learned to swim, the captain. Of course she had weights of her own beneath her skirts, weaponry and harness and whatever else she chose to carry against ill-chance, gold and more. Here she came, easy to know in the chaotic waters with her skirts puffed out around her like a jellyfish, like a ship's bell...

LIKE A BELL, YES. YES.

EASY TO KNOW, EASY TO REACH. Poor Sebastian was dragged by his neck again, though this time it was my arm curled about him; and I dragged him below the margin of his captain's skirts and thrust him upward, past her kicking legs to where the billowing fabric still trapped a bubble of air.

Just a bubble, but enough: enough for him, for now. I held him by the body, and felt it as he gasped, as he breathed and breathed.

Then pulled him free of those entangling skirts, and didn't let him see her as she fell below us: faster now, with that last buoyancy stolen from her, dwindling into the dark. He didn't need that face in his memory, those mute curses on his mind. He barely knew what I had done there, only that I'd found him air from somewhere.

Air for him. None for me, and I can't breathe water—but I can hold my breath longer than most, and think while I do it.

And look around, and see the vast bulk of the turtle sliding by, and act against all obvious good sense.

Tow my boy *towards* that surging shadow, not away.

Perhaps he thought that I was mad at last, mad for lack of air perhaps. He tried to kick against me, to pull me back.

He had no chance of that. I took a tougher grip and towed him on, into the currents of Her passage.

Turtles use their front flippers to drive them forward. Their back feet do quieter work, acting as vanes against the water. I wouldn't have risked this if She was coming at us, but that lethal front flipper was past already.

Besides, we were committed now, caught in the turbulent suck of the water She threw back. Rolled over and tossed about, I clung and kicked and maybe prayed a little; and saw what I was looking for, a break in a mighty wall, a gateway not quite blocked by the massive limb protruding through it.

YOU CAN TRAP AIR IN A SKIRT, UNTIL IT LEAKS OUT IN A THOUSAND STREAMS OF bubbles. You can trap air in a bell, and it won't leak; make a bell big enough, you can lower a man to the sea-bed and have him breathing all the way.

How much air can you trap in a cave, if your island takes a dive?

ENOUGH, THERE'LL BE ENOUGH.

I hauled Sebastian in, and the water flung us up, and there was air; and even a hint of light, that same phosphorescence that had clung to the whale. Enough to show that we floated in a chamber where half the wall was rigid shell and half was shifting leather, the obscene leg of the thing. It looked like seamed rock, but no rock ever moved with such purpose, this way and that like the rudder of a ship under steerage-weigh.

Everything about Her was slow and mighty; She had no reason to heed us little things. I helped Sebastian pull himself out of the water, up onto a ledge of Her leg, and found just strength enough to follow.

Then we lay against each other and only breathed awhile, painfully, gratefully.

When he spoke at last, his voice sounded strange in that strange space, distant and muffled and hollow all three. He said, "We, we're inside it. Aren't we?"

"Her," I said. All ships, all whales. All giant turtles, seemingly. It felt right. "I suppose we are."

"Like Jonah."

"Something like Jonah. Not swallowed, though."

He thought about that, then said, "What happens now?"

I didn't know, but lying's easy in the dark. I said, "She won't stay down long. When She rises, we'll go out and see where we are, who's about. There'll be someone to signal, or land we can reach. We'll be famous, shipwrecked mariners who survived Leviathan, like St Brendan survived Jasconius."

His head was on my thigh, wet and warm and welcome. He sounded sleepy, like a child. He said, "You're famous already."

"I am, I suppose. Not for anything particularly praiseworthy. Just for surviving, mostly; and here I am again. Doing that. And here you are, doing it right alongside me."

"I'll be a part of your story." No self-deception there. The fact of it, the act of it, the being with me: that could only ever be temporary, in the nature of the thing. He knew. But the story of it, that goes on for ever.

"You will," I said, toying fondly with his ear. "And you'll tell it yourself, to Sir Terence Digby yet. He'll invite us to his ball, and we'll dress up fine and dance all night," and take no prisoners and do no harm and perhaps Sir Terence could find a berth for him, some other life that he could love, not buccaneering. And perhaps I'd be there with him for a while, be a part of his story, however briefly told. "It'll be a masked ball, naturally. You can go as a pirate boy, you'll like that. Yo ho," I said, "Sebastian."

'Tis Pity He's Ashore

"SAILOR MARTIN. YOU SHOULD NOT BE HERE."

The voice came from the tangle of shadows in the back of the shop. It was salt-abraded, familiar, unchanging. Live long enough, go far enough, you will find those things that never change: the places, the people, the truths.

Not many of them, and not all are welcoming or welcome, but still: they stand like islands in the sea, islands in the storm.

Johnnie was, is, always will be one of those. Johnnie calls himself a chandler, and that's as dishonest as he's ever been. Johnnie sells much that came from the sea, but nothing that's useful to a sailor, nothing that any boat should ever want or need.

Johnnie and I, we've got history. He likes to say I'm his best customer. Sometimes I think I'm his only customer. The shop is a collection, more a museum than a place of exchange. The only trade is inward. Johnnie loves to buy, if a thing is rare or dark or strange enough; he hates to sell. Except perhaps to me.

"You should be afloat," he said. "Stood well off, in deep water. Bad weather coming."

I knew it, I could feel it: a tension all through the city from harbour to highrise, a breathless unease, a readiness. Not only for the typhoon in the offing, though that was the reason I'd put in. Any other trouble I preferred to meet at sea, but delivering a billionaire's new yacht to KL, I thought I'd best not turn her up storm-toss'd.

"What do you hear, Johnnie?"

"I hear everything. You know this."

Of course I knew. The true question was *what do you believe?*—which of course he would never tell me, and I could never believe him if he did.

This was how we dealt with each other, in hints and doubts and rumours. It was how he dealt with everybody. Even his name was not Johnnie. That was a joke, perhaps, or several jokes. Surabaya Johnnie for obvious reasons; Rubber Johnnie because he always bounced back; Johnnie-come-lately because he had been here on this waterfront, in this store for ever. I could attest to that.

For a man his age he was still robust, still unrepentant, and some of his teeth were still his own. The cracked and ancient ivories, those few. The gold ones, mostly not: he mortgaged them at need. A man needs negotiable wealth, and his stock-in-trade won't serve if he will never agree to sell it. I held lien over one of those teeth myself, from the last time I'd touched port.

"Go back to sea," he said, "sailor."

I shook my head. "Not until the storm blows over." That, or something other.

"Well, then. Come here. I have a thing for you."

Johnnie's storefront is neon-lit, as gaudy as any of his neighbours'; his window that season held a shabby stuffed bird of paradise, some unconvincing scrimshaw work at unlikely prices, a less-than-interesting kedge. This was the stuff he might possibly be willing to sell to strangers, except that nothing there would ever entice a stranger through the door.

Further back, where the goods were more curious and you might actually want to look at them, the light was correspondingly fugitive and unforthcoming: a few dim bulbs half-hidden behind stacks of tea chests and sea chests that might open up to disclose a seventeenth-century mariner's journal or a shrunken head from Java shore or a knotted mess of hooks and lines that was once a patented system for catching mermaids.

Take them out, carry them forward into a better light and perhaps you'd see that the mariner's maps depicted no known coastline; that the shrunken head was actually a monkey's, dribbling cold sand from an opening seam; that the fishing tackle was no more than a standard Whitby mackerel rig, somehow strayed half a century, half a world out of its proper time and place.

Where Johnnie sat, there was no light at all, unless he chose. He lurked in the crevices between the heaped and hidden stock like a wary spider watching his things, his occasional customers, me. To us, he was invisible; to him we were brightly lit, exposed. Untrusted, of course. Even me.

Especially me, perhaps. How could he trust the man most likely to leave here with something that used to be his own?

Nevertheless, he called me back into his absolute domain, the little cubby where he kept his utter treasures, utterly in the dark. I had to grope my way past the rough-iron touch of ancient spars, the salt-sour harshness of coiled cable, cold smooth polished wood that might have been anything. Then he lit a storm-lantern, and I laughed at him.

"Hush," he said, all wrinkles and wind-ruined skin, wizened but not wise, "storm is coming. Ready or not, Sailor Martin."

There was a kitten, asleep on an upturned barrel. He scooped it up with stubby misshapen fingers, sailor's hands; slipped it into a silken pocket in his sleeve. If it woke, it didn't stir or peep.

The lantern hung from a hook above, showing walls of furniture all around us, secret ways of access that might shift like channels in sand between one tide and the next.

"Now," Johnnie said, reaching into a darkness and drawing out a wooden box, laying that on the barrel-head, opening its lid. "I had this out of a condemned whaling junk in Kowloon. The binnacle I sold to a copper millionaire, to make a bar for his apartment; but I took this out under his eye, and he didn't know what he was looking at."

No more did I, except the obvious. It came from a binnacle, it had a needle under glass, above a card. "It's a compass," I said.

"Sailor. It's a *right* compass. This would find you your way through Hell."

One thing for sure, it would be small use to anyone at sea. The master of that whaling junk must have kept another needle to find his way from point to point, from port to port, to know his course across the wasteful ocean. A right whaler knows his fish from their spout, from how they blow; he can tell a sperm from a minke from a bowhead, a right whale from a rorqual.

Any sailor knows one thing about a compass. Never mind what the card says, in whatever language; what matters is the way the needle points.

This compass, this *right* compass of Johnnie's, it wasn't pointing north.

I lifted the box in my hands, felt the solid weight of brass and wood—dark and old and salt-worn, but not rotten—and saw how that needle shifted not one second from its line, however I turned or tilted it. It knew where it meant me to go, or what it was trying to tell me. The ignorance here was my own.

Held closer to the light, it was still reluctant to enlighten me. The card beneath the needle was no printed rose, it had been hand-written, and long ago.

And in Chinese, which would have been no trouble in a regular compass. Besides, I can read Mandarin a little. Enough to tell my northings from my eastings, *bei* from *dong*, that at least.

The thing about Chinese characters, though: they don't work like an alphabet, where you can spell out an unfamiliar word and have an idea at least of what it sounds like, what other words it might have come from, the general drift of its meaning. You know a character or you don't, and if you don't you cannot work it out.

Whatever this needle was inspired to point towards, I couldn't understand it. Johnnie might, but I couldn't quite understand Johnnie either, not tonight. He said, "I owe you money," which was no way to start a negotiation. Direct is one thing, open surrender is something else.

"You do, Johnnie." A gold tooth's-worth of money: more than the value of the tooth, in honesty—the mortgage was a token, an insistence, a gesture of honour—but not as much as this compass was worth, in its brassbound box with all the heft of its age and mystery and scientific question. Not by a distance.

Still, he said, "Take this, keep it, use it; we're all square."

"I don't know how..."

"Be smart, sailor. You will need it."

ANY OTHER NIGHT, JOHNNIE WOULD HAVE FOUND ME A BED OR MORE LIKELY GIVEN me his own, upstairs among the aromatic shadows of his stock, the smells of joss and camphorwood and dust from a thousand holds and homes and marketplaces, a thousand separate journeys from there to here. He'd sleep in the shop, or else shift himself to some back-alley dosshouse for a night or a week or however long I stayed, stranded between one voyage and the next.

Tonight, though, he was boarding up the storefront and moving out himself, heading for higher ground. And so I came from Johnnie's back to this: a room that I could almost call a suite, thanks to the way it bent around the hotel's corner to give me two walls of glass and two distinct spaces, one for bed and bathroom and one for sofa, television, desk. Properly meant for business, no doubt, but I had done all mine. I could use it simply for typhoon-watching, until the storm passed through and I could away to sea again.

I set the compass on the desk, still in its box. It could wait, and so could the typhoon. I wanted to sleep first, in a broad deep bed that didn't rock me, before I woke to wind and wuthering.

Before that a shower, hot and hard. Then I meant to call down for food, to sit at my high windows here and watch the lights of the city and the dark of the sea until I was thoroughly ready for bed; but I was still drying my hair when there was a knock on the door and a voice called, "Room service!"

I pulled on a robe and opened the door, although I hadn't ordered yet. I'm like that. Besides, I knew where I was.

There was a boy, a young man in the corridor with a tiffin-box in his hand, a stack of stainless steel containers that glistened with condensed steam.

"Hullo," he said. "I'm called Shen."

I quirked an eyebrow, and asked the obvious question. "Did Johnnie send you?"

"Of course." A swing of narrow hips and he slid past me as though he was oiled. Went to set his burden on the desk, found it occupied already by the compass in its box; pursed his lips, drew out a coffee-table and spread mats to protect its gleaming surface before he disengaged the various containers from their handle. Lids were marked with scribbled characters; lifted off, inverted, they turned into bowls. Chopsticks were supplied. As he laid out my dinner, Shen glanced from me to the room's mini-bar and back, so emphatically that I was almost apologising as I went to fetch beer. Beers.

Generous to a fault, Johnnie is, once business is put out of the way. To several faults, and some of them my own. Shen was hospitality, no more: a gift, that competitive generosity that encompasses, seems sometimes to define a relationship in the east.

To Johnnie, that is, Shen would be an expression of hospitality. Also a message: stay where you like, I can always find you, always trouble you with gifts.

To me, Shen was very obviously trouble: that kind I leap to welcome, to embrace. A man should seek his sorrow where he can, seize it when the chance arises.

He was one of those slender, short Chinese who look almost too young, although they are not; almost too pretty, though not that either. He looked seventeen, so he was probably twenty-five. He looked as smooth as a girl, as though he barely troubled shaving; that was probably true.

His smile was as solemn, as self-possessed as his hands were neat and swift among the dishes: the lustrous gleam of oyster omelettes, the powerful aniseed smell of chicken in basil. And rice, of course, and yard-long beans coiled in a sesame sauce, and thousand-year eggs with their grey yolks and translucent black albumen, that could only be there to frighten the foreigner. Except that he would never be so crude or so ill-informed, and I would not be frightened. So they were there for my pleasure, as it all was.

As he was himself, of course. Well-dressed, well-briefed, well ready.

He ate a little—half an egg, some of the beans, rice of course because no Chinese can ever not eat rice—to keep me company, and sipped at a beer for the same reason. Likely he was that kind of Chinese who has an uneasy relationship with alcohol, except that nothing in his life would be uneasy; if he could not drink in comfort, he would not drink at all except like this, for manners.

His chopsticks were busier on my behalf than his, nipping up choice pieces of chicken, a stray oyster, a slice of tofu, and laying them encouragingly in my bowl. To oblige him, I ate more than I might have done, though not—never!—as much as there was to eat. That would have been a mortal insult, to him first and so to Johnnie.

Questions are impolite, so he asked none. We talked lightly, inconsequentially, of the sea and the city, nothing personal. Time passed, food disappeared, the sky darkened and the wind built. I fetched another beer for myself but not for him, who did not want it. While I was still picking, filling up the corners, he drifted across the room in search of music, and found the compass instead. Opened the lid and looked, touched curiously, glanced at me, his face alive with questions.

There was one question I could legitimately ask him, a privilege I could lay before his feet: "Can you read the characters?"

"Of course." And was delighted, his sudden smile declared, to do it; delighted that I had asked.

He held his hand out, and I went to him.

His grip was soft, enticing; his voice the same. Between them, they held me entirely. "This here, at south, this is the character for sorrow, for lamentation."

O my prophetic soul: I had called him, privately, my sorrow. I could kiss him now. I did kiss him now. He tasted of tea and smoke, and no surprise.

"This at the west, this is pleasure. At east it is pain, or extremity. At the north, though," where the needle pointed, because I had set the box that way: straight out of the window, across the bay, south-westerly and directly towards the coming typhoon, "this is a character I do not know. I do not think it is a true character," though it famously took a lifetime to learn them all. "See, it has the radical from sorrow, and from pleasure, and from pain: it is a construction, a configuration of all three. I do not think that there is such a word."

He didn't say it like a confessional, *I cannot read this after all,* in shame at the breaking of a promise. Rather it was an excitement, as though the very strangeness of it were something achieved.

We talked about it a little more, we searched a Mandarin dictionary on the net until the connection went down, we disassembled the compass to see if there was anything written on the back of the card. There was not. I magnificently failed to explain how I had come by it, he magnificently failed to ask; we were both, I think, rather pleased with ourselves.

At last I took his hand in my turn and drew him from the table, from the box; drew his distracted gaze from the window, the line of the needle's pointing, the dark of the building storm; led him around the glassy corner to the bed.

NOW HE DID SURPRISE ME. He stood quite still, and allowed me to undress him. Not from shyness, never that. Not from shame either, though another man might have thought it, when he saw what lay beneath the fresh black shirt and jeans.

Shen stood in the shaded light of a single lamp on the nightstand, and that only made his scars stand out the heavier, as the sun's angle shows the moon's craters more clearly at the half than at the full.

The smooth, supple body I had been feeling for was...disfigured, disrupted by a regular pattern of deep scarring, a chequerboard effect all up his arms and across his chest, down his thighs and calves, wherever he could see and reach. If those scars weren't self-inflicted, they were surely administered by consent. It might have been a mark of passage, a ritual achievement, if he had belonged to another kind of people. As it was—no. I thought he had done this himself.

Here are the characters for pleasure, and pain, and sorrow. Here is another character, the roots of all three intermingled.

I thought perhaps that compass should be pointed directly at him; it seemed to encompass him. That must be why his eyes had gleamed above it, why he had seemed to yearn, or else to sigh in satisfaction. It had spoken to him, sung to him, far louder than it did to me. I was intrigued by the thing; Shen, I thought, was hungry for it.

Even now his eyes were moving in that direction, even while he stood with his body, his privacies exposed to my eyes, to my fingers, to my questions.

IT'S NOT POLITE TO ASK QUESTIONS. I took the boy to bed, and never mind what strange artifice his yearning called him to. With me he would find cleaner, simpler pleasures. At least, I had hopes that they would please him. For certain, he did me.

One thing about being so high above the city: you might feel disconnected, but you don't have to draw the blinds.

One thing about that night, that kind of night: neither of us was in any hurry. There was no rush to sleep, no rush to wake or fuck or be away. My time was my own, and so was his; the room was paid for, and so was he.

Through the darkness, then, there were times when we were only lying in bed, talking idly, playing idly and listening to the storm in its own hurry. There was a physical sense of rushing, of increasing solidity and urgency to the air, even before the rain struck, and the lightning.

Smoke and fire and hush in here, in the glass by my bed, in the Lagavulin that I sipped; smoke and fire and noise out there, beyond the windows, in the storm, like a battle fought at sea. God's man-of-war, the typhoon.

I may have said that aloud.

That, and other things equally foolish. The night was long, and short on sleep; he was interestingly delightful, even besides his unmentionable markings, and the storm brought an unexpected focus into the room and the moment. Every one of the moments, as though every single needlepoint jab of a tattoo mattered equally. Or, I suppose, every slice of a razor.

I said, "I'm sorry, did I hurt you?"

He said, "Don't be sorry."

I said, "Roll over, then."

Dawn must have come in some higher place above the clouds, sunlight trapped in the ridges of the whirl, sucked into the funnel of the eye. Even below, it did grow lighter.

Shen got out of bed, went to the bathroom; claimed to be surprised, a little, that we still had electricity. Half the city had gone dark, district by district, as the storm turned the lights out.

Then he went to stand naked by the window-wall, gazing out at the typhoon where it still thundered and rushed, young transient flesh and ancient eternal weather separated only by a fixity of purpose, glass as statement, *here I stand and there you are, and this is the gulf between us.*

Lightning made the patterns of his scarring stand out, stark and brutal.

Then I thought I saw another figure, stood beyond the glass.

In mid-air, that would be, on the solidity of wind, twenty-three storeys above the city streets.

It was naked too, that shadow-shape; and of course it was only a reflection, window turned to mirror, so that Shen was looking at himself and so was I.

Except that the storm must be distorting the reflection somehow, because the figure it held was none so straight as Shen and none so clean, it seemed twisted somehow and its scars were differently organised; I thought they cut a diagonal cross into its chest, from shoulder to hip both ways, as though it might unfold like origami. And then it moved, it lifted its hand to the glass, seeming as though it stood on the other side of a doorway, some place still and bewildering, hints of a labyrinth behind, where a man might need another kind of compass to navigate...

And then I put the lights on, one bedside switch to brighten the whole room. I wanted to see quite clearly how wrong this all was, what a nonsense, no figure at all out there once the light fell onto it.

And there was the figure in full light, and there was Shen staring at him, lifting his own hand in the irony of a slavish reflection, and I saw that he had the compass between his feet there, box and all.

And then the window blew in.

Blew out.

Blew away.

WAS GONE, ALL THAT GLASS IN A SUDDEN SHATTER, ALL NOISE. Like a blast without wind, or a wind without direction.

The glass was gone, that separation was gone between one state and another, and Shen was gone too. Just—gone. He had been standing in arm's reach of the window when it ruptured, and now that place was empty.

I hadn't been looking, not properly. I'd been flinching in anticipation of flying glass that never came, that never reached me. Even so, I had two contrary impressions in my head: one, that he'd been snatched away, that the figure outside had reached in and taken him; the other, that he had reached out. Stepped forward. Gone willingly.

Both were nonsense, of course. There had been no figure, stationary in a typhoon two hundred feet above the city. There was no such hell, to be glimpsed in storm and reached *in extremis*. Only a reflection distorted and a mundane tragedy, a window imploding under pressure and a young man seized by dreadful wind, carried off to a dreadful death.

That same wind was in the room with me now, something living, appalling.

It pulled the duvet from the bed and dragged it out into the sky; it took what furniture was closest, the television on its stand and never mind the weight of it, that lifted too before I saw it fall. The standard lamp was seized and thrown, hurled across the room to break a mirror in the other wall.

For a little moment, perhaps my body wanted to hurtle over to that missing window, in a desperate lunge after the vanished Shen. I know my voice snatched after him, I know my arm flew up in echo, instinct over intellect. And met that wall of wind, felt it against my fingers, and—well, no.

If a sailor knows one thing, it would be the wind. If he knows another too, it would be a lost cause, when not to reach for what is gone already. I have seen men washed overboard, lovers walk away. The trick is to survive them, not to chase.

I didn't shift a willing foot towards the window.

North Sea gale or Gulf hurricane or roar down in the Forties, your first massive wind will blow all pride, all shame out of you. I crawled from the bed to the door, crawled naked on my belly except to snatch my money-belt from the nightstand as I passed. I dug my fingers deep into thick pile carpet and dragged myself along, didn't try to stand even at the door. I reached up from the floor to work the handle, hauled it open and slithered through, let it slam behind me and felt my ears pop at the change of pressure.

STOOD UP CAUTIOUSLY INTO NO WIND AT ALL, THE STILL AIR OF A HOTEL CORRIDOR and the faint distant buzz of voices, someone having a room party, entirely safe behind their window-walls; and made it only halfway to the lift before a member of staff appeared, calm and utterly unsurprised. Perhaps she had seen me on the CCTV and come to intercept; perhaps it was purely routine to discover naked men astray outside their rooms, in times of storm or otherwise.

She took me into a linen cupboard, found me a robe while I was telling her about the window gone, my friend gone with it. Her shock was swift and professional, impersonal, efficient; my own was climbing me like a monkey in the rigging, I could feel the tremor of it in my fingers, knew what it was, could do nothing about it.

Then there were police, the hotel doctor, a large whisky and a little pill, another bed in a room without a window. I had tried to say, I had said—time and again, I think I said it—that I was used to this, I had seen men die this way; but to the hotel of course it was terrible and they were determined that it should be terrible to me too.

The pill gave me a deeper, perhaps a better sleep than I could ever have achieved on my own account; my body doesn't like to sleep in storms. I woke to the hush and ruin of what follows on land, and longed to be at sea where all the damage is swept away or left behind. When I called to ask for food, I got the manager instead, still horrified by the morning's news. A window gone and a life lost—a guest's friend, subtly and discreetly to be distinguished from a guest—such a thing might be common news in the typhoon, might almost be commonplace at other establishments but had never happened, should never have happened here. Should not have been possible. The glass was guaranteed, promised to be proof against the strongest wind. There must have been a fault in that one sheet, that triple-sheet, or perhaps an unregarded twist in the frame, damage from the last quake, though the whole hotel was promised to be earthquake-proof also. There would be an investigation, of course. And in the meantime, of course, I was a guest of the management for so long as I cared to stay; and if my, ah, friend had any family living locally, the hotel would do everything in its power to ease their transition through this difficult period...

Did Shen have family? I couldn't say; I found it hard to care. Johnnie would know, perhaps. I put him on to Johnnie.

The police, too, I sent them round to Johnnie with their questions and my apologies. It's no kind thing to bring the attention of the law down on a waterfront trader who may lack import licences and invoices, whose contacts might well prefer their anonymity; but I couldn't be kind that day. I answered what questions I could, not many, and most of those with "Best ask Johnnie."

I asked one question of my own: what of the yacht I'd left in the marina, had she survived the storm and the tidal surge? The management there had claimed their covered berths in their isolated dock to be typhoon-proof, but then, so did the management here make comparable claims...

They promised to let me know, as soon as practical. They implied that they had more urgent matters to attend to first, the recovery of bodies, Shen's among them, and how could I be asking about a boat?

I didn't say it, but I doubted they would ever find Shen's body.

I didn't say much of anything, indeed. I gently let them infer that I was still in the grip of shock or tranquillisers, both; I said I wanted to go back to my room, and they obliged me. Offered an escort, indeed, which I declined.

For good reason, because I had let them assume I meant the new room, the windowless, the safe.

I still had my original keycard in my money-belt, and they hadn't thought to recode the door; why would I go back there, why would I want to go back?

There was no watch in the corridor, for much the same reason. The police had been, had seen, had taken what evidence, what photographs they needed; why should they want to go back? Or to keep guard? It wasn't a crime scene, after all. Officialdom was done with this place. A minor tragedy, after all, in a city overtaken by them...

I LET MYSELF IN AND FOUND THAT THE ABSENT WINDOW HAD BEEN REPLACED WITH deadlights, boarded up. Otherwise, the room had been left largely untouched except by storm. The police would have wanted it preserved, of course, at least for their cursory inspection; the management would see no hurry in it now, when they had live guests to attend to.

My things: someone might have been sent to fetch out my things, but they had not. Not yet. They might still come, of course, at any moment. I didn't overly care. If they caught me here, they caught nothing but a disturbed guest among his own possessions.

Among what was left of his possessions. Anything that had been lying loose in the room was gone, scoured away by too much wind, *tai feng*, and its attendant water. But I'm a sailor, long trained to neatness and alert to storm; I had unpacked, of course, and put most of my things away.

The nightstand was gone, with its drawers. With my watch, my phone, my cash purse and medications. No matter.

The wardrobe was extant, built-in. The sliding doors were off their tracks, but only wedged more firmly in place; it took ocean muscles and a degree of ocean experience to shift them. Behind, everything was sodden that could be soaked: which meant my better clothes, but there were few enough of those. All my practical wear is waterproof by necessity, by definition. As is my bag, and the useful stuff it carries; and...

AND I WAS HERE FOR NONE OF THAT. Of course. I was only displacing the moment.

Close by the boarded window stood the compass-box, not quite where Shen had left it: set aside, I supposed, by the men who came to seal up that appalling breach.

I thought Shen had meant to take it with him, and had not been given the chance.

Left behind, it was closed up tight against the weather. Locked up tight, apparently, when I tried the lid: although there had only been one key and that was with me, in my money-belt.

When I tried it, the brass lock moved as sweetly as if it sat in an oil-bath. When I lifted the lid and looked inside, so did the compass needle.

It pivoted and spun, reacted to any movement of the box, paid no heed to any outside force or inclination: nothing to point at, nowhere to go.

Wherever Shen had been taken, you couldn't get there from here. Not any more.

NEXT DAY, I CARRIED THE BOX BACK TO JOHNNIE'S PLACE. On foot, necessarily, through streets still full of ruin, busy with people, no wheeled traffic at all.

I found him dealing with the aftermath of his own broken window, sweeping up glass in the street.

I put the compass down and helped haul out ruined stock—all those things that no one had ever wanted; anyone could have them now, if they would only take them away—and said, "I thought you were safely boarded up before the typhoon hit?"

"I was," he grunted. "Someone came, ripped down the boards, broke the window to get in."

"Christ. What did they steal?"

"Nothing. Nothing's gone."

How he could tell, I was not clear; everything was overturned, broken open, torn apart. He was entirely certain, though. And oddly phlegmatic, I thought. If he was angry that morning, it was with me. "Sending the police to me—to me!—over some whore-boy I do not know..."

"Wait, what? You didn't send...?"

"I did not. I am not your pimp."

That was a blatant lie, he had pimped for me for longer than either of us would credit, but I let it by.

And went on fetching and carrying, until there was as much sodden trash outside as in; and then, remembering, I glanced aside for the compass where I had set it down just by the step there.

No one had come, but it was gone, and I was somehow not surprised at all.

The Boat of Not Belonging

THE STORM CAUGHT US JUST OFF HARTLAND POINT, BLEW US HALFWAY TO Milford Haven.

In honesty, I thought it was a blessing.

You can shake a new crew down, just with a regular cruise: show them the ropes, help them learn about the sea, the ship, the world and each other. For a real shakedown, though, there's nothing better than a crisis; and there is no crisis like a real storm. I'd bottle one if I could, manufacture one if I had any gift in that direction. Storm strips you down to the bone, it takes away your choices. All you've got is what you are, is what you can offer to your crewmates.

My crew that trip was half a dozen gap-year students, filling in time. Nice kids. In the ordinary way of things they would have fallen in and out of love and in and out of bed, sulked and broken things and glued things back together again, talked and talked. Over a week or ten days they'd have shaken down into a decent crew, bar maybe the one who couldn't take it, who would have left in tears at the next convenient port.

They didn't get the ordinary way of things. What they got instead was a hard blow out of the south-west, seas like plough-hills, rain like they'd never seen it. What I got was memories of Fastnet in '79, the last thing I was looking for in these waters—and a sudden, unexpected crew, where they'd been a bunch of strangers just before. They were sodden and seasick and scared, desperately sorry for themselves and utterly out of their depths; but they worked like Trojans regardless, and took care of each other. The first time I saw a girl swear viciously at a lad for not clipping on his safety harness before he stuck his head out of a hatch to throw up, I knew they'd be all right.

Myself I'd never had any doubts about, nor the ship either. Kids are more susceptible: inexperience and bravado make a cocktail with hormones that doesn't always mix well in a storm. I've seen youngsters go over the side, foolhardy or unlucky, tempting fate either way.

Not these. On this ship, with me to watch them, they should have been safe anyway; if they had sense enough to watch each other, I could stop worrying.

I watched them anyway, of course, and drove them hard. When the storm finally blew over their reward was a slug of rum in their tea, and a reprieve. "This one night," I said, "I'll stand watch alone. Me and my electronics, that is, you're never alone with a GPS. You go below, find yourselves a dry bunk, get some sleep. You've earned it. In the morning, we'll see what's what."

MORNING DAWNED CLEAR AND STILL, NO SIGN OF LAND ON ANY HORIZON. One by one the kids came up on deck, sweaters and jeans, hands wrapped around mugs, woken by strangeness: voices or seagulls or the swell beneath the hull, something. They were sore and sleepy and deeply, unutterably pleased with themselves. It might have been their first taste of survivor's relish, that understanding that they could have died last night and didn't.

They strewed themselves about the foredeck, all eyes turned beyond the bow. I gave them five minutes to realise that we weren't actually moving in that direction, that the muted thunder of the engine was absent from the day and maybe after all it had been the silence that disturbed them, the loss of forward motion, something; then I left the wheelhouse and went to join them.

"Okay, here's the situation. The motor's out. Seawater in the fuel lines, maybe, or something more serious. I won't know till I take it apart. I've told the coastguard we're adrift, but not to worry: we've plenty of searoom, and we'll be back up and running soon enough. I need two of you to keep watch, just on general principles, but no one's coming anywhere near us; everyone has radio, everyone has radar, they all know where we are. Two more come down with me and I'll show you the inside of a diesel. The last couple makes a start on sorting out the bookroom, it's an unholy mess in there. Shuffle yourselves into pairs, if you haven't already; duties change every two hours. Everyone does everything. Clear?"

THE BOAT OF NOT BELONGING

One small voice said, "What about breakfast?"

"Everyone does everything," I said, "bar the cooking. I cook. Once I know what's going on in the engine. If you can't last that long, there are cereal bars in the galley."

WHO WAS IT SAID HE DIDN'T ENVY THE HEART OF YOUTH, BUT ONLY ITS HEAD AND stomach? Last night they'd been as sick as dogs, whenever they stopped to think about it. This morning they engulfed a vat of porridge so quickly, I made cheese butties to follow. And carried them around from one watch to the next: up to the wheelhouse, down to the engine-room, lastly to the bookroom where my heart lay and my business too.

Orcas was an old retired ferryboat. She used to ply between the northern isles, carrying cars and cattle, tourists and teenagers, bread and bricks and broadcloth. Now she was mine, and I'd refitted her; she carried books.

Books and seawater don't mix. I'd done everything I could to keep the boat tight and the cargo dry; I stowed the books in sealed crates and strapped everything down, and even so. The old passenger lounge was what I called my bookroom, and the floor was awash. Half the crates had come adrift of their strapping, as last night's seas tossed my poor boat about. I didn't know yet whether the sea had found its way inside the crates. The shelving was all steel and all bolted to the walls, but even that had taken damage: from flying crates, I thought, more than surging seawater.

There was mopping to be done all through the ship; there were soggy seabags to be carried out on deck, to dry off in the sun; but the bookroom mattered most. I had the kids set up trestle tables and inspect boxes one by one, laying damp or battered books to one side and sorting as they went. Learning the inventory.

"All this lot's new stock," I said, "picked up over the last month, when I was on my own, that I haven't had time to go through yet. I don't know what's here."

"Can you really manage this whole thing alone?" Kelly was wide-eyed; if I had any interest in impressing eighteen-year-olds, she was ripe for it.

"If I have to," I said, "I can. I'd sooner have a crew—well, you saw, last night. Sometimes I need you. On my own, I hug the coast and put into port at the first sign of weather. Actually, I mostly just go from port to port anyway. *Orcas* was built for sea, but yesterday's cruise was meant to be a treat, for her as much as the rest of us. Sorry 'bout that."

"Nah, it was fun," Luke said stoutly. He'd been the one throwing up through the hatch—nice boy, didn't want to do it inside—and she'd been the one who yelled at him. I try not to jump to conclusions, but—well, kids aren't so careful. I thought they'd probably be jumping each other's bones by the end of the week, if they weren't already.

"So do you just buy everything that people bring you?" Kelly asked.

"More or less. If it's a boxful, absolutely. You never know what you might find lurking at the bottom of a box. Real treasures, sometimes."

"You must have to wade through a lot of trash, though."

I shrugged. "Every book has its natural home, its proper reader. Even the ones you think are trash. It's my job to find that reader, and bring the two together."

"Isn't that what the internet's for?" Luke asked, picking disdainfully through a dozen ancient Zane Grey paperbacks.

"Sure—and I do trade online. But a lot of readers are still old-fashioned, they like the thrill of the chase, hunting through shelves of physical books. And when the bookshop is a boat, when it's only in town for a week, that adds to the allure. I do better business over the counter than I do over the net." As he'd find out soon enough. A couple of days hauling books around, he'd be more sore than he was after a night of storm. It wasn't sailing the boat I really needed a crew for, it was days in port.

"Hey, look, Martin—is this something?"

From under a pile of Jackie Collins and John le Carré hardcovers came a familiar shape, with a familiar heft to it. I could practically taste the dust already on my tongue. A foot high, four inches thick, heavily gilded and embossed: Kelly looked so excited I had to bite back the groan it wanted to drag out of me.

"That's a family Bible," I said. "Victorian. I don't even need to open it. Someone's found it in their attic, and they're just like you: they think age must equal value. It's not true. Sorry, but they're practically ten a penny. There are plenty around, and no one wants them."

"You said every book has its natural home."

"I did, yes—and that one belongs in the house it's just come from, or else to the family that used to live there. Open it up, it'll list the paterfamilias and all his descendants unto the third generation, in a lovely copperplate hand. If we could find them, the current generation, they might want it—but their forebears left it behind, remember. As genealogy it's not so much an avenue as a dead end."

She made a face, but put the book on one side carefully. As soon as I was gone, I knew, she'd be at it with a J-cloth for the dust, opening it up to find the former owners. Tonight no doubt she'd be full of intrigue over dinner, wondering who they were and where they'd gone, using her smartphone to Google names, getting excited all over again at the inevitable hits.

Hey-ho. I shrugged and went back down to my engine, where it lay in bits and diesel baths with anxious children trying to diagnose it.

I COULDN'T SAY QUITE WHAT BROUGHT ME UP AGAIN, BEFORE WE WERE HALF DONE down there. It can't have been the weigh that was on us, the slow momentum of the tidal drift; that hadn't changed. It oughtn't to be the quality of the silence, isolated as we were down in the engine-room. Uncounted years at sea give you an instinct, that's all: not for trouble, but for the conditions that can cause it. Sometimes that means a change in wind or weather; sometimes it's more subtle.

I left Scott and Michelle greasy and determined; I all but ran up the companionway, wiping my hands on a rag as I went.

And came out on deck, into a world of white and hush and stillness: that same feeling that in childhood fantasy Christmas is a thrill, because it means the snow has come, but at sea is always a dire warning, because what it means is fog. Fog without power.

It ought never to be a surprise in those waters, but it always is. It ought always to be a terror, in any waters. Fog banks have a natural affinity to rocks and sand banks; also to busy shipping channels, giant tankers running fast and heedless.

Orcas has a fog-horn. Of course she does, wise old boat. She might not have lived so long without.

I ran up to the wheelhouse, and punched the button that sent our presence blaring out, every thirty seconds. Nothing that was likely to harm us was likely to hear it, but you do what you can. It would make the kids feel better, that at least, and morale is always a factor.

I didn't clip Jason and Penny around the ear and demand to know why they hadn't called for me, the instant the fog showed. That could wait.

More importantly, I called the coastguard.

Tried to. Being adrift in known waters is one thing; being adrift in fog is something else.

Being adrift in fog with all your electronics dead? Something else again.

Radio, radar, GPS. Nothing.

"Okay," I said, sounding positive, robust for the kids' sake. They really didn't need to know that this was their second crisis, hot on the heels of the first. "We'll do this the old-fashioned way. One of you in the bows, please, one in the stern. I'm sorry to split you up; I'll dig out walkie-talkies if your phones don't have a signal, but I need a watch both ends. Take these," their compensation, a flare-gun each, "and fire one off if you see anything moving, any shadow in the fog. I'd rather waste a dozen flares than hit a ship unknowing. Or have a ship hit us."

I made sure the youngsters were settled, each with their exciting guns. I tested their cellphones myself—and no, no signal: no way to call the coastguard, something more than fog had closed in on us—and promised them the walkie-talkies when I had time, so that they could at least chat to each other, keep themselves alert. Then I went below just for a minute, to let everyone know the position.

And down on the deck below the wheelhouse, just at the hatch to the companionway where the fog had drifted and clumped together, just as I stepped through the bulkhead, just *there*—

Well. I stepped between two silent figures, shadows in the fog, standing like sentinels one either side of the hatchway.

A man and a boy, I thought they were. A child.

Colder than glass, I thought they were. Cold as the deep water, down where light never reaches.

I stopped dead. And despised myself for doing it, for standing there so utterly still, bereft; and even as I forced myself back into motion I was thinking that someone had stopped them even deader, dead indeed.

And then as I turned in the hatchway there to find them, I was thinking *no, don't be a fool, that's just the fog in your brain, thinking for you. Thinking fogthoughts. There are no boys aboard, except the crew. Big boys. This is a boy and a girl, that's all: she'll be the short one, Kelly. The two of them come up together in search of you, fog-bound and frightened, mute, waiting for reassurance...*

And I was ready almost to offer it, robust and practical—except that they weren't there. No crew, and no stiff silent figures like guardians at the door.

Instead, there was a woman: middle-aged, none of mine. Nothing that belonged here. Plunging at me through the physical air, entirely physical herself, entirely ruined: monochrome in foglight, blood like black ink flooding her face, soaking the white of her long dress, nightgown, wedding gown, whatever it was that she wore.

Just that glimpse, that moment. Then a gust of wind tore at the fog and she was gone, ripped away from me before I could stir to help her.

I clung to the frame of the hatchway, both hands, just for a moment, just to hold myself upright.

The sea is...a liminal space, vast but marginal, the ground between. Between one state and another, in any sense you like to use those words. Liquid, again in any sense. A boat is a bridge, always. No one actually goes to sea, we go to Rio de Janeiro or Surabaya or Hong Kong; the sea is only what we have to straddle between here and there, a condition we have to pass through. Quarantine.

They call me Sailor Martin, and even so. I use the sea, I don't belong to it.

It took me a while to understand that, and no one else believes it. Never mind.

The sea does have its people, of course, those it's claimed. Lost souls, and many of them: and yes, you may see them in the fog, hear them in the wind. Meet them, perhaps, if you're not lucky. But they're...diffuse. Dissolved. Diluted. Not like this.

I took a moment, took a breath. Turned again, and went below.

Needed more than a moment, apparently, more than a breath. Didn't go to the engine-room, nor the bookroom either.

Went to the galley, and started cutting bread. Put a pan of milk on to heat. It's a default position for me: when in doubt, make cocoa, make sandwiches. Feed the crew. Lunch is always the good news.

I bore gifts and tidings, then, to my oily workers, and then to my dusty ones.

"Beef and horseradish," I said, when Kelly asked.

She took her hand away. "I'm vegetarian."

"Don't be," I said. "Not here, not now. Food counts for more than principles. What if we had to eat the cabin boy?"

"You can eat the cabin girl instead," she said mulishly. "I'd volunteer."

"Luke's bigger," I said. "He'd go further. You'd barely make a mouthful, and then we'd have to eat someone else."

It's not my reputation, but I can be kind. I set that up deliberately to give him the chance to prod her slender parts and observe there was no meat on her, to win himself a fist in the ribs and a quick wrestle, a relief of tension all round.

When they subsided, I nodded towards one of the tables, where that family Bible lay predictably open. "Been reading through their begats, have you, Kelly?"

"Oh—yes." She pulled a face, seeming not to notice that Luke had carelessly left his arm lying across her shoulders. "I don't like it much."

"Why not?" That was unexpected, and useful: another distraction. Sometimes with a new crew you have to stop them thinking, or they'll worry themselves into paralysis.

When she came to show me, she tugged Luke behind her by the finger. Just to have him there, apparently, to lean into as she said, "Look. One of his daughters must have blotted her copybook."

Indeed. She'd been more than blotted, she'd been expunged: her name utterly blacked out, ink deliberately dribbled onto the paper and the surface scratched with a pen-nib to help it soak through.

I thought of her plunging through fog, sodden with disaster, nameless and lost, unsalvageable.

"What could she have done," Kelly asked, "to deserve that?"

I shrugged. "Elopement, pregnancy. Refusal to marry where her father said she must. That's the tradition, it's usually something to do with the line of inheritance. The selfish gene. Unless she went mad and murdered her maiden aunt. Burned down the stable. Sold the family jewels and ran off to Australia. Something. Drink your cocoa before it skins."

I still thought it would have been something to do with her person. Personal.

"How are the dilithium crystals, Scotty?"

It was, of course, irresistible. He gave me one of those weary obliging grins that say this joke is very old indeed; he humoured me with a mumble about how they couldn't take it, Captain, and could we all please be beamed out of this?—and then he offered his actual opinion, that he didn't know diesels from Adam but he couldn't see that we'd done anything at all, just taking the damn thing apart and putting it together again.

"It's like a hard reboot," I said. "Seawater gets where it shouldn't, or a bubble of air, fog in the system. You don't see it because there's nothing there to see, but you shift it anyway. Maybe. If we're lucky. Who wants to press the magic button and find out?"

Scott deferred to Michelle, only because he thought he ought to; you could see that he really wanted to do it himself.

She could see that. She smiled, shook her head, gestured to get on with it.

Which he would have done, his hand was halfway there and he was just glancing to me for confirmation—*turn this, press that, hold it down, right?*—when we were interrupted.

A scream through fog and steel comes muffled, but it does still come.

It was hoarse and horrified, and male. I was running before they had their wits together to follow me; I was halfway up the companionway when I heard the bang of a flare going off.

I got there first, because of that head start. Jason was standing backed up against the rail, shaking, shying at the sight of me, fumbling to reload the flaregun. I took that off him first thing, before I peeled him away from the rail and led him somewhere safer, into the anxious clutches of the others as they came.

"What happened, Jason?"

"I," he said, "I'm sorry, I shouldn't have fired, I know it's not—"

"Don't worry about that," I said. "I told you, I'd rather waste a dozen flares than miss something that mattered. What was it?"

"I saw...I saw something. Someone. A man. I think it was a man..."

My crew might be bewildered, but not me so much. Not now. I might have let him stop there, but the young are less generous; he provoked a chorus of questions, because they all think it's always better to talk everything through. Better out than in, they say. It isn't true.

He said it again, "I think it was a man. How can you tell, when their face has been all cut away? He was...all blood, all over. Flesh and blood. No *skin*..."

The kids gazed at him, gazed at each other and at the empty deck, turned at last to me. I said, "Okay, you're all off duty for a bit. We'll take a chance on some tanker running us down. Get yourselves down to the galley and find the rum. You can have a tot each. Just the one, mind."

"There's more space in the bookroom," someone said.

"No," I said flatly. "Not there. Take Jason to the galley." They'd pack in close and warm, and I'd know where they all were. Safety in numbers.

Me, I was going to the bookroom. Alone.

What's the opposite of safety in numbers?

Ah, yes. Stupidity.

YOU CAN MAKE WHAT JOKES YOU LIKE ABOUT L-SPACE AND THE INTER-connectedness of all libraries. It's still true, and it's still not funny. The sea is liminal, and so is fog—and so are books. It's only that books are more fixed, more focused. They still constitute a marginal land, gateways and fences, boundaries to breach.

A boat is a bridge, and so is a book. It's meant to stand between writer and reader, to bring them close to touching: to have them march in step a little way together, almost hand in hand, nothing between them but an unloved wall.

But a book is an object too, as well as a journey people take together.

It can be all too physically a bridge. Where the sea dilutes, a book can concentrate. There's power in the written word, power in a pen—and any book can be written in, by anyone.

I came down into the bookroom, into the sound of muttered voices, into an empty space.

There were footsteps at my back, but none of the kids was coming after me.

I went to the porthole first, undogged it, flung it wide to let the chill fog in. Then I went back to the table where the Bible lay open to that family tree, laid out I thought for sacrifice.

It was no surprise to see the name of the paterfamilias was gone. Not inked out this time, no. Cut away, rather: scraped off the heavy paper with a blade, a razor. Skinned.

There were still a dozen names remaining, children and grandchildren, generations long gone and yet to suffer. I wasn't having that, not on my boat.

When I reached to close the book, to lift it: that's when he spoke to me, a voice like bitter wire in my bones, that deep inside me. That cold, that vicious. That deadly.

"Don't you touch that. Let it lie."

He was too late, I was touching it already. Perhaps I leaned some weight on it; perhaps it only needed a touch, some books are like that, all too ready to turn.

It had been propped, but the spine fell flat beneath my hand and all the pages flipped so that I was looking at the endpapers suddenly, the back of the book.

At two more names written in a round, careful, difficult hand: *Elias Munstrum*, marked with a cross, and *Joshua his son*. Joshua who had been to the board school, as I guessed, for long enough to learn to write his own name and his father's, that at least.

I didn't know who they were, or how they stood to the family. Servants, tenants? Something. It didn't matter.

I stepped around the table and looked up and there they stood in the doorway, in my boat: father and son, man and boy. The one with an open cut-throat razor in his hand, the other with a pen.

"You let that lie," the father said again, "you don't touch that."

A book is a bridge, and they were using this one, in the fear, in the fog.

A book is a gateway, and we had opened it.

MY HAND WAS STILL ON IT, TO PROVE THE FATHER WRONG.

His razor was still in his hand. Absurdly, I was almost more frightened of his son, the silent boy dressed like a model of his father in his Sunday black, with his feet bare and that cheap pen clutched tight, steel nib ready to scratch and scratch.

The cold was everywhere, was everything. It came from them, from the book, from the open port.

I said, "How if I close it now, what then?"

"Then you have us," the father said, "cut loose aboard your boat. Do you want that?"

I said, "How if I throw it overboard? Through that porthole, still open, here and now? How if the sea washes out all the ink, you and them together, what then?"

Then was when the boy rushed me, mute and dreadful. I...do not know what would have happened, if that pen of his had pierced me. I have lived a long time and seen many things, seen and done many things, that he may not have accounted for: just a boy, after all. If he was ten years old, he was not more than ten.

Still. I do not know what would have happened. But they had taken some form, some solidity on my good solid bridge of a boat. Maybe they took it from the boat; maybe the boat forced it on them. They weren't fog, they were compounded of more than fog and fear now, and the table was between us and he couldn't quite come at me, he had to stretch across.

Which meant that I did just have time to do what I meant to do, because I would never have condemned the family to a sea-bed shared with these two. However diffuse, dissolved, diluted.

I stepped back, and tore that endpaper out of the Bible as I went.

I had their names in my hand, and I heard them howling as I went to the porthole.

I heard the crash of it as the table was knocked off its trestles, I felt the cold of them biting at my heart as they came, at the blood in my veins and the breath in my lungs.

Too late, they came. I crumpled that heavy paper between my hands and hurled it out of the port, into the dense fog and down to the sea.

Perhaps they followed it. Perhaps they had to. Perhaps there was an eddy in the fog as they went. I don't know.

I do know that it took me a minute to move, to turn around, to be sure that the room was empty now.

That the first thing I did was bend down and retrieve that heavy Bible. It had fallen on its face, open and askew, so that the family page was crumpled and torn. I was disinclined to smooth it; I didn't want to ally myself with any family that had earned itself such a cold and lingering hatred. I wouldn't send them down after their assailants, but the next port of call, this book was going ashore. And not being passed on to some other innocent's custody. Just in case. Who knew what else might not be written in its pages, sewn into its spine, glued behind its covers? I had drowned one page of it; I thought I might burn the rest.

In the meantime, I took it to my cabin: before I went to the engine-room to start the diesel thumping, before I went up to the wheelhouse to talk to the coastguard and see if we were back on their radar yet.

Villanelle

NOT EVERYBODY DIES.

War...happens. You choose a side if you're that way inclined, if you're allowed the luxury. More likely your side is chosen for you by birth or by geography, by loyalty or happenstance, by edict or by luck. Good luck, ill luck. Either way.

You fight or you don't fight, depending. On what you can get away with, if you're wise.

Sooner or later, one side is going to lose. As often as not, it'll be yours. You were in the wrong town at the wrong time, you listened to the wrong prince or the wrong god or the wrong recruiting sergeant. One way or another, it's your turn to go down. Fighting or otherwise.

There will have been battles; people will have died. In the fighting, and afterwards. In the cities, in the villages, in the fields.

Eventually there'll be an ending of sorts. A last siege, a final battle, some kind of surrender. And then more deaths to come: executions public or private, official or otherwise, in justice or punishment or revenge.

And then the hunger, because of course nobody brought the harvest in, you were all too busy fighting or being besieged, running away, dying in droves. And the sickness that follows the hunger, and the jail-fever in the prison camps, and the pox that leaps from one brothel, one harbour, one occupied city to the next; and...

AND STILL, NOT EVERYBODY DIES.

Some of us have to come back.

HOME. FOR SOME PEOPLE, IT'S WHERE THEY END UP, WHERE THEY SETTLE.

For some of us, it's where you start. Where you run away from. Where you *leave.*

For some of us, coming back would never be a choice. Only ever a thing we did because we had to.

STILL, HERE I WAS. HOME AGAIN.

"Djoran. Still too pretty to kill, then?"

I gave him half a shrug, half a smile. *Wry* would be the word. You get to be good at that. "Pretty boys don't mean much any more."

"They never did." He was a man who could never have been pretty, even as a boy; but his trade was intimate with beauty. He did know.

"True enough," I allowed. "These days, though..." The other half of the shrug, and no smile; that was all it took, to say what I knew too. That with a glut of prisoners, orphans and runaways, bandits in the hills and half the world in motion, the market was sodden with the likes of me. Boys had never been so cheap.

That mattered.

I still had to sell myself, but there was no better way to start. Beggar your own value before you begin.

I said, "Well, I'm back now. And still pretty. And I know the work." *Better than ever.* "Will you—?"

"Wait. You mean you're not just passing through?"

"No," I said, perhaps more heavily than I meant. "I'm home now. I've nowhere else to go."

"And you want your old place back, is that it? You want to put yourself under my roof, my charge?"

Want is a slippery word at the best of times, which these were not. One more time I shrugged, while I could still afford to. And said it again, "I've nowhere else to go."

"That I can believe," he said. "You left few friends behind you, when you... left."

That little hesitation was a little reminder that I'd sneaked away without his consent, which meant without leaving profit in his purse.

"I know it," I said. "But will you take me?" Put bluntly because I wasn't negotiating here, I was begging. "I'll cost you nothing this time, Largo. Only bed and board—and I'll share beds, of course, and I know what you spread on your board. And what you pay for it. You won't notice one more mouth, and you do know what custom I'll bring to your door."

"Trouble," he said dourly, "that's what you'll bring."

"Trouble pays, Largo. Trouble *drinks*, and is this not a tavern? Trouble eats, it keeps your kitchens busy; trouble has all kinds of appetites that we can satisfy for a price, you and I."

"Less of the *we*," he growled. "If I take you—*if*—there'll be no partnership between us. You're one more slut in my house, no more than that. And you'll take nothing from it, except what I give you. Bed and board."

"Of course, Largo. That's all I ask."

I stood meekly before him, waiting for his decision: the very image of a boy broken by a world too big for him, creeping back in search of whatever rough accommodations he could make. Not looking for kindness, any more than justice—gods, no, not that!—and almost afraid to hope, almost that. Absolutely afraid of everything else, including Largo.

Briefly, I even thought he might refuse. Maybe I'd overreached at last: come too far, asked too much. So little, and still too much. Maybe I really hadn't learned the lessons of defeat, capitulation, loss...

In the end, though, his snort of contempt told me I was in. "Not as you were before, mind," he said. "There'll be no tricks, and no deceptions. You're a servant, a dancing boy, a whore. You don't steal so much as a pin or a mouthful of meal, you don't cheat my customers or my people. You don't play and you don't wager. You'll have nothing of your own to wager with, I'll be sure of that; and you'll beg no more than you borrow, which means nothing at all from anyone. Agreed?"

I nodded.

"And I'll sell you on again, first fair offer that I hear. You'll have no say, and no share. Agreed?"

Again, I nodded.

"And just to be sure, I'll have Virelle put a binding on you. You bring nothing into my house when you come, and you take nothing with you when you leave. Nothing outside your own skin. That's how far I trust you, boy."

"Virelle?" I may perhaps have flinched. He may have been looking for exactly that. I blustered on, awkward and inevitable: "Virelle still with us, is she? I never thought that old crow would—Ow!"

His hand was no softer than it had been; he was no slower to use it.

"You speak of her with respect, Djoran, or you don't speak at all. I could have her place a binding on your tongue. Perhaps I should. I've other uses for it, but a boy don't need to speak much. Not in my house. One word out of place, one whisper that I don't like and it'll be my mute dancing boy that people come for. They'll enjoy that, the slippery glib Djoran silent and helpless under their hands. I will do that. Understood?"

I nodded hesitantly. No words now, only my uttermost need on display. He'd thought he had the most of me, the best of me before; now I was his again to use again, to sell again and again night after night, until he sold me one more time for true.

It was a bad bargain, and the best that I could hope for. Boys were cheap, and I was tainted goods.

Hell, I was a legend, and nothing good at all.

"Good, then. Come, then."

I HADN'T COUNTED ON VIRELLE.

Stupid of me. If tavern-keepers survive a passing war, then why not temple-keepers? Any soldier worth his kit will spend as much time at prayer as he does at table. And as much money, that too. For the priests, for the incense they burn and the blood they spill. For luck, if that's for sale; and for whores, who certainly are.

Temple or tavern, there are always whores.

It's how I started, as a temple boy. One of Virelle's. Looking like the streetrat that I was, all ribs and knees in a tunic that hid neither; burning resin and striking bells, dancing in lamplight and shaking down the faithful. Smelling of smoke and sweat, my own and older men's. Long ago, but—well. Fire and steel had swept these winding streets, more than once since I'd been gone. Not everybody dies, but even so. I really hadn't counted on Virelle.

Here was the street called Strait, because it was like honesty: narrow and difficult and not for us. We used to laugh about that, all her skinny children. Long ago.

Here was the old stone facing of her temple, unexpected among the high houses that stood all with their backs to the street and its people; here was a step up and an open door, the way we never came. Here was a perfume that seemed soaked into the wood and stone, into the air itself, that had soaked bone-deep into us.

Here were the lamps I used to light, the boards I used to scrub and polish. There in the shadows was the boy I used to be, swaying softly to a music not yet played, half out of his skull on chewing *kef*, dreaming maybe of a freedom never tasted or a body known too well.

Good dreams, bad dreams. Either way.

HERE WAS HIS MISTRESS, ONCE MY OWN: VIRELLE HERSELF, MUCH LIKE THE CROW I'd called her if crows come white and scrupulous, marked by time and temper, counting their age in accumulated scars and influence.

She looked at me and knew me from the inside, as Largo did. Her mouth twisted.

"Come crawling back, has he?"

"Aye that."

All of that. I wasn't going to argue.

"Well, and you're going to take him?"

"If you'll bind him to me. Keep him from taking anything, from me or mine."

She could do that. I wasn't the first that he'd had reason to mistrust. He knew where we came from and what we were. He knew that we'd steal coin from any purse and bread from any kitchen. We'd load a die and mark a pack of cards, we'd drug and cheat and lie from first to last if there was benefit. Why not? It's a cold world and it takes no account of need or innocence, so you might as well go guilty all the way, if guilt will keep you warm and fed.

They talked it through, he paid in coin and promises; I wouldn't have trusted either, but these two wouldn't cheat each other, they were too closely bound.

"Strip then, you, Djoran."

It was hardly the first time I'd taken my clothes off under her eyes, or his. I did hope it might be the last—but I'd thought that before, the day she sold me to him. I'd worked hard for it, so hard; I was on my way up, moving out, moving on. Each step higher than the last.

Now I was naked again, brought down again. *Starting again,* I told myself determinedly. Home was just a place to start.

Smoke and bells. A boy to swing the censer and the little bronze hammers, fetch her pots and simples at a run, watch bug-eyed from a corner when he wasn't put to use: learning, absorbing, storing away. Wise boy. It was almost hard to believe he wasn't me, so many times I'd stood just there and seen just this, how she used a twig of rosemary to splash bare skin with water and oils while she chanted under her breath in call of her shadowy gods. Seen it from about his height, too, and about his stage of dawning cynicism. She gave you a grand farewell to innocence, did Virelle.

She wasn't so kind once you grew older. To me, now, not kind at all. No reason to be; when I left the temple I left some trouble behind me, and another boy was taken and hanged for it. She had always been sure that the first fault was mine, and that I'd arranged to have blame fall on my friend.

She'd always been acute.

Now she murmured her words and flecked my skin, had the boy waft smoke and musk my way; and I didn't know now as I hadn't known then whether her words were potent or her various preparations or neither, whether it was all her own will that drew the attention of her gods; but I felt their purpose close about me like a sheer silk wrap, like a second skin, tight and all-encompassing.

I might have shivered in that moment, I might have cried aloud.

"He'll do," she said abruptly, cutting off her chant and waving her boy away. "Nothing into your house, Largo, and nothing out. Only what's inside his skin. You wouldn't want him chucking up his breakfast on your doorstep."

"No," Largo agreed magnanimously. "What he's eaten, he can keep. If he doesn't get smart," his big hand on my throat suddenly, "and try swallowing a patron's pretty ring. Anyone misses a jewel, boy, and we can't find it, you'll go in the hole until we do."

The hole was Largo's sewer, a cess pit behind the house. Most of his people spent a day or two in there, for one offence or another. Most only ever went in once.

"Yes, Largo. Ow!"

"You'll call me master now. As you did before."

"Yes, master." Some things aren't worth being stubborn for.

ACTUALLY, MOST THINGS AREN'T WORTH BEING STUBBORN FOR. Certainly nothing that I owned just then: not the clothes I'd peeled off, nor the various bits and pieces I'd hoarded this far in pockets and pouches and hems. I left it all on the temple floor, for her boys to glean.

Actually, I didn't have a choice. *Nothing in and nothing out*: I could feel that binding settle across my bare hide, as real as the bite of loose stones beneath my feet, the brush of cool air across my skin, the giggling attention of stray children as I followed obediently at Largo's heel through the streets of a city that I hoped had forgotten me.

No such luck. People called my name, mockingly. One flung a stone, but he was a fool; he did it where I could see him, see it coming and duck, and remember his face for later. His name was long gone, just one of the many I'd abused or robbed or insulted, cheated or exploited in my hectic heedless rise to where I thought I ought to be. Now his face was fresh in my mind, someone to be hurt again if the chance arose.

Things change. Not everybody dies, but some do. For some, it can be arranged.

Here again, back at the tavern. Round to the back of the tavern, naturally: and the alley behind was half blocked by a wagon, old Per Simon delivering barrels of fresh cider as he always had, war or no war.

He sat his wagon as he always did, hunched and heedless. Largo's people came and went, in and out of the stable yard, unloading. Kitchen boys, musicians, whores: it made no difference. If there was work to be done, they did the work.

We did.

I went to the wagon's tailgate without a word to Largo, willing to show willing. One quick hoist, barrel onto shoulder and turn towards the gate. This was heavy work once, when I was all bone and gristle; now it was easy.

Until I took that one significant step, under the arch of brick and into Largo's yard.

That feeling you get, when you know you're being watched? This...was like that, except that it was like being touched too, all over and all at once. Not like the breath of the wind, or silk on the skin, or a sudden rain: this was personal, intimate, *intended*.

Then the barrel was punched off my shoulder, to fall back into the alley behind me. I felt it tear from my grasp, I heard it thump to ground while I was still bearing forward, suddenly too light on my feet, momentum carrying me on although my mind was reeling.

My foot came down on familiar cobbles; I almost knew each separate stone by touch. I turned around bewildered, flinching, expecting a blow and almost hoping for it, something I could understand.

Largo stood under the archway of his gate. Those quick hard hands of his were set on his hips, and he was *laughing*. At *me*.

"*Old crow* did you call her, boy? Well, perhaps—but she's a crow with wisdom. *Nothing in, and nothing out.* Here." He stooped to retrieve the barrel, blessedly unharmed—he wouldn't laugh at a loss of coin, not Largo—and tossed it at me like a ball at play.

I caught it with a grunt, held it cautiously in both arms. Nothing tried to knock it free, now that I was within his bounds.

"Take that to the cellar, then get up to the kitchens. You're no use out here, if you can't fetch and carry through the gate. Ask Marta to find you something to scrub."

"Yes, master."

IN A BUSY TAVERN THERE'S ALWAYS SOMETHING TO SCRUB, BUT HE HADN'T taken me in for a scullery-boy. Neither for a whore, though he'd have me do that too. Largo keeps his people busy, and the town was full of soldiers. Liberators, occupiers, call them what you will. Victory breeds appetite. Food and drink and sex, of course; and entertainment, of course, that too. Song and dance.

Largo had bought me and trained me and kept me as a dancing-boy. *Too pretty to kiss,* he used to proclaim, till I was grown enough to prove him false. Then it was *too pretty to kill,* which was only half a joke; he had a killing temper, and I had a thousand sins in me and no conscience at all. I danced and stole, danced and cheated, danced and sold secrets and took my beatings and danced again. He made more money than I did, but we both did well.

Until my ambitions grew larger than my purse, larger than my opportunities. I left Largo—stole myself away, naturally, paying nothing for the privilege of freedom—and trekked my way to the palace, inveigled myself into the prince's service, rose and rose.

Rose and fell, when my foolish prince lost his war and his life too. Not everybody dies, but some must. Half his people were condemned, but who cares about a dancing-boy? I ran, and no one chased me; only there were too many thieves on every road and too many whores in every tavern, too many cheats and beggars everywhere. If I'd claimed palace skills—*I danced for the court, yes, and warmed their silken beds, that too*—I'd have been mocked for a liar or hanged for a prince's man. Or both, whether they believed me or not.

So I held my tongue and went hungry, went barefoot when my boots wore out, went down and down until at last here I was, back where I'd started. Scrubbing and screwing for Largo's purse, not even bothering to keep one of my own. *Nothing in and nothing out:* there was no point hoarding a single penny piece, if I couldn't take it with me.

Scrubbing and screwing but dancing, that too. That most. I'd been good before; by local standards now, by Largo's standards I was spectacular. I'd learned a lot in the prince's troupe, as much as or more than I did in his bed.

Every night I danced, and word spread, and people came specifically to see me.

Some came back, and back again.

Merrick was young to be a captain, but the New Army was like that, promoting men for merit rather than age or influence or name. It was the gamble I'd taken, me and thousands like me, that experience and long-established power would win out over hotheaded rebellion. Grind it down, stamp it out, crush it utterly.

We'd gambled; we'd lost. Now I danced for Merrick.

For Merrick and his kind, officers and men, a constant succession of faces, bodies, hands. Variously drunken, sweating, reaching to touch. They weren't all soldiers; they weren't all men. There were administrators, traders, the idly wealthy and the busily broke. Some nights, there were more women than men.

MOSTLY SOLDIERS, THOUGH—AND AFTER A WHILE, MOSTLY MERRICK, AT LEAST IN my head. I danced for him; the rest were only clutter.

He was sweet. It took him a week of watching from the shadows, until he found the nerve to step forward. He had to shoulder other men aside before he could throw a towel across my naked sweating shoulders, toss a coin to the lurking Largo and take a firm grip of my neck.

"Where can we go?"

"This way, master..."

When I slept alone, I slept with everyone; all Largo's people bedded down together in the hay loft. For customers, I had a room. Lamplight and soft comforts, wine and perfumes, oils and toys. Whips and chains, if their tastes ran that way.

Merrick found no need to hurt me, and I gave him no reason. The occasional clout if I bit too hard: it was nothing, an occasion for a laugh and a quick apology, the brush of lips over the offended spot and move on. I learned what he liked, which was simple enough: a boy both eager and submissive, occasionally wicked, always willing. When he wanted to fuck, we fucked. When he wanted to talk, or more often listen, we could do that too. He liked to hear stories from the palace, from my old high life; he liked to be shocked, a little, by the late prince's decadent behaviours and my own. With a cool goblet in one hand and his other resting on my thigh, with my head nestled into his shoulder and our skin sticking together, with my voice murmuring tales of a world unimagined, he felt something like a prince himself. That was all I wanted.

One morning I was scrubbing floors when I heard his voice unexpectedly, behind and above me: "Let me have Djoran for the day, Largo. How much?"

Largo named a price. Merrick dickered unconvincingly, overpaid shockingly, cuffed me lightly in embarrassment when I bounded to my feet like a whistled puppy. I rubbed my sore ear and beamed at him. "Where are we going?"

Largo snorted. "Wherever you take him, keep his hands tied and a rope on his throat or he'll make off with anything that's yours."

"I will not," I said. "Why would I? I can't bring anything back here."

"You'd find someone to hold it for you. I don't want him building a store of credit outside my house, Captain. Keep him close."

"Hands tied," Merrick agreed, "rope on his throat. Right. I might enjoy that. Do you have a rope?"

"I have better. Djoran? Fetch."

I fetched. A minute later, Merrick stepped out with wrist-cuffs and a chain leash dangling from his hand. I padded at his heels, naked and obedient. *Nothing in, nothing out:* I couldn't even wear chains before I was across the threshold.

In the street there, he cuffed my hands behind my back and looped the leash around my neck. And grinned, and kissed me; and said, "Maybe I should keep you this way. At least I can be sure you'll be good."

"I'm always good," I protested. "Master."

"You are, I know. Except when I want you sinful." His hand rested a moment on my hip; then he laughed shortly and gave the leash a twitch. "Come on, then."

He didn't make me trot at heel long. Soon enough I was settled against his side, his arm around my shoulders and his lips in my hair. He did keep the cuffs on me, though, and the leash too; he didn't think to stop at a market stall and buy even the simplest strip of cloth to mask my nakedness.

Turned out the day was all about nakedness. He took me to the city baths, and we didn't pass the door again till dusk, when he had to give me back to Largo. We bathed, we swam, we oiled each other's bodies; we drowsed and sweated in the steam; we fucked slowly, languorously, slept and fucked again. We drank chilly sherbets and hot strong coffee, and sweated again, and plunged recklessly into the ice-pool and came out gasping, shuddering, desperate for rough towels and rougher hands to work them.

I'd never felt cleaner or more contented, resting my weary head against his shoulder as he cuffed my hands again, kissing the scented skin of his neck, murmuring, "You don't need to do that."

"No, but I want to. And Largo'll be glad to see me being watchful. As I am. I'm not a fool, Djoran. I know your instincts. And how to overcome them."

"Yes, master."

That was our first day, maybe our best. There were more. Soon enough it was a rare day when he didn't come for me. One of those, we had excitements enough to compensate. A guest was missing a jewelled brooch; she was angry with Largo; Largo was angry with me. I was halfway to the hole, still protesting, when the brooch was found—broken, missing its pin—hidden among the scant belongings of one of the kitchen girls. She was whipped, poor fool, and sent to market, sold. Not listened to. Largo paid to have the brooch repaired, even though even he thought likely it had broken and fallen of its own accord and the girl had only found it, kept it, a simpler kind of stealing.

I DIDN'T NEED TO WAIT MUCH LONGER. A day came when Merrick came, but not to me, not first. Went straight to Largo, and came out with one finger light of its ring, a piece of heavy gold he'd had from his grandser. I knew the history of all his rings, and their value too.

First fair offer that I hear, Largo had said.

"He cheated you," I said bluntly. Boys were cheap, and rightly so.

"I know," he said. "I don't care. You're mine now. Come away. I've a month's leave; I'm taking you home. I might leave you there, if you settle. My people will be good to you, put some weight on your bones, take fair work out of you, teach you a new kind of life."

His people were farmers. I knew the kind of life they offered, I'd seen it. Passing by, on my way from one city to the next.

Still, he was master. It was his decision. He left me in no doubt about that. His horse was in the stable yard; he had to lead it out himself into the alley, I couldn't do it. Once we were out, though: then he could set his pack on my back, his new iron cuffs on my wrists. His chain around my neck, a lesson learned.

"There's blood on your thumb," he said, testing the cuffs as a careful master ought. "What have you been doing to yourself?"

"It's nothing, just a splinter under the nail..."

"You should take better care. I'll do that, I'll take better care of you than you do." He tipped my face up, fingers under my chin; and frowned, and said, "Tears, Djoran?"

I sniffed, shook my head, muttered, "It's nothing," again.

"I hope you'll be happy with me," he said fretfully. "I think you will. I'll be strict, you need that; but I won't be unkind, not ever. I'll treat you with all the love you deserve. Love and discipline together; you'll thrive, you'll see."

Largo stood in his gateway watching, approving. Content. One more ring on his finger, one less doubt on his mind. One less trouble in his house.

My new master swung himself up into the saddle, kicked his horse into a trot. His horse and me, necessarily.

IT WAS AN EASY PACE HE SET, AND DANCING KEEPS YOU FIT. I could keep this up for hours, running at his stirrup with his pack on my back; but I wouldn't need to. By the time we reached the city gate, I was already working the steel pin out from under my thumbnail, where I'd pushed it in a hard hour earlier.

Nothing in, and nothing out. Nothing outside my skin. So I'd thrust it deep under my nail, with only a bead of blood to show and an eye-watering pain to endure and disguise. Virelle's watchful gods couldn't touch me for it.

And now I had steel in my fingers, sharp and flexible. Even at a jog, even working blind behind my back with fetters on my wrists, I could pick a cuff-lock with a jewel's broken pin. Two minutes' work, and my hands were free. Merrick didn't know; I held them behind my back as though they were still chained there, one clamped hard around the open cuff to stop it swinging loose.

Half an hour later the road dipped to a ford, with trees on either bank.

There was no one before us, no one behind us.

Merrick slowed to a walk, and took us into the stream. The water was calf-deep and unhurried, no more trouble to me than it was to the horse. Just as my master smiled down at me, I brought my hands out from behind my back.

One jolted his boot out of the stirrup; the other slammed that steel needle deep into the horse's rump.

The horse screamed and reared. I heaved. Merrick fell heavily into the water.

Well-trained, he still kept hold of the reins. I'd been hoping for that.

The horse danced out of the way. Merrick was sitting up to his chin in the river, sodden, bewildered. I took a step forward, swinging my arm lustily. One iron cuff was still locked around my wrist; the other flew on the end of its chain at the end of my arm like a flail.

Dancing gives you muscles like a whip. That cuff caught him on the side of the head with a brutal thud, and I thought I might have killed him.

I snatched the reins from his slack fingers, calmed the horse before it could charge off with me still chained to the saddle, tied it to a tree and picked that neck-chain loose. Then I went back for its master.

An hour later, he was the one running sluggishly at the stirrup, cuffed and leashed and naked, with the pack on his back now. His clothes were still damp—and all too big for me—but I wore them gratefully, with stockings stuffed into the boot-toes to keep them on my feet. His rings wouldn't stay on my fingers, so I carried them in a pouch. The horse was equable beneath me. Its former master less so, but I'd gagged him once I tired of his moaning.

Boys are cheap after war and men too, but horses not. Horses never. Between the two, they'd fetch enough to buy me passage overseas. A new land, new opportunities. Put the war behind me, put it all behind me, start again. With quick feet, a quick tongue, quicker fingers. I could rise and rise.

MERRICK'S FAMILY WOULD BE EXPECTING HIM. When he didn't arrive, there would be questions asked, people sent in search. Of course they'd find their way to the tavern where he'd spent so much time in recent weeks. Of course they'd interrogate Largo; of course they'd see and recognise the ring he wore so blatantly on his finger.

He'd have nothing to offer but the truth, that Merrick had paid it fairly for a dancing-boy. But boys are cheap, and that ring meant much to him; no one would believe Largo. Not the family, not the magistrate.

A man, a captain gone, and his ring on a tavern-keeper's finger? I thought Largo would hang, like enough.

Not everybody dies, but some, oh yes. Some do.

About the Storyteller

CHAZ BRENCHLEY HAS BEEN MAKING A LIVING AS A WRITER SINCE HE WAS eighteen. A British Fantasy Award winner, he has also published books for children, thrillers, and more than five hundred short stories in a variety of genres. He is a prizewinning ex-poet. Chaz has recently married and moved from Newcastle to California, with two squabbling cats and a famous teddy bear.

CPSIA information can be obtained at www.ICGtesting.com
Printed in the USA
LVOW11s1025081114

412679LV00001B/9/P